ath Wears a
ocked Hat

ar and private investigator Richard Scott
aud and murder in his own business. In
oving mystery, he places himself in the
right-wing, pistol-toting evangelist and
lowy villains before falling into the arms
a Petry, once his college sweetheart. He
olve the quandary of her life: the murder
us beauty queen in which her son is a
ect.

ath Wears a
ocked Hat

John W. Brown

Guild Press of Indiana, Inc.

Copyright 2001 by John W. Bro

GUILD PRESS OF INDIANA, INC.
10665 Andrade Drive
Zionsville, Indiana 46077
317-733-4175
www.guildpress.com

ISBN 1-57860-093-6

Library of Congress
Catalog Card Number 20-01863

Cover art by Steven D. Armour
Text design by Sheila Samson

Printed and bound in the United States of A

Also by John W. Brown:

Death Rides a Carousel

Rogue's Bluff

(Both available from Guild Press of Ind

Prologue

FROM HIGH UP IN THE DARKNESS, Janie McNamara's nude figure tumbled past the jagged escarpment and splashed awkwardly into the water.

Roger Petry waited near the foot of the quarry's sheer wall.

Now he dove, his lean body piercing the black water. Surfacing beside her, Roger laughingly grabbed Janie's wrist to tug her close.

Her terror-stricken eyes tried to focus. Her mouth worked, straining to form words. Her lips framed a horrid, gargling rattle. Her staring, dilated eyes filmed over. Beneath Janie's jawbone, the neck of a broken beer bottle protruded, the bottle still capped.

For one insane moment, Roger strained to read the brand label. Then his agonized scream reverberated against the limestone walls, dying in a mewl.

Sweeping his gaze upward to the quarry's rim, searching for her assailant, Roger glimpsed someone momentarily silhouetted by the campfire's light. Before he could identify the shadowy figure, it vanished.

Chapter One

My name is Richard Scott, businessman, entrepreneur, sometimes private investigator. Usually, I sell steel. I stack it in hangar-sized warehouses and deliver it to customers who produce car fenders, skyscrapers, or anything else made from the metal. Lately, I've been solving murders.

A few years ago my father-in-law swindled me—and others. After investigating, the G-men signed over to me the whole company. I was again in charge of the business, but adding further intrigue, my accountant said recently that Architectural Design and Elaboration, an outlying division of the parent company, was losing money big time—and perhaps hiding murder. I was in deep trouble.

This morning, intending to delve into those problems up front and personal, I left my Indianapolis condo early to tie up loose ends at the Capital Detective Agency. Skirting downtown via the traffic-snarled spaghetti bowl, I parked in the agency's lot at precisely eight o'clock.

I hadn't made the scene for some time. Hadn't needed to. But as remembered, the two flights to the tiny office remained as steep as a Rocky Mountain goat run, and as cold and dark as a slumlord's heart.

After pounding up the stairs, I cut a hard left on the top landing, paused a moment to gather myself, then shoved open the door and ambled nonchalantly in, the picture of cool. "I'm Richard Scott," I announced. "The agency's prodigal investigator—make that knight errant." I extended my hand, thinking how Charles Richard Tracey, long in the detective business, never missed an opportunity to exploit his name or a beautiful face.

The new receptionist gave my fingers an especially warm squeeze. "I'm Stella Carlyle, Gemma's replacement." Pushing back her straw-colored hair, she rolled her eyes in mock distrust. "Before leaving, Gemma warned me about you and mentioned 'nights,' but they weren't spelled with a 'k.'" Stella laughed, the sound as happy as a baby's chuckle.

I unfastened my London Fog. "I'm here to see Charlie."

"May I?" she asked, sliding smoothly behind me and lifting the coat from my shoulders.

I'd really liked Gemma—now the boss's wife—and I instantly liked her replacement. It's always nice establishing quick rapport; when you do, a half-dozen words and a smile can confirm it. Hinting of jasmine, Stella's perfume teased my nose.

I watched Stella Carlyle when she moved from the battered gray desk to the tiny coat closet. Mid-thirties, I guessed—trim, but amply curved, with full hips flaring from beneath a slender waist. She wore her shoulder-length hair loosely. Certainly she outclassed the agency. After finding her in such questionable surroundings, maybe I'd discover a Monet original stapled to the office's Masonite paneling?

Having wedged my coat between an upright vacuum cleaner and a tall stack of document boxes stored in the coat closet, she buzzed the boss's intercom. She led me past my darkened and abandoned cubicle, down the hall to the president's office.

Charlie Tracey rose and grasped my hand. "Great to see you, Richard—been waiting for this. How about that NCAA tourney?" Playing it casual, he went on, "I'd want a bunch of points before taking Duke . . ."

As I was about to find out when I tried to resign, he wasn't in a mood to "give in" easily. Not on anything. I took a chair.

Stella brought in a carafe, two packets of NutraSweet, and my earthenware mug. I liked the mug, its insides imprinted with hairline cracks, each shallow line personally painted by uncounted cups of ink-black coffee. Grinning, I nodded my thanks and stirred in the sweetener.

"We kept the cup here, so you'd feel at home when you visit," Stella explained.

Tracey waved away the coffee offer. I studied him. Things had changed. The voice had cleared. The fingers, now playing with a manila folder, no longer showed yellow. "Aha!" I teased, "You old sneak, you've kicked the cigarette habit!"

"Yep. Gemma keeps the pressure on," He patted a flat stomach. "Best of all, due to the diet she's enforcing, I've dropped twenty pounds."

"Now, if she can just teach you to grow hair." That dig out of the way, I introduced my own, festering imbroglio. "Charlie, you know that while I was away playing soldier in Desert Storm, my ex's father stiffed me out of a lot of money—although it took him a few years of conniving before he took my job too. You're also aware that while I was private-eying for you, the IRS investigated him, and that more recently, the old man has used court injunctions, both to prevent my taking over the company and to keep the IRS at bay." I raised my coffee mug in an informal victory toast. "Finally, the feds have made their charges stick and jailed his sick, nitro-chomping ass for tax evasion."

"Yeah, it was a long road back, Richard. But word has it that the FBI has signed the company over to you." Twisting his face into a smile, he gave a knowing wink. "That should put you back, firmly, in the driver's seat."

"Yeah, but I got problems, lots of them; the company's losing money hand-over-fist. I scrambled management. That didn't help. My auditor isolated the source and suspects fraud—and worse. Charlie, I wanted to make it easy for you and gradually phase out of this operation. I'm sorry, but I must resign from the agency and investigate my own company. Immediately."

Facing pressure, smokers reach for a cigarette. Out of habit Tracey fumbled with his shirt pocket. Looking crestfallen, he popped a handful of TicTacs between his lips. His mouth rattling like a crapshooter's fist, he tossed the packet across the desk. I touch-passed it back.

"I'll cut you a deal," Tracey said, eyes narrowing. "Keep your ties to the agency, at least for a while. It'll help you in your company investigation."

"You're being too sweet, Tracey. What's the catch?"

"You began the Indianapolis building hoax case. Now finish it." He opened another packet of TicTacs, then went for my throat. "You owe me. I bailed your buns out of trouble when you were down and out. If we drop the ball on this case, I'll be ruined. Step up and give me a hand."

"You push a tough deal." I frowned, considering options. "All right. For you, I'll do it. You provide a body to run the leg work; I'll supervise the job on a part-time basis."

When he nodded a quick agreement, I suggested we review the case. With a crafty smile, he opened the manila file he'd been toying with. "Five years ago, as you know, a do-gooder religious organization in Indianapolis developed a low-cost housing plan for the poor. A local bank, pushed by the city, provided minimum-interest loans for the apartments."

He scratched deeper into the file. "The humanitarian agency went bankrupt and bailed out. The bank, still saddled with the original mortgages, got stuck with deteriorating structures, some so dangerously weakened the tenants have been moved to other accommodations.

"The bank, suspecting fraud, has been searching for the deep pockets where their money might still be cached. Adding to its woes, the original construction company has now levied a claim for unpaid building costs."

I nodded at his recount. "Okay, Charlie, you've sucked me in, so give me the name of this engineering hotshot who'll help me at the job site, supervising, checking prints, and taking quality samples."

Triggering his intercom, he called, "Hey, Stella! You ready to go?"

I exploded. "You've gotta be kidding!" I lowered my voice so Stella wouldn't overhear. "Those animals out there on the job will eat her alive."

Another phone call kept him from answering. Conceding the battle, I rose, nodding goodbye. He held a hand over the mouthpiece and whispered, "By the way, Richard, I've already closed your office here and shipped your decrepit desk and chair to your Bloomington factory."

At that instant, a metamorphosed Stella entered. Now dressed construction-worker-stereotypical, she wore denim jeans, a quilted jacket unzipped over a message sweatshirt, and thick-soled work boots. I was still reassessing the change when again the door opened behind her.

"Richard," Stella said, "meet Rhonda from the temp office. She'll fill in here while I'm working with you."

I welcomed Rhonda aboard, wondering how she'd make out trying to talk sense to some of the agency's harder-nosed clients. Rhonda weighed in at only medium height and weight. Her rounded face and boyishly cut hair gave her a far too youthful, inexperienced appearance.

I nodded a jaunty salute before following Stella down the stairs, then opened the driver's door on her Saturn. While she adjusted her seat belt, I maneuvered to read the sweatshirt's message without being tagged a voyeur.

She smiled. "It says, 'PCB's KILL.'"

"I hope nobody else does," I answered. Even a short stint in the private snoop business had honed my cynicism. About to turn to my car, I added, "How about your running on out to the job site, alone, this morning. Start by taking a look at the blueprints and conditions. I'll be back in town to see you as soon as I check in with my company, downstate."

On her nodded agreement, I climbed into my Jag and dialed Laureen Smith, who'd been my father-in-law's housekeeper when he visited the factory down in southern Indiana. "Laureen, can you open the hunting lodge for me? I'll be staying there while I'm in the area on business."

Her answer came slowly. "The place is kind of, uh . . . run down, Mr. Scott. It's been a while since anybody used it. Are you sure?"

Going for a string of mistakes, begun when I agreed to help Charlie Tracey, I told her, "Yes, Laureen, I'm sure."

"Okay, then, if you arrive before me, don't let the dog scare you. See, there've been some break-ins at the new house next door—"

"Fair warning," I said, interrupting. Dialing twice more, I called the Bloomington company and the post office and asked both to immediately forward all my mail to the A-frame. Cradling the cellular, I checked my watch and steered toward my condo. If I hurried I had time to pack my bags and still be at the lodge before dusk.

Five minutes later I circled the red bricks surrounding Indy's Soldiers and Sailors Monument before speeding past her "Magnificent Mile" of parks and monuments. Then, racing yellow lights, jockeying for position, I studiously guided my green Jag past the black ghetto as surely as a skipped rock clears a stagnant pond. I pictured myself as a faint blob behind a tinted windshield, my face an indistinct white speck on that skipped stone. Again, today, my attitude and habits pissed me.

My life was about to change.

Chapter Two

As I hit the highway, I chilled, remembering my accountant's parting words. His eyes riveted on mine, his mouth a grim hyphen, he warned, "Richard, you're facing fraud. Unless you can stop the company's hemorrhaging red ink"—his stubby finger jabbed at figures on the thick report—"your cash cow will bleed itself white! And the story gets much worse: rumor has it that your company has ties to a grisly murder! I'm surprised you hadn't heard of the killing."

"Don't be. During the last two years my work with Capital Detective Agency plus my court battles with the old man and his attorneys have kept me fully occupied. The factory down south could've fallen into a crater and I wouldn't've known. Somebody else has been running it."

But, now, I promised myself that I'd get the whole story. Why not? My stint as a private eye had made murder and larceny my business. Yet, an hour after departing Indianapolis, while I tooled around the Bloomington bypass, another memory tweaked my intuition: Laureen's mentioned break-ins. Today, I had something new for speculation.

"Richard Scott," I asked myself, "Why don't you play it smart and find a motel?"

But I'm stubborn. Faking a shudder, I turned from the main highway onto Rose Cutter's Pike. On the other hand, maybe the shudder was more real than imaginary.

My old British grandmother would have told me, "A dog just walked over your grave, Richard!"

The A-frame—loosely designated a "hunting lodge"—had been part of the deal when my father-in-law and I bought Architectural Design and Elaboration just after I returned from Desert Storm. Inasmuch as the smell of gunpowder and blood of animals didn't light my emotional fires, I gave the keys to him. Thrilled as a kid who paid fifteen dollars for a favorite jock's autograph, the old man designated the retreat as his hunting lodge.

Back then, he extended a welcome by saying, "Richard, you and Barb must come down for a weekend. The place is basic, of an earlier time. It's beautiful." Since that invitation, for all of us, the situation had changed: Barb and I had divorced three years ago; he was locked in the federal penitentiary; I had taken over the company. Now, belatedly, I accepted his offer.

I figured, Why not? It sounded good. While trying to make sense of the company's money shortage, I'd take a shot at some bucolic, country life, though it meant living farther south in Cavalier County and a longer commute to the factory.

Lonely country digs and criminal investigations don't always jibe, I knew, but I packed a Glock 19. That should make me the meanest top-gun in the valley. In local dogfights I'd accept no losses, no ties—only wins.

At three P.M. I left the county blacktop for a gravel drive. Abruptly, the lane climbed to the crown of a broom-saged hill before curving its way amidst a grove of maples and winter-stripped oak. A quarter-mile farther, the road passed between my ex-father-in-law's partially constructed mansion and the A-frame, then looped around the latter's front yard. Driving between the houses, I saw no evidence of any "break-ins."

I parked at the end of a flagstone walk. With a loud grunt, I dragged my suitcase from the trunk. Lugging it, a carry-on bag, and a briefcase full of business papers and notes about Architectural Design and Elaboration, I staggered up the sidewalk and mounted the front steps. Dropping the baggage, and ignoring the doorbell, I banged the moose head knocker.

The thickly paneled door cracked to show a single staring eye. The security chain rattled and the door opened.

"Hi, Laureen! Thanks for coming on short notice."

It was my first sighting of Laureen Smith. She now worked full-time for a company called The Cleaner's Solution, its logo showing in white lettering on her blue uniform pocket. When the old man was still optimistic about running the company and staying out of prison, he hired her to clean and tidy the place, and the company began mailing out monthly paychecks. Now, I'd see if she'd earned those dollars.

"I wish you'd called sooner. The place would've been shipshape." With that, she hoisted both cases. The muscles on her right arm rippling like a stevedore's, she whisked them through the living room and into the master bedroom. I followed, carrying the briefcase.

I gave a disappointed look around. Several lamps dotted the tables, but rough-sawn, darkly stained paneling and heavy lampshades absorbed most of the light before it penetrated the room. Not a ray reached the ceiling's smoke-blackened peak. Nor did the dull day and grime-streaked windows help. A rust-colored rug wrinkled its way beneath a dingy plaid couch's lacquered-sapling legs, adding more discouragement.

Stepping over an untidy mound of carpeting, I flopped down. Either miffed because Laureen had hoisted the suitcases easier than I, or suffering early stages of light deprivation, I lifted my eyes above the fireplace. "Jesus H. Christ!" I yelped, climbing to my feet.

Laureen had been bemusedly watching. "My, but don't that stag's glass eyes give you the willies?"

"Yeah, and that head's about to take a one-way trip to the crawl-space."

"You better be ready for a lot of work. He's got a lotta brethren in the spare bedroom."

I wasn't surprised. An avid hunter, the old man had stored his trophies in the basement of his Indianapolis home. Later, when we bought the Bloomington factory, he trucked them here, eventually to be relocated inside the new, more-spacious house he was building next door. At that point his dream of a taxidermy heaven died.

"We'll take care of those babies later," I promised and stomped outside onto the porch.

Across the drive, the partially finished mansion dwarfed the "hunting lodge." The property's title work showed a limestone quarry lying somewhere between the new house and the woods flowing over a tall hill and beyond. But where was the quarry?

Soundlessly, Laureen joined me on the porch. "Rose Cutter's Quarry is hidden in the middle of that grove of trees," she said, pointing.

"Yeah, I remember reading about the place."

"I've said enough," Laureen said. "Else you might not spend the night." With that, she scurried back into the house. I lingered, idly wondering about her untold story and the quarry's name. In the far distance, a broad lake shimmered golden in the afternoon sun. Side by side, two speedboats cut the water, their skippers hunched over the controls, the vessels' roostertails double the boats' size. Laureen's vacuum drowned the sound of their engines.

Walking back into the house and into the kitchen, my every move seemed followed by the stag's sad, glass eyes. I hate killing animals. After fighting in two wars, I never aim at anything that can't shoot back. I believe lions and leopards belong in the Serengeti, tigers in India. They should lie beneath acacia trees, licking their balls or stalking the savanna in search of prey and mates. They shouldn't die young and spend eternity staring through glass eyes at a succession of wizened hunters.

I pictured an army of decrepit old men creeping through darkened game rooms or perched around a table, and imagined their recounting how they bagged the polar bear from a helicopter, the gazelle from a Land Rover, and the big cat from atop a fifty-foot-high scaffold. All safe perches.

Now fully disgusted, I reached up and unhitched the stag's head. Risking another rupture, I half-carried, half-dragged it from the living room, out the door, and off the porch. I rolled it into the crawlspace. I was out of shape and nowhere near as strong as Laureen. It required five minutes to regain my breath.

"Good idea!" Laureen said, when I marched triumphantly back inside. Her mouth broke into a wide smile; I expected applause.

Together, without a word, we attacked the spare bedroom. One by one, we lugged out the whole sorry menagerie and crammed it into the crawl space. Inexplicably, I couldn't bring myself to incinerate the dreadful objects. Later, I thought, I'll seek a better solution.

Laureen brushed dust from her uniform on finishing. "I have to leave for another job, but like I do every day, I'll return tomorrow to feed and water George and let him tear around outside for his daily constitutional. He's supposed to stop the break-ins next door." She snorted. "I don't know why they call him a guard dog; he won't bite anything bigger'n a lamb chop or a dog biscuit. Nevertheless, I'd planned to take you over for a formal introduction."

"No sweat! I'll go it alone. By the way, how about picking up a few supplies before tomorrow?"

Her face tilted, her expression quizzical.

"Main thing, bring a case of Coors and two fifths of Stolichnaya vodka." I pondered a moment, then tossed her my AmEx card. "Throw in a loaf of rye and some eggs. Beyond that, you're the boss."

I helped by storing the big-bellied vacuum cleaner. For certain, I wanted the housekeeper to see I was capable of lifting *something*! That done and Laureen gone, I made my way next door.

A big, tail-wagging ball of yellow fur met me at the door. "I suppose you get exceptionally mean when the moon comes out," I said, patting him on the head.

George and I toured the nearly completed mansion. He had comfortable quarters, and a heaped dish of food and a full container of water stood close beside a plump mattress standing on the floor. It wasn't a cold day, but the furnace clicked on while we were making the rounds. The panes in a couple of basement windows shone especially bright, so I supposed they had been replaced after the break-ins. Although a lot of work was still needed, the bar, along with the rest of the house, appeared almost complete. "The old man must've been planning one doozie of an open house," I told George as I read the labels on a mixed case of twelve- and fifteen-year-old Scotches.

George didn't answer—too busy sniffing through an assortment of vintage wine. "Christ! You a lush too?" I asked.

Three other cases also caught my eye: the best sour mash Kentucky bourbon this side of heaven. Or at least the Mason-Dixon line. On leaving, I carried a case with me.

George didn't care. He was probably smart enough to know the old man would never again drink here. Come to think of it, maybe the dog was privy to other inside information as well—data still hidden from me.

I lugged my bourbon back to the A-frame, pondering. After depositing the booze, I admired the blank spot over the mantle, rearranged the sofa's thick cushions, and kicked back for a snooze.

That lasted thirty seconds.

The doorbell rang! I shook my fist. No rest for the wicked!

Was my past coming back to haunt me . . . already?

Chapter Three

WHEN THE DOORBELL RANG, it wasn't really a bell. Nor a ring. The sound had been customized: "Oo-rah-ah-oo-ah"—or something like that—as if mimicking the frustrated bellow of a rutting moose.

Fighting an urge to assume a defensive position behind the gun cabinet, I sped across the room and yanked open the door.

"I collected your mail at the end of the lane," a casually dressed woman announced, her face deadly serious. "A friend at the factory said you were on your way here." Then, unable to contain herself, she laughed. The sound was lyrical, music unheard for far-too-many years. I knew her!

Her hair, once jet black and worn shoulder-length, was now swept back from the face and showed touches of gray. It had been fashioned into a pageboy with bangs, but my recognition had been instantaneous. "Samantha Glasston!" I exclaimed, surely muffing both names.

Thirty years ago, in high school, I knew her as "Sam." We had dated, parted, and she had married after college, before *our* final, unexpected evening together, a memorable event that didn't occur until three years after her graduation from Ohio State, mine from Purdue.

"Sam, is this ever great! Many's the time I've thought of you." Yeah, that was the understatement of the millennium! I'd spent countless days and nights absorbed by the thought that, after our one romantic evening, I had lost her forever.

I ran my fingers over her upturned face, then decided against a kiss. That restraint took willpower. Although I'm six-three, she was gracefully tall and her soft, full lips were oh-so-kissably close.

Compromising, we exchanged hugs and air kisses. She reached up and brushed her fingers through my graying beard as I ushered her inside.

The pleasant scent of her perfume—rosewood and cedar—lingered. A fervent opponent of fragrance overkill, I especially liked the cedar—a hint of the outdoors, but not sufficiently lethal to zap moths.

Thanks to Laureen, a fresh pot of coffee already waited. I offered Sam a chair, then made the short walk across the tiny living room to the kitchen to fetch cups and fixin's. In a two-bedroom-and-loft house all trips are brief.

I reached for a pair of artist Laurel Burch's coffee mugs. I liked the Southwest motif picture with the stampeding horses and the saguaro cactus. Then I remembered the many months the old man had batched here and wondered how frequently he cranked up the dishwasher.

Fearing mold, and afraid the hand-painted pictures of the horses might sprout green hair like Chia pets, I upscaled into china cups and saucers. Playing it safe, I rinsed each with a blast of hot water.

I glanced across the breakfast bar cum room divider. In quick succession, Samantha tossed the handful of my letters atop the coffee table, removed and draped her khaki canvas pullover atop a chair back, and finger-combed her hair into submission. Ignoring the chair I'd offered, she sat on the sofa, seemingly as comfortable and at ease as if our last meeting had been yesterday.

She removed one silver hoop earring and placed it beside her on the end table. Removing the other, she absentmindedly touched her earlobe with a fingertip, then gently massaged it between thumb and forefinger. That really struck a chord!

Just like when we were teenagers, I thought. Even then, the

minute she relaxed, off went the earrings, followed by the watch and bracelet. Habits die hard, I guess, or this one resurfaced because of my company. I couldn't say why, but I preferred the latter premise.

I poured while she talked. She had aged remarkably little. The fair, delicate skin still stretched smoothly over those oh-so-magnificent, high cheekbones, and the lithe, slender figure showed nary an unsightly bulge.

Still, I sensed some obscure change, and tagged her overly casual attitude as a charade. "Okay, Sam, where've you been and what've you been doing?" I asked.

"For years, life was so simple," she said. Her deep-set, brown eyes fixed on mine as I slid into the chair across the table.

Then I knew with certainty. Her eyes, once virtual fountains of joy, were now mirthless. Afraid, perhaps? Awaiting reasons, I only nodded responses.

"So much has happened since you and I last met . . ." Her soft voice dwindled away as her expression grew pensive. She paused and watched me for an extended moment. Only then did she lower her eyes and continue, "As you remember, after our marriage, my husband and I stayed on in Columbus and I worked downtown as a stock and bond salesperson. Eventually, I discovered how much I missed academics, so I went back to the university as a graduate assistant. Joe was always determined that I quit my job, have a child, and stay home as a full-time housewife. For several years, I refused, because our relationship was shaky from the start. Then, I got pregnant and had to acquiesce. Unfortunately . . ."

Seemingly re-gathering her thoughts, she said, "But despite the problems, we lived together for nearly nineteen years before finally separating. Once the divorce finalized, I moved to Indiana. I've been here eight years."

I glanced at the wedding band. It was still there.

She noticed. "Joe wants a reconciliation. It's hopeless. Nevertheless, he insists I wear the ring. He feels it marks me as being off-limits to others."

"My God, Sam! You make the ring sound like a brand."

"Perhaps it is. Joe Petry is a violent and dangerous man." Her lips clamped shut. "Anyway, I don't wish to discuss that."

"Possibly you should."

Shrugging off the suggestion, Sam changed subjects, "I'm now teaching comparative religions at IU while working on my doctoral dissertation." She toasted with her coffee cup. "That's only the first chapter of *my* story." She paused. "Shall we now hear yours?"

I began hesitantly. "While I was away and serving in the Gulf War, my father-in-law devised a scam that cheated all the stockholders. I lost a fortune. Then five years ago, or thereabouts— three years after you moved back to Indiana, he finished the hatchet job by firing me—"

Sam interrupted. "I'm surprised that you'd continue working for the man who cheated you. It doesn't ring true, especially for someone like you." Again turning pensive, she rose and walked to the window. Hooking her fingers over the sash, she stared intently outside. Suddenly she shivered. I wondered what she had seen. Or recalled.

"I trusted the old man and attributed the loss to business reversals. The scheme didn't surface until after I had been fired and the IRS launched its own investigation. I won't bore you with details," I said, anxious to soft-shoe past the less tasty parts of my past.

When she had retaken her seat, her eager expression signaled that she'd gamble on boredom rather than miss a tantalizing story. Most would. That's not my way, however. I shield my privacy like a killer bee guarding the hive.

"But I want to hear," Sam insisted. "What happened between you and your Barb. Please tell me."

"Okay, here goes," I warned and leaped in. "Shortly after I lost my job, Barb and I divorced. She ended up marrying Darius Stalcup, our old high-school buddy, who, after college, founded the African American Land Holdings group. He's still very successful and they continue together and are very much in love. I wish them much more of the same."

With difficulty, I kept my voice light. "Following the divorce, my situation didn't turn sublime, like Barb's. Unemployed and trying to restructure my life, I signed on as a private investigator with Capital Detective Agency. I nailed a couple of killers in Abram's Trace, a small village just south of here, but still in Cavalier County."

"You mentioned Abram's Trace. I've been there. I've also read of your success in *The Indianapolis Star*. That's why I came. I need an investigator."

"I'm disappointed," I complained, "I'd hoped you were simply unable to resist a great-looking, macho stud with a knockout personality and a beard."

"Sorry," she said, wrinkling her nose and smiling. "Though I'll admit the salt-and-pepper beard adds a touch of elan—" She grew serious, and persistent. "Would you consider accepting another case?"

Trying for safe ground and innocuous schmoozing, I paraphrased a few lines of an older-than-dirt western, citing that I was "hanging up my boots and gun belt, and and catching the first stagecoach outta Dodge."

Quickly, I lost my audience. "Richard, surely, you haven't retired. Not while still in your forties."

"Oh, no, I'm back in business! What else remains for me? I've renounced gumshoeing. Now you just nipped in the bud a promising singing career." I rearranged my face into a suitably maudlin expression. "So I gotta go with what's available for me. Business is all that remains."

"Will I get to meet your fiancee—uh—?" She snapped her finger, grimacing when the sharp report didn't inspire a name. "Dammit! That other business executive who, doubling as an investigator, helped solve your last case . . . Help me, Rich!"

The impatient tone scraped a nerve. I did remember though, that usually Sam was serene and understanding and affectionate. There was more here than met the eye.

"You must mean Caitlin McChesney. Cait was always more business guru than investigator." I shook my head. "Skipping details,

I'm afraid the Cait McChesney-Richard Scott partnership was strong enough to endure headliners and daily features but not suited for a successful series. She's back in New York, CEO-ing another company."

I hoped Sam wasn't trying to read my eyes too. I wanted all the hidden chapters kept private. After all, at this point my relationship with Caitlin remained difficult to describe, even to myself. Especially since—through the magic of daily e-mail messages and telephone conversations—we were still trying to get a firm handle on our situation. Better put, we were struggling to reestablish a relationship we had once viewed as indestructible.

"I don't know which way to turn," Samantha continued. "I had hoped I could convince the two of you to investigate a local death *and* a terrible miscarriage of justice." She brightened. "Would you consider going it alone? Perhaps on a part-time basis. I can't afford a huge fee, but I'd pay as much as I can."

I shook my head, lips set.

Obviously tired of sparring, Sam swung for a knockout. "You don't understand. This death was a brutal murder. It's my own personal tragedy—I've lost two people." Her hands became unsteady and her eyes welled. "A wonderful young lady has been murdered. Though my son hasn't been charged, he has been run off because he's the leading suspect as her killer. I have no place else to turn." Her eyes pleaded as beautifully as ever. "Richard, I desperately need your help."

"I'm sorry, Sam! You have my sympathy and moral support— always. But as I've said, I can't get involved."

She almost upset the delicate porcelain cup, fumbling it onto the saucer. She leaned over the oval coffee table, her eyes boring into mine, "Like it or not, you *are* involved. And you'll also need all the help *you* can get!"

Chapter Four

LATER THAT NIGHT, after saying goodbye to Samantha, I flicked on the television, plopped deep into the Scotch-plaid sofa, and tried to concentrate on a television whodunit. My thoughts returning to Sam, I mused about our discussion, especially the part following, "Like it or not . . . you'll need all the help you can get." Not ready to deal with all the implications of our conversation, my mind wandering dangerously, I visualized her when she walked into the A-frame. I remembered the soft feel of her skin when I ran my fingers over her upturned face. I fancied I could still detect the rosewood and cedar aroma of her perfume. My pulse quickened, just as it did each time she came near back in high school. "Can mental programming last so long?" I asked myself aloud. "Nah! Surely not for thirty-odd years?" I answered, knowing I lied.

Unsettled by too-strong emotions, and reminding myself that I was here for company business and not an ancient romance, I ripped my thoughts away from Sam. I pried myself from the deep cushion, flicked off the television and retrieved my stuffed, leather briefcase from the next room.

Sitting at the corner desk, scanning papers beneath the circle of light from a tiny reading lamp, I recounted the rapidity of changes in my life. Since taking over as president, my duties had broadened quickly to include corporate investigator. To save my total company, I had to catch a crook at Architectural Design and Elaboration—ADE for short. The good news: I felt confident. For this job, I had a unique advantage: just after we bought the place, I had been the division's head honcho. I knew the business implicitly.

Opening a manila folder not seen for years, I reviewed the company's history. Immediately, I felt the dark side of the company. Since its founding, the firm had gained experience in building design, skyscraper erection, and—*surprisingly*—brutal murder. Maybe that was why we bought the place. After all, I'm a history buff and a sucker for a good story . . .

During the mid-1800s, U.S. cities overdosed in the construction of squat limestone buildings. Choices were minimal because ordinary humans can't leap to the top floors of high-rises. Then Otis invented the elevator. Close on his heels, Carnegie's mills began producing high-quality steel.

"In 1899," I read, "two Hoosier brothers, Silas and Archibald Williams, founded Architectural Design and Elaboration. Forceful men with big plans, they visualized skyscrapers. Their new company both designed the buildings and fabricated the steel skeletons for hundreds of the new structures.

"In the early thirties, Silas and Archibald caught a train to Chicago. Wanting a first-hand look at their handiwork, they rode a construction elevator to the top floor of a building carrying the 'Designed by ADE' crest. Archibald rode the same elevator back to State Street. Silas took the quicker route, a headfirst plunge from the twenty-sixth floor."

The report went on to say that the law credited Archibald with the assist; he was indicted for murder. He beat the murder rap to die in his own bed of congestive heart failure in 1951. Yet, under him, the company tripled in size. Had he murdered his brother? No one knew.

A year before Barb split from me, and I from the company, a business broker invited my father-in-law and me to tread the aisles that Silas and Archibald once walked. Ignoring the agent's hype but liking what we saw—maybe even enticed by its history—we bought the company.

The divorce intervened, my father-in-law defrauded me and I was forced away from it all. Now, after my sojourn as a PI, I was not only ramrodding the parent company based in Indianapolis, but trying to solve the problems at ADE, a division located in Bloomington.

Gathering the papers and snapping shut the leather briefcase, I flicked off the desk lamp and walked into the bedroom. Still guiding my mind like a difficult-to-steer machine, determined not to think of Sam, I sank beneath the covers.

Early next morning, I climbed out of bed to make a few uninterrupted phone calls from home before going to the office for paperwork catch-up and company re-familiarization. The phone beeped between outgoing calls.

It was Herschel Peters. "Can I bum a lift to work, Mr. Scott? I heard you were going in. I live just around the curve from your drive."

"Sure, Herschel. I'll pick you up at your front door in thirty minutes."

Herschel and I went way back. In 1994, just after we had bought ADE, and on my first day on the job at the new site, Herschel repaired my condo's furnace. He said he wanted a new job; ADE needed a maintenance man. I pulled strings. Human Resources hired him. Now, Herschel probably considered me more neighbor than company prez. Although, the down-home relationship wasn't management-by-the-book, it suited me.

On the dot, twenty-nine minutes later, I rounded the curve between our driveways. Herschel had already come down the long lane from his house and waited beside his mailbox.

"Mr. Scott, it's good having you back," Herschel said, climbing into the Jag. Carefully, he placed his sack lunch on the mat between his black, shop brogans, their steel toes shiny enough for shaving. "I've heard we got some company problems but, like I told my maintenance crew, you'll fix 'em."

"Thanks for the vote of confidence." I left unasked the question of where he got his confidential information.

Herschel wore a gray, freshly starched uniform and a long-billed cap carrying the ADE logo. Perched on the rim of the passenger seat, he looked tightly wound, ready for flight.

I knew Herschel to be a conversation minimalist, but after a half-dozen miles, he managed two complete sentences. "Me and the shop guys have a gift for you, Mr. Scott. Later on, can I bring it by your office?"

"Hey, Herschel, the door's always open." It would be too. I appreciate how difficult it is to define characters like Herschel. I believe that God, nature, or some supreme being keeps producing us humans from a DNA mix that, properly stirred and shaken, makes each one equally good or evil.

On occasion, the mix goes awry and produces a Hitler or a Mother Theresa type. Then there are small-fry exceptions like Herschel, people whose lives have limited reach, but who make their tiny realms better.

I remembered that, during the year I ran ADE, the company sponsored a charity for a mother of six who lost her husband in a car wreck. Of the hourly workers, Herschel and his wife Minnie contributed the most—a full month's paycheck. Now, probably suspecting I was carrying a tough emotional load, he had arranged a gift for me. I thanked him again, in advance.

After dropping Herschel off at the plant's side door, I circled to the front entrance and entered the lobby at seven o'clock sharp. While I was hurrying down the hall, a raucous screak of metal against metal grated on my ears. The sound came from Seve Jensen's wheelchair. Jensen had served as acting president during my company absence; now he would resume his former job as ADE's chief financial officer.

When he sighted me, his expression, chameleon-like, quickly altered from benign to vexed to congenial. I doubted that the final smile expressed much warmth, or enthusiasm at having me back aboard.

"It's a bitch when you're not certain you're loved," I muttered, hurrying to catch up. Aloud, I added, "Seve, for God's sake, don't CFO's ever sleep?" I stuck out a friendly paw.

After a millisecond's pause, he clasped it.

"Like always," I said, forging ahead, "you've made the scene ahead of me. You're even beating *our* secretary to work. I thought that was impossible."

I had emphasized *our*. After all, life is all about sharing. Unfortunately, for him, my returning as president hacked his duties in half. Now he must also share not only people but also authority and responsibilities. I suspected that sharing secretary Jeanie Robbins' talents would be especially galling.

He smiled and then again grew serious. "Welcome back, Richard. The company needs you."

His rapid changes revealed a pattern I knew. When angry, Seve Jensen showed a flash of anger, quickly followed by a big smile to smooth the waters.

Anyway, for the moment, I appreciated the smile. To some degree, I also understood his feelings. Temporary, high-profile jobs such as he'd been doing, quickly became thought of as permanent. When they end, the boss hears only enthusiastic lip service. It usually goes: "I understand. It's for the benefit of the company and, as you know, I'll make any sacrifice for the common good." Yet a husband, wife, or main squeeze catches the real spin: "Those bungholes down at the plant have repaid my loyalty, all right . . . this time, royally."

I attempted to ease the shock with, "You look good, Seve! You feeling on top of your game?"

"My back and my leg are kicking up a bit," he said, folding his body over the restraining seatbelt and massaging his right calf.

I fought showing pity. Here was a handsome, blond-headed guy weighing at least two-fifty, his legs and arms still knotted with muscles, but his paralyzed torso belted upright and captive to a stainless steel chair. That's tough! It seemed unreal. Even the wheelchair reminded me of a toy—a toy ready to topple because of the over-sized body riding it. I did wonder, though, how he kept so fit. Even on my feet constantly, I tend to go flabby.

"Let me know if you need the day off, Seve," I offered. "If you stick around we'll discuss the mall construction job sometime before lunch."

I planned to use the first day here to build rapport before broaching the money shortage. I foresaw prosecutions. I doubted they would involve Seve Jensen. Nonetheless, once more I recalled my Indianapolis accountant's caution about fraud—and murder.

While Jensen considered the day-off proposal, I recalled that during the short period since I resumed the presidency, I had talked to him several times on the phone and once in person when he visited the company's headquarters back in Indianapolis. I questioned why he hadn't outlined ADE's problems. Then his big square face broke into a smile. "I'll be here, Richard. Sorry I complained. Don't want to get in the habit." Grabbing the wheel with a rim-crushing squeeze, he yanked the wheelchair straight, and pushed off, squeaking away down the hall.

Some people say it takes guts for suffering people to bury their hurt inside. I don't agree that pain should always be hidden. If some poor schlemiel has to live with constant pain and wants to spend a half-minute describing it, we should listen. Anyway, nobody should forget that life's a crapshoot. Feeling strong and invulnerable, we offer some poor soul pity. A day later the karmic scales shift and we, as well, are up to our necks in alligators, hoping for a last-minute rescue before we go from being big guns to a gator's hors d'oeuvre.

Seve screeched around the corner en route to his office. I did have one bitch, though. I wanted to treat his chair to a grease job down at Luke's Quick Lube.

Chapter Five

TURNING, I TREKKED THE HALL to my old office. Charlie Tracey had made good on his shipping promise—the furniture from the agency had made the scene. The place looked precisely as it did all those months before when I left.

By seven-fifteen I was comfortably ensconced in my scuffed and wrinkled tan leather swivel chair planning the day's details. I'd heard that, back when I was head honcho, some of the office staff on the sly referred to the high-backed chair as my throne. Okay, I'd buy that! I liked the huge bugger, made ergonomic by my own expanding butt during the twenty years when I piloted this and other manufacturing companies.

I also liked my multidrawer, cubby-holed, and thickly painted desk with the carved-from-a-slug-of-tar look. The movers, giving the ancient and unsightly unit a place of honor, had plopped it down in the middle of a tribally patterned Tibetan carpet—the rug a pedigreed piece of wool that my ex-wife chucked out of the house when we split.

What the hey? I now had an office larger than my first factory—room aplenty for both whimsy and function. Feeling good, I gazed around the cavernous space. Yep, I had both.

One wall held a framed montage of pictures, including images of D.C.'s new Ronald Reagan Building, the Lincoln Memorial, the Pentagon, and New York's Empire State building. All built with

Indiana limestone. Of importance to me, ADE had been on the scene long enough to contribute expertise and materials for each structure.

Since I treasure that kind of background, I tended to forgive old Archibald Williams' malfeasance. Truth is, we build on foundations laid by pioneers. Many had more smarts than we cats who are fortunate enough to follow their clearly blazed trail.

Sometimes, a little history lesson lets us "big guns" know how tiny we really appear in the overall picture. Momentarily, I pictured a dwarf gnat astride a giant elephant.

Though ajar, my office door echoed a tentative rap on the jamb. "Hi again, Herschel!" I said. "I haven't seen you for a good thirty minutes."

Looking embarrassed, Herschel averted his eyes. Gaining confidence, he peeked from beneath his cap bill. "Mr. Scott, I'll say it again, the guys in the shop're mighty glad you're back," he said, his nose bobbing in time with his words.

Herschel's nose was his most prominent feature. It was as if God, at Herschel's birth, had first created the awe-inspiring beak and, only as an afterthought, attached a tiny bird-like body to one end of it.

"Thanks, Herschel."

He was hugging an irregularly shaped object against his chest. Through the burlap, it looked like a giant potato masher. He peeled off the wrapping.

"This is a cutting tool from the shop. The guys fixed it up real pretty, just for you." The tool had a foot-long broomstick-sized shaft with cutting teeth blossoming from one end like petals on a stainless steel rose.

"I recognize it." I ran my fingers over its surface. Normally, the metal would've been gouged and discolored from cutting through steel or stone. Evidently, in the interest of aesthetics, the guys in the shop had smoothed, chrome-plated, and polished the whole thing.

"Maybe I could stick it on that shelf with some of your other stuff," he said, hopefully, his eyes gesturing toward my glass and stainless steel bric-a-brac shelf.

I nodded and took a phone call. While I talked, Herschel rearranged the middle shelf to make a spot for my new acquisition. Finished, he examined the remainder of my "odd lots" memorabilia— a collection running the gamut from golf trophies to *objets d'art* picked up while in 'Nam and Kuwait.

His attention segueing from shelf to the wall, he then straightened the frames on a couple of my school and business bona fides. Cocking his head, he closely inspected a Lyonel Feininger print entitled "Sailing Boats," before moving over to examine a couple of random Picasso prints. He stepped back two paces for a better view.

I hung up the phone. "By the way, Herschel. What's the name of that whatchamacallit?"

"Sorry. Thought you knew, Mr. Scott. That's a 'rose cutter.' Sorta like the name of your stone quarry." He smiled. "That's one reason we wanted you to have it."

Handshakes have their place. I gave Herschel a big hug, then sat and watched him as he left the office. I suspected that, in the future, my new trophy would draw more attention from visitors than my bona fide art works.

That should've pleased me, but fighting a feeling of disquiet, I returned to the shelf for a second look. I turned the piece over and over in my hand. Still nonplused, I put it back and resumed my get-reacquainted tour of my office by going next to the drawing board that sometimes acted as a second table.

Periodically, however, I looked back at the rose-cutter tool. For some reason that hunk of gear gave me an eerie feeling.

Chapter Six

Two more quick phone calls aborted my tour completely. The first came from Jeanie Robbins, my secretary. She had a dental emergency and would be late. The second was from the lobby receptionist announcing a visitor.

I stepped into Jeanie's office just as my visitor hustled through the door. "I'm . . . Cyril Eads . . . from the . . . Cherished Days . . . Nursing Home," he gasped.

"Something's wrong with Mom, isn't there?" I tried to hide my alarm.

"It's nothing physical, be assured."

I offered to take his bulging briefcase; his thin frame was already listing windward. He refused. Changing direction, I led the way to the conference area where a pedestaled table—a new addition to the decor—seemed to grow out of the burnt umber carpet.

Still breathing hard, Eads swung his briefcase in an arc and guided it to a rough landing on the tan-leathered top. He pulled out a folder. "Just before your mother . . . joined us, you . . . funded a bank account in . . . her name."

"Sure did. Wanted her to feel independent. In fact, I authorized your nursing home to bill her account directly for monthly charges."

"That's the problem." Mr. Eads hesitated, seeming to give a lot of attention to the manicured grounds outside. Drawing a big breath, he said, "Mr. Scott, the account has been depleted!"

"Not another bloody evangelist! Surely to God, not that Bible-thumping, hypocritical son-of-a-bitch again!" Embarrassed by my own outburst, aware that there just might be another reason for the money shortage, I asked, "What precautions is the nursing home taking?"

"We're conducting an investigation." He went on to explain that my mother had been writing modest checks and having them cashed by first one practical nurse then another. He added that the cash had been returned to my mother. Preoccupied, he rubbed the tabletop's stainless steel trim with a slim finger and then un-smudged it with his cuff. "We have warned our employees: 'Cash no more checks!' But we have not the slightest idea what she's done with the money."

"I'm certain I do," I said. Knowing my mother's history, I surmised—or feared—that once again she had been suckered by a bogus charity. Only this time, my little, old, crafty mom was making cash gifts so I couldn't trace the recipient.

I moved to the other end of the office for my checkbook. While I wrote a check to cover the deficit, Eads stood by the window admiring the grounds. "I'll wager that those oaks and maples are as old as I," he speculated.

"Older. Far older, I imagine." I handed him the check. While writing, I harked back to the conversations with my accountant and Sam. Since I now sat in their old office I even factored in Silas and Archibald Williams, when I said, "And growing old in this world is a hazardous undertaking, Mr. Eads. Sometimes, impossible."

Chapter Seven

AFTER WALKING CYRIL EADS to the lobby, I keyed FTD on the Internet and, guilt-ridden, sent flowers to Mom. "Good boy," I *soto-voce*-ed. "Mom wants to hug a son, but must settle for pussy willows and freesias in a spring bouquet." Being a super son, I dialed her number, but got no answer.

Still fighting guilt, I pulled the thick, half-finished mall construction file from one of the desk drawers. Slipping on my half-glasses, I adjusted the green-shaded desk lamp and dove headfirst into the quotation's blueprinted lists of numbers mixed with drawings.

Classic fountain pens being my passion, I unclipped the Mont Blanc Octavian from my shirt pocket. In addition to lengthening the string of calculations, I added some class to the sheaf of papers. I maintain that a document isn't truly official until it has been signed in Waterman's black ink.

My attention held firm until eight-thirty. At that point, my mind strayed once more to Samantha and yesterday's conversation. I reconstructed and reconsidered her concluding comments after she bombed me with the earth-trembling announcement that a local killing had implications for me and my company.

"Before her murder, Janie McNamara was a part-time university student—and my pupil," Samantha had said. "She and my son, Roger, met one night when she came by the house to drop off a theme paper. She stayed for a few minutes of special tutoring. I think she stayed because of Roger, not my teaching."

Sam waxed thoughtful. "I hope you can meet Roger. I'm certain you'd like him." With the last words, her expression became even more intense, as if my liking Roger were of prime importance.

"Please go on," I urged. "You said Janie McNamara was a part-time student. Did she also work?"

Sam's lips tightened. "Full time at *your* company."

In a flash, I recalled my financial advisor's words about "rumors of a grisly murder." At the moment, choosing not to mention that statement, I said, "During my exile, Seve Jensen and I stayed in touch. Since my resumption of the presidency, we've talked both on the phone and in person. I wonder why he never mentioned a murder?" Though I kept an even voice, I knew my surprise bled through my musings. Certainly, an employee's murder involved the company. "Maybe Janie's killer is, at this moment, still on the company's payroll," I added. But needing support troops right then, not enemies, and feeling magnanimous, I mentally tugged at my judicial robe, adjusted my imaginary jurist's wig, and temporarily cleared Seve Jensen of blame.

I did regret that either the nearly two-year-old murder hadn't been adequately covered by the Indianapolis media, or I had been too preoccupied with Capital Detective Agency to notice. For whatever reason, I was facing an unpleasant surprise.

Samantha described Janie's final moments as recounted by Roger. "Janie knew her murderer." Sam had then gone on to describe how her then-twenty-two-year-old son and his date Jane McNamara, who was three years older, and another couple—both IU students—had gone skinny-dipping in Rose Cutter's Quarry the night Janie was stabbed.

That information chilled me. When she told me, I rose and peered out the window to see only the coming darkness. "Sam, can you believe we've talked until dusk."

She came forward to stand beside me. "Time flies when you're

having fun . . ." Also looking outside, her voice faded to a whisper.
Again Samantha shuddered.

Now I knew why—the infamous quarry, site of the murder, lay
out there, just beyond our sight. The very reason I had been drawn to
the glass.

Taking her hand I led her back and, this time, seated her on the
sofa beside me, continuing to hold and caress her fingers. "Sam, we
have strong emotional ties. Believe me, I'm sympathetic. However,
basically, I'm a business stiff. The presidency is a full-time gig. I haven't
time to backtrack into the shamus game. Anyway, my amateurish
detective work depends almost totally on persistence and legwork,
very little on skill."

I knew Samantha. I sensed her rejecting my arguments, one by
one, even as I presented them. "Anyway, I'll help you find a bona fide
professional," I concluded, very lamely.

She began covering the same ground once more. "But—"

"Sam," I interrupted and tried to reason, now taking both her
hands in mine, "you're only making this doubly difficult for both of
us."

She pulled away. Silence seemed to fill the room. Fighting tears,
surely unwilling to cede the fight, she fumbled with the letters left
scattered on the coffee table. Absently, perhaps because the square
envelope with its hand-written address stood out among the business
letters, she selected one and handed it to me.

The iron-gray envelope had no return address. Curious, I ripped
it open. It began with a simple greeting, "Dear Richard Scott."

The content exhibited greater, creative flair. Printed in block type,
the first two sentences took up one whole page: "I plan to deep-six
your carcass in the deepest part of Rose Cutter's Quarry. You have one
way out . . ."

Grim faced, I turned to the second page.

Chapter Eight

THE INSTRUCTIONS ON THE SECOND page were explicit: "Get your gangly body back to Indianapolis in that Jag, now, or stick around for a box. Private investigating will get you killed."

More same-tenor comments filled the remainder of the page. The note was unsigned—as one might expect. The letter had been mailed from Stonecrop, the nearest town and the county seat.

Disgustedly, I crumpled the paper. "Christ! I didn't know my gray sharkskin suit could generate such strong feelings. Maybe it's the yellow, power tie . . . ?"

Samantha didn't smile.

I too sobered. "Perhaps, the note's from somebody hurt by my private eye work downstate. Another thought: is a competitor trying to spook me?" I shrugged away the idea. "I doubt it. Successful business types usually out-think a rival, not snuff him."

"*Usually!*" Sam repeated the operative word.

For moments we didn't speak. Sam broke the silence. "Perhaps the threat is related to yesterday's *Herald Times* story."

I had read the Herald's business-section story on ADE, and recalled it word for word. First, it provided a rundown on my company. That part had been "on target" and good publicity. The blurb on my PI history said too much. Though it stressed my return as company president and CEO, it said I still carried a private investigator's license and would continue gumshoeing as a sideline. On that, I wanted to keep the opposition uninformed. What's more, whether here or in Vietnam, the company represents the worker's rice bowl. My employees needed to know my main aim was keeping theirs filled.Still, court appearances in the high-profile, apartment fraud case would've eventually blown my cover anyway.

"You should visit Janie's father, first thing," Sam urged, switching subjects, a leap of faith inference that, despite what I had said, our past relationship had sucked me into her case. "He lives downstate."

I searched for the right words. Hating to disappoint her, yet knowing I must, and wanting to make it easier, I found myself saying, "Yeah, he might shed light on the case." My wish-washy statement invalidated solid judgment. I hated myself for being a wimp and taking the easy way out.

But even during my self-exam, I knew I had but one—the right—choice. "Okay, Sam, I'll do what I can. I'll see her dad, but first, let's visit Janie McNamara's grave."

Sam ran her finger over the dateline of today's newspaper. Now smiling, she moved from the sofa to my chair and planted a wet kiss on my cheek. "We shouldn't delay. It's Tuesday and the cemetery is located a few miles south in Bedford. Shall we go later this week?"

I nodded, trapped, re-weighing my decision. Perhaps I hadn't resisted Samantha because of her obvious vulnerability. Could be it was the lightly tinted lips and delicately shaped mouth that did me in. Maybe the rosewood and cedar in the perfume was responsible, and I wasn't to blame at all!

I walked Sam to her car. She drove off with a wave. Farther down the drive, atop the hill, headlights flashed on. Sam's brake lights flickered as if she considered stopping. More slowly now, the Geo continued. In a few seconds, both vehicles disappeared over the hill, the second car plastered inches behind Sam's rear bumper.

"What have I done?" Turning, I trudged slowly up the sidewalk. "Here less than a day, and already, I'm neck deep, backstroking in a quagmire."

Chapter Nine

NEXT DAY, IT WAS TIME to start delivering on my job for Charlie Tracey, so I drove to Indianapolis. The disputed apartment complex stood forlornly in the middle of a forgotten neighborhood. Here, potholes deepened, curbs crumbled, and heavy-trash day should've been everyday. Obviously, the trucks never came.

Stella Carlyle met me at the curb as I eyed the mess.

"Stella," I commented, "compared to the other buildings, this red-brick complex looks like an oasis."

"Yeah," she said, wrinkling her nose, "but don't drink the water."

Briskly we followed a cracked and sunken sidewalk toward the middle apartment. Stopping near the door, Stella pointed toward the roofline. "Check out those drooping gutters and missing downspouts. Nobody cares. It's awful."

"Yeah," I agreed. "I don't suppose aesthetics are a high priority in this neighborhood, but *that* is too damn much." Stella's gaze followed mine.

A cluster of ragged bushes and shrubs nearly hid an abandoned, overturned grocery cart. Yellowing newspapers, empty booze bottles, and a dozen-plus used condoms mulched their roots. "You were dead right about the water," I growled.

It had been a tough winter. I couldn't help smiling as I pictured a new kind of investigation: "Officer, find the guy who's been taking advantage of our daughter. He'll be the one with the frostbitten willy. " In the interest of professionalism, I kept the thought to myself.

Stella climbed three steps and punched a doorbell. While we waited, she talked, "Twice, the city commission has forced the landlord to replace this building's plumbing. During vacancies, druggies stole the newly installed copper piping and sold it for scrap. Unsalable plastic replaced the copper."

I suspected that already this job was wearing on her. "It's a Catch-Twenty-two," she complained, sounding tired. "Someone steals copper; it's replaced; the buildings settle; plastic fractures; the pipes develop horrendous leaks. It's a bitch."

The door cracked open and a cafe-au-lait face peered out. "What ya'll want?" The woman's keen voice rode a smoker's cloud outside. She looked to Stella for her answer.

"Ms. Dempsie, we've plans to improve your living conditions. First, we need to visit your home."

The door opened, reluctantly.

Inside, Ms. Dempsie dragged an overflowing Budweiser ashtray to the corner of a thrift store coffee table. Scratching the longest butt from the heap, she uncrimped it. Between coughs, she sucked a light from one stub to the other.

Three children, stair-stepped from one to five years, huddled on a dilapidated sofa watching Roadrunner cartoons. Hotly pursued by Wily Coyote, the big-eyed bird skedaddled through a blinding snowstorm produced by the thirteen-inch TV's bum reception.

The youngest child wore diapers and sucked on the corner of a dingy blanket. The other two, dressed only in cotton briefs and goose bumps, struggled to gain owner's rights on a box of frosted Cheerios. All shrieked in anger and frustration when the box ripped open, showering them and fanning sugared cereal across the piss-green, shag carpet.

"Shut the M-effing-noise up!" Ms. Dempsie yelled, while, without missing a beat, leading us into the kitchen and pointing overhead. Like footprints from an embryonic earthquake, a two-inch fissure curved from the kitchen ceiling. It split at the intersection of two concrete blocks. Twin cracks, each wide enough to hold a man's fist, disappeared behind the kitchen sink. Beneath the cabinet, water from a broken garbage disposer flooded the linoleum, then snaked past an open garbage can and meandered to the outside door.

Grousing animatedly about ". . . a busted toilet, and ankle-deep crap," Ms. Dempsie led us toward the hall bathroom.

"Thanks, I've seen enough," I said. Holding my breath against the stench of garbage, dirty diapers, cigarettes, and stale booze, I bolted for the door.

I've heard that the perfumery business has two dozen gifted people called "noses," who can sniff any perfume and accurately identify all fragrance categories, from *head*, through *middle* and *base*. I've always believed that I possess a similar talent. Pity my gumshoeing trended toward *eau de la pauvreté*—and the stench of wretchedness—not essences of bergamot, ylang-ylang, and ambergris.

Stella rejoined me outside. Nearby, an air compressor "phlub-phlub-phlubbed" into action. Searching for the source, we walked to the next building and descended a steep set of stairs.

Somebody had filed his set of blueprints on the filthy basement floor. I supposed it was the boss employed by the bank, since that organization had also hired Capital Detective Agency to investigate the site. Dropping to a knee, I leafed through the yard-square, bound volume. "Have you checked the job against these drawings?" I asked Stella.

Removing a leather work glove, Stella traced blueprint lines with a slender finger. "Certainly! But you won't like my written report." She snapped her finger. "I almost forgot. I've also taken core samples of the soil."

"Good. Anything could be hiding beneath these buildings."

A heavyset construction worker started to stroll past us. Recognizing Stella he smiled and waved. Grabbing his arm, she steered him to an outside wall and showed him where to dig. Leaning a jackhammer against his stomach, he snapped on protective earmuffs.

Next, he tugged a full-face, cannistered mask into place. Tensing his arm muscles, he triggered the machine.

His overhanging gut and double chin vibrating in time with the chisel's strokes, he sliced through a first layer of concrete. Dust and earsplitting noise filled the room. In another cop-out, Stella and I retreated—up the stairs and outside into fresh air.

A bright red tractor pulled a lowboy trailer into the space between two buildings, just as we made the outside scene. I glanced at Stella, then checked my watch. "Right on time," she exclaimed.

She grabbed the truck jockey's coat sleeve and jerked her head toward the lemon-colored backhoe. "Unload that baby," she ordered. "We'll dig beyond the foundation and check the footers and the broken sewer connections—"

A hand snaked from behind me and grabbed my shoulder. "What in the holy hell are you doing?" A harsh voice demanded.

I wheeled around and stared straight into cold, dark eyes. I hoped height was our only similarity. I took in a broad, high forehead topping a tapered face. The chin was so wedge-shaped it could've been used as a replacement chisel for the construction worker's jack-hammer. Glimpse a face like his in a movie promo, you know the killer without shelling out eight bucks to see the flick.

Not buying his bluff, I carefully readjusted my shoulder pad. I feigned nonchalance and stepped back a couple of paces. My muscular friend, clad in a black suit, curled both hands into ham-sized fists and cocked his right arm.

Early on, I learned the intimidating power of bluster. "What in hell is *your* beef, pilgrim?" I bellowed, my voice so loud both he and Stella retreated.

Black suit quickly recovered. "I'm Karl Sprader, vice president of Consolidated Constructioneers, Inc." He jabbed a stubby thumb over his shoulder toward the building we'd just departed. "My company hasn't been fully paid for this job. No way I'll see you destroy it!"

"So sue us," I said, laconically. "You'll discover that Stella Carlyle and I can rip out this rotten concrete faster than you poured it."

Lips compressed, Sprader stepped forward until his nose was inches from mine. "Our attorney's seeking an injunction. Reverend Gabriel Goodall has the clout to get it. In the meantime, you stop dismantling"—he inched closer—"or without benefit of the court order, I'll have a piece of your ass!"

"Stella," I said, standing my ground, "run and get your wide-bodied, jackhammer friend. We'll either bury this creep here under his own building or schlep his battered remains outta here aboard the lowboy."

Taking a chance, I turned my back on Karl Sprader and stomped off to the Jag. Waving goodbye to Stella and ignoring Sprader, I maneuvered past his black, SR600 Mercedes.

The company veep stood, unclenching his fists, legs wide apart, sullenly watching me depart. I suspected Karl Sprader and I would meet again, too soon and much too often.

While maneuvering the first turn, I thought back. "Hey! He threatened me with Reverend Gabriel Goodall. Perhaps I'll finally meet the 'good reverend' face to face." I ached to do just that. Years ago, even from a distance, he had caused my family a giant amount of grief.

As I'd mused earlier, in a murder investigation, the private eye needs to get close to the victim. Nothing's closer than a grave.

Sam and I shuffled schedules and cleared a slot for an early morning cemetery meeting. We each drove. Just as I braked to a curbside halt, Sam rounded the corner and snugged her bright red Geo close in behind my Vanden Plas.

"As God is my witness!" Sam cried fervently on passing between Green Hill Cemetery's stone posts, "We *will* find your killer, Janie!" Then, just as emotionally, she addressed her son in absentia. "And Roger, we *will* have you back home again."

I tugged the wrought iron gate closed, waiting a long count of five for Sam to bring her emotions to ground level.

A half-block down the fence another steel gate creaked open and clanged into place. Hands on hips, a late arrival eyed us from the edge of the driveway. "Sam, we have company. And we seem to be the focus. Anybody you know?"

Sam's gaze followed mine. "Surely you jest," she chuckled, shielding her face in the crook of her arm. " 'Only the Shadow knows,' for sure."

Her imitation made the point. An upturned topcoat collar and a heavy scarf completely concealed the new arrival's chin. I wondered whether we were watching a slight figure bundled into a bulky coat, or heavy muscle in an all-weather shell. I strongly suspected that it was the latter. With frequent looks over a shoulder, the visitor ambled deeper into the cemetery. *Could this be the anonymous note writer?* I wondered, approaching paranoia, *or . . . did Sam write the note just to hook me into the case?* Knowing I now approached the completely delusional, I muttered a final "Nah!" aloud.

"Pardon?" Sam asked.

I shrugged. "Just growling."

We strode purposely along the blacktop drive. Frost muffled the sound of Sam's rubber-heeled boots and my leather-soled loafers. Our shoes crunched like jackboots when we turned onto a crushed gravel path.

Nearby, two gravediggers sat on the ground, dangling their legs into a newly dug grave. Hearing us, they turned and peered from deep within sweatshirt-hood tunnels.

I motioned a one-fingered "Hello." Each lifted his cup in a styrofoam salute then, in unison, they tossed their empties onto a pile of dirt. Both cups would end up in the grave, a McDonald's guarantee that one soul would spend eternity under the sign of the golden arches.

Cemeteries fascinate me. Tombstones chronicle the past. A history buff, I pore over shapes and inscriptions. Even the dying reach for the future and other people. Cryptic engravings become messages of history, pathos and an occasional smile.

"Read these, Sam," I pointed to a couple of small, weathered tombstones. "Joshua Barton, born June 16, 1842 . . ." The inscription faded. Tracing letters with my ignition key, I scraped away lichen. "Killed at Shiloh on April 6, 1862. Brought home for final rest, September, 1890." His next-plot neighbor, also twenty, perished a day later, same battlefield.

Sam's eyes misted. She searched through her purse for a tissue. "Those soldiers died too young . . . like Janie."

We continued on, weaving between stones and benches, skirting trees and bushes. The path next led to a whimsical, limestone statue of a golfer. His gaze surveyed a blissful green; his hands clutched a bagful of clubs.

Another monument replicated a stonecutter's workbench with hammer, mallet, chisels, and even an apron and broom. "For sure, we're in stone country," I observed.

"Jane's father was a stone carver. He once showed me through his shop." She stroked a corner of the inclined work-bench. "This is called a 'banker.'"

A bit farther on, Jane's grave lay beneath a thick, winter-dead maple tree. A drooping branch grated the top of her tombstone. The sound recalled Sam's comment, "While struggling to breathe, Janie tried to speak. She knew her murderer—I'm certain of it."

I leaned closer. JANE EDITH MCNAMARA, BORN JULY 3, 1973— DIED AUGUST 13, 1998. "Blast! That is young." Standing on tiptoe, I fingered the top of Jane's tombstone. "Why the broken-tree configuration, Sam?"

"It's symbolic. A broken, but not-quite-severed, branch hanging near the apex signifies a life cut short." She pointed higher. "Also, in local tradition, a crowning hat like the one atop her monument usually indicates a child's memorial."

"But Jane was twenty-five. Still," I concluded, "I suppose to hurting parents, a twenty-five-year-old may still be a baby."

"I empathize," Sam lamented. "Roger had a difficult time, too. He wasn't allowed to play out his grief in Indiana." She laid her hand on my arm. "Many times, I've felt lonely and longed for you to be near."

Thoughts of Caitlin McChesney flitted through my mind, but my finger was gentle when I touched Sam's cheek. "At least Roger's father could've been supportive."

Her words bitter, Samantha recounted that her son's traveling orders came quickly. "Frightened and lonely, he was aboard a Greyhound and away from Indiana in less than a week." She didn't say who gave the orders and I didn't ask.

"Richard, you haven't yet heard one of the most pathetic chapters in this whole tragedy . . ." She started to turn away, but I insisted she continue.

"Janie's tombstone was her father's last work. Next day, he closed his tiny shop, packed his belongings, and moved back to his boyhood home. He lives downstate, near the Ohio River."

More slowly than we came in, we walked arm-in-arm toward the exit gate. I read one more inscription: "Virginia Ashworth, Born in Hitchen, Hertfordshire, England—9 July 1863 . . ."

It being late March, English bluebells had just pierced the ground around the grave, and saffron crocuses and brilliantly yellow daffodils laced the bluegrass. Figuring no one would care about Virginia's neglected grave and that she might like to share, Sam and I plucked a handful of each.

We placed a few atop her tombstone. I found a discarded urn lying in the grass near the path. After tucking the remainder into the container, we carried it back to Janie's plot. I grimaced in sudden frustration. "Sam, I can't say why, but I feel certain we've missed something. Dime to a donut it's something obvious, and important, but for the life of me, I can't copy the message."

She hugged my arm in silent commiseration.

As we neared the exit, I glanced around the stone-laden field. Across the cemetery, our companion now leaned against the wrought iron fence. While we watched, he levered himself erect, and followed another gravel path toward an exit.

Hurrying, we tried to angle our way ahead of him.

He broke into a jog. Without another glance toward us, he hurried through the gate, trotted across the street and slipped around the side of a building.

When we rounded the corner, he was nowhere in sight.

Feeling protective, I followed closely behind Samantha's tiny car as we drove north toward home. WQIP, my favorite Indiana station, switched from the soulful, Appalachian/Country sounds of Gillion Welch and David Nowlings with their rendition of "One More Dollar" and gave a local weather report. The station then segued to news—which turned out to be another weather report.

A freak hurricane had just been spawned in the Caribbean. Designated Hurricane Aaron, and ". . . packing winds in the hundred-fifteen MPH range, it plowed into the Dominican Republic, killing thirteen, destroying hundreds of houses, and causing floods that have sent Dominicans and tourists fleeing for higher ground. If it continues on its present course, the rogue, out-of-season hurricane will hit Florida within days . . ."

I found myself concerned, a feeling going beyond the tragic deaths and destruction. I owned a Siesta Key condo, but the chance of damage to that was remote. Maybe it was because hurricane season usually runs from June to November, this storm had been spawned out of season, and being a certifiable ecology nut, I dislike rapid environmental changes.

In a voice of doom, the announcer mentioned El Niño and La Niña and global warning. I switched stations and didn't listen to the rest of the story.

Chapter Ten

Later that afternoon, I called Sam and we agreed to dinner at a small, cozy seafood restaurant. Unfortunately, the evening never got off the ground.

Samantha couldn't seem to pull her mind away from Jane McNamara and the cemetery. Neither could she tell me more about the broken tree monument with the wide-brimmed hat. And that, I definitely wanted to know.

Nighttime, darkness and a lone guy in a king-size bed can be a bitch of a combination. During the day, thoughts are illumined and softened by sunlight and activity. At night, scope becomes the inside of your head. It's an impossible trap.

Anyhow, thoughts tornadoing my mind, the night seemed a week long. There was little room for another woman in my life. Not even Samantha. Not when I still loved Caitlin McChesney. Also, I hadn't wanted another investigation. But, I had committed; I would do it. The threatening letter added another complicated dimension.

Being suckered by an anonymous, possibly all-bluff note galled me. I would dig for the cowardly miscreant who wrote it. Maybe hand feed him his own ballpoint.

In my *Richard Scott's Book of Truisms*—unpublished, but

positioned for quick recall—bluffs have limited utility. I'll admit that while playing poker I can admire some Cool Hand Luke flashing a four-aces smile over a loser's spread, but away from the table I'm a cat who treats bluffs and threats alike. I issue an identical challenge for both: "Show your cards or get the hell out of the game!"

Near one o'clock I finally slept. In what seemed minutes, strident voices woke me. Groggy, I sensed sunlight seeping through the drapes. I thought of the finish work yet to be done in my ex-father-in-law's dream house. Had a carpenter crew made the scene?

That would be good. Sunshine wasn't. Daylight had arrived much too early for my biological clock.

"What the hey, Richard," I asked myself, rhetorically, "Don't you deserve a big gun's perks? Give yourself a break! Let Seve Jensen open the store. He has successfully kept the wheels turning while you were away—even though somebody's stolen you blind."

Eyes clamped shut, and willing myself back to sleep, I became lodged in that no man's land between sleep and consciousness. I'm convinced that life has an overall harmony with a plan taking you where you're supposed to go, but sometimes, like tonight, mine seemed more like a fugue orchestrated by a mad conductor: the themes variant, all dissonant, many beyond my comprehension. My mind, drugged by sleep and two late-night double Stolichnayas, steered a route all its own. The road led backward, through years of twisting curves and deadly intersections, best avoided.

With nightmare clarity, I recalled Dad's last years when he stumbled around the house, a Second World War limp made more prominent by fifty years of manual labor—and frequent shots of cheap bourbon making him forget that he hurt.

I thought of Mom, warehoused for years in a nursing home after Dad died. Now, bereft of a meaningful life, she had grown nostalgic about all the years spent living with Dad, even during his binges.

I reflected on how she and Dad had always wanted to be a big part of my life. They refused to admit, or maybe recognize, that they had a fast-track son who couldn't—or wouldn't?—deliver on the kind of attention that parents long for. Adding to Mom's woes and humiliation, Reverend Gabriel Goodall's fraudulent charity suckered her out of her savings, leaving her vulnerable, ashamed and dependent on me for the cost of her care.

Not that I minded. I had plenty of loot, but the loss of her independence had driven her into a year of silence and remorse, and only recently had she again resumed talking.

Increasing noise jarred me back to the moment. Could they be burying more pipes? Before long—in this neighborhood—an earthquake would be impossible; the countryside would be laced solid with plumbing from this building project.

I dozed again.

Jerking forward, my up-close-and-personal phantasmagoria flipped another of memory's cards . . . 'Nam, then Desert Storm . . . my own last rites . . . my ex-wife Barb's abortion . . .

Light flickering across my eyelids intensified. "Okay Scott," I muttered, psyching myself, "Get your butt in gear."

I threw back the blanket. Throwing my feet over the edge of the bed, I heard a crash from the direction of the new house. I even imagined I heard a man's agonized shout. My eyes swept across the Seiko's glowing face. "Christ!" I yelped. "It's only two A.M.!"

Spinning round, I darted toward the window and yanked wide the drapes. "Oh, God, no!" I yelled, peering outside. Grabbing the phone, I dialed 911. That wasn't sunlight. It was fire! Flames engulfed, consuming, the new dream house.

Cramming my feet into my loafers, I charged outside, pausing on the porch's top step. A bitter cold wind stung my cheeks; an ember-filled cloud swept against the A-frame's top story and cascaded down, showering me with sparks.

I vaulted back onto the porch. "Maybe the fire department can save something."

The scene through the windows hypnotized me. Embanked by rafters, supported by intense heat, an upside-down, golden stream of fire raced toward the ceiling's apex. Outside, smoke licked from a third story vent. Growing blacker, the tongue climbed a gable, blasting into flame. Fire exploded through a third story skylight.

Too upset to watch, I wheeled around. The picture window reflected the conflagration. With a jet squadron's roar, the roof collapsed through three lower floors. The whole structure imploded into a basement inferno.

Crack! Crack! Crack! Gunfire! Diving to the floor, I rolled and dropped five feet onto frozen ground.

"Gunfire? No way!" I yelled, massaging an aching hip pointer. The booze bottles had exploded. "What a rotten way to break open a bottle of Booker's bourbon or pop the cork on a bottle of Vichon Cabernet Sauvignon."

At the height of the conflagration, I suddenly remembered George, the big, floppy-eared mongrel. Scrambling and twisting between evergreen shrubs, still not fully erect, I charged down the sidewalk and across the drive.

"George!" I cried. "Here, George! Here! What a shame, anyway," I groaned, my path blocked by a wall of superheated air and the hopeless feeling that no matter how fast I traveled, this trip was much too late.

I had a premonition that the dog wasn't all we'd find buried beneath those ashes.

Chapter Eleven

A DISTANT SIREN topped the fire's roar.

I stood next to the A-frame beneath the branches of a tall sycamore. High overhead, a clump of dead leaves flamed, then caught by a wind gust, they broke apart and soared into the night. If the limbs caught fire, the A-frame would go with the tree.

"Come on! Hurry it up!" I shouted, my attention shifting back to the narrow lane.

The siren seemed to wail in place when the fire engine slowed to make the left turn from county asphalt onto my gravel drive. A procession of cars followed as it lurched over the hill, its red and blue lights repainting in vivid colors the dead sage and brush along the berm. Seconds later, the fire engine's brakes hissed as it rattled to a stop.

Autos cozied near the fire truck like a mother hen's brood. A dozen, tousle-haired, half-uniformed, volunteer firemen piled out. Some appeared drowsy, others wide awake, but when their feet touched the ground, they all snapped-to as if on parade.

Appearing professional in a bright yellow firefighter's coat, the chief yelled instructions. His men scrambled atop the truck. After unhooking firefighting axes, hoses, ropes, and hook-ladders, they leaped to the ground and lugged the paraphernalia onto the lawn.

"Hose the other house!" the chief bull-horned and pointed.

The men fired up the fire engine's meager tank.

I ran to him. I leaned close, tugged a sleeve, and yelled directly in his ear, "You'll have to use the cistern!"

He was accustomed to the rural problem and flipped a circled-fingered okay. Grabbing his arm, I steered him toward the A-frame, and a roof-fed cistern twenty feet out in the yard.

Now twigs on one of the sycamore's bottom limbs blazed. Flames skittered a scaly barked path around the tree's trunk and raced toward the A-frame. A fireman drenched the lower limbs. He cursed when the hose quickly pissed out. Desperate for additional water, three firemen dragged an auxiliary hose toward Rose Cutter's Quarry.

Minutes later the fireman were again playing water onto the inferno. White-hot steam shot into the sky. Orange and yellow flames absorbed the water and, undiminished, reached higher, dispensing newly made clouds.

Pieces of the new house, now ash, landed on trees and ground like white-winged butterflies fluttering from the clouds. Maybe they were a supernal message that my ex-father-in-law's final dream had died.

The A-frame's asphalt shingles began to fry. One section burst into flame. I tugged a fireman's rubber coat and gestured at the roof. Forsaking the old man's doomed dream home, he played water across the roof and front wall of mine.

Just then Samantha's red car skidded to a stop behind the firemen's. I ran forward to her greeting. "One of your neighbors called after she heard sirens and saw the fire."

I shuddered with emotional tension and release, then expelling a deep breath, shut my eyes. She pulled my head near hers and made cooing and clucking sounds that had nothing to do with fire, but had everything to do with what I needed most at that moment.

I reopened my eyes. Despite the catastrophe, I felt remarkably better. Grateful to have her by my side, I hugged Samantha more tightly.

An hour later the battle concluded, the never-in-doubt outcome now a fact. "It's a shame, Mr. Scott," the good-looking, young chief said. Removing his helmet, he used a maroon shop cloth to swab the sweat streaming down his forehead and cheeks. "Who would've caused such a thing?"

"Welders, probably. Yesterday, they were splicing basement columns. I suppose they cut through the drywall. Who knows? The electricians were here too, so it could be I'm hanging the welders with a bum rap . . ." My voice rasped to a halt. Suppressing a cough, I sniffed deeply, in a futile bid to clear soot and grunge from my nostrils. Sam dug through a quilted coat pocket and came to the rescue with a tissue.

The fire chief stepped between us and grasped our elbows. Silently, he steered us nearer the fire. With his aimed flashlight, he traced a scorched path leading from the rear of the smoldering pit. The beam spotlighted a bright-red, five-gallon, gasoline jerry can lying on its side a hundred feet or so out in the yard.

"Aha! So it's arson, eh?" I asked, voicing a redundancy as we eyed the smoke-blackened answer.

Sam shivered. I supposed she was thinking of Jane McNamara's murder and pondering connections.

"Yes," he said. "It seems more threatening, knowing that the arsonist sent a message that the fire was no accident."

"Yeah, it would be difficult to miss that can."

Sam and I wheeled around and moved toward my house, exhausted, throats parched, faces covered with ashes and soot. I wiped my upper lip on my forearm and gagged at the smell of singed hair.

Slowly we climbed the porch steps, I despising whoever hated me enough to burn the house, she quietly reflective. A disjointed thought caused me to wonder which neighbor had called Samantha, since there had been no gawkers. Still, it didn't seem important enough to ask.

From deep in the hills a cacophony of canine barking broke the silence. Somewhere nearer a lone dog barked a vigorous answer, the sound tapering into a protracted, mournful howl.

"Earlier, while I was half asleep, I heard voices outside," I rasped. "Who could it have been?"

Samantha shrugged her answer. We moved directly through the living room and into the kitchen.

"You feel up to a cup of coffee?" I asked.

"Just like old times sake? Okay. Remember how we loved to meet in the kitchen and gab? Except, back then, it was always orange juice for me and my complexion, and a Coke for you because you"—forcing a smile, she reached up and playfully tugged at my beard—"because you worried about absolutely nothing." She wiped her smudged finger on a table napkin.

Seated in the tiny dinette, we didn't talk much. Too worn out. I recollected that the second bedroom was filled with everything from wader boots to water skis and a heavily stocked gun cabinet. "You sleep on the bed and I'll take the sofa," I suggested.

"That also sounds like old times—except, back then, Mom was there to keep us in line." For the first time tonight, Samantha laughed. "Anyway, time hasn't changed our chemistry. Perhaps staying over isn't such a good idea."

"Or perhaps the best," I kidded . . . I think. I remembered our last night together. It had been much more than a kitchen gabfest. Even bone tired, I felt a deep stirring, a forgotten awakening.

"Truth is, I have an early morning class and had best go to my own bed."

I bear-hugged her all the way to the car. Subconsciously I held her especially tight, hoping she'd change her mind and stay.

She laid the cellular phone from her purse onto the passenger seat. I watched as the taillights grew dimmer. Again, near the top of the hill, the brake lights flickered. On cue, just as before, another vehicle pulled in behind Sam's car and followed closely as she drove from sight. I recognized the shape of the taillights. That same car had followed her before.

Coincidence? Unlikely. Quickly, I dialed her cell phone number. "Hey, Sam, you have a bogey at six o'clock. Is everything okay? Stop for nothing! I'm on my way!"

"Not to worry," she said, her voice tired, then added, "I'll explain later. Good night, dear."

"Who in hell—?" A hang-up click killed the question.

My thoughts returned to big, friendly, bushy-haired George and my hatred for his killer.

Three hours after I hit the rack again, the alarm clock booted me from a restless sleep. After a shower and a stiff, black cuppa, I logged onto the computer, and got upset when my server sent a dozen busy signals before shaking electronic hands with the rest of the world.

I checked my e-mail. Since my split with Caitlin McChesney, this sequence had become my schedule's lead-off item. The red flag snapped upright:

Dearest Richard,

I like being back in New York, the job is great, and the company's performance far exceeds my wildest projections. But my career has become of minor importance. I miss you. Desperately.

Now, complicating matters, an old issue has once again surfaced. I had dinner with Christopher last night. He suggests that I cancel my apartment lease and move back in with him. He feels it would be best for Peter.

I know a twelve-year-old needs both parents. Maybe Chris has changed . . . but just now, I can't get you out of my mind . . .

With Love and kisses,
Cait

I reread the letter. With my blood two degrees north of boiling point, I hammered out a message of my own:

Dearest Cait:
Cait, how can you be so foolish? Today's Christopher is the

same low-life who, just months ago went to court and lied through his teeth so you'd be separated from your child; so Peter is his biological child; so what?

I've seen the two of you together, and believe me, the bonds of love between you and that child were much stronger than genes and bloodlines.

Now, again, he suggests that you have a legitimate place in your son's life. That's his wedge; he knows that you'll sacrifice anything for the child.

Please! Don't again go down the same road with that cruel bunghole; once again, you'll endure the same emotional turmoil . . . !

Love,
Richard

Our relationship had become so bloody complicated. With no money problem of my own now, I tended to discount the importance of her job, which was patently unfair. Not only did the presidency of a New York computer software corporation represent big bucks to her, it more importantly represented a tremendous personal accomplishment.

She was justifiably proud. Especially after all she'd been through with Christopher, who majored in ego-destruction.

Ignoring other options, I continued to insist that she return to Indianapolis and live with me. I never admitted that I could just as easily move to New York, once I had a handle on my company's cash problems.

Heaven forbid that we compromise. I could stay in Indy, Cait in New York, and we could commute, at least on weekends. For people in love, a half a loaf is better, et cetera, et cetera, et cetera . . . So where were we? Frozen in place, two strong personalities, each determined to call the shots.

Overwhelmed by either love, loneliness, exhaustion, or last night's hurt, I decided to reach out through Ma Bell. My thoughts soaring, I punched the first number on the speed dial, then remembered that I was in new digs with an unprogrammed phone. Feverishly, I dialed.

We would marry, I vowed! We'd force the custody issue with Christopher and bring Peter back to Indiana to live with us.

The phone rang in her apartment. No answer. Obviously, she'd left early for work. Once again, e-mail became the route.

I dashed off a quicky message. I advised that she "maintain the status quo while we sort out our lives."

"I can't propose on e-mail," I consoled myself.

But, admittedly, I had been relieved when she didn't answer the phone. Obviously we had a new problem—Samantha's lovely face had become superimposed upon the total picture.

The doorbell's honking broke my train of thought. I opened the door—introducing a delightful surprise along with a complicated day.

"I'm Gerald Camus, your building contractor."

"Good. The insurance adjustor should be here anytime—"

Cutting short my words, a brownish-burnt fur shape catapulted onto the porch. Forcing his way between my leg and the door jam, guard-dog George scrambled inside, tore his way through the living room and darted into the kitchen.

I found him peering from the pantry door. "Good boy, George! You made it!" Rubbing his head with one hand, I gave him a quickie examination with the other. Although covered with cockleburrs and smelling like scorched burlap, the old man's guard dog appeared none the worse for wear.

"Excuse me, Mr. Camus, I have a resurrected dog to feed."

I poured a saucepan of water and searched the pantry. A few cans of heart-healthy food remained from the old man's stay. Gerald Camus and I stood watching while George wolfed beef hash from a casserole dish. Not only had George escaped the fire, now we were guaranteeing him shiny-clean arteries.

Another door bell honk announced that the blue-suit from Fealty

Insurance Company had arrived dead on schedule. "Richard Scott, I presume?" He presented an embossed business card. "I'm Agent Felton Crenshaw." He extended his hand.

He had skillfully arranged three flattened ropes of hair to conceal a bald spot—a void big as a Buick hubcap. When we sat down, strands broke free and fell, hanging like bungee cords over one ear. By rote, he quickly palmed the hair—stroking it back in place and leaving it as smooth as sprayed paint.

"Thanks for coming early, Mr. Crenshaw. Please meet Gerald Camus, my building contractor."

I manned the sofa, the other men chairs. Hunched over the tiny coffee table, we concentrated on cluttered stacks of documents like seers, each with his private crystal ball. Only the rustle of papers broke the silence.

Laureen quietly entered through the back door as we were sitting down. Now she brought steaming hot coffee and found room for mugs between papers.

I arose to welcome her efforts and introduce her to my guests.

"Such a shame, Mr. Scott." She pulled a wadded tissue from her sweater cuff and dabbed her eyes. "I hoped to work for you full-time once the house was finished." Grimacing, she nodded toward the window. "Now, just look at that mess. Your father-in-law, Mr. Winters will just die."

"Yeah, it's a bummer. Still," I soothed, "maybe we'll rebuild after Mr. Crenshaw writes a check."

Harrumphing, Felton Crenshaw ripped the seal on another brown envelope. I sneaked a peek. The document had been signed by Fealty's arson investigator. Obviously, in prepping for us, Felton Crenshaw had called an early morning meeting with his own people.

Squinting through my half-glasses, I plowed through a phalanx of documentary whereases and exclusions. Pity the house hadn't been destroyed by earthquake or volcano. Both were covered. My pathological distrust of insurance companies intensified. Plus I resented being a suspect. Here's my read: in murder cases, cops automatically finger the spouse; in insurance losses adjusters immediately suspect policyholder skullduggery.

I could be wrong, though. I was wrong once—back when I was young and inexperienced.

From his lofty position, hair momentarily balanced, Felton Crenshaw fixed his eyes on mine. "Do you have progression pictures taken during the building's construction? Failure to produce those along with receipts for material could void the contract."

After scratching through his briefcase, Gerald Camus produced the pictures.

"We must be especially cautious with your company, Mr. Scott. Its history gives us cause for concern. I believe your father-in-law has been, uh . . . shall we say, incarcerated? Furthermore, another policy claimant has close ties to your company."

"Please provide a name," I demanded.

"Impossible. And absolutely unethical," he said with finality. He re-folded the policy.

I framed a harsh rejoinder, but then, studying the adjuster's face, its creased and nearly translucent skin thinner than an onionskin document, I reconsidered. I just couldn't do it. Felton Crenswaw reminded me of my dad. Even the worsted wool suit was a virtual twin to one my father owned, except shinier, probably having logged even more miles than Dad's. Plus, it presented a more creative twist. The three-button suit had been converted into a more modern two-button model with the lapels rolled lower and what had once been the top buttonhole now staring from the middle of one artificially lengthened lapel like a half-closed but malignant eye. It was a tailoring trick, long used by old-timers who couldn't bear to throw away a suit with serviceable miles left on the odometer.

Crenshaw restacked his documents and used the table surface to peck the edges even. Then, he opened a notebook and pencilled a series of notes, claiming the attention of both Camus and me.

With an effort, I tore away my gaze to stare through the picture window at the scorched rubble. The acrid smell even permeated the house. At first, I blamed George, then cleared him of blame when I saw him snoozing in a far corner.

Yellow crime-scene tape now draped the burn site's periphery. Through what had once been a casement window, I watched the investigators descend to the basement. I followed their progress as they meticulously searched the ruins.

Remembering the uncovered sump pit, I considered warning them to be careful. Still, I supposed that the deep reservoir would be filled with debris.

I again studied the insurance adjuster. When I noted the lapel's third eye, I smiled. Perhaps I could rent the coat for a hidden-camera gig? With the lens unobtrusively peering from that stitched buttonhole, I could snap picture after picture without raising suspicion.

Felton Crenshaw zipped his briefcase. I liked him. I suspected that in the long run, I'd get a square deal. Right now, however, I needed help that had nothing to do with a hefty cashier's check.

After all-around handshakes, Camus and Crenshaw—contractor and adjuster—exited the front door together. I called after them, then held my pen poised over a note pad. "Mr. Crenshaw, I believe you meant to provide the name of the other claimant, the one with close ties to my company?"

Suppressing a smile, he shook his head, "No."

Hey! It had been worth a try.

Chapter Twelve

With Felton Crenshaw out of the way, I joined the arson investigator outside and, being a hands-on type, offered to help.

"Thanks," he said, waving me away. "We've everything under control here."

Perhaps, he should've taken me up on it. I would've known where to dig. Since he didn't, I called Sam with the good news about George, ". . . so you two can bond properly, I'd like to drop him off at your house."

"I don't know . . ." Sam sounded doubtful.

I described how pathetic he looked peering from the pantry, then explained that Laureen would soon be leaving for the day. "George desperately needs a dog-sitter." I let my voice fade for effect. "Of course, he's just a big, cuddly, but worthless mutt, and who cares . . ."

"All right, Richard. It's not fair, but bring him along."

Next, Herschel Peters, the factory's maintenance man called, "Mr. Scott, my car's back in the shop. But if I had a ride into the plant, my brother-in-law would give me a lift back home, this evening." His words put the problem in my lap.

I cheerfully answered, "See you in five, Herschel."

While I dealt with Herschel, Laureen had contrived a makeshift leash from drapery cord. Thinking I wasn't looking, she wrapped George in her beefy arms and kissed his scorched head.

After twisting the cord twice around my hand, I coaxed him down the sidewalk and wrestled him into the Jag. The car looked like it had been parked near the Mount St. Helens eruption. I whisked a layer of gray ash from the windshield before climbing inside and speeding along the lane toward Herschel Peters'.

Again, sack lunch underarm, he waited at the end of the lane beside his mailbox. "Hi, Herschel," I said, as I opened the passenger door.

"Mornin', Mr. Scott." Herschel averted his eyes. After giving the matter serious consideration, he spoke again. "Dad-burned shame about your house." His head nodded in time with the words.

Aiming the Jag's head north on Highway 37, I flicked the radio onto WQIP Radio. The local newscaster reported that, "During the early morning hours, a partially constructed mansion burned to the ground—with an estimated loss in the low seven-figure range . . ." I wasn't named.

Following that, we listened to pop music with one interruption from my cellular phone call. According to the caller, I had won a new Blazer from "Vacations Unlimited." That was the third one this month, alone. "Who knows," I mumbled, "maybe I can soon start my own car dealership and sell Herschel a bargain Blazer!"

Herschel, staring straight ahead, now glanced over his shoulder. Spying George in the back seat, he turned downright loquacious, "At least everything didn't turn out bad." He scratched George's back. Grateful for the attention, George sniffed Herschel's ear, then licked the back of his neck.

"Yes, for awhile old George had us worried."

"Sorry I wasn't around to help. The company's Laser cutter went on the blink just past midnight. Clyde drove out and got me so I could repair it."

"No sweat. Nobody could've helped."

The music broadcast switched to a religious program and a

familiar voice giving a mini sermon. Yesterday the Reverend Gabriel Goodall had been haranguing abortionists; today he was trampling the gays.

It's a bitch, but even though I despise the man and the message, I still can't resist listening to radio- and tel-evangelists. Especially, Reverend Gabriel Goodall.

That's not just because Reverend Goodall rooked Mom out of her savings and I dream of getting even. I believe I envy their persuasive powers and subconsciously plan, somehow, to adopt their formula for my own business. If an evangelist can worm money out of the penniless, surely I could use the same technique to get more business from people who aren't broke.

Or, as I often ask myself, is it because my father once listened and gave 'em hell when they begged for money? I could still remember Dad's summoning up his best country twang to sing: "Spin the radio on,/And the sound of preaching fills the air./Flip the television on,/ Then mail in your fair share . . ."

Blame it on Dad and country-western music.

Today, Goodall, hard into his bashing of gays, warned, "You out there in my airwaves congregation, don't confuse *wild* times with *good* times. Don't speak to me of 'sexual orientation'; homosexuality is a mortal sin."

Pages rustled. I pictured an aide wadding paper while Goodall read from the Bible. " 'The sons of God came unto the daughters of men, and they bare children to them, the same became mighty men which were of old, men of renown.'

"Procreation is God's plan. Cloaked in goodness and wearing the armor of perfection and love, Christ will guard against evil. He will destroy today's abominable—just as the Old Testament Israelites fell upon and slaughtered the hated Canaanites . . ."

His voice a theatrical whisper, Goodall put the final whammy on gays: "For they have sown the wind, and they shall reap the whirlwind: it hath no stalk; the bud shall yield no meal; if so be it yield—" his words rose in volume "—the strangers shall swallow it up."

I hadn't heard such religious fervor since Charlton Heston had, a few years ago, become president of the NRA and pledged his everlasting love for gun nuts, pistols, and assault rifles.

I lowered the volume.

"Whadda you think of Reverend Goodall?" Herschel asked, pointing a skinny finger toward the radio. "Is he a good man? Would my wife Minnie and me be wrong to send him a few dollars? We like supporting the church."

"That's your call, Herschel." I didn't want to get into Herschel's head and cause him to think like me. On important issues, I believe people must make personal evaluations.

"I wondered about your idees. You being smart and all. He claims to be holy. Is he?"

"Look, Herschel. I have a difficult time getting in step with evangelists. Especially ones like Goodall who begin their ministry with magnificent promise, then lose their way and turn predator." For the next minute we rode silently, alone with our own thoughts.

I could only guess what Herschel thought, but in my mind, I summed up my belief that God is responsible for everything, the good and the bad. I figure that depraved characters like the Reverend Gabriel Goodall represent all the prejudices and hatreds making up the pernicious side of God's kingdom.

Herschel kept glancing toward me, expecting a longer answer. I tried, "Just think it over, and do whatever you and Minnie believe to be right. It's all guesswork. You and divinity Ph.D.'s. have an equal shot at the truth."

"Ph.D.'s?"

"Doctors. See, Herschel, the Jews, Moslems, Buddhists, and everybody else can enter the pearlies. I suppose a belief in the tooth fairy could get you there too, providing it caused you to treat your neighbor okay."

Looking somewhat confused, but still pleased, Herschel nodded, his nose now bobbing up and down in time to the tires as they kissed the cracks on the concrete road.

Once more, my cell phone beeped. I flicked off the radio.

"How quickly can you get to the office?" Seve Jensen asked, not panicky. But concern clipped short the intervals between his next words.

I listened quietly for a couple of secs. "See you in ten minutes." I glanced toward the back seat where George was chewing on one of my leather gloves. "Make that twenty-five," I corrected, "I have to make an important stop on the way in."

Evidently, Chief Financial Officer Seve Jensen had been vehicle shopping. He was seated in a new, motorized chair, its wheels snugged close to the desk. His fingers were tracing the top page of a computer readout when I walked into his office.

In contrast to his usual precise and immaculate appearance, Seve's cuffs had been rolled up two turns, his white-on-white shirt looking limp and rumpled. Drawing nearer, I got a whiff of Van Cleef and Arpels cologne like I once wore; only this batch had been supercharged by a stressed and overheated body. I figured my jittery financial officer had been sweating it out in that same spot for several hours.

"Jesus, Richard!" Seve began, obviously feeling my presence. He hooked his right arm over his muscular left shoulder to shake my hand, but kept his eyes glued on the financial report, "As you probably realize, along with its other problems this company has a big-league cash-flow deficit."

"Run that by me again, more slowly," I suggested, my voice calm. It surprised me to hear him introducing the top subject on my hidden agenda. It also made me immediately suspect his motive. I know the rule: "When you're facing disaster, be up-front and go on the offensive." He certainly knew that too.

"How could this disaster happen?" To make certain that we had no misunderstandings, I provided a history lesson before he could answer. "Look Seve, after my stint as an investigator, I spent years fighting the old man and his attorneys for control of the Indianapolis parent company. This factory—ADE—was part of the package. Then last year, I became principal owner and president of the whole shebang. To avoid hidden financial problems, I signed off on a cabinet full of due-diligence reports. And every document had been predigested and okayed by an army of high-paid attorneys and accountants." I leaned forward, my eyes locked on his. "You were one of those specialists. You were responsible for keeping us healthy." The last statements carried the acid chill of a court decree.

"I know." He avoided my eyes. "I don't believe the problems date from your takeover." He slammed the report shut.

"Yet," I walked around the desk to his work table and bent over to scroll the computer. "During the last business quarter the company showed a profit shortfall of almost a million dollars."

His eyes grew wide, then narrowed just as quickly. "So you already knew? Richard Scott, you've played me for the fool."

"No, Seve, I just analyzed the numbers." With that, I depressed the entry key. A year's worth of figures flashed by in a blur. "Now, call Joseph at Grover, Gable and Schwab. We'll go for a re-audit."

"I'm two weeks ahead of you. I called them at the first inkling of trouble. Wanted to save you worry. Some account entries could've been logged into the wrong month. The problem might've fixed itself."

"'Physician, heal thyself, eh?'"

Face grim and flushed, Seve waited for me to continue.

"Okay, Seve. First, let's verify, that we've been paid for all completed jobs," I ordered. I sensed that the timbre of my voice had dropped dangerously low like it does when I feel provoked or threatened. "Maybe somebody's cooking the books."

I rubbed my palm over the singed hair on my forearm. "Lately everything's growing pretty hot in Richard Scott's territory." Seve raised his eyebrows. Wondering how he had missed the news, I gave a thumbnail fill-in on the torch job out by Rose Cutter's Quarry. Probably glad for a change of subject, he clucked his sympathy.

Deep in thought, I traipsed down the hall toward my office—hoping against hope that Seve and I weren't facing insurmountable problems. Since I'm not a by-the-book kind of guy, I had to admire his independent attitude. I especially appreciate people who have so many of their own ideas that they're practically unmanageable. Staid, older companies tend to attract myopic people who can't see into the future, or brown nosers who can, but who are afraid to describe the view. Both hew to the company line and never create a solitary thing.

Without exception, however, I demand total honesty from my employees. Always have. After all, that's been the lynchpin of my business from the get-go. When fresh from 'Nam, I discovered that most people had become accustomed to a business world filled with smoke, mirrors and bulldust. Learning fast, I avoided promises I couldn't or wouldn't keep. As a result, customers arrived with dollars and stuck around to spend them with me.

I quit philosophizing. For now, I'd figure Seve was simply being especially creative. But I would keep my eyes open, my mind alert. That's part of my management style too.

In my own office again I plopped down behind my desk. Just as I liked it, the envelopes on today's batch of mail had been knifed open on one end with the paper inside barely protruding for easy removal. The first was from a Miami marine company.

The letter congratulated me on my decision to buy a high-speed Cigarette boat and said that a title had already been issued. That confused me. I knew the boat, all right. Don Aronow, who originally built it, straddled the drug-war fence by promoting his creation into the vessel of choice for both drug runners plying the Florida inter-coastals and for the government agents trying to intercept them. Feeling betrayed, the mob snuffed Don Aaronow.

Such a big-ticket boat, though, didn't interest me. I doubted I'd need it to cruise either Bloomington's Monroe Reservoir or that little lake out near the A-frame. But the message grabbed my attention. Especially when the next letter notified me that due to my heavy purchases in Florida, I'd maxed out one of my MasterCards—the one with a hundred-thousand-dollar limit. A misplaced pincer from last night's Alaskan crab dinner clawed at my stomach lining.

I called Jeanie Robbins and asked her to make a couple of calls. "Find out what's happening—please. I don't have time for another investigation, but it's crucial that we get to the bottom of this thing."

The last letter was from Jacobi's Real Estate. It said that an unnamed party "had a strong interest in purchasing the land around and including Rose Cutter's Quarry—for industrial development."

I pulled up the Jacobi name on the computer screen. Along with Rose Cutter's Quarry, Architectural Design and Elaboration, also known as ADE, owned several pieces of local real estate. During my absence, Jacobi had been an interim trustee of the outlying properties—including Rose Cutter's Quarry.

"Talk about convenience," I muttered. "After last night's fire, debris removal will be a pud. And, without the expensive home, the property's value will decrease. Perhaps the realty company was prescient and expected the fire. Hah! Fat chance!"

Tucking the letter into my suit's breast pocket, I dashed for the parking lot. Suddenly, I grew desperate for a friendly face.

Add beautiful to friendly.

"Now, that is a bonus!" I said, firing the Vanden Plas's big engine and steering for the parking lot gate.

I smiled inwardly, thinking of Samantha, eager to touch her, taste her, hold her in my arms . . . remembering how happy we had been just this morning, when I stopped by her house on the way to the office. Not bad for two people who had, hours earlier, watched a mansion turn to ashes.

That thought slammed me backward into the case: surely the fire had been an additional warning—just like the first by Karl Sprader on the job site back in Indianapolis, and the second in the threatening letter Sam showed me. But what was *this* warning suggesting? Stop the company's embezzlement investigation? Discontinue the Janie McNamara murder investigation? Abandon the apartment fraud investigation?

Like a bombshell, a fourth worry rattled my brain. Karl Sprader had said he and Reverend Gabriel Goodall had a financial involvement in the apartment case I was investigating. In the back of my mind I still carried a highly personal thought: "Gabriel Goodall robbed my mother. Someday, somehow, I'll get even." Goodall alone had won before. Now, he had an ally. God, what had I gotten into?

I steered toward Samantha's, my mind spinning, never realizing that the case, or cases, were on the verge of getting really complicated.

Chapter Thirteen

SAM SMILED A HAPPY INVITATION as she opened wide the doorway into her two-story, red-brick home. Dressed simply in a camel, sheath skirt and a mahogany tweed blazer, she appeared every inch the girl I remembered from our youth—the years between vanishing, seemingly, without a trace. Gently, I closed the foyer door.

A brown raglan coat lay draped over a living room chair in ready-to-go attitude. Sam had said earlier she would be leaving for class at eleven-thirty A.M. A glance at my watch showed I'd arrived just under the wire.

The chandelier shone softly on her dark hair, highlighting her high cheekbones and fair, flawless skin. Never had she been more desirable.

"My God, Sam," I gushed, suddenly wishing she'd skip class so we could spend the morning together. "You look ravishing, just like earlier this morning." My voice thickened. "You're exactly as you were that special night, years ago."

For a moment, she appeared uncomfortable with my compliment, but quickly recovered. "You lie." She laughed, fluffing her short hair. "My mother complains that I'm wearing my hair much too short. She also becomes livid about that ratty blue robe you caught me wearing this morning. Maybe Mom wants to believe I'm perfect." She screwed up her nose, obviously trying to lighten the moment. "At least *almost* perfect."

She had skillfully avoided the allusion to our romantic evening. Yet, I forged ahead anyway, "The girl inside is important, not the packaging. And for our one brief night . . ." I gazed deeply into her eyes as I moved closer. "This morning, I couldn't wait to leave the office. I longed to be near you."

Sam reached up and straightened my tie, her fingers pausing to rearrange my collar, then lingering to penetrate below the fold in my shirt and brush my neck. With her face upturned and her lips apart as they'd been that first day in the A-frame, I felt an uncontrollable urge—she must have felt it too. "Your tie was perfect," she whispered, her voice catching, "I just wanted to touch you."

"I know . . ." I eased my hands from her shoulders, slid them down to her waist, and stood there, holding her close. Lowering my lips to hers, I remembered that scant hours ago, I had been on the verge of proposing marriage to Caitlin McChesney. Abruptly guilt-ridden, embarrassed, and determined not to hurt Sam, my passion plummeted. My hands dropped from her waist.

"I can't do this," I said, turning away, then offering, "It's not the right time, Sam." A lame finish, but the best I could manage.

For one moment, anger sparked Samantha's eyes—then changed to hurt. "It's Caitlin, isn't it?"

I nodded. "Yes, but—" Paws clawed the gray marble tile and George tore into the foyer, providing an excuse for us to escape a dangerous hook.

Seeing me, George flopped onto his side, rolled onto his back, and kicked all four feet straight into the air. "He's feeling guilty about the fire," I surmised.

"Not at all. He's thanking you and Herschel for bringing him to me." Sam chuckled softly, with a catch, still recovering.

I raised my eyebrows, sniffing the air. "Jesus! Our George smells to high heaven."

"He's still damp from being freshly bathed," Sam protested, "but isn't he handsome?"

"Well . . . much improved." I ignored the burnt, smoldering

burlap bag odor, and dropped to one knee and rubbed his stomach. He whined, producing a noise akin to a cat's purr.

Obviously, Samantha wanted to be part of the rehabilitation project. She knelt beside me, adding her own version of TLC. "Guess what?" Sam asked, her expression a tad uncomfortable. "Earlier, I called Mom. She lives just south of Louisville and she wants a guard dog for companionship and protection. She feels George will fill the bill."

"I favor the idea. But I can't believe you're willing to swiz your own mom."

"How dare you speak that way about George," she chided. "He'll be 'our' special gift. And a precious one this little sweetie will be, too," she said, adding a touch of baby talk before rising to her feet.

We moved from the foyer into the living room. Sam offered a drink, but I settled for tea.

While Sam excused herself to go put on the kettle, I examined the house and her decorating tastes. The house was unpretentious, with many windows. Even on this overcast day, it seemed light and cheerful. She'd furnished it eclectically. A table-high, Art Deco entertainment center took up part of the far wall. Veneered in polished almond, the unit displayed a small television, a CD player, and a radio. Pastel tables on either side complemented its central arrangement.

Sam had successfully bridged the gap between Art Deco and traditional by adding a bergère, richly covered in burgundy leather. Nearby, a styled chesterfield and matching chair both showed brightly patterned prints.

After leafing through a Moroccan bound volume of American poetry, I perused a copy of a medieval manuscript. One originally handpainted page portrayed a man standing erect while pummeling a cowering woman.

I called to Sam. "Could we train George to attack your ex-husband?"

"Ah! You found *The Violence of Jealousy* book?" came from Sam in the kitchen. Grinning impishly, she peeked around the door frame to add, "Siccing George on him is such an exemplary idea."

I rose, and laying aside the manuscript page, studied the Oskar Kokoschka reproduction centered over the Baldwin spinet. The print showed two dreamily wistful children. Did she buy the print before or after Roger moved away? Either way, the scene might remind Sam of a simpler time.

I made my way around to the front picture window. A blue Park Avenue Buick sat at the curb. The driver looked directly at me. He turned his head so quickly that I barely glimpsed his face. The car left a trail of black-rubber tireprints on the street as it roared away. I turned back to the room as Samantha poured two cups of tea.

"You like what I've done?" Her eyes swept the room as she carefully smoothed her skirt and seated herself in the burgundy leather chair.

"Very nicely coordinated," I answered. "Still, it's an odd-on bet that most of your time is spent *there*." I indicated the combination office-library across the hall. All the shelves bulged with well-used books and the computer desk hid beneath more open books, notepads and papers.

We both took milk in our tea. She stirred sugar into hers. Trying to bank calories for tonight's dessert, I tore open a pair of Equal sweeteners while studiously ignoring a heaped pastry tray. I especially had to avert my eyes from a couple of chocolate-iced petit fours. In a sugary emotional context, each seemed to have my name written all over it—and I'm a pushover for sweets.

I couldn't ignore the case for long, however, and now, with my and Caitlin McChesney's relationship reduced to e-mail, phone calls, and indecision, I needed an up-close confidant. Sam had always been easy to talk to.

"Sam," I said, sipping my tea, "I know you want instant action on the murder and your son's problem . . . but let me fill you in on happenings down at 'Richard Scott's Jot-'em-Down Store.'"

She waited expectantly. When I filled her in on the money

shortage and recounted my latest conversation with Seve Jensen, she asked only, "Do you have suspects?"

"To paraphrase Inspector Clouseau, 'I suspect everybody, I suspect nobody.'" I stressed that even today, six years later, I still wanted to know how in blazes my CFO came up with enough jack to bid against us when we originally purchased Architectural Design and Elaboration. "Although I've known Seve Jensen for years, he's always been somewhat an enigma to me. Now, with the company's money problem and him a player, I must understand him, even his past. Does Jensen come from money? If not, does he have an angel?"

"An *angel*?"

"Small-time entrepreneurs sometimes lack the history and clout to get regular bank financing. So they find a deep-pocketed helper—an angel—who'll help an underdog either for altruistic reasons *or* to make a killing through unconscionable interest rates."

"Word has it that Seve had absolutely no money when he made his bid against you."

I nearly choked on a last sip of tea. "You've gotta be spoofing!"

"Seve's not only talented, he's also a gambler." Samantha pretended to shuffle and deal from the bottom of an imaginary deck.

"Certainly, he's far more clever than the old man and me. At least, we risked a few pesos. Had we not, we would've been laughed out of the boardroom."

"Seve relied on insurance proceeds."

"You mean, 'betting on-the-come'?"

"Right-o! He believed he could coerce an agreement from the insurance company prior to the buyout settlement date."

"Whoa, Betsy!" I protested, teeing my hands in a time-out gesture. "How could there be insurance? Isn't Seve's handicap genetic?"

"I thought you knew! Let me provide pertinent background: Seve entered Janie McNamara's life long before she and my son met . . ."

Sam went on to describe how the late Jane McNamara began working at ADE seven years ago, a year before the Indianapolis parent corporation bought the local company. Back then, Seve Jensen was employed, not by ADE, but by an equipment manufacturing company.

"A couple years out of high school, Janie became engaged to Clark Benefield, the Bloomington owner of a string of successful eateries called The Breaking Fast Restaurants."

Not only an invitation to breakfast, the name reflected Indiana's enthusiasm for ball-hawking, fast-paced basketball, and was familiar. "I remember when the chain franchised and went national. Then recently, I read a complimentary article in *Indiana Business and Industry*, so I suppose Benefield would've been a notable conquest for a young woman," I observed.

"Not really. Janie was so fresh and lovely." Sam lowered her head, sadly. "She was a honey-blond, a homecoming queen type with typically even, white teeth, and the full, beautiful smile. You know the sort. She always had her pick of men."

Sam went on to describe how Jane was sent out to a job site where ADE was the leading contractor. The second day on the site, Jane met the then-vigorous muscleman, Seve Jensen, who was there to settle a business dispute involving the equipment manufacturing company for which he then worked. She pursed her lips. "His looks were somewhat deceiving. He had physical problems even then."

"Janie and Seve met for lunch, then later got together for drinks, dinner, and a movie. Head over heels in love, within days Janie broke her engagement to Clark and spent all her spare time with Seve. Finally, she dropped the lease on her apartment and moved in with him.

"She was attending one of my night classes and I'd become a confidante. I advised her against the commitment because rumor had it that Seve was twice married, had fathered two children, and deserted the lot."

"Jesus! That's pretty tawdry. Tell me it ain't so."

"Janie pooh-poohed the story, saying he had married but once just out of high school, and while still childless, he and his young bride agreed to an annulment. I had no reason to pursue the matter further."

"So how did Seve get hurt?" I asked, growing impatient. I couldn't say why. The subject had little to do with my investigation, and nothing to do with Seve's abilities as a manager. I'd have been even less forgiving, however, had Sam confirmed the child desertion story. I would *never* allow a child deserter to work at my company.

"Seve was injured in a job-site accident," Sam answered, "One day, while working for the equipment manufacturing company, Seve walked along an idle conveyor belt. Inadvertently, somebody switched on the machine. Seve fell ten feet onto concrete. Paralyzed, he lay for hours before Janie found him."

Felton Crenshaw's name flashed through my mind. Aha! Was Seve the anonymous insurance claimant at our company? Sometimes, in those kind of cases, settlements aren't reached for years. Mentally recording the data, I said, "What a horrible experience."

"Horrible, yes, but no worse than he'd been through before."

I switched to another random thought, "How did your son fit into Jane's sequence of boyfriends?"

Sam counted on her fingers. "First there was Clark Benefield, then Seve Jensen. Roger and Jane dated after the first two romances cooled. That made him number three—and the last.

"Everybody loved Janie," she continued. "Even my ex . . . and that seemed almost miraculous. At one time I even thought him infatuated with her." Momentarily, Sam reddened. "I even accused Joe of having an affair with her."

Her expression turned inward as she added, "Yet I knew I was being foolish. Even though Joe was very solicitous toward Janie, she treated him coldly. Later she seemed to fear and avoid him."

Weighing the last startling bit of information, I massaged my chin, and managed merely a "Humph!"

"I must caution you," Sam said, also switching subjects. "Last night, Joe came by the house. He's jealous and warned me away from you. He can be very violent." She took a moment to say the rest, as if each word had become a challenge, "Once he was an abuser. Now Joe Petry has become a stalker!"

"Sam, we've gotta meet this head on!" I glanced at my watch, knowing her schedule. "Call the office. Now. Tell 'em you'll be late. Take a day off."

"No, I must go." She brightened. "I have a very qualified graduate assistant. The responsibility will be good for him. He can handle the load today."

While I called the office on my cellular, Sam phoned the university from her bedroom. I finished first. Now, with hours ahead of us, I was trapped. But the trap would be tender, and I was losing the fight to maintain my distance.

Sam returned wearing a floral cardigan and celery-colored slacks. This time, she seated herself beside me on the chesterfield.

I took her hand in mine and kissed her on the cheek, wanting to make long, luxurious love to her. Still, first, we had to deal with Joe Petry. "Sam," I said reluctantly—not wishing to disturb the developing mood, "let me take you back to your last comment about Joe. You can't allow a stalker in your house! Lock him out! Do something! Call the police!"

"Look, Richard—blast it! It's not that simple. I know the problem's complexity; you don't." She leapt to her feet and glared down at me. Clenching and unclenching her hands, she lifted them shoulder high and shook them in frustration. Virtually weeping, she exclaimed, "I know, that at any given moment, there are one and a half million stalking victims in the United States, two-thirds of them women. Four of five cases end in violence, but usually the police won't answer cries for help until there's been a maiming or murder." Expelling a deep breath, she collapsed onto the sofa and covered her face with her hands, knuckles white.

I finished the oration for her, "Yeah . . . and once they begin, stalkers seldom stop."

"Richard, I moved from Ohio to Indiana to escape Joe Petry. Eventually he quit his job and moved to Bloomington to be near me. Damn! Damn! Damn!" she concluded, her words full of bitterness and despair.

"At least cut all ties. Avoid mixed signals. Even though Petry insists, you must *not* wear the wedding band. That signals that you want to revive the relationship."

"Please, Richard, no more advice."

Although her voice reflected dismay, her eyes were dry. I suspected she had run out of tears, like I did after my wife Barb and I eventually tired of whacking at each other's emotions and called it quits. And, more recently, as I'd done when Caitlin McChesney and I mutilated what had at first appeared to be a solid relationship. Only recently had we again begun to communicate.

I squeezed her hand. "I'm sorry, but I can't ignore this," I said, forging ahead. "I know solutions always seem easier to outsiders, but I must know more if I'm to be of help. What *did* you do last night when he came here?"

"First, I pretended to be away. He yelled through the door, 'I know you're in there. I'll kick the goddamn door off the hinges.' I opened up. What else could I do?"

"Get a restraining order."

"Injunctions seldom help." Her voice, turning tiredly monotone, implied she was explaining a subject many-times covered. "Anyway, nobody believes that an upstanding citizen like Joe Petry could ever be threatening."

"Tell me more about the bugger. I need background."

Samantha explained that in the mid-nineties, after he'd followed her to Indiana, Petry had been in line for a police chief's job in a major Indiana city. One night after he'd been drinking, he came home and accused her of being unfaithful. Outraged, she reminded him that they were divorced. He beat her unconscious. She brought charges.

"Joe pled guilty. Since a new federal law made it illegal for people convicted of domestic abuse to carry handguns—a restriction also applying to policeman—he lost out on his big law-enforcement opportunity.

"Later, he appealed and had the misdemeanor battery charge dismissed. Like a fool, I softened and took him back—for a short period. Many people thought he had been railroaded. Now, he turned into a solidly grounded state lobbyist for energy interests, including coal mining and power utilities." She winced at the memory. "I suspect that his anger is fed by the thought that my charges cost him his 'greatest career opportunity,' and all the prestige that would have gone with it."

"Unbelievable, but typical for a stalker," I said, voicing my agreement as sourly as she had her statement. "He *would* blame you."

"It gets worse. He's become a big contributor to both political parties—and a frequent guest on several of the far Christian right television and radio shows. All the right wingers love him and his 'family values' message."

"What! I can't believe any cat expounding such popular buzzwords could also beat his wife, or his ex-wife—and neither can they, right?" I asked. "Or they don't care?"

"I doubt they care. Spokesmen and activists in far right organizations are always 'good ol' boys.' Never, ever, are they 'good ol' girls.' " With that outburst, her lips tightened, her eyes blazing with suppressed anger. Unable to contain herself, she arose and, this time, paced the floor, wringing her hands.

"Joe has never been there when Roger needed him." Her expression softened. "Thank God, Roger now has someone else who cares enough to help." She gave me a warm smile, seemingly forgetting that my interest in the case was strictly for her and had nothing to do with her son.

Just then, the grad assistant called for advice. Still mulling all the implications of Sam's comments about Joe Petry and Roger, I stomped to the window and scowled through the sheers.

The blue Buick and its occupant had returned. "By the way, what kind of car does your ex drive? Peep out the curtain and see if the bozo is parked by the curb?"

She yanked back the sheers, but before she could answer, my cell phone chirped for attention. I didn't recognize the number in the phone's tiny display window. A gruff male voice said, without preliminaries, "Mr. Scott, this is Sheriff Casey DeLyle. We need to talk . . ." I listened for a moment before hanging up.

"What's wrong?" Sam exclaimed. "You look dreadful! "

I supposed I did. The Alaskan crab from last night's supper ripped at my gut with its second claw. I could feel the blood draining from my face. "They've discovered a mutilated body at the burn site!"

Chapter Fourteen

I OUTRAN TWO SPEEDING TICKETS—one on the main highway, another on Rose Cutter's Pike—while streaking toward the fire-gutted mansion. I braked the Jag to a skidding halt in the drive, then sprang outside, skirted an ambulance's gaping doors, and stooped my way beneath a loop of crime-scene tape, before dashing down the basement entryway.

Ash-gray clinkers littered the stairs; they cracked like mini-gunshots beneath my shoes. At the bottom, I planted one foot on the bottom step, the other on a wad of melted sheet metal that, hours ago, had been the top floor furnace, and surveyed the ruins.

A third-story drainpipe had wilted during the inferno. Now, formed into a walking-cane hook, it leaned against a brick chimney; still attached, an inverted bathtub dangled from the pipe like a white-enameled, clapperless bell. Around me, charred timbers floated on a lake of ash and sodden embers.

Stung by the acrid odor, I gagged, then more furious about the destruction than repulsed by the smell, said, "Forget the stench, Richard!" Stepping down another tread, my voice aimed toward a clot of men circling the sump reservoir, I called, "I'm looking for Sheriff Casey DeLyle."

A pair of young guys wearing bright orange coveralls glanced toward me before returning their attention to the sump pit. I supposed they were ambulance jockeys.

The sheriff and his deputy, dressed in Vandyke brown, stood slightly apart from a work crew sporting dark blue coveralls and billed caps. As one, they turned to observe me. "Get back!" an authoritative voice bellowed from among the pack. "Move back up the stairs! You're violating the crime scene!"

This was my turf. I scowled in the direction of the voice, then took the final step to the basement floor and stayed put. After getting my bearings, I walked deeper into the basement. I noticed that indeed the old man's bottles of high-priced booze had melted. Stopping, I kicked a chunk from the colorfully, variegated lump.

A brown uniform broke free from the group and worked its way across the basement. "I'm Sheriff Casey DeLyle." He tipped his sheriff's badge with a fat thumb. I waved my private investigator ID beneath his nose in reciprocation. He glanced, but didn't deign to touch it.

DeLyle, my height and carrying at least forty extra pounds of fat-muscle beef, must have weighed at least two-fifty. Peering from beneath a cap bill—positioned exactly two military fingers above the crown of his nose—he looked me straight in the eye. His non-regulation nose pointed toward my right shoulder.

I figured at one time he either boxed, played college football, or had been tagged by a left hook during a roughhouse arrest. "Are you out of Bloomington?" I asked.

"Nope. That's Monroe County. This property's platted in Cavalier County, and I work out of the big city of Stonecrop. You new around here, Scott?"

"Somewhat. My company is proud owner of all this," I said sardonically, my sweeping gesture encompassing the ruins. I took another pace toward the crime scene.

Sheriff DeLyle blocked the way. "You don't want to see that—"

His warning came too late. Across the basement, two men poked around in the sump pit with grappling hooks. A cameraman readjusted his tripod for an unobstructed camera shot. I stepped closer.

A grappler yelled, "Hooked his butt this time!"

His partner answered, "A-okay, good buddy! Hoist 'im!"

A pair of sodden, tan chukka boots cleared the water's surface. Dripping argyles wrapped a set of blanched ankles. I glimpsed charcoal gray pants . . . and a black belt.

Fire had obliterated the upper torso. A blackened skeleton dangled beneath the soggy lump. Breaking free, a fleshless skull plopped back into the pit.

Shocked, both grapplers recoiled and stood motionless, gaping. Losing momentum, the body ripped from the hook and splashed back into the pit.

Black water splattered the younger man's face. He ran a few feet to one side and clung onto a concrete column, vomiting.

"That's tough duty, Sheriff."

"Believe it." Then DeLyle elaborated. "It's difficult lifting a chunk of cooked meat." He furtively glanced at me to check my shock quotient.

"I've been to both 'Nam and Desert Storm, Sheriff. To shake me, you'll need to add special effects."

Looking disappointed, he turned and yelled, "For Christ sake, bale out the pit!"

Two helpers went searching for a sump pump, but returned with scorched paint buckets from the fire. Casey DeLyle scowled and warned, "Keep secret the condition of the body, Scott. That's evidence."

I could visualize last night's scene and I'm into sharing. "Sheriff, dime to a donut I know what happened."

"Okay," DeLyle directed, his tone dubious. "Give me your take."

"Early on I heard a pair of voices; later I caught one agonized scream. So there were at least *two* arsonists. Also, prior to the fire, there was a loud crash. The way I see it, they first kicked the outside basement door from its hinges.

"After that, both intruders lugged cans of gasoline downstairs. One of them saturated the basement; the other splashed a gasoline trail up the stairs and into the yard. They undoubtedly planned to light it after they'd both cleared the basement.

"Unfortunately for our charcoaled friend, they didn't take into account the gasoline fumes. While one person was still outside, the basement's gas furnace probably sparked on," I spread my arms wide. "And whoosh! Flames blocked the stairway.

"Instinctively," I continued, "the man in the basement jumped into the uncovered pit. Head above the water, he lived until fire consumed all the basement's oxygen. Dead, his body popped above the surface of the water like a fishing bobber. Or maybe most of the water boiled away leaving his torso exposed. The fire consumed the flesh on his head and chest, leaving only a skull and skeleton—a cooked stump below the water line."

DeLyle considered my statement. "You said *two* gasoline containers." He twisted his lips for a sardonic finale. "We found only *one* five-gallon can outside in the yard." He held up one finger. "One, and only one."

My gaze swept the basement floor. "There has to be another." Figuring it to be within throwing distance of the sump pit, I maneuvered past DeLyle, hooked my toe beneath a section of galvanized, heating duct. No luck! I booted another piece aside. "Voila!" I pointed to the second jerry can's scorched and battered remains.

DeLyle's eyebrows lifted. "Okay, here's another theory for you to gnaw on, Scott. Maybe the man who got away made sure that his partner didn't." With that, Sheriff Casey DeLyle wheeled and stalked back across the basement to the sump area.

Minutes later, the two grapplers completed their recovery. The one who'd vomited tried to put a macho face on his earlier wimp's performance. Either that or he subscribed to the showman's credo: "Always keep 'em laughing." Dropping his grappling hook, he regaled us with his opinion and a joke.

"Gonna be hard to find out who this poor sucker is. In this condition they all look alike. It reminds me of a joke." He gazed around to see that he had our attention. "See, at a golf club, a naked peeper got his ass trapped in the ladies' dressing room. The attendant had took the guy's clothes. Wrapping a towel around his head to hide his face, this guy hauled his friggin' naked ass through the *nineteenth* hole, where the good ladies who had finished playing golf were now sipping cocktails.

"One blue hair said, 'That's not my husband.'

"Another said, 'It's certainly not Jim.'

"A third glanced up. 'Hell, he doesn't even belong to this club.'"

All the men except DeLyle and I guffawed. But it wasn't a bad analogy—and it showed that the sheriff faced a major problem. With little to work with above the victim's waist, DeLyle might try to have the face reconstructed by a forensic sculptor, although, first, the skull would require major rework. From what I'd seen, the fire's intense heat had exploded the head like a superheated melon. Still, I suspected DeLyle would rely more on clothes, buttons, zipper parts and DNA testing. Maybe he'd even get lucky and find a few stray teeth in the bottom of the pit and make an ID that way. With this victim's condition, he couldn't rely on fingerprints.

A van from WQIP-TV, Channel 1, pulled onto the scene. DeLyle immediately straightened his shoulders and tie, fingered his jaws for whiskers, readjusted his cap and like a shot, took off in the reporter's direction.

I left. I could see—or I could visualize—DeLyle on the six o'clock news. Even now, in my mind's ear, I could hear the interview: "Here's WQIP-TV's own Carla Diston, on the scene with Sheriff Casey DeLyle," a background voice would announce.

"Is a break in the case imminent?" Carla Diston would then ask, her mike held inches from the sheriff's big smashed honker.

"My men are working on several good leads. An early break in the case can be expected. However, we haven't yet identified the alleged victim." DeLyle, meanwhile, mugged for the camera, enjoying his fifteen minutes of fame.

On my return to see Samantha, I forgot to switch on the radio. But despite the oversight, my thoughts tuned in on Reverend Gabriel Goodall and a recent meeting at the WQIP-TV studio. I had just finished taping a promotional spot for the limestone industry.

A sign in the studio lobby welcomed Reverend Gabriel Goodall. He arrived as I was leaving. I was certain he saw me. After a slight glance down his aquiline nose, he made a major point of turning away.

I whispered, "Nice threads." The comment fit perfectly, like his tailored suit. I believe that an evangelist who sucks his money from the poor should at least refrain from wearing thousand-dollar suits. How about a double-breasted number in pinstriped sackcloth?

Goodall pivoted on one cowboy booted heel. "I remember you, Richard Scott!" His voice thundered like Moses' must have when he came easing down the mountain with two stone tablets tucked beneath his arms, each engraved with five of the "Big Ten."

"I *know* you well!" he bellowed again.

Recoiling, the blond receptionist knocked over a glassful of pencils and ballpoints. They noisily skittered across the floor. Alarmed, a couple seated in a side vestibule ran to the door and peered into the lobby through terrified eyes.

Goodall stood dead still, his wrists brushing back his carefully tailored suit coat, one hand landing on an empty holster, the other hooked into a western-style, tooled-leather belt. He never carried a weapon in the holster, but during sermons, he always laid a pearl-handled, silver, Colt .45 somewhere nearby. When he wished to impress his far-right supporters, his schtick involved picking up the pistol and waving it theatrically before the congregation.

I recollected that, at key points during his sermons, the technicians also over-amplified the sound. Then Goodall would pound the podium. I gathered that the moment was an orgasmic experience for his redneck followers. I actually heard the fervent cries of, "Amen, brother. Amen!" from the over-testosteroned men. By cupping my hand to my ear, I fancied that I also detected the musical sound of rattling ovaries among the female parishioners.

"We will meet again!" he thundered in promise.

"Where? In Bloomington, Indianapolis, or hell?" I asked, now so angry my ears and cheeks burned ember red.

Keeping the same pivot foot, he wheeled and marched out the door. I was sorely tempted to speed him along with another booted foot in the most tender part of his posterior.

Then, I confronted another thought: maybe the good reverend kept the pistol loaded—and could be induced to use it. *That* would make a juicy story!

That night, Sam and I talked about the arson victim over dinner at the Fourth Street Inn. In return, Sam described her afternoon, breaking the spell with, "Who killed the nun, Rosata? That's another mystery haunting my life."

I screwed my face into an expression of avid disbelief. "You mean somebody else in this case has been snuffed?"

Samantha giggled. "No, Richard, that was years ago. I'll give you the details later."

Always chic, she was dressed in a charcoal and vanilla wrap dress with a revealing slit that elevated my blood pressure. I brushed my fingers across her sleeve, liking the sensual feeling of silken chenille, as well as the soft skin of her upper arm. Across the room, the white-jacketed waiter surreptitiously eyed the slender, shapely legs that had long driven me to distraction. I smiled, and he self-consciously turned away to slosh water into already overfilled glasses.

Complementing her dress, Samantha wore a gold Cleopatra necklace, matching earrings, and a diamond solitaire ring. Last time, she'd worn her wedding band; tonight she didn't. That especially pleased me. Perhaps she'd listened and made a final emotional break from Joe Petry. More importantly, the missing ring might help convince Joe Petry that the separation was final and he should get on with his life. Good logic. I doubted it to be a good bet.

Over my first Stolie vodka, I went on to recap my talk with Sheriff DeLyle. While listening unemotionally, Sam toyed with her gin and tonic.

I motioned for the waiter. "I'll take a change of pace—Chivas on the rocks. Please bring the lady a Treviso Sling." Sam raised a quizzical eyebrow until the waiter explained that it was delicious, a chilled concoction of champagne, fruit nectar, lemon, and cassis.

Now, sipping our drinks, the conversation turned personal. "At one time weren't you seriously ill?" Samantha asked, her expression concerned.

"Courtesy of Saddam Hussein, I had a two-year bout with Gulf War Syndrome. At one time the situation was pretty shaky. Once, I even had last rites! Now I'm in remission." With a palms-up sweep of my hands, I tried bidding goodbye to that chapter of my history.

"How did your wife respond?" Samantha persisted, probably seeing through my faked nonchalance.

Her question opened the flood gates. "Essentially, the sickness led to estrangement and finished our marriage, although it was five years before our divorce. Oh, it wasn't Barb's fault," I said. "For years she'd wanted a baby. But the docs handling my case tabbed me a dreadful bet for fatherhood and warned us we might have an afflicted child. With my adding the final shove, Barb agreed to abort. She never forgave the doctors—or me."

I left out the part about the U.S. military trying to avoid responsibility for what we GIs had been through. Thinking about it can cause me to mount any handy soapbox. I was afraid I'd already sounded too self-pitying. With romance somewhere in the air, I wasn't about to risk tainting the evening with a honked-off vet's diatribe as well, so I guided the conversation back to Samantha. "Tell me more about good ol' Joe, Sam."

"Our marriage appeared solid in the beginning—still from day one it wasn't a soul-mate relationship." She sighed, a long-drawn expression of wistful nostalgia. "I sometimes wonder how it lasted so many years." She breathed the sentence rather than saying it. "My life could've been so different, had I made the painful break earlier—or chosen the right man to begin with."

From there the conversation drifted to her teaching job and her doctoral dissertation. "My paper will be fantastic reading," she laughed. "It stars Henry the Eighth, his six wives, and the dastardly thing he did to the Gilbertines—"

"Along with killing his Anne Boleyn and some of his other wives, and . . . uh . . ." I fumbled for a name. Sam filled in the gap by naming Katherine Howard. "Anyway, in addition to executing his wives, His Majesty wiped out the Gilbertine family, eh?" I twisted my lips into an expression of distaste.

Sam rolled her eyes feigning reproval. "Family! Come on, Richard, the Gilbertines constituted the only religious order ever founded in Britain." She chuckled. "Henry the Eighth destroyed them."

I nodded solemnly. "Now, back to Rosata . . ."

Sam turned coy. "Although it's a spellbinding mystery, you'll just have to wait." I feigned a sad look and she relented. "Rosata, a Gilbertine nun, had an affair with a Chicksands Priory canon. Once her delicate condition became known to the brothers and sisters, the enraged prior of the house ordered that her lover be executed and that she be walled up alive in the cloisters. A plaque inside the twelfth-century priory explains it all." Sam recited: " 'By virtues guarded and manners graced/Here, alas, is fair Rosata placed.' "

"What a sad story," I said.

"Yes, and now, on the seventeenth of each month Rosata walks the halls of the priory, forever searching for her lover."

"But the good news is," I said, smiling, and lifting my glass for a toast, "for the first time since I arrived in Bloomington, we now have answers to a mystery!"

After a shared laugh, she informed me that Indiana University was sponsoring a joint student-teacher trip to London. "The trip has been in the planning stages for several months. Now, they've had a cancellation and invited me along." Her smile faded. "Of course, I'll miss being here with you."

"And I'll miss you . . . but you must go." I reached out to cover her hand with mine.

The waiter interrupted a tender moment to take our orders. Retrieving her hand and grasping the menu, she ordered penne with spit-roasted salmon. I asked for the same, then grimacing and lightly patting my stomach, changed from the rich cream sauce to salmon grilled. An instant later, I did another about-face and broke my resolve by ordering lobster bisque for myself and artichoke-dungeness crab appetizers for us to share.

That done and the waiter's back vanishing into the kitchen, I said, "This morning, you implied that Seve Jensen had endured debilitating problems almost as tragic as his paralysis. Skipping from Great Britain and ancient history, to Bloomington, Indiana, and the here and now, can you fill me in on the rest of that story?"

"Well, Seve suffered terrible injuries during Desert Storm," she answered.

"Strange, he never mentioned the Gulf War," I observed. "Especially since my service there is well-known around the company, and veterans of the same battles usually develop a special camaraderie."

"That *is* surprising. For that experience must've been a defining period in Seve's life—as well as a terribly traumatic episode. While there, Seve suffered cervical and lumbar damage. During reconstructive work to deal with those injuries, the surgeons removed and fused vertebras along with repairing muscle damage. He ended, I heard, with extensive scarring and scar tissue. Not good. Not good at all."

I must've looked puzzled. "I'm confused. I thought you said he was hurt in an industrial accident."

"After the industrial accident, the doctors could hardly differentiate between the old war injuries and new damage from the conveyor accident."

"Was his injury claim settled strictly on the basis of medical findings or was the insurance company influenced by Seve's war record?"

"All my information came from Jane McNamara; I asked if

emotions influenced the trial's outcome. She wouldn't—or couldn't—answer. I suspect that in a confusing case, with a hero plaintiff, an insurance company might wish to avoid facing a jury." Sam placed her drink on the table to eye me with a straight, tight-lipped, look. "Surely you don't *seriously* doubt Seve's integrity? After all, after you first purchased ADE, you hired him based on your own personal judgment. Perhaps those people wanting to buy your property are more solid suspects." Again sipping her drink, she mused aloud, "Seve Jensen had yet another insurance suit still left to settle. I don't know the name of the company nor the amount of the claim."

This time, my antenna really quivered.

Once more, before I had time to fully explore a clue, the waiter brought our salmon and suggested we complement it with a Chateau Souverain zinfandel. Enthusiastically, I signaled a circled thumb-and-forefinger okay.

"Sam, you have one mystery remaining: Janie. I have five: your student-friend Janie's death; the money shortage at Architectural Design and Elaboration, Inc.; the apartment fraud case in which Karl Sprader and Reverend Gabriel Goodall have an interest; an unidentified body in the basement of my torched house; and the arson itself—who set the fire?"

The zinfandel not yet in place, I killed the last of my Chivas. "To add a touch of acid to the recipe, we have your ex-husband the stalker."

The waiter arrived to begin the wine protocol; I hurriedly tasted and okayed the vintage and taste. Immediately, I leaped back to the case. "Sam, I know you feel protective toward Seve Jensen. Obviously, he would be physically incapable of a violent killing. Yet, he does have the brains to shipwreck my company and the motive for doing it.

"You see, Sam, the company has additional stockholders. A failure on my part, would send the other owners scurrying for a new CEO. Somebody, perhaps Seve, can end up with my job."

"But, once again, I must say: you hired him. Now, how can you be so distrustful?"

"I know my attitude confuses you. But, see it my way: I'm facing a money problem that could destroy the company. I suspect fraud. I must look first at the people who've controlled the money. Immediately, that brings me to the chief financial officer's and the president's positions; Seve Jensen has served in both jobs." Satisfied with the rationale, I leaned back in my chair and crossed my arms over my chest. "Jensen has to be a leading suspect."

Sensing, from her nonresponse, her reluctance to further discuss Seve Jensen, I moved onto an even more dangerous subject. "I know Joc Petry is a right winger. Does he have an association with Goodall?"

"I don't know. I'm unaware of a close relationship, yet they might."

Our happy evening already nosediving from my meticulous probing, I ground ahead. "That FIPRO organization of Goodall's— what does the acronym stand for?"

"Only yesterday, one of my religion-class students mentioned that." She concentrated, her hands fluttering before her face as she tried to recall. "Oh, yes! It stands for 'Final Prophet.' I suppose that's the way Reverend Goodall views himself."

Continuing, she verified that the movement's objective was to isolate gays, minorities, liberal Democrats, and all others who didn't fit the right wing's agenda.

She went on to say that prior to becoming FIPRO, Goodall's organization had a different designation. "They were called C-R-O . . . something, something. It had to do with children."

I slammed a fist into my palm. "You're thinking of CROWN! That's an acronym for 'Children Relief Organization With Nurture.' "

"That's it!" Obviously, my intense interest excited Sam. "How did you know?"

"Easy," I growled. "That organization defrauded my mother out of her savings."

"Although Goodall is reprehensibly right wing," Sam said, her expression grown dubious, "I'm surprised he would be involved in fraud."

"More than surprised, I was stunned when I heard the full story. See, during the sixties, when this good looking, charismatic, up-from-poverty guy came on the scene, my parents backed him with a lot of cash. And when they learned he had been an abused kid, they wrote even bigger checks."

"I'm the religious studies prof, but you know him better than I," Sam said, sounding surprised.

"Yeah, you've met him through media and books. My closeup and personal lessons carried more impact." I stopped talking long enough to sip my drink and survey the dining room. Our heavy-duty conversation had continued for so long that the tables had begun to empty. "Anyway, Goodall had an international following. He preached to presidents and during a revival, his congregation filled London's Wembley Stadium. He raised a lot of money for the homeless. I'm convinced; he was a force for good."

"I wonder why he changed."

"Greed, I suppose. See, like I said, he came from abuse and poverty. Sometimes, those things can brand a man's soul; formerly devout men become fishers of dollars, not souls." I went on to explain that just after my dad's death, Goodall's CROWN organization deluged my mother with letters offering condolences and requesting contributions. "They said the money would take care of starving children, but I investigated and discovered that little of the money was reaching the children. However, I couldn't dissuade Mom. She responded with check after check. She squandered nearly every penny of Dad's life insurance money. Too late, I wised up and stopped payment on her final pledge."

"What did Reverend Goodall do?"

"At that time I had no idea Goodall was personally involved. However, his organization brought suit trying to enforce her pledge. I said, 'Be my guest, pilgrims. I've a bundle of cash, a stable full of attorneys on retainer, and I revel in a good fight. I'll see you creeps in court.'"

"And then?"

"CROWN withdrew the suit. They couldn't risk exposure with many donors just to salvage a single gift—even a big one."

We finished our salmon and after-dinner drinks over small-talk, but the evening had lost its sheen. When our words became desultory, I asked for the check.

What a bummer! I thought. It's difficult combining romance with murder and fraud investigations. Maybe—just maybe—I was peeved by Sam's protective attitude toward Seve Jensen.

We had driven to the restaurant separately, so we each departed alone. A brief interval by her door, trying to salvage the warmth of our former intimacy, ended futilely.

While the Vanden Plas purred south on Highway 37 toward the turnoff and the lonely blacktop leading to the A-frame, I mused at the strangeness of events. "Just fifteen minutes ago I was ready to conclude the evening, now I wish Samantha were in the seat beside me. Funny that? No, not really for an old romantic like me."

Our conversation about Seve Jensen hadn't been at all satisfying. At the first mention of his name, I recalled his bitterness when I outbid him for the company way back when.

In another mental flash, my thoughts leapt cross-country to New York, and I wondered what, at this minute, Caitlin McChesney was up to. I heard a man can't love two women at once. Perhaps I would end up proving or disproving the theory. I wasn't prepared to make a final break from Cait, yet I felt myself becoming closer and closer to Samantha Petry . . .

That brought me full circle to the deeper bitterness, vindictiveness and hatred that must surely be percolating through Joe Petry's mind. Also, I recalled the car parked in front of Sam's house. Was it his? To me, the man had the earmarks of a dangerous monster. That thought urged me to turn around and return to Sam's rescue. But I didn't.

Later, I wished I had.

Chapter Fifteen

THE FOLLOWING MORNING, fulfilling that promise to Sam, I drove a hundred miles to Indiana's southernmost border to meet Jane McNamara's father. Detouring from a county blacktop, I paused to read the name on a battered, rusty-galvanized mailbox, and then followed a narrow, pea gravel lane down the sheer edge of an Ohio River knob.

Cedar trees lined both sides of the drive and shielded a clear view of the river. I skirted a woodsman's homemade guardrail spiked to some cedars' knobby trunks. The Jag's fenders barely cleared the split logs' splintery surfaces so I drove slowly. Multi-colored paint streaks recorded the previous passages of those who had hurried.

Part way down, I reached the only flat place on the bluff, and parked in front of Hugh McNamara's house. Perched on tall, skinny stilts, the white, clapboard bungalow faced the river.

I climbed tilted-askew concrete steps to the front porch, and knocked. I held my private investigator's ID, chin-high, so the murder victim's parents could see that the face in the little picture and the one smiling through the door belonged to the same guy.

The inner door rattled open. "It's a bitter wind off the river, today, Mr. Scott," stated a strong, male voice issuing from a wizened figure. "So's you can quickly return to the warmth of that fancy rig, tell me what you want."

Sensing he was about to slam the door, I stepped nearer and phrased a quick and brutal, no-finesse question. "Mr. McNamara, do you have any idea who killed your daughter?"

"Everybody has the same question. I always give the selfsame answer. The killer still walks free." For a moment, he studied me through the screen. "I don't reckon you'll be different." He slammed the door, leaving me with my back to the muddy waters of the quarter-mile-wide Ohio River and my nose six inches from a rusted screen door.

A piece of red twine darned a hole in the screen. A stiff wind skimmed the frigid river, pasting my trousers to the back of my legs and teasing the frayed end of the twine.

I knocked again.

Waiting, I ran my fingers over the white surface of a roughly sawn porch column. A black band encircled the post and crude printing said: 1937 FLOOD LEVEL. The painted surface below the band had a different texture from that above the line. After the flood, I figured somebody, making repairs and pushed for time, brushed paint right over the Ohio River mud.

Even though the flood came before my time, I liked the thought. I see today's world roaring along like a high-speed locomotive. I like riding the caboose and catching last looks at historic stations.

Having waited and speculated a reasonable time, I yelled at the still-closed door, "Samantha Petry told me to come."

This time, easing wide the door, Hugh McNamara reached out and clicked open the screen door's safety lock. "Come in. I can't leave a friend of Samantha's outside in the wind."

He turned and led the way into the living room and motioned me to sit. I put my coat on the chipped floorboards beside a dun colored chair, then sank deeply into its thick cushion.

Maneuvering his way between a television and an oak library table with carved legs thick as crossties, Mr. McNamara dropped heavily into my chair's twin. He sighed expansively—or resignedly—surely the latter.

The furniture looked huge in the three-room, shotgun house, as if Gulliver had moved in with the little people, but brought along his own stuff. Some appeared to be antiques.

I explained my relationship with Samantha. Nodding without comment, McNamara excused himself and hurriedly left the room.

Gazing around again, I leaned over my chair arm. Touching the wallpaper with a careful finger, I traced the outline of a faded flower. Beyond an arched doorway, identical paper covered the walls of the combination dining room and kitchen. Although the tiny house appeared spotless, odors of rancid grease, sickness and stale air permeated the air. I suspected the windows always remained tightly shut and thus the miasma of decomposition never changed. Defensively I—as I had in Ms. Dempsie's house—rerouted my breathing from nostrils to an open mouth.

A black-walnut grandfather clock stood beside the arched doorway. I like clocks so I crossed the room for a closer look. I fingered my wrist and discovered the clock's ticking matched my pulse. I wondered how many hearts the six-foot-tall antique had outlasted since first delivered from a Philadelphia clockmaker.

After a toilet flush strong enough to suck oxygen from the tiny house, Hugh McNamara returned. Now I took my first real look at him. Terribly emaciated, his blue dungarees and plaid lumberjack shirt hung loosely on a slight frame. My British grandmother would've said, "He's nothing but a death's head on a mop-stick."

McNamara collapsed into his chair. "I still think we're wasting time."

It struck me he might not live to see a solution to his daughter's killing and—suddenly—I wished he would. Sensing his vulnerability, my providing the answers became even more important. "You'll find me different," I promised, and told him about the company we bought a half-dozen years ago, and how I'd once lost it. I explained that, once again, I was back in the driver's seat. My information about ADE carried a lot more clout than my PI card had.

"Architectural Design's a good company," he said. "The name

takes me back. I worked there once. Heck, everybody in the industry learned the ropes while working for your company."

The furnace fired, the mini explosion ending his comment like an audible period. A moment later, the furnace fan kicked on. Air from the duct behind him lifted and moved stray wisps of his thin gray hair.

"Thanks, for liking the company," I said, glad he had worked at ADE and somehow proud to be part of his special fraternity.

"Yep. Until Janie's death, my job was my life."

"Samantha said that the shock of your daughter's death caused you to lose interest."

He nodded. "That, and my wife's sickness. Gertrude's been in poor health for years. Janie's death nearly finished her off. She's in Louisville's Humana Hospital for observation and the doctors suspect an aneurysm. In a way, you might say that whoever killed Janie should also be prosecuted for what they did to my wife."

"I agree."

"Anyway, back in my prior life, when I was earning my daily bread . . ." He lowered his eyes slightly, and rubbed the white stubble on his chin. "I'll pat my own back—I was a fine artist. I carved statues of both Saint Peter *and* Saint Paul for Washington's National Cathedral. Loved every minute of it. Although doing work for the National Holocaust Museum was a darned tough go. Sometimes, I'd cry while carving inscriptions. It embarrassed me. I feared my workmates might notice the wet limestone dust when it caked on my cheeks."

"Thoughts recorded by tears, eh?" I liked Hugh McNamara and supposed his daughter's death would've been doubly difficult for the sensitive man.

He struggled from the chair and walked around to my side of the library table. Yanking open a drawer, he extracted a thick stack of pictures. He pulled one free and a rotten rubber band binding the packet together snapped and dropped to the floor.

"Look!" He handed me the picture. Waiting for my response, he fumbled around the tabletop and uncovered a pair of wire-rimmed glasses. Searching for a handkerchief, he patted his back pocket. That search a strike-out, he polished both lenses with his bare thumbs, then bent over and brushed his hands across the floor in a futile search for the yellow rubber band.

I turned a snapshot to face him. "You sculpted this gargoyle?"

"Yep. And not just one. In the early sixties, I spent months carving dozens. Of course, no Frenchie would admit it, but word has it that my carvings were repair parts for Notre Dame Cathedral in Paris.

"Now, instead of carving stone, I'm living astride it. Like a warrior who's retired from the fighting and spends his time still in the saddle, but watching the battle from atop a hill. See the limestone strata up your way runs all the way through here to the Ohio River . . ."

Losing his animation, he again appeared years older. "Care for a drink?" He struggled to his feet. "I only got Seagrams."

"Good enough," I observed. "That gives me three choices: Seagrams straight from the bottle; Seagrams out of a glass; or, Seagrams, 'No, thanks.' "

"Or a fourth. If you want, I'll slosh some branch water into that glass." His laugh was weak but not an old man's cackle.

He returned in seconds. "I'm locked in here now"—his gaze swept around the room—"with memories of *three* loved ones, and talking about the past seems to help. You want a science lesson?" he asked hopefully, tapping his glass against mine.

I said, "To your health," then glanced at my watch. "I'm a bit pushed for time. About Janie . . ." Looking disappointed, he began to rise from the chair. "No, no," I said quickly. "On second thought, there's no big rush."

He looked pleased again. "See, knowing about limestone teaches you humility even before life itself enrolls you in a much tougher class." Earlier, just forming words had seemed to sap his vitality. Now, his voice seemed to grow in strength as if revisiting the past brought him back to life.

"Three hundred and forty million years ago a shallow, tropical sea covered much of what is now middle-America. That was way before dinosaurs, or even trees. Thinking about such a broad stretch of time seems to make me feel better. Makes me know that Gert's, and Janie's, and my problems are short in duration and less significant in God's big plan—"

He paused to stifle a cough. His lungs won the battle. Covering his mouth with a gnarled fist, he unleashed a volley of rapid-fire, hard, dry coughs. "Sorry."

He talked on and on, describing how sea fossils formed the limestone he had ended up carving. When he described the sea's currents, he made a stirring motion with one finger as if one gnarled finger were reaching back in time to mix water in an ancient ocean.

Again I checked my watch, this time seriously. "Who do you think killed your daughter?" I asked.

He looked disappointed by the interruption, but this time accepted it. "Roger Petry," he said with conviction, then matter-of-factly added, "Who else?"

"According to Samantha her son had no reason."

"She just hasn't admitted the truth. Samantha's a good woman, but for a mother—especially the best—facing that kind of truth's a difficult pill to swallow."

He looked out at the ever-flowing river. "There's no other way. You have an obligation to go back and talk to her. She has to face the worst about her son's guilt . . . just like I've had to face up to Jane's death as well as the truth about Gertrude's health."

I pried myself from the chair. I believed he had more to tell me, but I couldn't even think of the right questions to ask.

I walked outside onto the porch and stood facing the river. Just below me, three loaded barges slowly rounded the river's curve and headed upriver to Louisville, Cincinnati, Pittsburgh, or dozens of other berthing places along the river's muddy banks.

I supposed each stack of steel plate in the lead barge's hold was much larger than the boats Abraham Lincoln once maneuvered around that same sweeping bend. By using a little imagination, I pictured a youthful Abe manning the rudder on his flatboat as it rode the channel downstream, then visualized it swinging wide on the curve and Abe scurrying to pole the vessel away from the Ohio River's muddy, north bank.

Old Abe would've been surprised had he known that there would eventually be a Panama Canal, and that the Ohio River would continue to grow in importance until it carried more bulk freight than the isthmus waterway his generation only dreamed about.

McNamara struggled down the stairs behind me, breathing hard. Feeling philosophical, and remembering Sam's comments about symbolic carvings, I turned to face him. "I was touched by your monument to your daughter," I said. "Although she died in her twenties, the wide-brimmed hat atop Jane's stone lets the world know that you still thought of her as your baby—"

"She'll always be my baby!" he agreed, his voice growing angry. "However, I wasn't honoring Janie because she was my baby."

"Pardon?"

"I was trying to do something for the baby in her belly. She was pregnant. With her, the baby died too." Tears welled in his eyes, and for a moment his quivering lips wouldn't form words. "I lost two members of my family: a daughter and a grandbaby."

I hid my surprise. "Who was the father?"

"Ask Samantha!"

With that, he turned and, grasping the pipe rails, began to tug himself laboriously up the steps toward the porch. I opened the Jag's door and stopped, remembering the bottle of Canadian Club stashed in the trunk.

"Here, Mr. McNamara," I called. "Have your next drink on me." Reclimbing the steps to him, I handed him the liter of Canada's best.

For the first time that day, he favored me with a full smile. "You come back any time, Richard Scott. Not because of the whiskey, but because you might be a man worth knowing."

He paused, carefully observing me before adding, "Remember: you've got *two* murders on your hands. I'd like to see you solve 'em both before Gert and I pass on."

We each had the same target. Could he help me more? I felt certain Hugh McNamara hadn't been completely open with me. I'd find out—I'd return here again.

While driving home, I had plenty of time to digest McNamara's comments. The strength of his convictions about Roger Petry perplexed me. I planned to explore that at greater length. Yet, right then, I needed to freshen up and slip into a sweater and jeans before meeting Sam.

But first, I would call Jeanie Robbins, my secretary. All day long, while I traveled, I had split my worrying time between the major criminal cases and the one involving the stolen credit cards. Now, that too had become another perplexing, even dangerous mystery. I needed to get to the bottom of it. I knew that as an investigator Jeanie was inexperienced. Had I relied too heavily on her? Had she even called the Indiana police . . . the Florida police?

I phoned the office. Jeanie was in a meeting. I decided to shower and shave, then try again later.

The doorbell rang just as I put the finishing touches on my beard trim. I yelled, "Just a mo'," and threw on a robe and clogs. I peered through the living room window before answering the door.

A tall, slender stranger stood on my porch, well dressed in a striped tie, black slacks, and a gray cashmere blazer that came close to hiding an embryonic paunch. Straight, steel-gray hair, trimmed long on back and sides, added to his distinguished mien. While waiting, he carefully polished his horned-rims, fastidiously examining each lense before carefully slipping the hooks through his hair and over his ears.

I opened the door. "May I help you?"

He stuck out his hand. "I'm Joe Petry." He showed strong even teeth, but I sensed the smile had been predesigned in front of a mirror and involved voluntary muscles, not warm emotion. "May I come in?"

Ignoring the outstretched hand, I nodded reluctantly. He chose a chair, I, the sofa.

"Mr. Scott," he said, his voice unctuous. "I'll come straight to the point. Samantha and I wish to reconcile, although admittedly, she's waiting for the exactly appropriate moment. I know that you've long been friends." He spat the word, like a man who's just discovered a roach's leg in his consomme. "But now is not the time for you and Samantha to renew past relationships. Surely, you'll both rise above such tawdriness." His slate blue eyes bored into mine.

My anger flared. "Look, Petry, you're an abusive husband!" I strained to control my emotions, yet this, most certainly, was not a relationship I wanted to develop. "You have no right to Samantha. She detests you. You're not welcome in my home." I shot to my feet. "To you, Samantha's only a stage prop for your twisted, right wing publicity stunts."

He leapt from his chair and placed his palm, flat on my chest, shoving. I plopped back onto the sofa. "Scott, I'll say this but once." He stopped to inhale, his face a mask of fury, and I witnessed the rage usually aimed at Samantha. "If you continue seeing Sam I'll ruin you in this community. If I let you live. And, believe me, I can see that you don't!"

While he harangued, I pondered. I know peacemakers are blessed, the meek shall be rewarded, and a willingness to choose reason over violence is the mark of a civilized man. But I also know valid arguments are difficult to develop, frequently misunderstood, and dreadfully slow to persuade when confronting anger. In an instant all that flashed through my mind; I elected for a concise, hard-hitting approach.

I unleashed a fierce kick. My wooden clog speared Petry dead in his crotch.

"Jeee-sus!" he yelled, the first syllable expelled from deep within his lungs, the second and third fashioned from sucked air.

He doubled over. Using both hands to coddle his injury, he collapsed onto the floor, his body tightly tucked into the fetal position.

Crossing my legs comfortably, I leaned back in the chair, watching his every move. "You about ready to hit the road, fellow?" I asked in my warmest voice.

He struggled to his knees. I rose from the chair. Grasping his arm, I tugged him to his feet, then gently guided his bent frame out the front door, down the sidewalk, and all the way to his car. When I opened the front door, I cupped the top of his head protectively in my palm like they do in the movies. That seemed to piss him more than the kick—he slapped away my hand.

Face contorted, he started and yanked his blue Park Avenue into gear. Watering eyes aimed straight ahead, the grimace locked in place, he sped down the drive.

I waved goodbye with my fingertips as he braked at the top of the hill. The Buick's taillights matched those on the car that always followed Sam. Now I knew!

I remembered that same car following Sam when she drove away after the arson fire. Her ex-husband had even been a witness to that conflagration. I swept all thoughts of credit card theft from my mind. I had to get to Sam. Immediately. I charged down the flagstone walk to the Jag.

Chapter Sixteen

EVERY LIGHT BLAZED INSIDE Samantha's house, though it wasn't yet dusk. She didn't answer the doorbell or my frantic pecking as I dashed from window to window.

My thoughts fixed on Joe Petry. An hour ago he had driven from my house, enraged. He could've driven directly to Sam's. I cursed my stupidity for not immediately considering it.

Running again to the porch, I twisted the knob and rattled the locked door. My mind redrew Petry's face—eyes crystal hard, upper lip drawn so tight it was bloodless. My face probably mirrored his as I sprinted down the sidewalk between houses and pulled the latch chain on Samantha's garden gate.

A flagstone walk led to the middle of the back yard and a waist-high concrete statue of Saint Francis of Assisi before forking into two paths. The shorter one veered left to a pergola trellis; the other meandered to a daffodil-filled rock garden in the far corner of the garden.

There, near the pathway, stood Samantha. Her parka-clad back to me, a spading fork in her hand, she dug furiously around a rotten stump.

Adrenaline spent, knees weak, feeling foolish about my panic, I slowed to a trembling walk. At once, elements of this benign environment snapped into sharper focus. Ignoring me, a pair of crested cardinals sorted seeds in an overflowing feeder, their beaks bright orange blurs. Below, on the ground, a half-dozen doves performed clean-up duty. As if questioning my passing, they tilted their silver-gray heads inquiringly before they resumed eating.

Sam wore her jeans tucked inside a pair of Wellingtons mired ankle-deep in muck. Grasping first one boot top, then the other, without losing either her balance or her boots, she tugged free of the mud. Carefully, while she repositioned each foot, I sneaked closer.

The next time she pried, I added my weight to the end of the spade handle. The stump fairly leaped from the ground. Surprised by the unexpected assist, she turned, "Again to the rescue, huh, Richard?" It earned me a bright smile and a kiss.

Her cheek was icy cold and the air tinged with the earthy smell of peat, but her breath tasted deliciously sweet. When our lips touched I felt the softness of rose petals.

Grasping me by the arm, she led the way up the path to a point where she plucked a tear-shaped snowdrop, cradling it between her fingers. "Aren't these precious?" She grinned impishly and touched it to her lips then tucked the delicate stem into my vest pocket.

A few steps later, she stopped again. "I love tulips. I've planted dozens along here." Leaning over, she fingered the tip of a newborn shoot, then recited names like White Fire, Burgundy Lace, Angelique, Apeldoorn, Groesbeek and Nijmegen.

"I favor tulips named after Dutch towns."

"And why might that be?"

I explained that during World War II, those villages had figured heavily in Montgomery's and Eisenhower's campaign to free Holland. Though the battles came before my time, through books and with a kid's imagination, I spent hours piloting Sherman tanks through those towns and miring half-tracks on the exposed tops of muddy dikes.

"Romance is difficult when you're a history buff," Sam said, laughing again.

Samantha indicated another flower bed. "Tulips will replace daffodils as the season warms. After that, lilies will bloom. Later, perennials will take over and flower all summer." Reverting to unique gardener's language, she glibly named flowers with names like bleeding hearts, coralbells, cranesbills, and chamomile.

"That's all Greek to me," I said, stumped by the names, yet delighted by her joy. We had been holding hands. It happened so naturally that I, just then, noticed.

Inside the back entryway, I played boot-jack to her muddy Wellingtons. While she changed clothes in the bedroom, I searched through the liquor cabinet. Figuring she needed a quick warm-up, I splashed a triple-shot of rock and rye into a an old-fashioned glass.

Testing it, she said, "This mixture takes me back. Joe kept this for IU football games on briskly cold days." She made no attempt to separate the good times from the bad.

For me she located a brandy snifter. She snuggled into the sofa as I fixed myself a brandy and benedictine.

"My day's been spent teaching students, more interested in spring break than learning," she said, drawing her legs beneath her on the sofa. "How did yours go?"

Going into rich detail, I described her ex's visit. My leather chair shifted on the carpet when I demonstrated my exuberant kick.

"Oh, Richard, no! Joe Petry never, never, *never* forgets," she exclaimed, sucking in a deep breath. "You shouldn't have!"

Still, underneath, I sensed her pleasure. Holding nothing back, I added my conversation with Hugh McNamara.

"Dammit!" she cried, "I've always adored Hugh, but he has no right to intimate Roger is guilty, or even capable, of murder." She pointed out that the stabbing took place on the rim of the quarry, while Roger was far away, down below, waiting for Janie to dive. "And the police discovered footprints in the ashes and puddles of blood near the campfire."

"Did I hear correctly? You said 'puddles'—plural?"

"More accurately, I should've said one puddle, plus a spatter.

Rumor has it that the killer nicked his hand leaving a sample of his own blood. The police never publicized that." She chewed her lip, thinking. "The night of the murder, the police checked Roger's shoes; even carefully examined they didn't match the footprint. Since then, they've asked for, but never demanded, a blood sample."

"Did your son father Janie's child?"

"No!" She reached for the phone. "I'll call Hugh."

"Don't try," I advised. "Hugh doesn't have a phone. Nor even a nearby neighbor. He's virtually incommunicado. That's why I risked a hundred-mile wild goose chase without calling ahead."

"I've forced you into this investigation; now you must believe in Roger's innocence. If not, turn back, and I'll go on alone."

"The warning's too late." Still embarrassed by our first fiascos and my feelings for Cait, I didn't go into my emotional involvement with both Sam and the case. I did insist I would stay the course.

Frowning, she placed a finger over her lips. "You must be careful the road you choose." Whispering, she recited: " 'I shall be telling this with a sigh/Somewhere ages and ages hence:/Two roads diverged in a wood, and I,/I took the one less traveled by,/*And that made all the difference.*' "

"I hope you're never sorry you took this road—for *me*," she concluded softly, "because, like Robert Frost, you may always wonder, 'what if?' "

"Professors are so complicated." Moving across the room, I lowered myself to the sofa beside her. "And I've chosen this road *with*, not just *for*, you." This time I kissed her more deeply. Her breath quickened and I tasted the flower's musky scent. I felt her heartbeat accelerate through the silk blouse. I wanted her . . . and knew she wanted me too.

Murder cases, however, especially ones involving a mother and son, are passion killers. Almost immediately, her breathing slowed and I knew she was thinking of Roger again. I sensed her withdrawal even before she pulled away. "I'm sorry," she said, running her fingers through my beard.

How ironic, I thought. Last time, Caitlin McChesney murdered our music. This time, Roger killed the dance. What next? Ever the optimist, I brightened. At least tonight we'd made it from the foyer to the sofa. Who knows? Could the bedroom be our next stop?

Frustrated, I took a couple of cool-off laps around the room and staggered away to freshen our drinks. Recommitted to Stolies, I returned to the Bergere chair and we both went back to the case.

"Where does Roger live, anyway? Do you ever talk to him?"

"For months we lost all contact. For awhile he lived in Pittsburgh, but sneaked back into Indiana. I still don't know his home address. But one of my students, an Internet freak, ferreted out his workplace." She spent a moment rummaging through her purse. "Here, write down this information. It gives his Social Security number, birth date, work address, and even describes the job. Take this picture also."

I took the picture. "Okay, I'll go see him next week." I knew the general location. It was a tough section of town. That would be okay. For Sam's sake, I'd go through a firestorm to help advance the case.

Later that evening, with Sam's safety filling my mind, I fixated on stalkers, not my next-day trip to Indy. Despicable, cowardly, evil *bastards;* contemptible, craven, depraved *stalkers.* No matter the adjectives, in my book the two nouns held identical meanings.

My primary cases, the ones I should've been focusing on, encompassed a litany of felonies—from fraud, to arson, to murder. Emotionally, though, I was unable to concentrate on crimes already committed, when Samantha faced another risk, much more immediate and potentially far more ferocious.

In her life, violence had become more of a probability than a possibility. Joe Petry, having terrorized Sam for months, now had a new nemesis—me! Now he and I had fought. Although my crotch shot had reduced our battle to a short campaign, I knew he must be lusting for revenge.

As for me, I'm impatient. I detest the defensive. I strike first, rather than react to some creep's first hit. My private eyeing hadn't included stalking cases. I needed to know the new territory.

Back home, I searched the Internet for the case law on stalking and spousal abuse. What help was available for victims? The answers were clear; help sources were limited. Screen after screen filled with nightmare cases where help came too late, or never. Disappointed— my gut knotted with worry about Samantha—I hit the sack.

My first stop next morning was the public library and more reading, my second, police headquarters. I had a life or death question: Could Sam and I look to the police, or were we strictly on our own?

I shifted from foot to foot waiting for the duty policeman to acknowledge my presence. Between gulps of coffee from an extra-deep Hardy's cup, he busied himself arranging a stack of citations into numerical order. I tire quickly.

A sign above the hallway's first door read "Sergeant Clyde Smith," the next, "Lieutenant Jason Humphreys." When seeking help, I always grab for the highest rung on the command ladder. This time I skipped by a couple of second louies and went for a big gun. I found a "Major somebody," distance obscuring the name. Reversing fields, I settled on Captain Raphael Redonzo.

The policeman rose slowly from behind his desk. "Sir, may I help?" His pithy voice grated, like an actor on *Law and Order*.

"I'm here to see Captain Redonzo."

"Got an appointment?"

"Nope. But I have a reason," I answered, confident and cocky, like the characters on *Nash Bridges*.

Shaking his head, the cop sat down again. "I'll need some information." Stretching to reach the forms, he upset his giant, bottomless coffee cup. "Damn!" He tried sweeping stacks of paper beyond the surge of spilled coffee. "Dammit!" followed failure.

Throwing his hands in the air, he yelled, "Paper towels!" He hopped to his feet and scurried down the hall to the ladies' restroom.

Seconds later, a uniformed policewoman followed. Retreating, hands palms-up before her, she shrugged disgustedly and continued down the hall. I watched through a window as she crossed the parking lot and climbed aboard her police cruiser.

A spiffy uniform walked in from outside. Its owner detoured to investigate the coffee fiasco, rolled his eyes, and turned to go. I glimpsed a name tag. This was my man!

"Captain Redonzo, I'm the president of Architectural Design and Elaboration, aka 'ADE.' I need your help in the worst way." Instead of my PI identification, I handed him an embossed business card.

Mid-thirties, the officer looked basketball-forward trim. His carefully barbered hair had been combed straight back with every coal-black hair oiled into place. He glanced at the card from beneath hooded lids, then scanned my Armani suit and Donna Karan silk tie. My clothing and I must've coalesced into a non-threatening package.

Smiling an easy smile, he motioned for me to follow, and led the way down the hall to his office. He placed my business card face-up on his desk.

"Captain, I can't yet name names," I said, laying my PI card on top of the ADE card. "But I have a friend being badgered by her estranged husband. Can you help? What's the law?" After hours spent on the Internet and in the library, I believed I knew.

I'm experienced enough to know language alone doesn't determine ultimate law. The law's effectiveness and clout gets tied to local police attitudes and priorities, and how they choose to enforce it.

He asked me to explain my private investigator connection, nodding okay when he'd heard. Without rising, he twisted around and tugged a thick tome from the bookcase behind his desk. "Let's start by describing a stalker as the Indiana courts define one," he suggested.

"Every state has its own interpretation. Paraphrased, our definition is as follows: 'A knowing or intentional course of conduct involving repeated or continuing harassment of another person. This conduct must be such that it could, or did, cause the victim, a reasonable person, to feel terrorized, frightened, intimidated, or threatened.'" He paused to study my response. "Does any of that apply to your friend?"

"Every bloody word!"

"Then you'll need our help. The threat always tends to escalate. The stalker's interest is domination and abuse, not love. Typically, there's a continuum from harassment, to physical violence—and that violence frequently proceeds to murder."

Thinking of Sam alone in her house, I almost recoiled from the strength of his words. "That's why I'm here," I said and gulped while responding evenly. "My friend hasn't called you, and although I've suggested it, there is a reluctance to seek outside help."

"She must consider legal measures. A restraining order could be the answer. Perhaps she—it is a *she*, isn't it?" I nodded. "Perhaps she has grounds to have him arrested. We're on her side. We'll help . . ."

Again remembering my Internet and library hours, I asked, "Do you always help? Or even usually, help? It seems to me that most injunctions merely cost the victim money and rile the stalker. And that if there is an injury, case law says that the police aren't responsible."

"You're absolutely correct about police responsibility," Captain Redonzo responded, his voice still carefully modulated. "Both the Declaration of Independence and the Due Process Clause of the United States Constitution proclaim that all men have the right to life, liberty, and the pursuit of happiness. However, neither instrument says that our police departments are accountable for guaranteeing it."

My face must have revealed my chagrin at hearing his confirmation of my own dark thoughts. "Essentially, then, we are S O L," I said. "We're dealing with an escalating situation, yet you can't—or won't—help."

"Look, even in *DeShaney v. Winnebago*, the court ruled that 'special relationships' exist only as regards certain incarcerated individuals—"

"Yeah, yeah, yeah," I said, cutting in. "Basically, your legal obligation is restricted to people the system has put in jail, prison, or a mental institution? You must feed, clothe, and medicate the inmates, all the while trying to keep them from being raped, beaten, or murdered. Right-o?"

"Exactly!" He leaned across the desk. "But, look. Although I want to clarify the law, that interpretation doesn't tell the Indiana story. This is a tight little community. We care. We'll do all we can, but visualize it from our standpoint. We just are not sufficient in numbers."

Again he spun around in his swivel chair and pulled another weighty tome from the shelf. This one quoted an eminent civil rights lawyer and criminologist. He scanned a ream of statistics. "Simply put," he summarized, "the numbers show there are too many victims for the police to look after everyone."

I climbed to my feet. "I'll tell her you're on our side. Unfortunately, you're short of horses." Rising to go, I tossed a bundle of reproduced papers across his desk. "Other victims may request help. Here's another case to quote . . ." I spoke slowly and quietly, my voice tinged with the acid of disappointment. "Maybe threatened people will wish to hear about Lisa Bianco; she made all the right moves and became a *cause celebre*—posthumously."

"At least give us your friend's name."

"Sorry, Captain, I can't betray a confidence. No matter how you cut it, no matter how many times you plow through the legalese and rationalizations, you reach one final conclusion." Raising my voice, I stabbed my chest with a thumb. "Except for me, my friend is on her own!"

He didn't disagree. "I suppose you complement that PI card with a weapon."

I nodded. "So the answer is, buy a gun!"

Redonzo pursed his lips and watched silently from beneath those hooded eyes. I wondered if I detected an almost-imperceptible nod.

Saying, "Thanks," I offered a snappy salute. Not angry, but totally frustrated, I walked from the police station and went back to confronting the cold, dangerous streets. It took but ten steps for me to realize our full peril.

There would be no official help. Sam and I had each other. We would go it alone. Period.

Chapter Seventeen

JEANIE ROBBINS, MY SECRETARY, wore a nautical blue blazer and knife-pleated, gray skirt—her typical office garb. Her cream and mahogany blouse, emblazoned in a retro print pattern, looked a lot like some of the neckties I'd recently worn. She backed her businesslike appearance with strong words, "Your identity's been stolen."

I had just withdrawn my prized Blue Ocean Pelikan fountain pen from my desk drawer and held it poised for signing a memo. Smiling, I flipped it into the air and with a flourish, caught it just before its nib speared the desktop. "You also, have a great routine, Jeanie! Please feed me the good-news, bad-news punch line."

I realized she wasn't joking. I waited, my expression matching her serious frown, my gaze boring into her dark amber eyes.

She tugged a chair closer to my desk, smoothed her skirt, and sat. Unfolding a Florida boat company's sales brochure, she fast-fed me the info exactly as I had asked, "The good news is: you now own one heck of a boat. Dimensionally, it's a forty-two-foot-long by eight-foot-wide Model 42 Revolution Cigarette Boat; sports three, four-hundred-fifteen HP Mercury Cruiser I-O engines, and attains speeds in the ninety MPH range. It carries a sticker of $285,000, and was produced in 1996."

She paused to catch her breath. "The bad news: it's not only titled under your name but, at last report, the new operator was tooling around Miami Bay using your identity. He's even using your platinum American Express card to buy boat fuel."

I kept my voice calm. "Have you called the police?"

"I've tried. First thing, when the problem started. Neither the Indiana nor Florida police departments are interested. Each says that the bank advancing the money is the victim. The merchant will get paid—and couldn't care less. As owner of the credit card, you don't have to pay. You need worry only about your good name and your credit rating."

"Yeah, as if those things weren't important," I groused, scanning the boat invoice. "This bill first went to another local address before being forwarded here. It's over a month old, the sighting two weeks later. I wonder what this character has been up to during the interim."

Sitting back against my leather chair, I ran my fingers through my mop of hair. "One problem—identity theft is a new swindle in my repertoire. Over the years I've encountered every form of shell game, trickery, deceit or con game known to man."

"Being a PI is difficult?"

"No way. I was speaking of the chicanery I've faced while running my ordinary industrial business." I paused for effect. "Now, you talk gumshoeing; that really gets squirrelly."

Satisfied with my one-upmanship, I sobered. "My case load's already too big. I have a premonition, though, that this credit card theft involves more than reputation, so I need answers. Post haste!"

I pondered a solution. "Jeanie, you either make the calls for me, or I'll lean on Capital Detective Agency. Either way, I must bottomline what's happening. I've gotta know where the crook is getting his info."

Drawing herself up to her full five-foot-two-inch height, Jeanie exploded with indignation, "I introduced this problem to you. I'll see it through. Or do you prefer that I remain in the background as others in management insist?"

"Hey, Jeanie, cool it," I objected. "Your job is to try anything you feel capable of doing well. You'll have every opportunity to grow within the company—"

"Well, weelll!" she interrupted, tripling the last word's length, "Seve Jensen wouldn't agree. He says I should stick to my knitting— only he calls it, 'your typing, letter writing, and calling either Richard Scott or Mommy when you have a bitch.' "

"Jeanie, be my guest. Run with it." I stuck out my hand. "And thanks."

While we talked, Peggy Murdock from the typing pool waited and listened beside Jeanie's desk. Sullen as usual, she dropped a stack of papers on the desktop and hurried out.

I was still wondering what, exactly, was chewing Seve Jensen, when Jeanie handed me a hot-off-the-Internet copy of a *Sarasota Herald-Tribune* news article. "Here boss, there's another storm brewing down on the beaches."

I read: " 'Although hurricane season normally begins in June, two computer models suggest a rogue weather system. When it reaches the Florida keys, it will be carrying winds in the 120 mile mph range. The National Weather Service suggests this catastrophic storm may be the result of global warming . . .' "

Obviously remembering my condo on Siesta Key, Jeanie had managed to have the last word after all.

Pondering Jeanie's latest info and anxious to meet Roger Petry for the first time, I cranked the Vanden Plas.

On long drives, I first review jobs I'm working on. Once tired of that, I scan the radio dial. This morning, boredom came quickly. When I tuned to WQIP and found Reverend Gabriel Goodall once more on the air, grappling with his interpretation of sin. Today, he added a new twist: "I take pleasure in announcing to my faithful parishioners that I will be running for a United States House of Representatives' seat in the next election."

I remembered his biting tone when he chastised me in the WQIP-TV studio lobby. Today, Goodall's sonorous voice dripped with honeyed sincerity. The pitch lowered. Again, I thought of Moses.

Maybe Goodall's voice sounded deep and resonant like God's when he met Moses on Mount Sinai. One major difference. Following *His* greeting, God gave us the Ten Commandments. Following *his* morning announcement, Reverend Goodall asked for liberal campaign donations. Cash, check, money order, or credit card, the listener could pick his poison.

"Remember," he intoned, "Barnabas sold his field and gave the proceeds to the Apostles. Ananias and Sapphira connived to keep their money from the Lord—and were struck dead." Here his voice dropped as if he were displeased with two low-life, but frequently encountered, neighbors. "Don't risk eternal damnation by depriving the church and FIPRO of your abundance," he warned.

"Now that I'm running for office, you must commend twice as much to your God: not one sheaf but two. Before, you had only the church. Today, you must support the campaign as well. Both are God's works. Send us your love offerings: I will send a three-CD set of sermons with all my thoughts on the Rapture . . ." Goodall emphasized his own statement—the sound of his fist striking wood told me he was pounding the table. At least he wasn't hammering it with his trademark .45 caliber, silver-barreled pistol—that was the good news.

After shushing the congregation's cheering, he announced that on the following Monday he'd have a campaign kick-off breakfast at an Indianapolis downtown hotel. He mentioned appearances in other cities and towns, but one in Abram's Trace caught my attention.

"Hmmm! Maybe I'll go . . ."

Switching off the radio, I rethought the dogfight between Seve Jensen and myself when three years after the Gulf War, in 1994, we competed to buy Architectural Design and Elaboration, Incorporated.

I'd had one objective: ownership for Barb's dad and me. Seve had two: he wanted ownership; he wanted the company presidency. Those reflections made me re-visualize Seve that day, his lips twisted in fury and those friendly blue eyes turned ice-cold when he discovered how—through a complicated buyout arrangement—my father-in-law and I would buy the company while risking little of our own cash.

Unfortunately, my carefully contrived plan kiboshed a bundle of Seve Jensen's dreams and he launched into a bitter tirade. It ended with his snarl: "You bandits are muscling me out of the play!"

"Look, Seve," I said. "With your limited resources the company would die." I talked "Return on Investment" and "Violated Credit Restrictions." Building my case, I spit financial jargon and accounting acronyms like a carpenter's pistol firing nails. Wrapping my argument, I showed him the numbers, then closed with, "Figures don't lie."

"No, but *liars figure*," he responded, bitterly.

Not letting emotions intrude on a business deal, I kept my cool. "Think about it, Seve," I said. "This business has to grow—or die." I stopped talking long enough to present more data on my handy-dandy laptop computer, then hammered home the conclusion. "See, Seve! Had you bought it, the company would've been belly up in six quarters, max." I flipped the laptop screen around to face him.

Stubbornly averting his eyes, he ignored the numbers and objected, "I could've made it. Through hard work I could've succeeded. With time, I could've located a business broker with the confidence to bankroll me.

"Even today," he continued, "Dollars for Mankind will provide financing. You squeezed me. The company squeezed me. ADE should've extended the signing deadline." Acid acrimony corroded his words.

For my part, I had no part in the contract-closing deadline. I did wonder about Dollars for Mankind.

Buying peace during the rest of the conversation, I buttered my words for easier swallowing. Nevertheless, despite logic, I know it's difficult learning to love the bugger who's just drop-kicked your butt in the final play of a losing game. I also know a man's dreams are ethereal and a mind hitched to gossamer can seldom be re-hooked by reality.

Yet I made one last try, "Seve, how about coming in with me as chief financial officer? Continue with the company. It takes a lot of imagination and moxie to build a business. You showed both during the negotiations." Even back then, I knew the wheelchair wouldn't be a factor in his performance, because business success comes from having a bright mind, not strong legs. Also, I liked his iron will. But most of all, I admired his intelligence, because, although a manager can teach his subordinates many things, he can't teach them to have brains. Getting Seve on board seemed worth the risk.

After I made my offer a secretary interrupted to remind me that more papers required signing and notarizing. Face livid, tightly locked jaw muscles distorting his rounded face, Jensen glowered at us both. Leaving his rage to cool I turned and scurried from the lobby into the conference room. Fifteen minutes later, finished with another set of documents, I returned to find him still waiting.

It was as if he had double-clicked on his personal computer screen's "I now love Richard Scott" icon. His attitude had completely changed. That day his quick change surprised me. Now, I took them in stride.

"Congratulations, Richard!" Straining forward in his wheelchair, he extended his hand. "If the chief financial officer slot is still open, I'll remain aboard."

"It is. Thanks for staying! You can even help me conclude the buy-out."

Following another set of paper signings and a few minutes of additional conversation we went our still closely related, but far separate ways. He wheeled down the carpeted hall to his smaller office and the CFO's desk. I marched in the opposite direction toward my ancient, high-backed and richly leathered, captain's chair . . .

Now, while speeding toward Indianapolis, I pondered coincidences. Reverend Gabriel Goodall and Karl Sprader had built the apartments in Indianapolis. Years ago, Goodall cheated my mother out of money. Samantha suspected her ex-husband, a stalker, of having some relationship with Goodall. Samantha's student, who was a friend as well, had been murdered. The murder occurred but yards from my house. Seve Jensen, my second in command claimed he could've borrowed money from Dollars for Mankind, a group that sounded suspiciously like the arm of a religious organization—and for all I knew, Seve's relationship with that religious organization might still be flourishing; that might be good or bad.

I might've thrown up both hands, but merging onto I-65 took my attention. "Richard Scott," I muttered, "this bucket of worms is becoming downright confusing. Where will this winding road lead? Downtown, certainly." Two miles ahead, skyscrapers speared the gray clouds. "But where else? Who can tell?"

Chapter Eighteen

THE LOW-RISE, YELLOW-BRICK Chez Royaliste Hotel squatted between two taller buildings in an un-renovated section of near downtown Indianapolis. The hotel's red and green neon managed only Chez and Roy—before flickering out. In spots, the aged, dingy brick had flaked away, leaving the pocked walls looking as if they'd been struck by stray gunfire. Maybe they had.

Anyway, Roger ought to be easy to locate. Samantha had described her son's job here. He probably worked, slept and ate his meals under the same roof.

I parked the car in a side lot. Inside the lobby, I tagged onto a line wending between crimson-velvet ropes toward the check-in. Just ahead, a thirtyish, blue-suited man placed one arm around the younger woman beside him and, leaning close, whispered into her ear.

Blushing, she poked him in the ribs. "Poor baby," she whispered, tenderly laying her hand on his arm.

He pulled her close, squeezed her waist, then, inserting his fingers beneath her waistband, he gently massaged the small of her back. Giggling, she grasped his hand, removed it, and held it firmly against her side. His fingers kept twitching, although now with diminished potential.

The waiting line split apart. While the eager couple filled out a room request form for a harried clerk, I waited for another female employee to sort and stack a bundle of receipts.

The peroxided blond banded and tossed a the sheaf into a tray before reciting a dull litany. "A single's sixty-five dollars, plus tax. You want king-size, it'll run you another twelve. There will be a six-dollar surcharge for each additional guest. Parking's free. HBO, Cinemax, and Showtime three dollars extra; Playboy costs five . . . we don't take debit cards. Which room do you prefer, and will you be paying with cash or credit card?"

I said, "No room. No cash. No card. I'm looking for Roger Petry."

"Rog, honey, you've got a live one," she yelled over her shoulder while simultaneously motioning me aside so she could tend to a paying customer. When "Rog, honey" didn't answer, she ducked around the corner to get him.

Blondie smiled a secret smile as she resumed her post. Following close behind her, a young, skinny guy sauntered from the office. I read his attitude and surmised that Roger's perks included not only room and board, but entertainment as well.

"Can I help you?" Roger was taller than either parent with Samantha's black hair, except his was worn longer, reaching to his shoulders. He also had the same deep-set brown eyes and a hint of her smile but his cold expression wasn't his mom's. I attributed that to Joe Petry's DNA, although he hadn't a single of his father's features. Of course, living with the threat of a murder rap could stunt personality growth as effectively as bad genes. Still, there was an up side. Since he didn't favor his dad, I might find bonding easier.

Roger wore a blue shirt, a nondescript tie, and an oversized, blue pinstriped suit with shoulder pads draping his arms like raglan sleeves. I felt a touch of pity. I could just see him, new in town and taking this job, only to discover the hotel's dress code called for something classier than tee shirt and jeans.

I'd have laid odds he had been flat broke and had upgraded his wardrobe shopping Goodwill. But surely he'd brought the green and white running shoes with him. Even Goodwill wouldn't have had the nerve.

I flashed my ID. "Your mom asked me to come." I indicated the crowded counter and the romantic couple now swapping cash for a room. Watching them, I reckoned they had other partners at home and dared not risk a credit card, paper trail. "Roger, we need a place to talk. This lobby is a madhouse."

"Yeah." He nodded his head in agreement. "At this hotel, each day's occupancy rate's over two-hundred percent."

"Very impressive," I smiled. "Couples probably get sleepy during morning work hours, come here for nooner relaxation, and leave feeling completely refreshed. Sometimes, a short nap works wonders . . . and the room can be rented again for evening trade."

"This no-tell takes pride in its appearance," Roger said. "We furnish white blankets to hide semen stains—"

I interrupted. "Except by request, I doubt you give body counts on the various mites, mildews, rusts, and smuts sharing the percale."

We were on a roll. "You called that right." He nodded, chuckling. "We also specialize in early check-outs. Everybody skips breakfast in bed—"

I finished for him. "And nobody reverts to childhood and chews the corners of their white blankies." Our easy rapport pleased me. Maybe it came from a shared relationship with Sam.

"Carrie, cover for me."

When the peroxided blond mouthed an okay, Roger skirted the end of the counter. He led the way across the lobby, through a door, to a coffee shop's corner table. I checked my watch. Lunch time! I ordered a bagel and lox with a coffee chaser. Roger settled on a triple-decker cheeseburger with the works, seasoned fries, and a Coke.

I baited him, "Roger, I spoke with Hugh McNamara, Janie's dad. He's convinced you killed his daughter."

His lips tightened. "If you believe that bull, you should've stayed home." His words came out tougher, but the thought mimicked Sam's. Changing subjects, he asked about her.

I assured him that Samantha missed him and suggested a letter or phone call would ease her angst. He preferred e-mail. I wasn't certain Sam used Internet. Checkmate.

The waiter brought the food and drinks. Squeezing a plastic bottle, Roger laid an artistic, red spiral atop his cheese-covered, real beef patties, following with layers of onions, tomatoes, and lettuce. Using all ten fingers, he compressed the sandwich, licked away a stray globule of ketchup, and opened wide his mouth. He scarfed up the food as if he were starving.

"How do you stay so skinny, Roger?" I teased, chuckling. "I've never encountered an appetite like yours—except maybe my own, when I was your age."

Leaning so far back in his chair that it teetered on its hind legs, he patted his stomach and smiled. "Working this place and daily workouts'll keep you skinny."

Back to the case, I blindsided him with, "Hugh McNamara also talked about Janie's pregnancy. He believes you're the father."

Roger didn't choke, but lowered the cheeseburger and bobbed it up and down for emphasis. "That's impossible. We only did the dirty deed"—he waggled a finger, stressing the final word—"once."

"Come off it, Roger! The numbers involved in sex are simple. It takes one egg, one sperm, and one time—at the right time—to usher you into fatherhood."

Roger turned a bright incandescent red. "Well, you see, I was pretty innocent," he said, squirming in his seat. "Not Janie. I got so nervous and uptight, my whole system crashed early on . . . if you get my drift. Janie could've killed me." He smiled, ruefully. "Believe me, when I was also slow rebooting, she threatened to do just that."

He stopped, waiting for a response. I stifled the urge to tell a Viagra joke. Still, he seemed a tad young to need a booster pill. I played it nonchalant as I bit through the cream cheese and into the fresh bagel. My mouth watering, I carved a piece of smoked salmon while waiting for Roger to continue.

"She could be tough," Roger added. He paused for a moment as if remembering; he dabbed at the corners of his eyes when he did. "People loved Janie because she seemed so sweet and innocent. Being young and inexperienced, I went ape over her because she had been around a bit. To me she was sophisticated."

His eyes strayed toward the check-in desk. "That was before I met Carrie. Now, I know what sophistication and hot action really are."

"I understand that the night of the murder, you and Jane and a couple of friends took a midnight skinny-dip in Rose Cutter's Quarry. Tell me about it. Everything."

"We doubled with a couple we'd bumped into a couple of times over beers. You said friends? Nah! I thought the guy was an up-front dude. He wasn't. And the girl was nothin' but a PHAT player—"

"A what?"

"You know—*pretty hot and tempting*. A good-looking chick, with gazongas the size of melons, always involved with one dude, but with hot pants for some other cat."

"But they were your friends, weren't they?"

"Let me give you the whole scoop. You'll see—they turned out to be real finks."

Expression gone from angry to downcast, Roger recounted how he'd balanced midway up the cliff while he waited for Janie to conjure enough nerve to join him and the others. "I had my toes hooked on this ragged-edged rock shelf and my fingers stuck knuckle deep in a crevice. I looked straight up into a coal-black sky and yelled, 'Come on, sweetheart! Don't be chicken. The water's fine.'"

He explained that, by stretching his body nearly horizontal to the water, he could make out the glow of their campfire up on the quarry's rim, but the perpendicular limestone face hid Janie. "I shouted for her to quit thinking about it and just dive."

"This so-called friend joined in," Roger said. "He was about fifty yards out in the quarry. I remember his words, exactly. He shouted, 'The water's warm as fresh piss . . . uh . . . bath water.' Said it would be even better'n the peppermint schnapps and warm blankets waiting for us after the swim."

"Was his girlfriend also in the water?" I asked.

"Yeah. She was freezin' her hooters off and had been bitchin' about it earlier. When her guy shouted at Janie, she answered, 'Humph!' Or something like that."

"Where in the water was she?"

"Both of 'em were mid-lake, treading water together. Earlier, we'd placed a lantern on a rock down near the water. I could see its beam flicking off her gold bracelet. Somebody had given her the piece of jewelry and she wore it every mother-lovin' minute. I figured she and some dude had to be this close together." Making the point, he raised his hand with the index and middle fingers pressed tightly together.

"Then Janie dove?"

"Yep. She yelled, 'Okay, guys! Here goes noth—' I thought it was nervous tension, or the running start to the edge that cut off her words." He grimaced. "Now I know better. You know the rest. Mom surely told you about the broken beer bottle used to kill her," he concluded as if it left a bad taste in his mouth.

"Did your swim-mates back your story about Janie being stabbed atop the quarry rim while you were standing down near the water?"

"At first, they did. But after an umpteenth questioning session, they changed their stories and said that while they had heard me calling for Janie to dive, they didn't see me hanging on the rock ledge before Janie hit the water. They lost their nerve and shagged me. Royally. The cop came away thinking that I was the second coming of *Fat Bastard*. They did a first class number on me, plain and simple." The acrid memory didn't tear him away from his sandwich. He stuffed the final bite into his mouth and stopped speaking to chew.

He swallowed the last of the burger and used his straw to search amidst the ice cubes and slurp the last drop of Coke, then wiped his lips on a wadded napkin. After pounding the ketchup bottle with the heel of his hand, he paused to decorate the fries with his trademark spiral, before carrying my cup and his glass to the counter.

"Where are your two turncoat friends now?" I asked, when he returned with our refills.

"They graduated and went back to Nashville. Not Indiana's over in Brown County, but the country-western biggie in Tennessee."

"Who ordered you to leave Bloomington?"

"Nobody ordered me. Clark Benefield, Janie's old boyfriend, was tight with one of the county deputies. He came to see me and Mom. He didn't believe I killed Janie. He said, according to his sources, I would be smart to get my skinny buns out of town until things simmered down."

"Okay, Roger, now for the biggie. If you didn't father the baby, who did?"

"Can't say. I guess you know that Janie was once engaged to Clark Benefield and that after that she shacked up with Seve Jensen. That gives you two additional prospects." For a moment, he mulled the statement. "Strike that additional bit," he concluded, dryly. "I don't even belong on the list."

I nodded my head deliberately, beginning to believe.

"Beyond that," Roger continued, "I don't have a handle on her other boyfriends. She had a carload. She was forever getting tight with one joker, then moving on to another sucker."

"As a first step for clearing you, I'll call Capital Detective Agency. Stella Carlyle will arrange for you to be DNA tested. Then we'll check your results against those of the fetus."

"No way, Jose!" His voice was vehement. "I wasn't the dad. I won't see Janie's body dug up to prove something that I already know is pure, unadulterated bull crap."

I tried arguing.

"Heeey man!" He pled. "Forget about it! Just plain damn-well, forget about it!" Roger rose from the table. Shoulders slumped, slender body wiggling loosely inside the huge, blue pinstripe, Roger moved slowly back across the lobby to his work station.

Feeling sorry for him, I wheeled, and left for the parking lot, puzzling about the real reason why he resisted a DNA test. Was he being super sensitive? Or had he been Janie's sperm donor? Or, absent an order from the county police, did he prefer merely lying low and trying to ride out the investigation? So far, the police had exerted little pressure, anywhere, and our Roger had been lying low for months.

Or was he guilty as sin?

Twenty minutes after I left Roger, I was inside the walnut-paneled offices of Grover, Gable and Schwab, and waiting to meet with my accountant. From the window where I was standing, I could hear Meridian Street traffic seven stories below. Gazing across a cornfield and into the distance, I had an airplane pilot's view of my condo nestled inside a grove of maple trees. Its red-tiled roof stood out like a beacon. With all the problems waiting for me downstate, I was tempted to follow the signal, kick back in my old digs, and remain in Indianapolis.

I heard the door swing open and turned in time to see rotund Joseph Schwab pad across the thick carpet to greet me with a pleased, "Good afternoon, Richard!" greeting, and the question, "What brings you to town so unexpectedly?" He motioned me to a chair and seated himself behind his massive desk.

"Same problem. What else?" I answered. "Since you warned of company fraud, I've had long talks with my financial officer." I went on to detail my conversations with Seve Jensen and an update on the Jane McNamara murder investigation. "Jensen assured me that you were working on the problem. Which I already knew. In the meantime, we're losing money hand over fist. What are you doing about it?"

Today's answers usually come pre-filtered through a computer screen, and Joseph wasn't about to answer without the benefit of his seventeen-inch Packard Bell. Propelled by a vigorous movement of his leg, he rocketed backward, and spun to face the worktable. His stubby finger gently touching the mouse to wake the sleeping computer, he said, "We've examined your company records. Meticulously. Thus far, we've been unable to locate the source of your problem."

He turned slightly, and leaned back toward me, the overhead light reflecting on his bald dome, and his lips narrowing like they did the first time he announced the money problem. "Your business hasn't grown. But your expenses have skyrocketed. Follow the money." With that, he zipped the mouse across its pad, clicked once, and watched as the printer whirred alive. "Here, Richard, you might wish to examine the names on this sheet. You may find an outside culprit."

Chapter Nineteen

IT FELT GOOD, AFTER A TOUGH DAY in Indy, to steer south on College Avenue toward downtown Bloomington. I relish the obvious; I'm delighted by a university town's ambience.

Years before, just after I moved to Bloomington, and immediately following our ADE buyout, I had time to burn. I explored the IU campus. My first trip took me through the stone, "Sample" gates leading into one of IU's magnificently flowered plazas. I strolled by the Student Building and a passing student informed me that its clock and bell tower inspired Hoagy Carmichael to write "Chimes of Indiana."

From there, I hustled to Maxwell Hall, which had been around since 1890. Stopping, I tugged at one of those ivy ropes that clung to its ornate stone wall until curving over the roof and beyond sight. I found myself feeling somehow connected to the past.

After that one stroll, even when driving, I tended to plan my trips east from downtown Bloomington so they'd take me through the campus. But I couldn't let sentimentality hide the fact that I'm a hard-nosed engineer with a master's degree from Purdue. Year in and year out, while living in Indy, I'd always cheered for the Boilermakers to clobber the Hoosiers in basketball, and stayed frustrated about the NCAA titles that at one time seemed to arrive downstate in clusters.

Anyhow, I tend to have strong opinions on most subjects, and my viewpoint about the special relationship between universities and towns goes far beyond buildings and grounds. I'm talking knowledge.

I believe that if mankind is ever to learn how to live successfully on this planet, revelation will have to come from education, not religion. Religions support fundamentalist beliefs by citing their own supportive dogma. So, whenever trapped in destructive orthodoxy, escape to truth and compassion becomes impossible.

Most of the time, since the "anointed" can't win arguments, they try to destroy the dissident. That can mean killing the heathen—although the death sentence will be pronounced in the name of the Lord, and deemed both righteous and okay.

Genuine scholars differ. Searching for answers, true "seekers" embark on any road having the potential to lead them to ultimate truths. That's my read.

I'm convinced that close physical proximity to academia provides a town with a special energy and conscience. Even better, students and profs, coming from different parts of the world, constantly toss new and diverse concepts into the intellectual process.

What's *my* answer? Sometimes my thoughts carry me too far from the case I'm working on. Maybe I'm developing a hybrid religion too. Perhaps I should get my own radio and television shows. I can just see it: "The Reverend Richard Scott, private eye for the confused. Hey, you brothers and sisters out there in radio and television land—it's tithing time! Make those checks out to read 'cash.' Cash and credit cards cheerfully accepted. The address is . . ."

A sign reading "Seventh Street" came into sight, interrupting my fantasies. I wheeled left for a couple of blocks, and turned right on Washington. I waited for a dozen book-carrying students to laugh their way across Kirkland, then motored east toward the Breaking Fast Restaurants office.

I wanted to meet the chain's president, Clark Benefield. He *was* a man of contradictions. Once, engaged to the late Jane McNamara, later, understanding of Roger Petry, her new boyfriend, and a suspect in her murder. He even warned Roger to skedaddle outta town just ahead of the posse. Yep, quite a guy!

The office was a few blocks beyond the business section, located inside a white, weatherboard bungalow. Parking was parallel with the curb, as-you-find-it, and restricted only by a neighbor's hand-lettered signs saying: DO NOT BLOCK DRIVEWAY—VIOLATERS TOWED. A smaller sign on the same post said: STUDENT APARTMENT AVAILABLE. CHEAP. NO PETS. A conflict of interest?

I climbed five wooden steps, took two long strides across a concrete porch, shoved open the door, and entered. "I'm Richard Scott," I announced, "I'd like to see Clark Benefield, please." It was my day for signs: one on her desk read: LISA CRUMB, RECEPTIONIST; the one beside it said: WE KILL EVERY THIRD SALESMAN. TWO JUST LEFT.

Lisa Crumb eyed me from a hood of thick, sandy hair. She reached for the phone, exposing long fuschia claws, coordinated nicely with her lipstick, eye shadow, and a skimpy, v-necked sweater. Pursing thin lips, she reconsidered, "You got an appointment, huh?"

"Sorry," I apologized, "I tried calling. First your line was busy. Next try, my cell phone went on the blink."

"Stuff happens." She smirked and I knew she didn't believe me. "Ya can't see Mr. Benefield without an appointment. He's always so busy. What's that name again?"

I repeated it.

She managed to write "Richard" before her ballpoint shot craps. She yanked a second pen from a glassful. Same old, same old. "Crap! Oh, pardon me. One moment, please." She dropped her wire-framed glasses on the desk and scurried into a side office.

I plopped down on an armless, red-vinyl and chrome chair. When trapped, I'll read almost anything. I opened a June 1995 issue of *Franchise Restaurants—Promises and Problems*. Concluding I'd finally hit rock bottom in the reading department, I lay aside the magazine and surveyed the surroundings.

This sure wasn't a Fortune 500 outfit. A window seat held two broken NCR cash registers, both with drawers open and askew. Some nighttime raider had subbed a pry bar for an ATM card and made a cash withdrawal. The living room-office floor was almost totally covered by a multicolored, woven-rag rug, probably a leftover from a previous owner. The white vinyl tile in the next room looked more serviceable except for circular spots in front of each of the two gray metal filing cabinets. There, pivoting feet had worn through, exposing the black-varnished, tongue and groove boards beneath.

I overhear an animated conversation in the next room. "But what'll I tell him?" the receptionist asked. "I've gotta say something."

"Tell him . . . oh, I dunno! Tell him Clark's out of . . ." The male voice faded.

Lisa Crumb returned. "Mr. Benefield's out—"

I interrupted. "Out of town, I'll betcha. When will he return?"

She blushed. "Don't know. His partner called to tell us it was an emergency. He said one of 'em would call later with Clark's itinerary."

On my way out I reached the door, then snapped my finger at an afterthought. "Breaking Fast Restaurants are located statewide. A going concern." I scanned the office and rolled my eyes. "I'm surprised at the size of the corporate office."

"Me too. Up until a year ago, we were big-time—right downtown on the square and planning to move north to Indy. Now this." She too surveyed the room, lips twisting disdainfully. "What's a poor girl to do? 'Course, Clark still uses the downtown office for some really important stuff."

"Perhaps he's there now." But I blew it by sneering, remembering the receptionist's earlier, surreptitious conversation in the side room.

Twisting the knob and stepping outside, I wondered why my simple request had caused such perplexity. Was Clark Benefield in hiding? Yep. I remembered that Mafia members, sensing trouble, often threw a mattress on the floor in some unfurnished dump and hid out until the threat disappeared. I had a feeling Roger Petry's benefactor followed that time-honored example. Our Clark Benefield had "hit the mattresses."

Earlier, during introductions, I'd told receptionist Lisa Crumb that my car phone had zonked. Miraculously, during our meeting, it had healed itself. Making a run for some good news, I called Seve Jensen to check on our missing money mystery. Nothing new. My gut tightened at the news, but I stayed cool as if losing a few more million wouldn't be a big problem. Then, I told him I visited Indy, but not the reason.

"I did make a trip downstate that might interest you, though. I called on Jane McNamara's dad, down on the Ohio River. Quite a guy." The phone went silent. "You still there, Seve?"

"Yeah, sorry. Dropped my pen."

Now, I read something other than eagerness in his voice. The conversation went dead, so I asked him to transfer the call to my secretary Jeanie Robbins.

"Hey, sweetheart, how about calling the Musical Arts Center and picking up a couple of tickets for their Saturday evening performance?"

"You're taking me?" Jeanie teased, "God! What a marvelous boss. I'll check." She grew serious. "Richard, you've just received an unsigned letter from some crazy. May I read you a portion?"

In response to my agreement she read, " 'Dear Miss Robbins . . . Please tell your boss that he should stay away from Rose Cutter's Quarry . . . Swimming there can be extremely hazardous to his health, and I'm not talking bullets, stabbings or drownings.' "

"No signature, I'll bet?"

"Of course not."

Pondering that riddle, I hung up. Hoping Samantha Petry and I might spend the evening together, I dialed her number. Zilch.

More mysteries: another crazy's letter; Seve Jensen's sudden quiet when I mentioned my downstate visit; Clark Benefield's disappearance. Now, compounding my disquiet, I faced a long evening alone. Where could Samantha be?

Chapter Twenty

IT WAS DUSK. I'D HAD a long day. Maybe it was my mood, but I dreaded another long night out in the country alone. Or was my concern hooked to a premonition? It's possible. I believe in psychic precursors, although most of the time I blast full-speed ahead, not listening. Sometimes I pay a price.

Jeanie called back to say good seats were still available for Saturday's performance. Killing time, I dropped by the box office and personally picked them up.

That done, I decided to stop at a local pub for a lonely guy's fish and chip dinner and a glass of Dead Guy Ale before heading for the A-frame. I felt remotely guilty about the ale. It seemed intrinsically wrong to wash down the Britisher's national repast with a mug of German Ale.

Once home, I figured on kicking back, catching a Pacers game on the tube, and sucking up a couple Heinekens while rooting against the Bulls. But, I desperately wanted to see—had to see—Samantha. One final time, I punched redial. On its second ring, I was rewarded with her most lyrical voice, answering, "Hello, this is Samantha." I envied her students, thinking how much fun it would be to monitor one of her classes, knowing I didn't dare.

"You busy?" I asked. "How would you feel about a little Chinese?"

"Height isn't important to me," she answered, suppressing a laugh. "Will it be a blind date?"

Obviously Sam had been holding out on me. All along she'd been a closet punster. I rushed right to her house.

Smiling broadly, maybe because she was still celebrating her pun one-upmanship, she opened the door and welcomed me with a hug. I drew her to my chest. Her damp hair against my cheek suggested my second to last call must've caught her in the shower.

Tonight, dressed in an all-tan pant set, her button-studded, woven-lattice jacket showed tiny, square sections of a more deeply colored shell underneath. I helped her on with her coat and we went from house to car, to drive directly towards Chan's Sizzling Wok.

"Remember," Sam said, "tomorrow I'll be attending an Indianapolis convention."

"Are you booked for the evening? *La Bayadere's* showing at IU's Musical Arts Center. And, my dear, guess who's come up with a pair of ducats?" Producing a set of tickets from my vest pocket, I waggled them under my nose ala W. C. Fields.

"Sorry," Sam said, grimacing unhappily. "I won't be back until Sunday, late."

"Shame, I'd planned to surprise you . . ." My words tailed off as the now-familiar blue Park Avenue pulled from a side street and dropped in behind us.

"Anything wrong? You don't usually give in so easily."

"I'm afraid we have company."

Glancing into the outside mirror, Sam paled. "There's just no escaping him."

Incensed, muscles tensed for a fight, I yanked the wheel and swerved to the curb. The Buick nearly rear-ended us. I leaped out. Joe Petry gave me a cold look, and crammed the accelerator. Tires squalling, the Buick reversed for a hundred yards.

I gave an ineffectual shake of my fist. Then, climbing back inside the Vanden Plas, fought down the shakes from a surge of unused adrenaline. "Sam, sweetheart, if he bothers you while I'm around, he'll whisper his goodbyes in soprano." Briefly, I again savored the moment when I'd delivered the classic, hall-of-fame crotch-shot. "Maybe he's squeaking 'em out already."

I wheeled down a side street and encountered Petry again going the other direction. I vigorously motioned, "Come on," with a raised hand. Ignoring the invitation, he drove straight on.

Chan's, located in one end of an abandoned train depot, rated the best Chinese food in the area. I'd never eaten there, although Sam said the restaurant had been around for years.

The building appeared inviting in the early evening, with its barrel-tiled roof and softly aged limestone. Wandering to the edge of the platform, I pointed overhead, toward the track overhang. "Sam, the exhausts of a thousand old coal burners painted that stone black when they were slowing to pick up passengers or high-balling through on their way to Indianapolis, Chicago, or wherever."

I cupped a hand to my ear. "If you listen closely, you can still hear the 'chuh-chuh-chuh-whoosh!' as the engine flashes by the platform, its iron stacks barely clearing the roof." Grinning, I reveled at pretending I was twelve again. "Can't you smell coal sulphur, and imagine the soot and cinders falling on your clothes?" Really into the spirit, I brushed imaginary particles from my shirt cuffs.

She nodded appreciatively. Turning, she kissed me gently on the cheek. "Somehow, dinner here seems extremely appropriate. Over the last century, this station has undoubtedly dispatched and welcomed thousands of travelers. In our own way, we're on our own mystery trip."

"Yeah, you're right," I agreed. "And it's a pity we're not riding the rails. That way we'd have a straight shot at a known destination. Better yet, we'd know when we got there."

Placing my arm possessively around her waist, I guided her into the restaurant.

The crimson-jacketed maitre d' escorted us to a center table. Sam touched my sleeve, then signaled, "No," with a slight lifting of eyebrows. Catching on, our host led us to a secluded corner table.

Behind Samantha the wall was decorated with a repro Kerman Vase carpet, now doing duty as a wall hanging. The thick partition behind me doubled as a divider and display base for an assortment of brilliantly colorful porcelain vases. A small Chinese lantern in the center of our table matched the chandeliers scattered overhead. I flicked it off.

"Perfect," I said. "We can talk in privacy."

"And if Joe comes snooping, we won't be so prominently displayed."

"Yeah." I pointed out. "Stalkers hate losing control over their victims. Our relationship could drive him berserk. Completely over the edge."

We ordered glasses of California chardonnay and after a first sip, I filled her in on my visit with her son. Holding both her hands in mine, I absently traced each finger as we talked. She wore no jewelry except for tiny, jade earrings. Touching the impression left by her wedding ring, my fingertip lingered in place. I must have looked pleased.

She smiled, but didn't comment. "Did Roger appear happy?" She asked, her eyes fixed intently on mine.

I thought of his co-worker girlfriend. Barely suppressing a chuckle, I nodded, "Oh, yes, very much so."

She responded with a quizzical look and I described blonde-haired Carrie. "And Roger does wish to improve communications with his mom." I squeezed her arm reassuringly. "But both he and I need your e-mail address."

She jotted her screen name on a napkin. "Surely, he knew I use Internet. I doubt any prof can stay in tune with today's students without it."

I scanned the menu, my eyes straying to the brightly printed, Chinese Zodiac place mat. I switched the table light on, but still had to slip a pair of half-glasses onto the end of my nose before reading. "Hey, Sam, we've got big trouble. You're a year younger than I, and a dragon." Squinting, I followed the minute type with one finger. "'You are healthy, energetic and passionate, but somewhat stubborn.' Right on all counts, especially the stubborn bit. Being laid-back and undemanding, myself, I definitely would've taken the first table offered by the maitre d'."

Sam scowled in mock perplexity.

As she lifted her wineglass, I added, "However, although you are 'well-suited to the rat, serpent, and monkey,' there's nothing here about compatibility with me."

"And you are . . . ?"

"A hare. I'm 'talented and affectionate,'" I read, chewing my bottom lip and lowering my eyes, "'Yet painfully shy, most compatible with the ram, pig, and dog.' Oh, wait, it also says I'm one of the world's greatest lovers and a perfect catch for any beautiful woman, especially, one born under the sign of the dragon."

After glancing at her own placemat for confirmation, Sam lifted a doubtful eyebrow.

"Well, okay, so I cheated a tad. I figure all's fair in love and war." Suddenly, I remembered Cait and felt uncomfortable about using the word "love." I noted though that my guilt had become less knife-edged, maybe because Cait wasn't near enough to defend her turf.

Fun and games over for the moment, we chose a Szechuan dinner for two. "Now, let's recap the case while waiting."

Sam winced. "Don't you ever stop?"

Quickly, I ticked off pertinent points on my fingertips, ending with, "We've learned nothing new about Jane McNamara and the night she was stabbed at Rose Cutter's Quarry. Oops! We now know that Janie was pregnant when she died, but can't ID the dad. We know that, with the exception of you, me, and possibly Clark Benefield, everybody in the world, including Janie's father, believes your son killed her."

Her lips tightened. Ignoring the signal, I said, "Sam, Roger should agree to DNA testing. I'll bet the test will clear him." I didn't say that a positive finding could hang him.

Sam was noncommittal. I suspected she tended to nurture, not suffocate Roger, a difficult balance when parental advice pertains to a "Murder One" investigation. I wondered: Does she prefer ignorance to discovery Roger fathered the fetus?

"How do you think Clark Benefield, Janie's one-time fiancé fits into the picture?" Sam asked.

"Placing him in the puzzle is difficult, at least for me, especially, now that he's MIA. Obviously, he knows I'm a private snoop and doesn't want to be enmeshed in the investigation."

While we switched our talk to the torching of my house, I gently caressed her hands, slowly stroking her wrists and arms. At one moment while she spoke, I lifted her hand and kissed the palm. She shivered, then asked, "Are you certain your mind is on the case?"

I destroyed the moment by asking, "Were you aware that the day following the fire, Jacobi Real Estate offered to buy the now-vacant land where the old man's dream house stood?"

"But the letter would have been posted prior to the fire." Sam said. "The timing must have been coincidental. Surely you don't believe they anticipated the fire?"

I shrugged a nonanswer. "The police still haven't identified the body in the sump pit. Was the house burned as a warning for me to stop investigating Janie's murder?"

"Or did the arsonists plan to kill you?" Sam's eyes widened in alarm at her own question.

"I suspect they did. But one's parboiling saved me."

I moved off on a tangent, "We mustn't forget that my ADE still has a huge cash shortage and is being robbed by a company employee. If the shortage turns out to be as large as I suspect, it'll constitute a motive for murder. Especially mine."

"Once again, is Seve Jensen a bonafide suspect?" Sam asked.

"Definitely. He works for me in a position of trust. The CFO slot provides opportunity. My question is, has he forgiven me for outmaneuvering him when we competed to buy the company?" I spread my arms, hands palm-up, and shrugged. "Who knows? He's a strange duck anyhow, or better yet, a chameleon. One moment, he burns with anger. Seconds later, he's dispassionate and amenable to calm discussion. In hindsight, I probably never should have hired him when we bought the company, but he seems to have done a decent job for the last half-dozen years—until now."

I had a flashback to my Indianapolis trip. "Sam, have you ever heard of an organization called Dollars for Mankind?"

"Certainly. Like FIPRO, it's another of Reverend Gabriel Goodall's organizations."

"Ah, so! Seve Jensen and Goodall *do* have a history together." That proved, I told her of Seve's obvious eagerness to hear about my trip to Indy, but his reluctance to discuss my visit with Hugh McNamara.

"How odd! I thought Hugh McNamara once lived in Seve Jensen's old neighborhood. I'm almost certain that Seve grew up and attended high school down on the Ohio River."

Mentally cataloguing another small mystery, I resurrected the fraud case in Indy and its tie-in with Consolidated Constructioneers, Inc. "That has the potential to get mighty nasty. The company's veep threatened to whack Stella Carlyle and me. And, as you know, the Reverend Gabriel Goodall has a passionate hatred for me."

The waiter parked beside us a roll cart filled with covered bowls and side dishes. Without speaking, he took our empty wineglasses, jigsawed the servings into place on the tiny table, removed the hubcaps from atop bowls of hong sue gai and beef chow mein, found room for a pot of tea, poured, bowed, and again vanished into the kitchen.

With the sensitivity of a pit bull, still not able to leave well enough alone, I broached another aspect while we ate. "Now, somebody in Florida has stolen my identity—"

Alarmed, Sam interrupted. "What else can happen?"

"I'd like to know." I squinted at Sam over the hot food, then stopped talking to decide between fried and steamed rice. "We're talking big bucks here, with the boat's price sticker nearly three hundred thou. Could there be an Indiana connection?"

She chewed her lip thinking, then said, "I doubt it."

"Samantha, that covers everything. And now, you've even told me who killed Rosata, the nun? And, most importantly, why?"

"But the story is far from finished," she said, in a teasing voice. "Are you prepared to hear about Saint Gilbert of Sempringham who was born in 1083? Do you want to know that Chicksands was called the Manor of Chicksands way back in 1086, during William the Conqueror's Doomsday survey? Do you wish to learn how Britain's Royal Air Force and the U. S. Air Force conspired to convert Rosata's final home into bedchambers for hundreds of airmen?" Slowly, Sam moved her head from side to side. "I think not." She lowered her voice to a whisper. "Not after such an already difficult day."

"Hey! Sounds like a darned good yarn to me." Chuckling, I glanced at my watch. "But it's time for me to head for the hill country."

"Stay at my house. I don't wish to be a Cassandra, prophesying doom, but I can't bear to see you out there alone." An involuntary shudder emphasized her statement. "Not after Janie's murder at your Rose Cutter's Quarry, and the fire and the unidentified body."

Tempted but still skirting long-term personal commitments, I made a lame excuse, featuring pieces of mail that urgently required attention and unpaid bills, desperately late. Feeling backward, embarrassed, or confused—perhaps all three—I declined her offer.

Sam excused herself for a few moments. I spent the time berating myself. My love life had never been so complicated or arid. When with Sam, I felt guilty because of Cait. When telephoning or e-mailing Cait, I felt rotten because of my association with Sam.

Again I pondered the old saw about a man simultaneously loving two women. Yep, I was field testing the proposition. In spades! Topping that, most men my age were married with grown children. Barb and I had tried and failed. Now, I was at an age where I would never have a child. That hurt too. Almost every man believes that a son or daughter would be life's greatest blessing. Of course the kid would make out too, because each potential father thinks he would be the perfect dad. I knew I would've been .

I held the chair for Sam on her return, still fighting my internal demons. "Anyway, Sam, you're the one in danger, not I." I described my visits to the Internet and the library, and repeated my conversations with Police Captain Raphael Redonzo. "I'm convinced that stalkers like your husband have the patience of a wolf or jackal. They'll sit for hours watching their prey's house. Memorizing every move. Ready to strike."

"Do we have to go into this again, Richard?"

"Yes! You must understand: Stalkers want to dominate. They don't love. Even if they once did, they've learned to truly hate. But even though the relationship nose-dives, they won't share their victim with anybody else. They'll kill rather than do that!"

Sam glanced around the dining room and I suspected that, involuntarily, she was conducting a quick search for Joe Petry. "Richard, I take a firm position," she said, her voice calm. "Then I tend to reconsider. I'm convinced you should have been more patient. Joe would've left your house without violence. In my heart, I don't believe he'll hurt me again."

"Look, my darling, even the most reasoned and sophisticated women feel compassion and give these creeps a second, third and fourth chance."

"Perhaps we focus on the few good years . . ."

"Could be, but hey! I watched from the chair as your husband stood over me, spouting a stream of threats. I've been around the block. When Joe Petry's hot, he has a Billingsgate vocabulary and a killer's eyes. He wanted to kill me. He will kill you unless I protect you from yourself. Get real, Samantha!"

I raised my hands in supplication. "Will you please go to the police?" My voice rose on the last sentence. Alarmed, the foursome at the next table stopped speaking and turned toward us.

"No! They're never around when they're needed. I fear publicity.

The propensity for embarrassment horrifies me. What would my students think? I fear members of the administration. I just . . ." Lapsing into silence, palms clasped together, Sam clenched her fingers until the knuckles whitened and her hands shook.

I hadn't planned it, but I decided it was time for shock therapy. I pulled from my vest pocket the copies I had carried since showing them to Captain Redonzo. "Here. I know that the circumstances aren't the same. Nevertheless, the fierce hatreds and frustrations felt by Joe Petry and Alan Matheney are surely identical."

She took the copies, but held them at a distance as if deadly afraid of their contents. Sam read the Lisa Bianco story, visibly paling as she did. It was a shocking story.

In 1988, Lisa Bianco lived alone with her children in Mishawaka, Indiana. Her husband, Alan Matheney, had been jailed on a seven-year term for beating and kidnaping her. The law had promised to notify her if he was released from prison.

After serving a short time, they released him on an eight-hour pass. She wasn't notified.

He drove a hundred and twenty miles to her house, and with her six- and ten-year-old daughters witnessing, beat Lisa to death with the butt of a shotgun.

The waiter came with the check.

That night, at least, I should've stayed with Sam.

Chapter Twenty-two

MY PREOCCUPATION WITH THE CASE and unremitting questions having cooled the night's romance, I swung left on the main drag and aimed the Jag towards home. High-beam headlights tucked in behind me at the first light. Joe Petry? Couldn't be! I doubted he'd hang around for hours just to walk me home.

At the next light, a huge, black Mercedes pulled up beside me. Glancing over, I did a double-take. Impudent as hell, I tooted the horn. Karl Sprader stared straight ahead. Still, although he didn't speak, maybe our relationship had improved. After all, when last we met on the apartment building job site, the burly vice president of Consolidated Constructioneers had threatened to clobber me. Nevertheless, I wondered what business he had in Bloomington. I made a whispered wager: "Richard, I'll lay odds this guy means trouble wherever he goes."

Angling across to the 7-eleven market to buy toothpaste, I watched the Mercedes roar away, down the road toward Cutter's Pike. Back inside the car, I spent two seconds thinking about Karl Sprader before reviewing my conversation with Samantha. What did I really want? Revenge against Jane's murderer and the arsonists? Most assuredly! One person perished in the sump pit. Did that help square the debt? Nope! He died without my personal involvement.

I'm an old fashioned, hands-on, eye-for-an-eye type of guy. If somebody hammers me and gets clobbered by a freightliner, that's not good enough . . . not unless I'm driving the truck. I wanted both the second arsonist *and* Janie's murderer to pay double.

A new thought intruded: I had been considering the case's coincidences. Instead, I should picture a tapestry, with the possibility that every complexly woven thread would eventually coalesce into one interrelated design.

My company was being robbed. Along with that investigation, I had agreed to find Jane McNamara's killer. Years ago, Reverend Goodall fleeced my mother. Goodall and Karl Sprader were connected to the Indy apartment scam. My house had burned. An unknown arsonist had been boiled . . . and I had just seen Sprader here in Bloomington.

My mind spun. Maybe, I shouldn't be thinking in terms of coincidences, nor tapestries, even. Actually, I was piecing together a crazy quilt, with most of the threads and pieces still missing. I didn't know the primary color was blood red, but I suspected it.

Turning into my lane, I fancied I saw a light inside the house, which I surmised to be the Jag's headlights reflected against a windowpane. When I parked, the car's high beams swept the crawlspace and highlighted the old man's trophies. Glassy-eyed stares died with the killed headlights.

Climbing out, I yanked my topcoat from the passenger seat, then looked around for another car. None.

Both the front porch lamp and the light at the end of the sidewalk were light-sensitive and should've been on. Burned-out bulbs? Two at once? A resounding *no*!

I moved cautiously up the sidewalk and mounted the porch. Long in the sleuthing business and longer in the army, I heed tiny warnings. I keyed the lock, shoved open the door and, dodging imaginary bullets, jumped aside. The strategy worked in 'Nam.

Darting inside, I crouched, listening. After a moment, I fumbled for the light switches. My finger brushed the porch toggle. Off. A floorboard across the room creaked. The hair on my neck stood erect.

Maintaining my infantryman's crouch, I crept across the blackened room to the entertainment center. I felt for my Glock 19 which I'd stashed behind a stack of records. Missing!

I bolted for the door. A sledgehammer blow rattled my skull. Whirling pinwheels and exploding planets lit a trip into a black hole.

My nose slammed against the floor, relighting the fireworks.

I rolled to the side, then launched myself back onto my feet.

I heard a loud *crack-crack-crack* as my own gun or its twin splintered the silence. A bullet tugged my sleeve. Another nicked my arm. A third whistled by my ear.

Again diving for the floor, I grasped the handle of an antique flatiron doorstop. I haymakered it knee high—and felt the satisfying jolt when it struck bone.

With a shrill "Oh-h-h, damn you!" my kneecapped assailant collapsed, squashing the air from me.

I swept the floor for the Glock. My fingers circled a wrist; one brushed cold steel. I clawed for the piece. I ripped away a shirt pocket instead.

I scrambled free and through the door. I dropped from the porch and scrambled into the crawlspace. Tucking the piece of cloth inside my pant pocket, I snugged close behind a lion's head and buried my cheeks and nose in coarse, musty mane, my eyes peering above the neck.

At the end of the sidewalk, a flashlight kissed the Jag's door panel, then swept its interior. A black figure ran toward me. Stooping, it hosed the crawlspace with the flashlight beam.

"So much for kneecapping," I mused silently.

Crack! A shot ripped the lion's fur. Rolling away, I found another hole to the outside.

I sprinted blindly for Rose Cutter's Quarry. My foot smashed against a concrete block and I slammed face first into the ground. I rubbed my wingtip, kneading life into my now-numb big toe and foot.

Recovering, I ran top-speed straight toward the quarry. "I must be near the rim!" I thought, gasping and hopelessly disoriented.

A flashlight switched on. Wheeling, I dove blindly from the exact spot where Jane McNamara died.

Splitting the frigid water, I dove deep and resurfaced near the edge. Clutching a jagged stone, I levered myself onto a ledge. Plastering my back against the jagged stones, I tried to hide.

The flashlight beam swept close. Two bullets splintered rock beside me. I felt my way along the ledge and dropped back into the water. I clambered ashore on the far side. My nose throbbed in time with my heartbeat. I gingerly reshaped it.

Minutes later, an engine roared to life somewhere above. Headlights flashed on and a vehicle pulled down the driveway, turned onto the county road, and sped away.

I stumbled my way back to the house and crept inside. I lay on the varnished boards, panting and considering alternatives.

First thought: I'll call Samantha! She would want me to come to her house. Not fair. With a seminar on tap, she needed her rest.

Second thought: Call 911? I'd end with cops fruitlessly crawling the grounds and rafters, and a prime-time spot on radio, television and the *Herald*.

I stopped cogitating and scrambled to my feet. I found the bedroom gun cabinet untouched. Tonight I would sleep close to a loaded twelve-gauge and tuck it inside the Jag tomorrow. A .45 would sub for my Glock.

I reached for my own personal anti-fogmatic—Jack Daniels sour mash, straight-up and doubled—like the revenge I'd be looking for. Cold air brushed the back of my neck. Checking the back door, I found a broken pane. The phone was also dead, the line probably cut.

"Sheriff DeLyle," I said, growling into my cell phone, "I've had a break-in and been clobbered to boot." I explained I'd found traces of blood. I checked my watch—it was after one o'clock.

DeLyle sounded groggy. "Scott, I'm lucky there's just one of you."

The sheriff arrived quickly and just as efficiently took care of business. After he'd gone, I remembered I hadn't given him the pocket ripped from my assailant. I blamed it on my being overly sleepy. On the other hand, I liked having a hole card.

I dropped onto the sofa, shotgun at hand. It seemed but minutes until the phone woke me from a deep sleep.

"Darling, this is Caitlin. Sorry to call so early." Her voice sounded breathless and excited. Outside, the sun shone weakly, barely up.

I rubbed my still throbbing nose. God, it *was* early. "No sweat," I reassured her. "It's never too early for your call."

"Richard, why don't you come to New York for a few days? I'll have tickets for *Beauty and the Beast.* We'll do lunch at Tavern on the Green. God! Seeing you, holding you, being held, would be divine."

Since she lived in the East, the sun would be higher there. I pictured her, curvaceous, willowy, and graceful, standing at her apartment window, her dark, almond-shaped eyes studying the people down in Central Park, their figures made tiny by distance and height. Impatient for my answer, she would probably be fiddling with a strand of darkly auburn hair.

"It sounds marvelous, Cait. However, this case has a dozen facets, and every one of them is driving me bonkers—"

Cait interrupted. "Surely you could take a few days off." Her voice became lower, guarded. "Maybe there's someone there you don't want to leave."

"Wrong spin, Cait." For a moment, I thought of Sam. That thought beaten back, I carefully searched my own personal thesaurus for benign words to describe a convoluted situation. "This case is a tangled skein. It's a case with a dozen faces—"

Cait again interrupted. "Are any of them beautiful?" Now her voice wasn't smiling.

I forged ahead, "Believe me, I'm talking evil. Later today I'll give you an e-mail description of it. For now, take my word for it. I *can't* break free, no matter how badly I want."

Her voice broke. "I'll come there."

"Cait, what's wrong. Are you okay? Is the job okay?"

"Oh, yes—Computers With Software, Inc. is everything a cutting edge company should be. But . . ." Her voice faded.

"Is it that worthless ex of yours?" I asked, fighting an urge to combine an oath and "ex" into one word. Also, I suddenly realized a major part of my life right now was being influenced by ex-husbands. Sam had a stalker. Cait was still involved with a cruel scoundrel who'd killed her relationship with her adopted—his biological—kid.

"Yes, now that I've refused to go back to him, he's threatening to separate Peter and me. Permanently." Her words faltered. A tissue rustle, I knew she was fighting tears.

"Tell you what. Let me think this over. I'll call back quickly. I won't have you hurt . . ."

Frustrated, I planted an elbow on the table and sat silent, my ear resting heavily on the headpiece. What a fiasco! I'd just spent the night rekindling my affection for Sam, and here I sat, trying to protect my relationship with Cait.

I pictured Wynn Dunne, the antebellum mansion a few short miles south in Abram's Trace. Wynn Dunne—Cait's and my "love nest." Majestic. Beautifully furnished but empty of people, and still waiting for Cait and me to return.

We hung up simultaneously, leaving a lot unsaid, and even more unfinished.

Chapter Twenty-two

WITH SAMANTHA AWAY at the Indy convention, I decided to spend the remainder of the day working at the shop office. Alone. Except for Herschel, my factory maintenance man who again rode in to work with me.

"This is Saturday, Herschel. Why not a day off?"

"We got another machine broke down back in the assembly area. Ah, but we'll have 'er workin' good as new 'fore Monday morning." He paused a moment, his tiny feet scuffing the gray carpet while he planned his next words. "I hope you don't mind, but years ago, I useta fish out at your place. Before knowin' you'd be transferring here I ordered some fish from the Indiana game and fish people—"

"So?"

"Along with a fingerling shipment, I got some bigger ones. I got small and big mouth bass, cats, croppies, and a bunch of other fish, all good eatin'." He cocked his head like a finch pecking at a thistle seed, then glanced at me from beneath the oversized cap bill. "Even though Mr. Winters had gone to prison and you weren't yet around . . ." He looked guilty. "Mr. Scott, I went ahead and put 'em in Rose Cutter's Quarry anyhow. That okay?"

"Sure, Herschel. For fishing rights, you own the quarry." I had another thought. "By the way, last night I made a late visit to the quarry." I pointed to my left wrist. "I seem to have lost my watch. You find it, let me know."

"You s'pose would it be on the path from your house or more likely 'long the bank?"

"It fell in the water. Maybe too deep to find."

Herschel, apparently not at all surprised I'd chosen to take a late night swim in the quarry, said he'd be on the lookout for my watch, then, smiling happily, stayed silent for the rest of the trip.

Once in the office, I called Jeanie Robbins. "Jeanie, you and your boyfriend can have tonight's *La Bayadere* tickets. Sam's not going to be available after all."

"Oh, Richard!" she cried, then held her hand loosely over the phone to speak to somebody in the background. "I should nominate you for 'Boss of the Month.' Or 'Boss of the Year.' "

"You can pay me back by finding out who snatched my credit card." I said, rising from my desk. "Because with my case load, I can't spare a minute to help find a solution." Jeanie promised she'd be on top of the matter first thing Monday. Still feeling angst about that situation, I hung up the phone, hurried out of the office and down the hall toward the accounting department—and bigger problems.

Just as I had hoped, the department was totally empty. With Joseph Schwab's list of suspects clutched in my hand, I sat down at the computer station nearest the door. The rationale for the list was simple: ADE had hundreds of satellite suppliers who furnished goods or services for ADE; during Seve Jensen's reign, many of the company's old friends had been fired and replaced by Seve—or somebody working for him. Now, although ADE's business remained flat, its outside expenses had skyrocketed. That was why Joseph said, "You may find an outside culprit. Follow the money."

Arvet Consolidated, the largest supplier, and the one topping Joseph's list, was located in northern Indiana. A supplier evaluation report said that, both because of the supplier's high quality *and* its top-notch research department, business volume with ADE, had surged. At least the logic was reasonable.

Surprise! Benefield Enterprises was another rapid-growth supplier, with offices here in Bloomington. Busy guy, that Clark Benefield! And he was an ex-boyfriend of the late Janie McNamara. Most interesting! At one time he had been a good Samaritan to Roger Petrie. Now, he was performing manufacturing services for my company. My, my! That company's evaluation report had been left blank.

Several times, Pasha Industries had been penciled into paperwork margins, then erased. I wondered why?

I, however, was searching for lost bucks. Lost big bucks! Growing more certain that one or more of my own employees had cooked up vest-pocket deals, I wondered how? Where? How did they hide their trail? The expenditures had been huge, but both on paper and on the CRT screen everything looked orderly and copacetic.

Leaving one copy of the list on my desk to give to Jeanie Robbins, I tucked a second in my briefcase and cut for home. What the hey? After last night's blast on the noggin, my head felt filled with more maggots than memory.

First thing in the door, I dialed Cait in New York. After a brief description of the case and an almost verbatim but desultory recitation of this morning's conversation, we again hung up simultaneously. At the moment, we weren't together on much of anything, but—on coordinated hang-ups—we were way off the scale. Far beyond "ten"!

Sunday, the seventh day, I rested. That statement sounding too omniscient and god-like, I amended it to include, I also recovered.

Monday morning, just before eight I parked the Jag on the street facing the ornate, limestone courthouse that centers Bloomington's downtown. After walking halfway around the square, I climbed two flights of stairs to Clark Benefield's office, and dropped my ravaged and water-puckered body onto a chair in the lobby.

The sign on the door said kickoff time for regular business was eight sharp. I was still alone twenty minutes later.

Although I could hear furniture being shifted and a vacuum cleaner gobbling dirt on the other side of the door, no one showed. Both the lobby and the office faced the street. I got up and peered outside. From the window, I saw a few early birds like me already entering the courthouse. In a neat touch, lettering on a plaque inside the window where I was standing, said, "Please gaze up and to your right to see Bloomington's famous gilded fish weathervane, originally atop the cupola of the 1826 courthouse, now gracing the copper dome of this classical renaissance, Beaux Arts structure, erected in 1907. Now, lower your eyes only slightly and enjoy Gustave Brand's stained glass . . ."

"Mr. Scott!" I turned around, expecting to see a Benefield secretary. Instead, I was greeted by Laureen Smith, my housekeeper.

"Laureen! Are you two-timing me?" I winked. "I thought I was your only client."

"I wish 'twas so! And if that big house hadn't burned, maybe I would've been doing your stuff full-time." She lowered her eyes, looking apologetic, as if she'd spoken out of turn.

"I'm finished in there," she said, a toss of her gray hair indicating Benefield's office. "I'll be stirring up a lot of noise and dust in the lobby. And nobody around here gets to work on time anyway." She handed me last month's issue of *Time*. "Why don't you take a seat in Mr. Benefield's office and catch up on the news while I tidy up out here?" Flexing a muscular arm, she yanked the vacuum's electrical cord and the canister cleaner zipped through the door like a trained mutt.

Feeling good about an unexpected sleuthing opportunity, I slipped inside and closed the door behind me. In truth, I hadn't the foggiest about what I was looking for.

My confusion was understandable. I originally entered the gum-shoe racket out of rent-paying necessity. Persistence, not technique, had always been my primary game plan. I've always rooted under gaggles of rocks to find a single clue. I've even been known to mix a metaphor or two.

Clark Benefield's walnut-paneled office was expensively, but sparsely furnished, as if he spent little time there. An elegant rococo partner's desk, flanked by three Art Deco armchairs, almost hid his own softly upholstered leather chair. All looked new and little used.

The desktop held a stuffed in-and-out basket, a phone, a pen and pencil set, a phone number tickler file, and a picture of a sturdy, strong-jawed man, decked out in a pair of red-checked plus fours following through on a classic golf swing. It also sported a trophy from a local club, honoring Clark Benefield for a second hole-in-one, so I knew that, thus far at least, his life hadn't been lived in vain.

After a cursory tugging of the locked desk drawers, I moved around to his worktable and studied the new, high-tech, LaserJet printer. A brochure beside it guaranteed the printer produced high fidelity, detailed text and graphics in a million color shades.

The state-of-the-art copier standing next to the table was large enough to be fitted with firestone tires, street-driven, and carry a gas guzzler classification and surtax. It also had multi-color capabilities. I didn't suspect Benefield of counterfeiting, but with this fancy set-up he could compete with the big boys, if he chose to enter the racket.

I switched on his PC. I punched three keys. The screen screamed ACCESS DENIED. Confidently, I punched three more. The screen now shouted "Program terminated."

Pushed for time, I concentrated on the in and out baskets. Fortunately the company wasn't yet highly enough computerized to have gone to a totally paperless order entry and processing system. Along with miscellaneous letters, there were several invoices from other companies billing Benefield Enterprises for work done. I wrote down the names.

A new electronic daily planner served as a paperweight on a stack of expense receipts. I keyed it and checked the phone numbers against those in the mechanical tickler file. Identical information! Two files in the same office, each holding the same data was an extravagance and a redundancy. Doubting the outmoded mechanical model would be missed, I tucked it into my vest pocket.

I moved across the room to an unlocked, fireproof safe. I snapped my fingers. "Bingo! I wonder—"

Just then, voices in the lobby replaced the sound of Laureen's tornadoing vacuum cleaner. Furtively, I eased the drawer shut.

Charging back across the room, I flopped into an armchair and aimed my eyes at a sales brochure. At that moment, Lisa Crumb from Benefield's other office came slinking through the door.

She removed a faux fur to expose another of those too-tight, V-necked blouses, similar to the one she'd worn last week. This one was blue, but it too exposed a lot of Lisa Crumb. Much more than enough. She hung the coat in a small closet, then gazed around the office as if counting pieces to ascertain that the furniture was still in place.

I checked the curtains to see if her perfume had melted the fabric. "The cleaning lady said she let you inside. She shouldn't have. The story's still the same as last week. Clark Benefield's working on a super-colossal deal and is unavailable. I'll tell the custodial president—he's the guy who signs really important documents in Clark's absence—that you were here."

She rearranged her lips into a twisted smile. "By the way, do you have any other duties besides chasing after Clark?"

I answered her question with one of my own. "Can I have the custodial president's name?"

"She handed me a card. He'll call you if he needs you."

"Hey, thanks for the help," I growled. Casting one last, longing look at the fireproof safe, I walked through the door, waved at Laureen, and moved on down the stairs.

Now I would do a bit of sleuthing here in town. Maybe on these streets, I might begin to unravel the riddle in the crazy's letter about Rose Cutter's Quarry.

Back in the car I searched for less hidden secrets. I hurriedly keyed the tickler file's A and B sections without uncovering a significant name. The J's showed Seve Jensen—as expected. I didn't become really fascinated until I flicked open the S's. Karl Sprader's name had to be important; it had been underlined in red. That sewed another tiny fragment into the crazy quilt.

The known material remained small, scarcely enough fabric to diaper a Lilliputian. Yet, I felt I was getting there.

Chapter Twenty-three

STASHING THE BENEFIELD ENTERPRISES tickler file in the glove compartment, I phoned my secretary.

Jeanie said Stella Carlyle's briefcase bulged with bad news about the derelict apartment buildings in Indianapolis. "What's more, your agency partner urgently needs to share the info with you."

I checked the car's dash clock. "Ask her to be patient. Offer her a plant tour to entertain her. I'll see her at three sharp."

Energized by my success, and certain I deserved a reward, I crossed the street for coffee and a chocolate donut; feeling guilty, I walked on around the square to Jacobi Realty's office.

Classy place. Pictures of expensive houses filled the plate glass window. I slowed to read the advertising copy. "Does your taste run to a carefully appointed modern residence in an area of distinctive new homes? Or would you prefer a gracious, historic Queen Anne, Free Classic, or Period Revival style home on Prospect or Vinegar Hill? Either way, Jacobi can provide a perfect answer to your most cherished dreams." I went in.

"Perhaps I may help," offered a distinguished-looking, salt-and-pepper-haired model of a gentleman.

I read the scroll-lettered name, Windemere Clairton, printed on his gold-plated desk nameplate. I supposed his business cards carried the same elaborate script. "Yeah, I'm confused," I grinned. "What's a 'Vinegar Hill'?"

He pulled his slender, but perfectly straight shoulders even more tautly erect. "It's a gentle rise south of Third Street. Years ago it took the name from the smell of the rotting fruit that fell from apple trees growing on the property." His tone suggested real estate wasn't a laughing matter.

He turned the computer monitor to face me and scrolled past pictures of two English Tudor Revival houses with half-timbered end gables and clay- tile roofs before parking on a Spanish Colonial with a copper-roofed balcony. "I presume you wish to purchase a home in that area. It's a wonderful choice. These homes have ultimate in historical authenticity both because of their ties to the university and because they were exquisitely built by old-time Italian and German stone carvers."

"I'm sorry, but I'm not really looking for a house on Vinegar Hill—although my business certainly involves rotten apples." I waited in vain for a smile or laugh. "Actually, I'm looking for Leonard Rankles." I produced the letter earlier received from Jacobi Realty in which they offered to buy the Rose Cutter's Quarry property.

Grimacing, he carefully flicked a microscopic stray particle from a dark blue coat sleeve. "Mr. Rankles no longer works here," he sniffed.

"You mean deceased, or removed—like the lint?" I smiled.

"Putting it crudely, removed. Our techniques and objectives diverged. In some instances, like your own, we have encouraged his clients to accompany him to his new company." He wrote an address on a pink, message reminder slip and proffered it across the desk. "Also, here's my card in the event that you sometime seriously seek a new home." The card was fancy, like the nameplate.

Companies seldom willingly relinquish clients. So why would Jacobi Realty be willing to lose a top notch account like ADE? Trying to establish distance between my company and theirs?

"Humph," I snorted, for a moment mimicking Windemere Clairton's persona, then offered a curt goodbye nod.

The address was only a brisk, two-minute walk off the town square, the building a narrow, two story, stand-alone structure. Chalky paint scaled from rotting window frames. A lightning bolt crack zigzagged the brown brick facade from roof-to-door cornice. Obviously, the structure wasn't new to the neighborhood. Certainly, the tenant was. A newly painted sign over the door shouted a cardinal-red greeting: RANKLES' BUSINESS BROKERS—*SALES AND BUSINESS CONSULTANT SPECIALISTS*.

Masking tape x-ed the two front windows. Tunneling my eyes, I peered inside.

Leonard Rankles' new office was a work in progress. A bevy of workmen swarmed the place. In the front office, one spackled a wall. Another clumped around on tall aluminum stilts while stretching to brush a spiral pattern onto the ceiling. For a second, he teetered, then rattled through a four-step dance routine before regaining his balance. A third man nailed prefinished walnut trim into place around a door frame.

In the back room, a brightly scarfed, tightly blue-jeaned woman smeared a cement trail across the floor, followed by her knee-padded partner slapping foot-square, mottled green tiles into place. The tiler divided his attention between the job and the jeans.

I pecked on the window with my car keys.

The tall, skinny drywall spackler aimed his trowel in the general direction of a water bucket, wiped his hands on the legs of his white uniform, stuck his fingers through the empty doorknob hole, and tugged open the door. "What th' eff you want, partner?"

"I'm looking for Leonard Rankles."

"Me too." He yanked his cap bill aside and swabbed his forehead with a dirty bandanna. "Me and my mates'll be out of this place by tomorrow afternoon—day after, latest. If you hear of a three-alarm fire in the near downtown, you'll know that mother humper, Leonard

Rankles, didn't get back to pay for the work, and I flat-out burned the place."

"Why the sweat?"

"He paid five percent down, with thirty-five percent due when we nailed the final two-by-four into place. We done that in three days. We ain't seen hide nor hair of Mr. Rankles since the first day. We're still working, but we're doing it on faith and right now that's getting mighty thin, like my bank balance." He fished his trowel from the water bucket.

I offered a card. "You see him, tell him another friend is also hot on his tail."

I stepped back out on the street, racking my brain. "How in the hell do you investigate fraud and murder," I wondered to myself as I hied my way back the way I'd come, "when every trail leads to another missing person?"

Chapter Twenty-four

RETURNING TO MY OFFICE, I lolled briefly in my leather chair while Stella Carlyle yanked folders from a bulging briefcase. When last we met in Indy, she had been all smiles, calm, even that day when I confronted an irate Karl Sprader, the Consolidated Constructioneers VP. Today her lips pressed themselves into tight, white lines as she organized the papers on the worktable between us. "As you might've expected, building codes have been flaunted."

I craned my neck to read the papers on the table. She flipped the copy of a certified computer document so the printing faced me. "The concrete hasn't been reinforced with steel rods and mesh. None of it has been pre-tensioned."

"I suspected as much," I replied.

"Indianapolis Hi-Testing Lab performed destructive testing. Concrete's strength is measured in pounds per square inch or kilograms per square centimeter of force needed to crush a sample of a given hardness—"

"Yeah, I follow that," I said, impatiently. "On this job, I suppose very little agrees with codes or prints."

Stella resumed command, "All else being equal, more cement like the prints specified would've meant a stronger building. This dreck was undoubtedly poured during freezing weather without the addition of calcium chloride or protective coverings."

"Look, Stella. Don't sweat it!" I leafed ahead through the report. "There are no surprises here. It's an investigator's three-legged stool. We suspected crooks. We searched for crooks." With my palms, I beat a tattoo on the desktop. "And we've found crooks."

"Surely you aren't that cavalier!"

"Of course not, but we've done our job. You've verified our suspicions. The tenants have been inconvenienced, but not injured. Unlike my last case, nobody's been snuffed. We're dealing strictly in impersonal dollars. All's right with the world. Hallelujah! We've made the case! The bank can win their suit," I exulted.

Why shouldn't I celebrate? Now, I could forget Indy and concentrate on my arson, murder, and fraud cases.

"Dammit Richard!" She objected. "Please allow me to finish. It isn't just about dollars!" Leaping to her feet, she glared down at me. "The building's subsidence wasn't caused solely by poor foundations. Part of the complex was built on an unstable landfill." She speared a document with a yellow pencil, then swept broken lead from the table without looking. "Who knows what this has done to the children?"

"Come off it! I repeat—nobody's been injured."

"Not true, Richard! The story gets worse. Much, much worse. As promised, I had soil samples tested! The tract where the apartments were built once held a salvage yard. Among other contaminants, the soil is loaded with mercury, lead, cadmium, arsenic, beryllium, dioxin, cyanide, and polychlorinated bephenyls."

Zeroing in on the last, I hand-signaled time-out.

"Sorry, Richard, you know them as PCBs."

"Like on your 'PCB's Kill' sweatshirt, when we first met in Indianapolis?"

"Exactly." She managed a tight smile. "The shirt was almost prophetic."

"Stella, back at Purdue I anchored the lower third of the Chem 101 class. Can you define usage and risk."

"PCB's are the oily fluids used as a fire resistant liquid in electrical transformers. They're also used in carbonless copy paper, pesticides, and small electric parts. They're even utilized as protective coatings for wood, metal, concrete and wire."

"What effect do they have on humans?"

She yanked another paper from the stack. "Liver and intestinal cancer, pituitary tumors, leukemia, lymphoma, and birth defects. I also have information on the other toxic chemicals." By her expression, I could see the recitation was painful.

Steeling herself, she carried on, "Beryllium is used in jet fighters, bombs, and missiles. Its dust causes beryllium disease, a killing lung ailment. Shall I continue?"

"Enough already. The reprehensible scum!" I rose and stomped to the window. "That complex is loaded with kids." Despite my investigator's need for objectivity, I personalized the story by remembering Ms. Dempsie and her three Cheerios-munching tykes in that dingy apartment.

"You're right about the kids, Richard." She began to gather her papers. "It appears your case has substantially broadened."

"But why would any businessperson knowingly build an apartment complex on a toxic site?" I asked rhetorically.

"Greed. What else?" Pursing her lips, she reached out a hand and brought me to a halt. "The concept of evil is out of vogue, but how else do you adequately describe those who willfully poison children? God, the problem is so huge ..." Her words tailed and Stella helplessly hung her head.

I helped her on with her coat, then walked her to the lobby's outer door. I continued talking while moving down the hall. "I've long been an eco-nut, Stella. That's why I'm generating such a white-hot head of steam. I despise lowlifes who trash the planet. There should be a death sentence for those who persist in ruining the earth."

Stella nodded agreement. "They kill far more people than a serial killer. Or a dictator's genocide."

"Only they do it slowly through cancer and gene destruction," I added.

"Worse than that," Stella pointed out. "While a murderer's weapon simply kills today's victim, these poisons become part of the DNA strand and continue to maim and kill through eternity."

Staying atop my soapbox, I complained that the corrupt businessmen killing today's people and destroying our children's future were, at the same time, amassing fortunes and spinning their stories, to become role models. "With greenbacks their only credentials, these creeps are featured on radio and TV talk shows and honored in newsprint and magazines. Filthy rich, they're viewed as valid spokesmen on every issue. "

On a roll, I went on to complain about investigative reporters and how they ignored the really important problems. "Their beats cover celebrity murders and politicians' sexual preferences. Was sex consensual? Was it oral? Was it on the desk? Behind the door? On the floor? How frequent? Are there videos? The American people need to know!"

I promised to see her soon back in Indianapolis. As I waved goodbye and she disappeared around the corner of the building, I made a silent bet: I'd lay odds there was even more behind this story than we'd yet uncovered.

Still trying to assimilate the new information, I stopped to see Jeanie Robbins and waited at my desk while she cleared a phone call.

She joined me in a flash. "Your alter ego down on the Florida beaches has somehow managed to buy a new Mercedes and have the cost charged to a credit card backed by one of your investment accounts," Jeanie said.

"But how did they use the card? I not only never use it, I distinctly remember opening the envelope and tossing the card into a desk drawer." I yanked open the drawer. "See! It's still here!"

"I know. And I've already checked with the brokerage company. Although you never used the credit card, the thief called the 1-800 activation number. Completely versed on your background, he provided your zip code, social security number, driver's license number, and your mother's maiden name. Naturally, having available all the valid information, he was able to trigger the activation code."

"Jesus!" I moaned, "This cat has my complete skinny."

Mini-skirted Peggy Murdock waited just outside the door. Jeanie excused herself momentarily and handed Peggy a stack of human resource reports. "That girl waits for nobody," Jeanie complained, "not even the president."

"Maybe she wants my job."

"Anyway," Jeanie continued, "for an identity thief to get much of that information is no big deal. I know that at one time, while you were in the army, you had a Florida driver's license. Well, when I talked to Florida law enforcement, the officer provided a neat little tidbit of information. For years Florida's Department of Highway Safety and Motor Vehicles collected millions of dollars by selling the information on driver's licenses to the highest bidder. That information included photos and social security numbers. How does that strike you?"

"In the solar plexus." I juggled possibilities. "But Indiana's just as high-handed. They recently had an out-of-state contractor do a tax mailing for the state. They printed the addressee's social security number in bold letters on the outside of the envelope. The story made the *Star*'s front page."

"Oh, yes," she added. "We also checked your investment account's balance. One million plus dollars there. Amount subject to credit card withdrawal: seven hundred thousand big ones. Think of it."

"Yeah," I groaned, "that's a lot of walking around money."

"I canceled the credit card and will schedule a meeting with the insurance company. Your financial loss should be covered."

"Yep. But again, the loss of my privacy and personal control can't be covered, and I find that hard to live with." I slammed my fist against the desktop. "I don't like being an open book for anyone."

I glanced at the newspaper on Jeanie's desk. According to the

Indianapolis Star, there was an increasing likelihood that another of my assets could be battered by a second Florida storm: "Carrying sustained winds of almost a 150 MPH, Hurricane Aaron was within one hundred miles of the Florida keys," the article read.

Grabbing my coat, I said goodbye to Jeanie and headed for the parking lot. On the way out, I nodded to Seve Jensen, but didn't go inside. He probably wondered why I wasn't putting pressure on him to come up with answers. Of course, he didn't know about Joseph Schwab's suspect list or my Saturday morning accounting visit.

Playing a hunch, I detoured into the accounting department to pick up a thick set of ADE's most recent financial reports.

I frequently lug paperwork home. Some accumulates in my car. Passengers face a choice: either sit perched on computer runoffs or risk a hernia by moving them.

Today I stayed and plopped down at a vacant desk. Keying the computer, I searched for the latest, unprinted scoop. I quickly picked out a few of the company names I'd copied while sleuthing through Clark Benefield's office. I needed more than a peek at Benefield's papers. I needed a face-to-face meeting with the president of Breaking Fast Restaurant and Benefield Enterprises. Where could he be hiding?

Hooked for the next three hours, I again electronically probed company records. ADE showed a limited history with the smaller companies on my new list. Money owed them for services or parts manufacture: negligible. As I had before, I reviewed the amounts being billed by Arvet Consolidated and Benefield Enterprises. The dollar amounts of their invoices continued to mount. But as before, the transactions didn't appear irregular.

Carrying a note-filled legal pad, I returned to my office. Standing just outside the door, I heard papers being shuffled inside. Then silence. At first I thought it was Jeanie, then remembered—whoops! She had been sitting at her desk when I walked by her office door. I sidled around the jamb, and inside. Quietly, I stood watching, glued to the spot by my own amazement. Seve Jensen, his wheelchair parked behind my desk, stood erect, part of his weight balanced on a hand

and muscular arm, punching buttons on my computerized daily planner. Although I wasn't certain, those supposedly paralyzed, but saw-log-sized, legs seemed to be bearing some of his weight too.

"You finding everything okay, Jensen?" I asked, my quiet voice loaded with venom. I didn't mention his newly recovered leg strength. Perhaps it had been there all along.

Glancing up, he did a double-take and dropped like a rock into his chair. His face turned chalk-white, then segued to its normal ruddy, before reddening to a vivid scarlet.

"I, uh, was checking your schedule," he stammered. Quickly recovering, his color reverted to ruddy. "Without your input, and the name of our construction contact in Albuquerque, I can't proceed on the shopping-mall job." His voice now came forth, exuding confidence. I suspected if he were ever caught with his pants down, he would quickly blame a defective belt or rotten suspenders.

He rebuckled his seat belt. From memory, I provided the name of the contact he needed. "Now, Seve, I have some heavy-duty questions of my own. Why have we consolidated so much business with these two companies? We're vulnerable when we don't spread around the business."

For an instant, Jensen's expression changed. He appeared almost defenseless himself. Without doubt, I thought, he's hiding a big problem. He's clinging to a ragged edge and fighting a fall. What could be tormenting him? Theft? Murder?

Quickly, he recovered equilibrium. "The machining, casting, and processing they do is too sophisticated for us to do it ourselves," he said, a mellow voice dismissing my concerns.

He must've read my skepticism. Again I witnessed a complete metamorphosis in attitude. His face grew crimson, a vein on his forehead throbbed. Seve tapped the power button on the chair's arm. The chair surged forward, its wheel slamming into the front panel of my desk. "I monitor all major business accounts," he hissed. "It's my job. My name's on every single major-dollar invoice." His body leaned forward until it strained against the seat belt. "Say the word if you wish to supplant my authority. You are president. You can sign off on every document, even the simplest, yourself!"

"Cool it, Seve! You're getting this out of proportion." My words were drowned by the motor's whine as he wrenched the chair around and powered through my door and up the hall.

I sat at my desk, shocked speechless. Not quite. Words are always abundantly available, but this situation was a Catch 22. As president I was the proverbial eight-hundred-pound gorilla. I could search wherever I wished. Seve, however, as second banana, couldn't tolerate further questions about any decisions he'd made. Ergo, ADE had an unstoppable president on a collision course with its immovable CFO. Presently, he held the edge. I couldn't perceive his plans. I couldn't fathom what he was concealing. I would've laid odds he nevertheless discerned his own chosen course with absolute clarity.

Yet I still didn't want to drive him away. Not yet. If he were guilty but still aboard, the case against him would be easier to prove. If he had helpers, I could better root them out too.

From habit, I glanced at my wrist and remembered losing my watch during hell night out at Rose Cutter's Quarry. I checked the clock on the wall. Seven P.M. I needed nurture. Make that at least a friendly voice. I dialed Sam's number.

"Hello, Samantha Petry residence." Her tone was flat. Or aloof? Or disinterested? Or apprehensive?

"What's wrong, Sam?"

Silence. Then, "I'm . . ." Another phone was plucked from its cradle. Would Seve eavesdrop? Abolutely, I concluded, remembering the desk planner episode from only minutes ago. Could Sam have a secret listener at home? Yes—that, too.

"Sam, are you still there?"

"Yes, Richard. And no, nothing is wrong." She said it reassuringly, but her subdued tone didn't back the words. "I'm just tired. It's been a long, tedious day."

"No sweat, I'll be over to cheer you up. On the way, I'll pick up a bottle of Pine Ridge cabernet sauvignon." Voice unctuous, I began to bogey my way through a list of wine descriptions. "It's the fruitiest, most high-spirited wine, with a full, rich mouth feel, yet with gentle aromatic overtones so evocative and oh-so-tempting to lovers—"

"No!" The phone dropped onto the cradle. No dial tone. But a surreptitious click as another phone followed suit.

Alarmed, I hit redial. Busy. Inspiration: I dialed her cell phone number. Pick up. Breathing, no answer. Click!

Chapter Twenty-five

My gut wrenched tight as in 'Nam and Desert Storm. Sweat greasing my palms, I charged through my office door and down the hall, knowing Sam faced countless hazards. Had she, like I, been attacked in her home? Was she this moment fighting for her life? Possibilities ricocheted through my brain.

Tires burning blacktop, I fishtailed the Jag out of the parking lot. It caught traction and fairly exploded onto South Street. Traffic picked that exact moment to slow, then stop. Like a bad dream in which the killer's gaining ground and you discover your shoes cemented to the floor, I was stuck in place.

Today, I had a glue-melting answer. I steered hard right. The Jag bounced atop the curb. The passenger-side wheels tracking the sidewalk, I slammed the accelerator. Ignoring horn blasts, vertical fingers, and shaking fists, I sped on.

"Hang on, Sam!" I screamed into the dusk. "I'm on my way!"

From a block off, I saw Joe Petry's Buick parked in front of Samantha's house. All the curtains were drawn, including the front drapes, which Sam never closed. I charged up to the sidewalk, jumped onto the portico, and punched the buzzer while pounding the front door with my free hand.

No response!

Vaulting the railing, I tore down the flagstone path toward the back of the house. George, one rear leg tucked beneath his belly, hobbled to meet me at the gate. Leaning over, I gingerly stroked his leg. He yelped, then locked his huge muzzle onto my hand, not biting, but telling me his bum leg hurt like hell.

I pounded the back door. Again nothing!

Grabbing a brick from a flower bed border, I smashed a pane and reached inside for the doorknob. Phone pasted to her ear, a next door neighbor glared down from an upstairs window.

Sam and Joe Petry stood just inside the front foyer, her shoulders wedged against the door, trapped in an imprisoning embrace, struggling to break free. One set of Petry's bony fingers were locked vicelike onto her upper arm; the other clenched a Glock 19.

"Turn her loose, Petry!" I thundered, my voice echoing through the tiny kitchen and down the hall toward them.

He aimed the weapon toward me. Realizing my .45 lay tucked inside the glove compartment, I hesitated. I dared not risk Samantha. Yet, if I had my piece, I'd willingly blast her ex into Hades.

"No, Joe! Please!" Samantha pleaded.

I hoped he listened. That lethal killer snugged inside his skinny fist held fifteen shots.

"You're a dead man, Scott!" Petry bellowed, trying to get a bead on my weaving body.

I dropped behind the refrigerator. "I'll shoot!" I bluffed, then counted, "One . . . uh . . . twoo . . .uhhh . . . threee . . ." stretching the numbers further than the long count in the Dempsey-Tunney prize fight. That count reached thirteen and saved Tunney from a KO. My count bluffed murder.

Buying my ruse, Petry bolted out the front doorway. The anonymous creep who'd dry-gulched me at home had stolen my Glock. Could Petry's be the one?

Sam staggered into the living room and collapsed onto the sofa. Rushing in, I cradled her in my arms as I heard Petry's car tear away from the curb.

"Darling," I whispered.

A siren drowned my soft words. Seconds later, the doorbell chimed. "Are you Samantha Petry?" A young, spit-and-polished policeman asked through the open door.

Before she could answer, Captain Raphael Redonzo barged in. "Hello, Scott," he barked, then turned toward Sam. "Is this man—this Richard Scott, bothering you, ma'am?" He aimed his pistol at my bellybutton.

"For God's sake, no!" Between deeply drawn, ragged breaths, Sam described the scene with her ex. Elaborating, she outlined the whole stalking story, telling even the parts I'd skipped when Redonzo and I met in his office.

His expression skeptical, Redonzo tucked his cap beneath his arm and patiently listened. "I can't believe it. I've known Joe Petry for years. I even vouched for him when he was up for the police chief's job." Obviously noting Sam's darkening expression, he switched his approach, "Was Joe—er—I mean, your ex-husband here by invitation?"

"Certainly not! First, he pounded on the front door. I ordered him to leave. He then went to the rear of the house and tried to unlock that door. That's when he kicked George." For the first time, tears welled in her eyes.

"Yeah," I said. "Hurting animals seems to be a typical step in a stalker's escalating violence. Next, the sneaking cowards hurt people. Finally, they kill. He appeared to have reached the third step just as I arrived—"

Giving me an icy stare, Redonzo cut in. "What happened next, ma'am?"

"He returned to his car and lay on the horn. God, what must the neighbors have thought? Finally, I couldn't stand more raucous noise. I shouldn't have, but I opened the door and motioned for him to come inside."

"Your propriety could've proved fatal," I observed, dryly.

"Richard, you were partially at fault," she retorted.

"Please run that by me again. At quarter speed."

"When you described, on the phone, that the cabernet was a 'wine for lovers,' Joe went berserk. Or as my students say, 'ballistic.' He started to slam the phone down, then quickly realized you would hear it. After you hung up, he threw it."

I could see into Sam's office. The phone had crashed through the computer monitor screen. Still attached by its serpentine cord, the headpiece dangled from the desk. Glass slivers littered the carpet.

"Will you press charges, Mrs. Petry?" the captain's sidekick asked.

She shook her head in an unequivocal "No!"

I understood. Like Redonzo earlier told me and I later recounted to Samantha: "In a stalker's world, the victim is pretty much on her, or his, own."

"I'd like to see him charged with cruelty to animals, though. He kicked this poor baby," Sam cooed. George licked his back leg, then sharing her affection, licked Sam on the nose.

"The animal cruelty charge will be your word against his, I'm afraid," Captain Redonzo warned.

"Not really. I have a witness. Miss Jarrett, next door, saw it all."

Ironic? You betcha! The law could probably jail the sleaze for kicking the dog. For assaulting his wife? The case would need to be stronger. A victim and two witnesses wouldn't keep him jailed. He would be out on bail before midnight.

Sam brought a cordless phone from the kitchen and I called the vet. While Sam went for her coat, I also called Capital Detective Agency and left a lengthy, voice mail message for Stella Carlyle, my sidekick in Indy.

Despite the storm clouds shadowing me at work and at Samantha's, the day had been unseasonably warm, with bright March sunshine hinting of spring.

Later that night, plunging temperatures rode in on a Canadian weather system. Two hours later, a sharply gusting wind whipped sodden flakes about the yard as if they were tiny snowballs. By six P.M. the snow had changed into a bone-chilling drizzle. A heavy fog rolled in, as though winter was trying to hide the season's last mistake behind a dense, gray curtain.

I woke at five the next morning, eager to hit the road and check the dilapidated apartment buildings. I hurried outside. At the end of the sidewalk, the Jaguar stood like a faint ghost, its green enamel washed out by the high-intensity, overhead floodlight.

From a hundred feet away, a coyote surreptitiously watched. I muttered, "Hi, Wily!" With a disdainful glance, rejecting my sense of humor, it casually turned and slunk inside the protective fog bank.

I seldom eat breakfast. Today, with time on my hands, I smeared a couple of pieces of toast with heavy coatings of butter and orange marmalade, and chugged them down with a mug of black coffee. Two hours later, I reopened the blinds. No change.

In the distance, a beech's silver trunk remained invisible. Its black limbs appeared unattached, as if beseeching the sky. Maybe it knew I needed to be on the road.

The coyote returned to sniff the Jag's Michelins. Detecting my movement, he slunk away once more.

Good news! The fog concealed all traces of Rose Cutter's Quarry.

I brewed another pot. Over a second and third cup, I reviewed Stella's report on the apartment buildings and the chemical dump beneath them. Now, even more concerned about Ms. Dempsie's Cheerios kids, I grew impatient. Fighting the odds, I pulled away from the A-frame at eight-thirty, bound for Indy.

For the next thirty miles I followed a faint trail, the car's fog-light beams spearing bleached-cotton fog banks, then piercing deeper and sweeping over the concrete lane like yellow tracing pencils.

I drove the fast lane knowing saner people would hug the slow. Certainly, nobody would be traveling fast enough to rear-end me. Why would they? Who else drove like a maniac because he was on the trail of environmental idiots? Eventually, the fog became spotty and gradually changed to drizzle. I stabbed the accelerator.

I keyed my way through Capital Detective Agency's doors at just past ten o'clock. Stella Carlyle entered on the same door swing. Her, "Hi, Richard!" greeting was cheery, but feigning anger she raised her oak-handled umbrella, brandishing it like a shillelagh.

Tucking her black faux fur into the small closet, she added an over-the-shoulder explanation. "There's been another huge pile-up on the south leg of I-65. Market Street was wall-to-wall traffic."

The memory of an interminable morning spurred my impatient tone. "Any luck at the courthouse, Stella? I need history on the apartment buildings." Immediately feeling churlish, I smiled my forgiveness.

She was dressed expensively in a cream blouse under a black and cream boucle cardigan. Turning first one way and then the other, she observed her reflection in the glass door, then, glancing over her shoulder, adjusted her kick-pleated black skirt. Seating herself, she motioned me to the armchair beside the desk.

"Until recently, the apartment tract has been owned by . . ." All business, she rapidly keyed the laptop. "By Reused Resources, Inc. During recent years, Karl Sprader has been president of both Reused Resources and Consolidated Constructioneers, the company that built the apartments."

I pecked on a front tooth with my pen, trying to assimilate the information. "Does either Reused Resources or Consolidated Constructioneers now own the apartments?" I asked, half my mind still trying to comprehend why Karl Sprader would at one time be president of Reused Resources, Inc. and still later appear as vice president of Consolidated Constructioneers, Inc.

"Neither one," Stella answered. "To clear the land, Reused Resources moved all its inventory to an unknown address. The inventory consisted of surplus electronics, chemicals, fuels, and other miscellaneous products which had been purchased for later resale at reduced prices."

"First glance it looks like a sound concept," I said. "Reduced prices, products recycled, everybody a winner . . ."

"Perhaps, but with the inventory removed, Reused Resources hauled in fill dirt and graded the land flat. Unfortunately, the fill dirt was contaminated," Stella said, her voice grating. I recollected the sharpened pencil episode in my office and felt grateful she was now using a laptop.

"Why weren't they forced to remove the toxic chemicals? Surely the city demanded a clean-up."

Stella cackled a deliberately dry laugh. "Reused Resources drove the city fathers to distraction. First, they refused to mow the weeds. The city did, and levied a charge. Reused Resources countered with a suit, charging damage to two rusty Quonset huts."

"The city negotiated to buy the property as part of a near-downtown sports complex. Reused Resources nixed the contract. To force their hand, the city threatened eminent domain. Reused Resources sold to a third party, unnamed. Consolidated Construc-tioneers then built the apartments for a third party."

"I suppose the city was delighted to be relieved of a long-running problem," I groused. "I can picture the roomful of bureaucrats, none daring to ask questions and rock the boat."

"You've pictured it correctly," Stella said. "The city even helped arrange financing."

"Yep. I remember that story making *Indianapolis Star* headlines. Problem solved. Low cost housing available. Indianapolis had a new taxpayer on the rolls. Everybody winners."

Taking her investigation a step further, Stella had researched the Internet. "Karl Sprader now lives near Bloomington," she announced. "I called his phone number. He's a bachelor, but has a talkative, live-in housekeeper, a Ms. Smith. I'm sorry, but I didn't catch the first name."

"Un-bloody-believable." I groaned. I had spent half the day listening to horror stories, with Karl Sprader the heavy. Days earlier I had met four of his helpless victims—Ms. Dempsie and her three tots. Now, he'd become my neighbor. Karl Sprader and I must meet again. Quickly.

Would he willingly provide answers about himself and his colleagues? Would he be pleased by a visit from me? Would he invite me in for a friendly drink? Would elephants fly?

Chapter Twenty-six

With frequent stops to study a county map, I drove far into the countryside searching for Karl Sprader's house. I located his numbered mailbox at the end of a long, skinny gravel lane. Unlike his neighbors, he hadn't cooperated with prospective visitors by displaying his name on the box.

I wheeled into the drive. The temperature had warmed since last night's snow and this morning's fog. Rolling down the window, I inhaled deeply, and held the fresh country air in my lungs, like a smoker trying to absorb a heftier jolt of nicotine.

I listened to the tires grinding gravel before squashing it deeper into driveway mud. I knew spring neared.

Looking far into the woods, I slowed the car to a crawl and watched as a five-member deer family browsed slowly through the underbrush. The deer paused occasionally to snatch a bite from a tree branch or to chew a tender shoot near the ground. In concert, they halted. Heads immobile, planted legs mimicking slender saplings, they watched my car.

Spinning through a patch of mud, the Jag's front tire caught a rock and zinged it against an oak's thick trunk. The buck pronked high into the air and landed running. The does strung out behind him, all five gracefully twisting between trees and stone outcroppings like open-field runners. Each white tail waved like a touch-footballer's flag.

For me, it had been a camera moment. I supposed it would have been different for an avid hunter. I imagined his response: "C'mon guys, let's kick Bambi's body the hell out of the way, so's we can count the points on that friggin' rack."

Of course, that's a weakness of mine. I invariably mix beauty, personal philosophy—and murder. It's a recipe that can get damn hot. But it won't always cook . . .

A locked, ten-foot tall chain-link gate halted my contemplation, and the Jag's progress. "That conniving Sprader arranged the idyllic scene so I'd lower my guard," I groused through tight lips.

I eyeballed the security system. The surroundings were heavily wooded, but the house stood in the middle of a cleared and fenced three-acre tract. Sharply barbed concertina wire topped the chain-link fence that encircled the property.

"Anybody home?" I called, aiming my words at a tiny speaker and my warmest smile toward the television camera's eye atop it.

"May I help, please?" A not-unfriendly, female voice asked. I supposed she was the housekeeper mentioned by Stella.

"I'm here to see Mr. Sprader about—" Three electronic beeps sliced short my words.

Six fierce-looking dobermans tore around the corner of the house, and chasing their own wave of canine noise, charged the gate. I fought an urge to raise the window, rip the Jag into reverse, and scurry back to civilization.

The conversation lag persisted for a full thirty seconds. That aroused my curiosity. Was Sprader at this moment studying me like a laboratory specimen, and preparing a special greeting? Had all the beer and savory foods I'd eaten turned me into a tasty repast? Would I end up as a doberman's hors d'oeuvre?

"I'm sorry, Mr. Sprader is away."

My mind spun fast. "No problem," I said. I felt certain even a surreptitious visit could pay dividends. "I'm Jerome Riddle from

Communications Responses. I'm here to repair the left diode on Mr. Sprader's Internet engine. I can do it in his absence. He'll be pleased knowing I was here."

Another lengthy pause. "One moment please." The gate clicked open. I pulled through. With the Jag surrounded by the pack of growling and frothing dobermans, I drove to the front of the house. A side door opened. Obediently, the dogs trotted inside the house.

From the car's safety, I surveyed the structure. It was a flat-roofed, two-story Frank Lloyd Wright knock-off, with its cantilevered front wall reminiscent of a ship's prow, except that the hull was all glass, not wood nor steel. In sailor lingo the front door was located a dozen feet from the vessel's "stem."

I got out gingerly and rooted around in the Jag's handy-dandy tool holder for equipment, then headed up the sidewalk. I trusted the dogs had separate quarters and weren't regrouping for a front door attack. Also, I prayed the housekeeper expected diode repairmen to arrive not only carrying a screwdriver and pliers, but wearing a Emeregildo Zegna tie and an Armani suit.

When I touched the doorbell, the remote-controlled door latch clicked open. Cautiously, I edged inside. I scoped my surroundings. A flight of stairs faced me and led to the second floor. I recalled the outside expanse of glass and assumed the steps led to a second-story living room.

I glanced at the ceiling—and into a huge eyeball. What an ingenious place for a peephole. A miniature door beside the lens slid open.

I leaped backwards. A bullet whistled by my nose and drilled the carpet. I flung my body against the outside door. Locked! Skirting the foyer's center—and the peephole—I darted for the stairs. Following a scramble of padded feet and toenails, the dobermans guarded the top landing. I touched the bottom step. The dogs broke into a barking frenzy. One took two paces down the stairs. Another scrambled over its back.

"Down boy! Down girl!" I recognized Sprader's voice. Never

before had a voice sounded sweeter. The dogs clawed their way back upstairs.

"Scott, that last shot was just for effect," he said, his voice gravel-tough like the crushed stuff on the driveway. "Now, throw down your weapon and stay on the bottom step. Move a muscle and I'll feed your balls to the dogs."

Tossing the .45 onto the carpet, beyond range of the ceiling door, I risked another, closer look at my surroundings and the possibilities of escape. They appeared nonexistent.

"Now, why're you here, Scott? And is your reason worth dying for?"

"I know you not only built those screwed-up apartments, you hung onto a piece of the ownership," I said. "The bank wants its money and I figure to pry it out of your deep pockets, or your fat ass."

"You're not only a gutsy S.O.B., but in no position to do either one, so listen up. You don't know what you're talking about. If you show up here again, you're a dead man." He walked to the top of the stairs. The pistol a lethal pointer, he gestured toward the dogs. "Those six dobermans are reading my lips." A big man anyway, Sprader looked ten feet tall standing there looking down.

Like I've said, I always try to achieve the offensive. "Your company also poisoned the land and the people. The city wants it cleaned up." Building a full head of emotional steam, I inched forward. "I want answers, Sprader."

Leaving me to address the dogs and vacant steps, he vanished from sight. A moment later his swarthy face filled the tiny, overhead door. "On second thought, I'll feed your balls to the dobermans now!" A pistol hammer clicked.

"No!" Ms. Smith screamed. I heard arguing, one voice harsh and demanding, one softly pleading.

"Okay, sweetheart," Karl Sprader said, resignedly. "You win—this time." Had the argument been pure theater?

I did not—could not—know. But the outer latch triggered open.

I picked up the .45. Moments later, I pushed the gate's exit button. The gate stayed closed. "Okay Sprader, quit playing games."

"If you ever show your face here again have a better cover story. Along with her other talents, Ms. Smith knows computers." A loud guffaw concluded the warning.

I pictured his choking on his laughter. Better yet, I pictured myself doing the choking. Turned out, being ridiculed was the day's brightest highlight.

Chapter Twenty-seven

My BLISTERING TRIP THROUGH HELL didn't require Dante's Seven Rings of Hades, or Virgil as guide. A Jaguar Vanden Plas, a tankful of high-test gasoline, and forty tons of rampaging steel got me through quite nicely.

Back from Sprader's house, and before going home, I swung by ADE to pick up Herschel Peters. I arrived at the plant's front gate during the four-forty-five shift change. Cars, pickups, and SUV's sped both directions past the guard shack. For a few minutes, I pulled to the side of the drive and watched.

I don't intrude, but I like knowing and understanding my employees. Paternalistic? Perhaps. My office door's always open and I have a "will-help" policy. Sometimes people can use a leg up when they're dealing with emotional problems. Also, despite good company pay, life sometimes deals rotten hands and people needs often outrun hourly wages.

Day shifters exited the factory with urgency. Seeing their faces, I wanted to read their minds. Would the laid-back guys and gals meet a buddy for beer at Big Bert's? I pictured the more disciplined as rushing straight home where they'd give their wives or husbands a quick peck on the cheek, wolf down a microwaved dinner, then head for Sally's or Junior's basketball practice. I visualized others kicking back for a night of dozing, reading or TV.

Each departing employee nodded, waved or honked at the guard. All accelerated toward a rolling stop onto Gustin Avenue, freedom, and happy times. Most were luckier than I.

Since Cait and I split I hadn't anybody to go home to. Though Samantha and I had grown closer, we both seemed wary of commitment. At least, I was. I was still psychoanalyzing myself. Maybe I was gun shy or lacked confidence. After all, I'd helped to blow both my marriage to Barb, and a good solid relationship with Cait.

I pulled back into the night shifter's lineup. Entering workers, rushing to beat time clock zero-hour and a fifteen-minute pay docking, barely slowed, holding their plastic passes flat against the car's side window, received a curt nod from the elderly guard, and drove the rows of parked cars searching for a spot near the time clock entrance.

Recognizing me, the guard drew his ancient back ramrod-straight, rendered a snappy salute, and motioned me onto factory grounds. I rolled down the window, and said, "Good evening, Mr. Curl," while driving past. Mentally, I pledged to transfer him to an inside job, out of the cold.

Usually, I dropped off or picked up Herschel Peters at a plant side entrance. Today, I elected to follow the structural steel warehouse's middle drive toward the rear of the factory. I'd collect Herschel at the overhead door separating the two departments.

That block-long drive ended up being eighty-nine miles of killer road.

Any building, whether a squat one-story or a towering skyscraper, shares one characteristic with man. The structure requires a skeleton in order to stand erect. The H- and I-shaped steel beams used to produce those skeletons were stored inside the hangar-sized warehouse through which I would be driving. And ADE's primary manufacturing job these days was to produce those skeletons, although the company, on occasion, still continued to design buildings.

Anyone entering the storage building, including jaded old salts like me, pay but slight attention to the ground-level storage area. Instead, their eyes are immediately drawn to the giant overhead crane that transports the steel sections from the warehouse to the factory for prepping. It's a magnificent piece of equipment.

Painted an electric-lemon yellow, and positioned three stories high in the air, its length extends from wall to wall in the double-gymnasium-width building. Each end is supported by a trolley consisting of four flanged railroad wheels.

Like an Amtrak train, the crane's wheels run on rails. There is another similarity. Like a train engineer, the crane operator controls his vehicle from a seat inside a glass-paneled cab.

There are two main differences. While Amtrak's rails are spiked to creosoted crossties, which, typically, are half-buried by mud and crushed stone, the factory's rails are supported by tall steel columns. Also, while Amtrak highballs the main line from city to city, the crane's route extends only from one end to the other of the long storage building.

Tonight, I'd safely driven slightly more than midway through the building when a siren's intermittent "wa-ruuppet, wa-ruuppet" announced the crane was prepared to move. A second, solid signal bansheed that the crane was on its way.

The giant monolith lumbered toward me, its chained bundle of beams swinging below it in a stork's carry. Only this baby had been diapered in high-strength cable, and weighed in at a massive forty tons, the weight equivalent of twenty automobiles.

High in the air, two maintenance men had been servicing the track. Warned by the siren, they scurried a few feet along the rail before leaping to safety on a metal catwalk.

I slammed the car's brakes. Looking overhead, I saw the operator's profile inside the crane cab, but barely. His hands were a blur as he punched buttons and manipulated control levers.

With a dozen car-lengths still separating us, the operator repositioned the load to the exact center of the crane. Fear tightened my gut. Two walls of steel locked my car into a narrow aisle and that forty-ton-load would pass directly over the Jaguar—and me.

"What are you doing, partner?" I shouted, although the car windows were rolled tightly shut, and my voice was drowned by the wailing siren. Yet I tried. "You ever read the bloody regs? Stop that goddamn thing!"

In its own ponderous go-to-hell answer, the crane increased speed and thundered closer.

Abruptly, the load dropped a dozen feet. A gust of smoke and a burst of sparks erupted from locked, over-burdened hoist brakes. The barrel-sized reel stopped spinning. The tightly wound steel cables snapped to a halt.

The load of beams continued its downward plunge. Reaching a critical yield point, with a thunderbolt's crack the nearest retaining cable split in two. One of the frayed ends lashed high into the air and whipped the metal roof joists. Retracting from within a black cloud of debris, it wrapped itself around the body of the crane. The other end flayed ground and air before forming into a tangled coil. A second cable ripped apart. Then the third and final restraint.

Freed, but still powered by the crane's momentum, steel beams nearly a hundred feet long and half as tall as a man hurtled toward the concrete floor. I dove to the floor.

One smashed head-on into the Jaguar. The car's sheet-metal hood crumpled and peeled back like a sardine can's top, shattering the windshield. Another beam ripped away the roof and skidded to rest on top of the squashed Jaguar. With an eardrum-splitting din, other beams screeched along the floor, gouged deep into the concrete, and ground to a halt beside the car, their bulk forming a steel cage and pinning shut the car doors.

Silence. For a brief moment, a hush descended over the disaster area, except for the hiss of steaming radiator fluid and the creaks and groans of stressed metal. Then, with a pop and a hiss, in quick succession, the car's four overloaded Michelins exploded and the car settled, its undercarriage flat on the concrete floor.

Trapped! Jagged metal pierced my shirt, gouging my shoulder muscles and backbone, pinning me to the frame. My face buried in the plush floor mat, I strained to breathe. I struggled to turn my head.

Excited but jumbled voices grew nearer. Finally, a voice nearby shouted, "Stan, dial 911." A whistle of shocked disbelief. Then the same voice. "Could the poor devil still be alive?"

"Not a even half a chance! His guts'll be smeared all over that freakin' Jag! What's left of it."

"Who was herdin' that baby, anyway?"

"The prez. El prez-i-dente Richard Scott. Poor S.O.B. All that lousy money, and then to end up squashed like a freakin' insect!"

"You got that right!" I visualized the speaker's open mouth and shock-widened eyes. "High ticket wheels"—short, two-beat pause—"made a junk-yard casket."

I struggled to yell. "I'm—" My voice squeaked. Metal groaned and a ripped piece pressed harder against my backbone. Terrified and, even though my chest was too cramped to fully expand, I managed a loud, "I'm alive. Help!" I struggled and got my arm beneath my face. I felt sticky blood painting my cheek. A couple of synapses fired wildly inside my head. I tried to form another plea, but I faded away.

Later, outlined by an overhead light, a face peered through a crack. "Help!" I squeaked again, more weakly.

He tossed a lighted match inside. Barely feeling the pain, I squeezed the flame between two fingers. Again I passed out.

"Fire!" The alarm propelled me back to consciousness.

Flames crackled somewhere in the rear of the car. Acrid black smoke curled around the front cushion and stopped inches from my face, but close enough to sear my eyes and nose lining. Half conscious, my eyes streaming tears, I knew I was doomed as I recognized the odor. The black smoke was plastic-fed phosgene, the stuff that suffocates trapped airplane passengers. The lethal gas had been around for most of this century, after first being introduced to mankind by the kaiser's army, who used it to poison French, British, and American troops sheltered in World War I trenches.

"Please, for God's sake—help!" I pleaded.

Now, fully expecting to die and sleep eternally, I grew wider awake. I knew this was the end.

Unraveling this twisted-metal cocoon wouldn't be a job for local wrecker operators manipulating "Jaws-of-Life" equipment. Ordinary Jaws would be the equivalent of frail boys struggling to do a burly man's job.

I was terrified that even with heavy duty equipment it would be an unsolvable puzzle. This was pick-up-sticks—six-ton sticks. Any mistake could reduce my ten-inch-high cave to zilch, leaving me a bloody smear on a Vanden Plas floorboard. Any delay and I'd be cremated.

"Great choice, Richard," I muttered to myself. Claustrophobia clawing at my guts, my mind spinning almost beyond control, I strained to hear. The smoke thickened. Finally, the factory's electric-powered fire truck whined to a stop alongside the wreck. I heard the blessed hiss of extinguishers as plant firefighters killed the fire.

Finally, Herschel's voice broke through the clamor. "Careful fellows. Don't wrap the beam with the chain. Just hook the end, and winch 'er back. Sloowly. Sloower. Good!"

I glimpsed light. The overhead illumination from a high-pressure, sodium flood shone directly into my eyes, blinding me. Twisting my head, I saw Herschel. He winked, chirped, "Thank God, Mr. Scott!" He gave me a thumbs up.

"Sorry, I'm late, Herschel," I said, managing a weak smile. "Your wife will panic when I don't deliver you home on time." I didn't know why I said it, but at that moment, taking care of Herschel seemed the most important thing in the world.

Seve Jensen's wheelchair sat parked off to the side. Face impassive, he watched as four medics maneuvered me onto a stretcher. Catching my eye, he smiled and waved, but somehow, the greeting didn't seem to be as warm with feelings of relief as Herschel's. I suppose he was still remembering our latest office confrontation. Maybe he figured that contesting with him was a capital offense and my being squashed and cremated would've been a fitting punishment?

I awoke sometime later to gaze around at an expanse of hospital white and suspected I was seeing something divinely gossamer, like I hadn't made it past the promised land after all. That was the bad news.

There was good news. During my ordeal, the word "Fire!" had been pretty deeply imprinted on my mind. With relief, I realized the smells here were antiseptic, not brimstone, so I'd definitely chosen correctly at that good-guy, bad-guy fork in the road.

Hearing footsteps, I painfully turned my head. An angel walked into the room. It wasn't the classic blonde with alabaster complexion and pinched smile, but a creamy-skinned beauty smiling brightly from within a frame of near-raven-black hair. "Samantha!" I croaked.

"Oh, my darling," Sam whispered softly. Arranging herself carefully on the edge of the bed, she wrapped me in both arms. Through my thin PJ's, her black leather jacket, still cold from the outside, felt cool and comforting. Like always, her familiar aroma of rosewood and cedar enticed me. "I love you, Richard," she whispered, her breath quickening.

"I love you too, Samantha." This time, perhaps because of what I had just endured, there were no fears of entanglement. All thoughts of Caitlin McChesney had been blocked from my mind, and the words came easy. And what a pleasant contrast, burying my face in hair instead of the Jag's floor mat!

Carefully, without moving my fatly bandaged left arm, I hugged her close with the other. Gingerly, and gently we kissed.

In the immediate future I would have to win all arguments with logic, not fists. Lips seemed to be my only body components effectively working and not aching.

"God, you must've been so frightened," Sam said. She shuddered, remembering. "I was on the way to the supermarket and had just pulled away from the curb when WQIP-Radio's Carla Diston interrupted programming."

She deepened her voice, and using carefully measured words, mimicked Diston's: "'Ambulances have been dispatched to the Architectural Design and Elaboration company. According to reports, somewhere within the plant, one man has been trapped inside a car.' "

Sam shook her head. "Today we're inured to on-the-scene news reports. I felt a flash of compassion for some poor unfortunate, but not alarm. Then an eyewitness described a green Jaguar—" She closed her eyes in recollection, wincing. "I knew it could be only yours."

Frantic with worry, she had wheeled down a side street and sped toward the factory. In her excitement, the words almost ran together. She paused and took a deep breath. "Do you remember the young policeman who called at my house along with Captain Redonzo?"

I nodded.

"He followed me, inches from my bumper, his cruiser's siren blasting away. I refused to slow. We arrived simultaneously. Recognizing me, he didn't arrest me, but sought retribution for my scofflawry." She shook her head in frustration at the memory. "He refused to allow me inside the factory."

"But, now, thank God, we're together . . ." My words trailed off. I couldn't help myself. Slowly, involuntarily, my eyelids closed.

"Thanks a lot, sweetheart," Samantha teased, her voice soft and a hundred miles away. Stooping, she adjusted the blanket around my shoulders. Brushing her lips softly across my forehead she eased quietly from the antiseptic room.

The sound of her high heels against the vinyl tile diminished. I longed to call her back . . . I dozed.

I woke again during the night. My thoughts centered on Sam. I remembered the touch of her lips and the smell of her hair and perfume. My thoughts flowed on. I pictured Cait, alone in New York. I needed to call her and tell her I was okay . . . but she knew nothing of my latest escapade and had no reason to presume otherwise. Suddenly, I wanted to see her.

Earlier today, had I allowed myself to be entrapped by emotions? I brooded about Cait and was wracked by guilt. Abandoning thoughts of Cait, I longed for Sam. My emotional state was as perplexing as the case.

I awoke again, early in the morning, mentally replaying the wreck scene, certain the crane operator had targeted me. Yes, I was convinced he intended to overtax and fracture the cables. Was it because of a personal beef, or had he followed orders? That baffled me.

Ironic! Killer employees! My own workers drawing paychecks from my company while plotting my death. That scraped deeper.

Fading in and out of sleep, I worried the scenario through hours of darkness. How could I capture my enemies before they snuffed me? As a sunless dawn finally crept into the room, I chose one positive: I'd never forget the operator's facial profile. But, try as I might, I couldn't put a face on the guy who'd tossed the lighted match.

Chapter Twenty-eight

I'M AN OPTIMIST. I needed a fancy, new fountain pen. Hey, why not? When it came time to sign complaints against all my murderer, arsonist, and thief suspects, I wanted to do it with flair. Anyway, of late, I had been dreadfully mistreated. I calculated that a four-grand goodie would salve my wounds.

After three days in the hospital, the doctors released me. My body still sore as an unlanced boil, I stopped by Katasha's Jewelers. Along with mundane stuff, like three-carat diamonds and solid gold necklaces, the store sold fountain pens.

Because I'm a history buff, I normally stick with used fountain pens. I like imagining the "Dear John" letters and the "I love you, Sherry" messages that once flowed from some of those hand-carved beauties with the gracefully engraved gold nibs.

Today, I broke my habit. I bought a brand new, bright yellow, Michel Perchin Fleur-de-Lis pen. With a start, I realized the emblems on the pen were almost exact replicas of the floral design on the shirt pocket I ripped from my midnight assailant when I was attacked in the A-frame. Even the color matched.

Previously, based on the design, I figured I'd been sacked by an overzealous New Orleans Saints fan. Now, I was unsure, and worse yet, I hadn't given that evidence to the sheriff.

Next stop, I bought Jeanie Robbins a fancy box of milk chocolates. Calling from the hospital, I knew she'd been struggling with my work load along with her own. This was one way to say thanks, although a pay raise would follow.

"Good morning, Jeanie!" I laid the chocolates across her computer keyboard.

Jeanie forced a smile of appreciation, then jerked another baby-blue tissue from a Kleenex box. Her voice was hoarse and nasal from a late winter cold, but her announcement that my guest had arrived was, to me, pure music.

Why not? While tripping down the hall, my mind replayed a picture of the dense black smoke's roiling around the Jaguar's front seat. Just now, I was a new man, and the new, lucky me was Indiana's—make that the world's—most gentle and appreciative guy. Even as a baby, I could not have been more lovable.

Felton Crenshaw greeted me with a warm handclasp. "Remember me, your claims representative from Fealty Insurance Company?" My bandaged left arm was in a sling. Noticing it, Felton reached out and tweaked the fabric so it covered my wrist.

"Thanks for coming, Mr. Crenshaw." Today, I liked seeing him. He still reminded me of my dad. Last time we met, I had been fighting a bum mood. Then, the cinders from the previous night's conflagration had barely settled to the ground. Come to think of it, things hadn't changed too much. Today, the Jag had scarcely quit smoldering.

"I'm here about the house fire and the car accident. We insure your factory. Also both your homes. And your automobile. Incidentally, there are only scraps of the car remaining." He reached into his briefcase. "I did salvage this, just in case you'd treasure a memento. Here."

"Thanks. Very thoughtful." I turned the Vanden Plas's hood ornament over and over in my hand. During the wreck, its face had been hammered flat like a pug's.

"I'm also here"—his voice, already grave, deepened an octave—"about another matter of utmost importance!"

"Mr. Crenshaw, you wear many hats," I said, approvingly. Along with the hats, he was also sporting a new hairpiece. I kind of missed the classic comb-over. The new brown thatch was a deeper shade than his own wispy, freshly dyed, and graying fringe. Though the malignant buttonhole eye still stared from the center of his lapel, today's vividly dyed and computer-designed tie detracted from its impact.

"Although arson destroyed your home, we are prepared to settle the claim. Since the fire victim was an uninvited guest, our company is absolved of any fiduciary responsibility toward him." Crenshaw ceased speaking while he scratched through his briefcase. "Here!" he announced excitedly. "I have two checks." He paused to raise his eyebrows. "You, of course, must sign a number of release forms."

Clearing for action, I yanked my new, silver-and-gold-nibbed fleur-de-Lis pen from its gold case and pulled the cap.

I inked a dozen x-ed boxes, and signed forms; within minutes they again rested in the insurance adjuster's briefcase. I studied one check made out for sixty-three thousand bucks and another for a little over a million big ones.

"Hey, this baby does have special powers," I teased, turning the new pen so the light hit it just right. "Maybe it's due to the floral design. Maybe, it'll help solve the murder case."

Puzzled, Crenshaw murmured, "Pardon?"

With an open hand, I waved away my foolishness. "Now," I urged, "give me that bit about the other 'matter of grave importance.'"

His eyes dropped to the speaker phone on my desk. "Do we have complete privacy?"

In answer, I punched a speaker phone button, then rose and walked to the door. "Jeanie, please hold my calls for the next few minutes." I pulled the door closed behind me.

"During our first meeting, you may have noticed some indication of distrust?" The agent asked.

I nodded.

"Although I couldn't discuss the matter, in the early nineties, your Mr. Seve Jensen had sued us for injuries incurred in an industrial accident. That policy was held by another company. At the time, we had some . . . um . . . concerns . . . uh . . . reservations about the claim. Of course, our distrust must appear obvious, since we've contested the claim for so many years. Since the two of you were so closely affiliated, our association with you was also colored."

"How has that changed?"

"Last week, Fealty decided to settle with Mr. Jensen. Partially because we were pitting our legal department against a war hero. Although our position was viable—and just—we knew any jury would side with your Mr. Jensen.

"We were also influenced by our association with you. You are a valuable client. Also, we respected your reputation. We were certain you wouldn't employ an executive of questionable character."

"When will Seve Jensen's final settlement be made?"

"Oh, I've misled you. Mr. Jensen's check has also been delivered. And cashed, I might add. I can't divulge its size, but you have my word, the amount was significant."

After I thanked Crenshaw once more, we said our goodbyes. Felton Crenshaw, struggling under the heavy burdens of lost claims, pried himself from the armchair, and walked slowly from my office. I understood; insurance companies are into collecting premiums, not settling claims. With both Seve Jensen and me as his policyholders, Crenshaw had two costly clients.

The new me was finding it difficult to remain placid and understanding. I wanted Seve Jensen to be treated fairly. Yet, something dormant in my psyche rose closer to the surface. An acid bile of growing distrust chewed my esophagus from gut to throat. But, still, how could Felton Crenshaw feel that his company's previous refusal to pay *was just,* when the accident had given Seve Jensen a life sentence. A lifetime strapped into a wheelchair? Or had that life sentence been commuted? I remembered his standing tall, while hovering over my desk . . .

I gave Jeanie Crenshaw's two checks for deposit in the company account. That done, I went looking for new wheels so I could drive to Leonard Rankles' office, and interview the former Jacobi Realty agent; I needed to find out what functions his company provided for ADE during my extended absence. The dealership furnished a green Jaguar Vanden Plas, identical to the last—as I expected.

Leonard Rankles was about what I expected as well.

I caught him seated behind a veneered, pressed-wood desk, the kind peddled by discount houses for home-basement offices. The tri-sectioned print of a six-foot-long swordfish decorated the wall behind his chair. The first frame held the sword-like proboscis, the second the dorsal, the last, a finned tail. On his desk, a liquid-filled paperweight featuring Indy's Soldiers and Sailors Monument held down the cover on an executive's vinyl-bound daily planner.

When I introduced myself, he leafed through the planner as if to see if he could fit me into his schedule. A sneaked glimpse revealed I was the sole entry on today's page.

"I'm Richard Scott." I extended a card, gingerly, with my bandaged left hand and offered my right for a handshake.

Leonard Rankles stood. "Sorry my secretary wasn't at the receptionist's desk to greet you. She's temporarily indisposed. On another important assignment, you might say."

He was decked out in a blue-and-red patterned tie, a tightly tailored white shirt, and gray, pleated slacks that looked ready to lose their hold on his skinny butt and slide to the floor. While on his feet, he removed his navy blazer and hung it on a wall hook.

"Mr. Rankles, during my sabbatical from ADE, what functions did your company perform for mine?"

Pointedly ignoring my question, he bent back in his chair. He was balding, with slickly combed-back hair. With a practiced, backward stroke, he smoothed the hair over his ears with both palms while lovingly fingering the bare channels beside his widow's peak.

Hard-driving executives sardonically refer to those bald spots as

"Power Grooves." Leonard seemed to feel good having something in common with the "Big Boys."

"Nice suit you're wearing, Mr. Scott. I'll lay odds that baby's an Armeeny." His smile stretched his thin lips, exposing yellowed rodent teeth without the usual overbite. He lifted my business card from the desk. "Richard's the first name? Can I call you Richard?"

I nodded twice.

"Truth is, Richard, Windemere Clairton's the big gun over at Jacobi and I did whatever he ordered me to do."

"Okay, let's try again. What sort of things did he order you to do?"

"Rich, when your father-in-law's ticker went on the blink—that was years before he started doin' time down at the fed's barred 'Hilton'—he quit using the A-frame as a hunting and fishing lodge, and I rented it to corporate out-of-towners. A cut on the rental income became a perk for Jacobi Realty."

Buying time, he lifted the paperweight, turned it base-up and watched appreciatively until the heavy snowfall descending from the monument's steps eventually covered the head and staff of an upside-down Lady Victory.

"Please, go on," I urged.

"After a few months, I got a call that a company south of here would like to access your land for some kind of storage. They were hyper for an answer. Big rushes and big-time money sometimes go together like this—" He raised two adjoining fingers to make his point. "Smelling big scratch, I went to Clairton. He yanked my skinny butt off the assignment and glommed onto it for his own."

Leaning across the desk, he held his nose to signal maximum disbelief. Obviously, even today, the injustice still galled him. "Using modern management techniques, top managers share the wealth by giving bonuses. You can bet your sweet bippy, however, that old tight-fisted Clairton wasn't into sharing. That horse's butt would rob pennies from a bell-ringer's bucket."

Rankles' voice rose in volume and pitch. "That hoity-toity,

sanctimonious hypocrite would sure as I'm sittin' here, steal pop cans from a bag lady's cart."

The front door opened and closed. I lost Rankles' attention. "Well, well, well! I guess it's feed-bag time. Desiree," he said, rising to his feet, "I want you to meet Dick Scott, the big gun at Architectural Design and Elaboration. In fact he's President *Richard* Scott." His eyes flitted between Desiree and me. "Dick—I call him Dick—this is Desiree Martin."

I stood and bowed. After that intro, I could do no less.

Desiree studied me from my graying brown hair and full beard to the comfortably rounded toes of my wingtips. "Pleased to meet you, I'm sure," she squeaked in a little girl's voice.

She plopped two Big Macs, a large carton of fries, and a chocolate shake on the desk pad for her boss, sliding the phone to a corner of his desk to make room for her own order of chicken nuggets, a regular carton of fries, and a Diet Coke. She unwound a long woolen scarf and removed her coat, then parked both on a corner peg beside Rankles' jacket. She turned, revealing that despite the childish voice, a spectacularly proportioned woman was beneath the quilted car coat.

Having followed my eyes with his own, Rankles winked and smiled at me. Then his attention returned to his secretary. "Sorry, hon—uh, Ms. Martin—today you'll have to dine at your own desk."

"Awright!" She puckered her lips in little girl's petulance. "A lady knows when she's not wanted! In a manner of speaking, that is." Desiree regathered her lunch, and with a flounce of her hips, made for the front office.

"Sorry about fouling up your lunch plans. Anyway, after Clairton removed you from the assignment, who did he usually work with?"

Yanking open a lower drawer, Rankles withdrew a manila folder and placed it on his desk. "Since I never trusted that cheapskate Clairton, I decided on a personalized do-it-yourself C-Y-A insurance policy. That being the case, late at night, I snuck in and made copies of the motherhumper's letters."

Leonard leaned back in his chair and cackled. "He almost caught me the last time I stole a folder full of originals. I was out that back door like a turpentined cat." He paused to share the moment. "But I took the documents with me."

"Life's about sharing, Leonard," I said, extending my open palm.

"Life's more about selling, if you get my drift," he objected. His gaze swept around the office. "This here newly renovated Taj Mahal costs a millionaire's mint to run. Desiree wants hers—paycheck that is—whether the company's cuttin' the mustard or not."

He took out and waved a solitary letter above his head. "I can sell these babies as singles, or as a unit, because there are other takers. Nah—come to think of it, I prefer lettin' 'em go one at a time. It's more like a pension from those high-binders at Jacobi. What's your bid? Just remember, originals are like high-class art, triple the freight," he said, trading an original for a short stack of C-notes.

Seconds later I roared, "Would you look at this!" fully knowing Rankles already had. The letter, just purchased for five hundred dollars, had been signed by Karl Sprader.

Sprader sure got around. Once, president of Reused Resources, then VP of Consolidated Constructioneers—the company that built the derelict apartments—and now, according to the letter, he was once again heading Reused Resources. The company, formerly in Indianapolis, had moved to southern Indiana.

Unfortunately, the introductory letter, though announcing a willingness to do business with Jacobi Realty, provided not one clue to the exact type of business.

Now, Rankles gave me a smile similar to the one he'd given Desiree. Maybe a four-letter word would accurately describe his intentions toward each of us. "That, there, is only the first letter. They get better. Much better. Some're downright juicy."

"Does Karl Sprader . . . ? By the way, I met him," I said, reassuringly. "Does Sprader still operate out of this address?" I tapped the letterhead.

"Nah, I think that place has closed. Permanently. However, he still has the same sweetie who works in a local club. The club's name is on the tip of my lips, but it's not coming. It's something suggestive—" He scratched his head. "It's something hotter'n young love on a first date."

"The joint's name is 'Delilah's Temptation'!" Desiree squeaked from the next room. "You should remember. You were there with that skanky Delores Jones the first night we met."

"Yeah, hon." For a moment, Rankles appeared almost embarrassed. "You might try to reach him there," he advised, quickly recovering his cool.

"Sprader's bitch is named Serendipity Smith," Desiree called through the open door, then following her tiny voice into the room, opened a closet door behind Rankles' desk. "Her sister Serpentinity will be there with her in a couple of weeks. Maybe you'd like to come with us to see her. It should be one heckuva show—"

"Yeah, man!" Leonard Rankles said. "I've seen pictures. She wears this live, big-ass—six feet if it's an inch—marble-eyed python wrapped around her neck."

"And it never quits squeezing and twisting." Desiree paused and shuddered deliciously, hugging herself in imitation. She giggled. "Of course, twistin' and squeezin' with a big one's not all bad."

Leonard cackled until his face turned red and his lips blue. I suppose that, in an earlier century, he'd have suffered from apoplexy.

"Sorry—I'll have to take a rain check. Next time she's here, I'll go for sure," I promised. I supposed a writhing, reptilian stole could be the perfect gift for a woman with everything. I made a mental note to tell Sam. She could try one on at the Indy zoo.

Desiree began searching through the closet. I could see that the closet, now converted for storage, had once been a staircase. Reaching high, she plopped a stack of papers onto a hidden step. Turning, she tugged down her tight skirt. Smiling flirtatiously at me over Leonard's shoulder, she moved around his desk. Leonard craned forward until she disappeared into her office.

I waited for Leonard's attention to return to me, then rose to leave. "We'll talk again, Leonard."

"By the way," Rankles said, mixmastering metapors, "Rankles' Business Brokers is primarily here to provide help, or a way out of the tall timber, for small companies that have hit rough water. I could just as easily help a big company like yours. You needin' any managerial advice?"

"For now, just the letters, Leonard. Just the letters." Rankles looked crestfallen. "Hey, cheer up! Those babies are good enough to kill for. Maybe later, after we settle the letter situation we can make bigger plans."

Rankles' broader smile stretched his thin lips, exposing rotten gaps left by missing molars.

Through the closing door, I heard Rankles yell for Desiree. "Come on in here, honey." I peeped over my shoulder. His attention gone from me, he waved the five hundred-dollar bills in the air. "There's no reason for you and Big Daddy to eat alone."

I wished Rankles would stow those letters in a lockbox. They offered rock-hard solutions for me. They could also get a greedy and careless man whacked. I would've promised the moon to make him preserve that packet of letters—for me.

I debated doing it, then thought aloud, "Nope, I'll wait till later."

During my first meeting with Captain Raphael Redonzo, I had been certain he suspected me of being a stalker, not the protector I pretended to be. Obviously, Samantha's 911 call and my being there at the scene cleared the picture.

Back in the car after my visit with Rankles, I dialed police headquarters and Redonzo's extension. Spared a voice mail purgatory, I reached him first ring. "Captain," I asked, "in this region, would a murder victim's facial reconstruction be done locally or at a State Police lab?"

Hesitation. "Why do you ask?" I could almost hear an invisible barrier snapping into place. That and some invisible antenna cranking higher so he could better detect nuances and inflections in my words.

I jogged him about the dead arsonist found in the sump pit.

"No, Mr. Scott, here in Bloomington and in surrounding counties, law enforcement assigns the reconstruction task to a retired IU professor. Your house is outside our jurisdiction, but the town of Stonecrop would do the same."

"Care to share the name?"

"Sorry, no," he concluded, dryly. The phone's click provided a period to end the sentence. And the conversation.

I called Samantha. "Sam, Captain Redonzo tells me that one of IU's retired professors now does facial reconstruction on corpses."

"Could you be more explicit?"

Previously, I'd told Sam about the body in the sump pit. For the first time, I described its parboiled condition. "The police hope the prof can produce a recognizable facsimile of the original."

She asked where she could reach me and said, "I'll have an answer in ten minutes, tops."

I started to toss the phone into the passenger seat, but heard Sam's voice. "It's undoubtedly too late to visit the professor. Tonight, please drop by for a drink. By then I'll have the name. We'll talk about that," she paused, the silence absolutely pregnant, "and we'll certainly have other things on our minds, as well."

I yelled, "Yippee!" then glanced in my rearview mirror. Joe Petry's Buick was parked no more than five feet to the rear of my car. His eyes fixed on the back of my head, he raised a clenched fist and shook it.

I pulled from the curb mumbling under my breath. "What a deal! I didn't bring a weapon. Both my .45 and the shotgun are still sealed inside the wrecked car."

Was Petry still toting that hog-leg? I supposed so. Then, three on the couch—Sam, Joe Petry carrying the Glock 19, and me—would certainly add challenge to our evening's romance.

Chapter Twenty-nine

S UDDEN AS A MONGOOSE slithering into a muddy hole, Joe Petry's car disappeared from the street. I scratched my head.

Driving in a straight line, I'd just gone ten blocks. For most of it, dark eyes glaring, Joe Petry followed within two car lengths of my bumper. Glancing into the rearview mirror, I made a fast run through a corner. When I again looked back, I did a double-take. Petry's car had disappeared.

For certain, with Petry dogging my fanny, I couldn't continue to go unarmed. I dialed my cellular.

A small voice answered, "This is Herschel Peters, Maintenance Supervisor, at your service."

"Herschel, see if you can pry my .45 handgun or my twelve-gauge shotgun from the Jag's wreckage. If either still works, how about dropping it off at Samantha's house."

"Okay, Mr. Scott." But his voice sounded doubtful. I pictured him wearing a concerned look, his gentle, dark brown eyes flitting from side to side beneath the huge cap bill. "Don't forget that fire got mighty hot . . ."

"Yeah, Herschel, I was there," I said—too abruptly—then rethought my comment. "Of course, without your help, I would've been fried along with the guns."

Herschel's outlook brightened. "If you're expecting trouble, I can come right over. I'll bring a pipe wrench for you and a tire iron for me. Or, if you'd like, you can have the tire iron, I'll . . ."

"Thanks," I said. "Teamed up, we'd certainly take care of business."

Saying goodbye, I curbed my car in front of Samantha's house and switched off the key. Two blocks away, tires screamed as Joe Petry's Buick skidded around the corner and roared down the street.

Mine was the only car parked on the block. Petry's car hugged the curb, aimed straight for my trunk lid.

Yelling, "You suicidal S.O.B.!" I dove for the floorboard. Clenching my teeth, I waited for a crushing impact. Tires screamed as Petry yanked the steering wheel hard left. Careening by, inches from my door, his auto sped off down the street.

I leapt from the car.

Her silhouette framed in the doorway and her body paralyzed by fear, Samantha stood watching. I shook my fist in fury before moving rapidly up the sidewalk. As I cleared the top step, I extended my arms, and walked into the circle of hers. "Oh, my darling!" she exclaimed, burying her face in my chest. "Are you okay?"

"Yeah . . . I guess. But I'm getting bloody tired of diving onto floorboards. First, I was almost squashed at the factory: now this. Next car buy, the salesman will ask if I'm into big engines, CDs and super sound systems. I'll tell him the only required options are a crash helmet, a roomy floorboard, and an extra-plush carpet."

I tipped an imaginary glass, and silently, Samantha and I voted two-to-none for stiff drinks. We retired inside and moved down the hall to the alcove bar and searched the booze cabinet. "Hey, hey, hey!" I exalted. "My favorite, Knob Creek bourbon—"

"It's a left over from Joe. It was his favorite too."

"So? The guy isn't a complete loser, after all," I said, my tone dryer than the two bottles of Bombay Sapphire gin I'd just moved while reaching for a liter of Stolichinaya vodka.

I pondered the contradiction: I wanted to avoid all contact with

Joe Petry. I wouldn't have borrowed his gloves, even if my solidly frozen fingers were breaking off at the knuckles. Nevertheless, I felt a keen sense of revenge while uncapping his favorite booze.

My ex would've said "it's a guy thing"—a testosterone-fed reaction to successfully one-upping a courtship competitor. I conjured an evil grin as I sniffed the bourbon's mellow aroma. Undoubtedly, Barb had nailed my motivation!

While Sam waited in the living room, I returned to my past by going into the kitchen and mixing a couple of especially muscular drinks. For myself, I knocked back a shot of the Knob Creek for luck, then poured a double vodka. For Sam I sloshed in two generous shots of bourbon, went light on the vermouth, added a dash of bitters, and decorated my handiwork with two maraschino cherries.

I handed her a glass and raised mine in a toast. "Here's to happy manhattans and delightful stolies, Samantha, followed by a glass of Chateau Souverain, and . . ."

"To us," Samantha said, the ice in the glass tinkling a joyful sound. "May this be the most exciting night we've ever spent together."

It was a most meaningful moment in a very confusing evening. My eyes drank her in. A charcoal pullover with a black polo collar complemented simple earrings and a Celtic horse broach. The combination of silver jewelry and dark clothing accented her creamy white skin and black hair. Carefully smoothing her hip-length sweater and knit skirt, she seated herself on the sofa. Kicking off her ballet style flats, she folded her shapely legs onto the cushion and sat facing me.

For a moment, I thought of Cait back in New York. I felt a twinge of guilt, but brushed it aside. "God, Sam!" I gasped, "You're ravishingly beautiful tonight."

"Even though being near you fills me with excitement, I can never feel totally beautiful," she said wearily. "Joe intrudes on my every thought. If only he would allow us to live our lives peacefully."

Incredible! I thought to myself, Joe Petry couldn't prevent us seeing one another, but—even at a distance—he had the power to dictate our emotional states. "Sam, with Joe, or any stalker, it's all about control, and he's managing that. Keep remembering, he wants you to never find happiness. If he ever suspects you have, he'll become even more dangerous.

"Right now, his emotions are totally unsettled, because he's sharing you with me. He knows I'm here. This minute, he's probably grinding his teeth or chewing on the barrel of my Glock because he pictures you in my arms." I hesitated before sharpening my next statement with a knife-edge of sarcasm. "He'd be delighted knowing he's still the focus of your attention."

Sam sighed. "But no matter how many times I consider it, this situation with my ex-husband seems so patently impossible, and no matter what he does, I keep remembering him as a young man, and the tenderness he once showed . . ." This time, it was she who took a moment for reconsideration. "Surely, an educated, *professedly* religious man like Joe isn't ever expected to become a stalker . . ."

"The cowardly lowlifes come in all shapes and sizes, sweetheart: Getty rich or dirt poor; blockhead dumb or Einstein smart; family doctor or chicken plucker; men or women. Creeps of every sexual preference play their own special games. Hell, today, children of eight are terrorizing and killing other kids just as young, or younger!"

"It still seems impossible that Joe is involved."

"Try this on for size, Sam." I called up more of my library and internet time, "Not long ago, New York Judge Sol Wachtler was a big political gun with career choices of becoming either a U.S. Supreme Court justice or state governor. While a jurist, he chose to menace and threaten a past lover. He even threatened the woman's child while trying to extort money from the kid's mother. After enduring years of emotional turmoil, the woman, with the FBI's help, nailed and jailed him. Christ, I could go on and on and on and on and on!" My voice faded, tiredly.

She brightened. "For ages, Joe seemed to constantly stalk me. Now it's more sporadic—"

"Without doubt, Sam?" I tried to keep my frustration from

showing in my voice. "Now Joe's running a tighter schedule. Half his time he's terrorizing me. Come to think of it, Sam—we are not only stymied by your ex, we're are also batting zero on your case and mine."

Sam nodded, buying into my ploy. "But I've been thinking. Perhaps, instead of defining the cases as 'yours' or 'mine,' we should designate them as 'our' cases. We've crossover suspects who touch each one."

"Hey, Sam, you're right!" Her eyes glowed with excitement.

I knew her high-octane Manhattan, and hopefully, my presence, would do their job. I maintain that there's never too much of a good thing, so I got up to fix new, and stronger, drinks. I tried to ignore the pain still lingering in most of my limbs from the factory fracas; the alcohol helped dull its edge.

Sam walked with me to the bar. "But Richard, although I know you're working a third case for Capital Detective Agency, I've never fully understood the story, nor the implications."

"My old boss pressured me into it. See, some creeps back in Indy built an apartment complex on a poisonous chemical dump. Karl Sprader of Consolidated Constructioneers was involved in the apartment's construction. Talking about dovetailing cases! Now, while I'm investigating his involvement in the Indy case, he's surfaced in Bloomington."

She took a long sip, lifting a questioning eyebrow at my incomplete explanation. "I don't get it."

"Leonard Rankles says Karl Sprader has a special relationship with Jacobi Realty, that the company once watched over the Rose Cutter's Quarry property."

I ambled to the coat closet and pulled the letter from my vest pocket. I gave Sam time to read before continuing, "See, darling, this letter—sold to me by Leonard Rankles, proves that Sprader *once* had ties to Jacobi Realty, but still, I can't figure Sprader's connection to this area, today. Especially, now that I'm back in charge of the company, *and*, once again, my company is responsible for the A-frame and Rose Cutter's Quarry."

Samantha's nose wrinkled, a sure sign of puzzlement. "I'd say the letter indicates your land provided some service for Karl Sprader. What could it be? How could he possibly use bare fields? Or a modest A-frame?"

"You've got me. There are many, many things I can't figure out," I said, then once again plowed through my litany of questions. "Who were the people who torched my new house. Why did they do it? Did they believe I'd moved in? Were they merely trying to frighten me from my fraud investigation within my own company, as the jerry can in the yard seemed to indicate?

"Or were they concerned I'd find Jane McNamara's murderer? Had they originally planned to lure me outside and kill me?"

My mind running in circles, I kicked back another slug of Stolie before continuing, "Then consider this: who died in the fire? Your ex-husband threatened me in my house. Later, somebody dry-gulched me in the same room? Was it Joe? Sprader? Who?

"That night, on the way home, I saw Sprader's car. It was traveling the route leading to my house, but that's scarcely a reason to hang him."

"And don't forget another unsolved mystery," Sam said. "You've a determined enemy within your own company. Perhaps he's the person responsible for crushing your car, and attacking you inside your own home."

"Yeah," I muttered, again seething. "Him too. I must be underpaying that ingrate for whatever job he does during the time when he isn't plotting to snuff me."

"And lastly," Sam added, "I suppose that, once again, you'll suspect poor, helpless Seve Jensen."

"Well, without doubt, he's hiding something. And certainly, his health is improving along with his financial condition, now that Fealty Insurance dropped a huge settlement check in his lap."

Sam's face fell. "Oh, Richard! How can all these things be related?"

"Can't say I know—so far. But, I'm going to keep tying the flesh onto the skeleton. I'll find out! Somehow, they're all interrelated:

Gabriel Goodall, Sprader, the Indy fraud case, Sprader's being near my house, Sprader's doing business with my company. Even your ex has a relationship with Goodall who has a relationship with Sprader! And you can bet your last dollar, the good reverend will always be the brains behind anything he's involved in."

"Let's forget all that for the remainder of the evening," Sam suggested, her voice dropping to a seductively soft whisper as her lips broke into a gentle smile. "Or weren't you interested in my promise that this would be 'our' night?" She took the glass from my hand and, leaning forward, placed both our drinks on the coffee table. The subtle movement also brought her face and her heated breath closer, her nearness stirring my desires, her fragrance arousing my libido. "It's been so long since we've really been together."

"Too long," I agreed, my mind melding with hers, my thoughts spinning backward through the years, even as I moved nearer . . .

Our special night had been three years after she graduated from Ohio State and I graduated from Purdue. Our Indianapolis high school class arranged a seventh anniversary class reunion. I suggested that we have our own celebration dinner the following evening. We met at a downtown Indianapolis nightclub. We hadn't planned a romantic interlude—after all, she had married Joe Petry right out of college, and Barb and I had wed two years later after my graduation from 'Nam. But the evening turned into much more than planned.

After a romantic dinner featuring delicious, but long-forgotten seafood and much too much wine, we strolled hand-in-hand toward the lot where we had parked our cars. Passing the Canterbury Hotel, we paused. Without a word, I gently guided her across the sidewalk and through the lobby doors. She opened her mouth to object—but didn't. I diffidently approached the desk.

"Mr. and Ms. Rowinski," I said. "That's Samuel Rowinski." Later, in the room, she teased me about the choice of names.

I remembered her shyness when she ever-so-carefully removed and placed her pleated skirt over the back of the armchair and meticulously arranged the thin, floral shell on the seat cushion below.

But then, without turning away, her eyes fixed on mine, she removed her bikini bra and panties, and dropped them to the floor.

My passion growing, for the first time I saw her trim, graceful body as she moved to the bed and covered herself with a sheet, waiting for me to undress. Her long, dark hair festooned the snow-white pillow. Most of all, I remembered the way she smiled when she held out her arms and whispered, "Richard, come . . . oh, come . . . please hurry . . ."

Tonight, after all those years of waiting, we would be in each other's arms once more. I moved slowly down the sofa and took her in my arms, ever so gently, tenderly, and sweetly. We kissed, ever so deeply. Tonight, there was no resistance as there had been a few nights ago when we moved from the garden to this sofa for our first kiss after so many years.

Finally, neither her son, nor her ex-husband, nor Caitlin, nor anything else could possibly come between us.

I ran my hand beneath her sweater and for the first time in so many years, reveled in the sensual feel of her smooth, silken skin. I fumbled loose her bra strap and cupped her breast in the palm of my hand. Her breath quickened. Mine came in gasps.

"Sam," I murmured, rising and taking her hand. "This will be our night . . ." Our bodies pressing closely together, we kissed again.

Sam took my hand and led us toward the bedroom.

The doorbell rang. The *damned* doorbell rang!

Our eyes riveted on the front door. Then an impatient rapping rattled the door knocker.

I ran over and peered through the peephole lense. Nobody.

"Joe, I'll bet!" I'm a believer that an aggressive offense beats the best defense ever devised. Even if he still had the Glock, I was furious enough to absorb a bullet and still make him eat the barrel.

Grabbing the fireplace poker, I charged back to the door. Flinging it open, I stood balanced on the balls of my feet, my arm tensed, the poker poised.

"Good heavens!" A prim, blue-haired lady cried, while retreating to the far edge of the portico. "Do you always answer the door in this fashion?"

"Mom!" Sam cried, "You weren't expected!"

Sam's octogenarian mother stood her ground though trembling, as if with the ague. "Samantha, why must you persist in associating with violent men? Joseph Petry—an absolute brute. Now . . . this . . . this . . . this Neanderthal!"

"I must say I agree," said a male voice from the edge of the portico. The voice's diminutive owner stepped forward and tilted his head so he could stop eyeballing my shirt pocket and aim a double-whammy glare directly into my eyes.

"Sam, this is my friend Archie Blessing. May we come in or shall we spend the night on the porch? Will you allow us to sit and converse like civilized people or shall you present us with a leashed George and suggest we be immediately be on our way?"

As they came in and sat on the couch, Sam explained her relationship with me and reminded her mom that it went all the way back to high school. She pointed out how, at one time, I had been one of the young punks—although she didn't describe me in those exact words—who stopped by their house after school for chocolate chip cookies. Eventually her mother's scowl gave way to a tentative smile and she looked pleased; evidently she remembered me. Her companion made a slower turn-about, but gradually reversed gears as well.

"Would either of you like some coffee?" Sam asked.

"No, but each of us would like one of those." Sam's mom pointed to Sam's Manhattan and my Stolie.

Wanting a complete break from Joe Petry's booze, I located a bottle of Jack Daniels. First slicing a lemon, I stirred together some apricot nectar, lime juice, and a few other ungodly ingredients. In the end, I presented our two guests with a colorful bombshell masquerading as "Heavenly Aprijacks."

An hour later, Sam's mother and friend finished petting big, shaggy George, and downed the last drops of their deadly, high-octane drinks. "George, we'll be on the road early, so you go immediately to sleep," Sam's mother said, waggling a finger in the dog's direction. Reciprocating, George wagged a golden tail in a happy answer.

We watched as, unsteadily, they climbed the stairs to their respective bedrooms. My dreams of a romantic night snafued, I gave Sam a long, reluctant, goodnight kiss and shagged back into the Jag, once more on the road again, planning to trek the same old route to an cold, empty, womanless bed in my desolate A-frame. But the thought chilled me.

Feeling vulnerable, I recollected a previous night when I had been attacked in my living room. The house should be empty. But what if it weren't? Oh, well, I had to stop by the factory, anyway, to pick up Herschel.

"You ready to go, Herschel?"

"Thanks, but my car's fixed, so I won't be needing a lift home." I watched as he polished the grease from a saucer-sized roller bearing. Lovingly, he turned the piece over and over in his hands, smiling at his own reflection.

"By the way, I'd planned to bring these to Miss Samantha's." he said, producing my weapons. "See, the pistol is good as brand-new, but the shotgun's stock is splintered and scorched. I sanded it as best I could and was waiting for the glue to dry."

I slipped the .45 in my coat pocket. Rubbing my fingers over the shotgun's still-tacky glue, my index finger strayed inside the trigger guard. "Thanks, Herschel. At the next dance, I'll call the tune."

Chapter Thirty

As I ROUNDED THE FINAL curve before reaching my driveway, the Jag's brights highlighted Herschel Peters's mailbox and swept down his driveway. Two dozen yards beyond, they reflected from another pair of headlights sitting well back in a sassafras copse. I glanced at the dash clock.

Young love's still cookin' at three in the morning? I mused. Thinking like a curmudgeon, I said, "Don't teenagers have homework or curfew, or jobs anymore?"

Suppressing a smile, the comment sent me on a nostalgic trip down memory lane. Sleepy and still focused on Sam, I recalled the late hours she and I once kept in high school, and how fresh and lovely she had been the next day—even after a three o'clock session. Today, in her forties, she still retained her youthful good looks. Back then, although she was a well-developed adult with full, ample breasts, I could almost encircle her trim waist with my hands. What's more, she was studious. Where most of us scratched for excuses to escape classes, she buried herself in her books; few classmates ever really knew her. The girls thought her unfriendly and unapproachable; the boys were perplexed. She studied too much, yet was far too attractive to write off as a nerd.

Though I conspired to spend every available minute with her, her mother stymied my most creative schemes. Because of her mother's machinations—or because of our own fears—we dated throughout high school, but never slept together. Tonight would have been only our second night together, but her mom had queered that deal as well! Perhaps it was fate. Considering the interruptions and frustrations, backseat necking might still be our best, or only, option.

Steering into my driveway, I quit smiling and imagined the driver's view from that parked car. The A-frame was visible. Was that same creep again waiting for me to arrive home?

The thought wasn't preposterous. I'd endured some memorable moments since moving into the old homestead. I shivered, remembering the night I sat with my naked, wet butt glued to the sandpaper surface of a block of limestone. It had seemed hours before my attacker lost patience and drove off.

I decided I had to know who was in the parked car. At this encounter, however, I would take the offensive, but with a bonus—surprise!

Spearing the accelerator, I sped to the front of the house. In the space of a hundred heartbeats, I doused the high beams, hurried inside, turned on all the lights, pulled the blinds, rushed through the kitchen, baled out the back door, and scurried back to the Jag. Leaving its lights off, I drove slowly to the end of the drive and parked where passing traffic couldn't spotlight my car and make it visible. Moving fast now, I yanked the shotgun and a flashlight from the trunk, then eased down the lid. Thinking like a soldier, I reverted to my first hitch's basic training mode. Dropping into a grunt's crouch, I maintained a low profile on my way toward the partially hidden, parked car.

The ground was frozen. That was good. This would be my first lesson in Anti-stalkers 101, the Richard Scott edition, and I didn't want to leave tracks. Unfortunately, on the hard ground, my wingtips resonated like hobnailed boots.

Easing through the thicket, I stepped into the middle of a bramble thicket and felt the briars bite into my calves and thighs. I swallowed a heartfelt "Holy hell!" but pushed on. For a moment, I lost my bearings and halted mid-stride.

Now what? Not wanting to stumble into the side of the car and either frighten the romance out of a couple of kissy-facing lovebirds or—worse yet—get shot by a jerk motivated by hot-blooded hatred, I edged cautiously forward a foot at a time.

The car's interior lit up. Inside, a squinting, blinking Joe Petry checked his watch. I eyeballed him, and the seat beside him. My Glock lay on the cushion, inches from his fingers.

I teetered on the tips of my toes. The shotgun wavered in my hands, its barrel inches from the car's front door.

In the distance, Herschel Peters' dogs barked. Farther away a hound bayed a long, mournful answer.

Petry rolled down the window, placed his ear near the opening, and sat listening.

I was so near the car the smell of his cologne rode the wave of heat from the opened window.

After a moment, Petry raised the window, fired the engine, adjusted the heater and switched off the overhead light.

Afraid of catching the shotgun on a twig or limb, careful to stay clear of the car, I eased my way around to the passenger's side of the car. Now, I vowed, Joe would find that—although it's easy to bluff the helpless—playing around with the "Big Boys" is a dangerous game.

Drawing way back, I slammed the gun butt into the side window. Flicking the flashlight on, I reached through the shattered window and grabbed the Glock.

Cursing, Petry recoiled, his body slamming against the driver's door. Quickly recovering, he grabbed for the shift lever.

Falling to the ground, I aimed the flashlight, then the shotgun. I pulled the trigger and blasted the rear tire.

The hubcap ripped free of the wheel and rattled into the darkness. Rubber laden air, dirt, and spent gunpowder swept through the flashlights's beam and into my nose and eyes.

The car lurched forward.

Rolling to my left, I blasted the other rear tire.

Front-drive wheels clawing for traction, the car roared onto the road. Rear bumper barely clearing the blacktop, the Buick clattered away. Spinning rims sliced the tires and hurled shredded rubber to either side of the car. The other rear wheel cover tore free and clattered across Herschel Peters' driveway.

I shook my fist in jubilation, then quickly aimed once more. The blast blew an advertising frame from around the license plate.

My job was done. As planned, I hadn't injured Petry. Even the last shot had been carefully aimed so it wouldn't hurt him or explode the gas tank. I had sent a buckshot-laden message: "Sam and I are no longer thinking benign supplications or easily ignored court injunctions, Joe Petry. You screw around with Sam, I'll shotgun you into the netherworld. Get it, sucker?"

I hoped the message totally changed his emphasis from Sam to me. I wanted him to believe he had to kill me to get to Sam. Of course, it was part bluff. I wouldn't kill him. Or would I?

More good news: I'd reclaimed my Glock.

Back in the house, I checked the piece, then tossed it on the table in disgust. Now, I was a pistol thief. This Glock was a stranger. Mine was still MIA.

Chapter Thirty-one

SAM ARRANGED THE MEETING with Simon Leveroux, the forensic artist who proposed to mold a face onto the skull found in the mansion's sump pump. To keep the appointment, I made the twenty-mile trip from Bloomington to deep into Brown County, Indiana's miniature answer to the Smoky Mountains. But I didn't mind.

An avid environmentalist, I enjoyed the drive. I like woods and hills, although I prefer visualizing the land the way it appeared when moccasin-wearing Delawares and Shawnees padded along its trails. I feel cheated that we had lost those first settlers, along with the land's original magnificence.

Perhaps my Granddaddy Scott shaped my attitude. An early twentieth-century peddler, he said even when he was traveling, much of the land around Brown County still retained its original splendor. He painted word pictures of rutted wagon roads meandering through densely forested hills with oaks, poplars, maples and sycamores sometimes towering two-hundred feet into clear unpolluted air.

He claimed that, during his dad's lifetime, squirrels could've walked across Indiana, from border to border, without touching earth. Wide-eyed, certain an eight-year-old such as I could've done it equally well, I pictured my pony-league buddy Jimmy Smith, a dozen pet squirrels, and me, swinging from tree to tree, high enough in the air to escape black bears, happily on our way to the Buffalo trace down near the Ohio River.

Today, however, was a real-life adventure. At ten A.M. sharp, I parked and sat gazing at Simon Leveroux's unique home. Fitting! The retired art prof, who could restore the facial structure of dead people, lived in a picture-postcard house.

I stared at a nineteenth-century, one-room schoolhouse, converted into living quarters, an ancient, red-brick building now forming the crossbar in an H-shaped, wood-framed residence. The entrance remained in the crossbar portion, and I suspected that the adze-carved door had been originally used by pioneer school kids. I did wonder about the sign on the arch above the front gate: HOUSE OF WEEPING WALLS.

I followed a winding stone walk to the central porch and knocked. A tall, angular man with shoulder-length black hair answered, "You're Samantha Petry's Richard Scott, I presume." His broad smile showing white, even teeth, he stepped back and held wide the heavy-timbered door.

Winking, I said, "Yep, I belong to Sam."

In a warm handshake, he wrapped my hand with long slender fingers. "Pardon my attributing the possessive to Samantha. However, in describing you, she gushed like a schoolgirl with a first boyfriend. For her, I would do almost any favor, so I quickly agreed to allow you a peek into what would normally be confidential police business."

"Thanks. It'll be our secret." I chuckled. "And certainly, I won't repeat the schoolgirl-boyfriend simile."

"Yes, Sam deserves the best. She's a good person, and such an excellent teacher with tremendous rapport with her students. Her ex-husband is an absolute ass. A bullying Neanderthaloid. And I hear he continues to be involved in her life . . ." For a moment, the retired prof appeared embarrassedly trapped by his own outspokenness. A phone's interrupting beep took him—and he took it—off the hook.

When I followed the sharply curving driveway from the main road, I had glimpsed forty-foot-high, wooden stilts supporting rear sections of the house. While Leveroux talked, I strolled from the old schoolhouse section and into a window-enclosed back room.

Even as I watched, a red-headed pileated woodpecker landed upside down on a cage feeder, its red crest blurring as it rat-a-tatted a greasy blob of suet. I shifted for a better view. Alarmed, with a flash of wings it just as quickly shifted to the top limb of a distant maple.

Further away, a panoramic view encompassed a seemingly limitless wilderness, with the tall, leafless trees almost hiding the few houses, cabins, barns, and outbuildings scattered throughout the deep valley.

Several miles in the distance, the land sloped up into tall hills that walled the far edge of the valley. I supposed this was about the way things appeared when the world was in its infancy, Adam had just met Eve, and together they nibbled the first apple . . . back when the chainsaw had yet to be created.

Leveroux finished his call and rejoined me. "You've got Brown County's best view," I marveled.

He nodded agreement. "And to think those trees are all second and third growth. Imagine it before the loggers stripped the hills." He continued, "The prime growth went for buildings and bridges, smaller trees for barrels and crossties, and much of the oak to tanneries. They used the bark for tanning and left many of the huge logs to rot."

I added, "Along the way, I suppose, they sawed the lumber needed to build Indianapolis."

"Yes . . . and much, much more."

Like any good teacher, he seemed anxious to share and expand on the history lesson. "After the hills were denuded, the local farmers kept a few plots open for corn, sorghum cane, pumpkins, truck gardens, and grazing land. Unfortunately, through poor agricultural practices, even the strength of the land was depleted.

"Those not farming settled in, letting new trees grow up around them. Later in the century, they needed a more lucrative cash crop and sold plots of land to city people wanting to build vacation or retirement retreats.

"Now, the people in the village of Nashville pull their dollars from the tourist trade. Out here, land speculators flourish along with the second growth of timber." His lips tightened. "The speculators thrive on selling and developing the land so Brown County will eventually become much like the places our new immigrants were fleeing when they departed from Indianapolis, or Tucson—or wherever."

"Do you attempt to save the land, or have you surrendered to the inevitable?" I asked.

"We who love this place will never quit fighting. People such as I—especially the local artists, musicians and environmentalists—wage a constant battle, but it's almost impossible to save people from their own greed." He suddenly looked weary. "Holding back the influx of dollars and people is as difficult as pushing water uphill."

Simon Leveroux abruptly snorted his disgust and, turning, took me by the elbow, guiding me through a side door. "I mustn't forget that you've come to solve a felony against individuals, not the crimes against nature which ultimately injure us all."

Inside what appeared to be a lab, I gazed around the room. "This is where I do my work," he explained.

A blackboard took up the top two thirds of a far wall. I suspected it was an original from the days when this part of the house was a one-room schoolhouse. Now it held sketches and notes about the human anatomy instead of arithmetic or Johnny's "I love you Suzie" notes of decades ago.

Beneath the board, a number of wire busts stood on a work bench, each topped by a skull. Several of the skulls had been plastered with modeling clay; faces were in various stages of completion.

"My God!" I exclaimed. "This part of the country must be in the midst of a crime spree—" Pointing toward the skulls, I counted aloud, ending at ten.

"Not at all. I do work for surrounding cities and counties as well. One body was found in an interstate ditch near Cincinnati. Abraham—there, on the far end—came from a Louisville archeological dig. The two on his left came from an aircraft crash."

"Which is mine?" I asked.

"This one," he said, gently caressing the forehead of a semi-completed skull. "For a while, it was a terribly difficult project. That fire must've been intense. Like cremation."

He explained, "In cremation, the body is burned at temperatures in excess of fifteen hundred degrees Fahrenheit and for periods of time ranging from thirty minutes to three times that, depending on the corpse's weight. This individual's skull not only exploded, part of it completely disintegrated. I've had to do a great deal of repair, both with super glue and with filler plastic."

I described the house where they discovered the skull, along with other body remnants, and pointed out that the house had a gas-fired boiler and that the supply pipe had broken within inches of the sump pit. "I suppose the gas gushing from that line contributed a few degrees to the conflagration."

He nodded agreement.

"Do you feel optimistic that you can develop a realistic clay facsimile of his original face?"

"Certainly. We have many advantages. Through recovery of the lower torso, we know the victim was Caucasian. Different racial groups have different skin thickness properties. We know sex. Age is estimated to be between thirty-five to forty. We also know hair color and approximate weight—"

I interrupted. "What can you tell about eyes and ears and lips? Seems that those characteristics would be required for a definite ID."

"Again, we have our own techniques. For example, the mouth will always be the width of the six front teeth. I can say with reasonable certainty the thickness of this victim's skin at his glabella, his gonial angle, his inferior malar—"

"What about eye color? Ear shape, size?"

"Due to skin coloration, I believe this subject probably had brown eyes. The ears are a question mark. Ears, being soft tissue, are quickly lost to fire or decomposition."

"May I return for another look-see when you're further along?" I asked.

"Certainly. Come back in a week."

On my departing, he sent his best to Sam and then went back to cementing tiny rubber washers to specific facial points. He explained that those would guide him when he applied clay, in varying thicknesses, to different parts of the face. The washers, he said, were cemented into place with soluble glue. Later, they and the clay could be removed without harming the skull.

I left, believing the far-from-finished product already resembled somebody from my past. But, racking my brain, I couldn't dig out a name or place. The feeling rode herd on me, sending chills skittering up and down my spine throughout the entire return trip to Bloomington. Who? Who? Who?

Chapter Thirty-two

FOUR MILES UP THE ROAD, while I was still pondering the "House of Weeping Walls" sign, my cell phone beeped. It was Sam with two pieces of news she couldn't wait to share.

"Do you remember the night at the Fourth Street Inn when I mentioned that the university planned to sponsor a joint student-teacher tour to London?" She allowed a pregnant interval to lapse while I racked my brain. "Well, Richard, it's now firm: Our group departs from Indianapolis International airport one week from today!"

Her voice filled with excitement, she went on to explain that while there she'd work on her doctorate. "That'll involve traveling fifty miles to Chicksands Priory where the nun, Rosata, was entombed during the time of King Henry the Eighth."

"Do you plan to meet her?" I asked, chuckling.

"Perhaps. After all, she's on a clockwork schedule. Remember that, most dependably, she strolls the halls on the seventeenth of each month."

I heard the rustle of paper and supposed she was checking her itinerary. "Great!" She exclaimed with relief. "I'll be there in time to see it."

"Don't end up cemented into the same wall," I warned. "You will always be needed back here—badly. Especially by me."

"Perhaps I'll cancel," Sam laughed. "Oh, yes, and the Chicksands Priory has been home to both the Royal Air Force and the United States Air Force, as a communication base. Under the British it received and sent to Bletchley Park the signals that helped decipher the German's 'Enigma' code, a big factor in defeating Hitler's forces."

"God, you'll be into international espionage as well!" I teased.

"While at Chicksands, I also plan to visit the site of what was once the world's largest elephant cage." She ended the sentence with a mysterious laugh, but I didn't pursue it.

"No ADE employees are scheduled for work this weekend, so I'm staying home and spending the time examining company records."

"Hmmm! I was hoping to see you, but I guess I can use some catch-up time prior to my trip. Oh, say—here's the other important item." She read me a just-published announcement in today's newspaper about Reverend Goodall's political fund-raiser in Adam's Trace. "Will you plan to go?"

My antenna waggled. "You betcha, sweetheart! No way I dare miss a big-time event in Abram's Trace, especially one with that cast of characters."

"Good idea! It'll keep you out of trouble, Richard."

"Yeah," I agreed, "But it doesn't seem fair. You began with the question: 'Why did Henry the Eighth destroy the Gilbertine religious order?' Now, you're delving into the murders of Anne Boleyn and Katherine Howard, chasing a spook around an ancient priory—plus discussing more modern, W-W-Two spooks of the James Bond variety."

"But, darling, you have a multitude of mysteries here—"

"Don't try to soft-soap me, sweetheart. While you're flitting around the globe, and dealing with ancient history, British royalty, and international espionage. I'll be staying home and chasing down-home killers of the Hoosier variety."

Somehow, I didn't agree with Sam—the meeting in Abram's Trace was far more likely to get me into trouble, than keep me out of it. How could I forget? That was Caitlin McChesney's and my old stomping ground. Cait had said she wanted to come see me. If she picked that time to visit, it could lead to the worst kind of complications for Sam's and my relationship.

Still, I keep saying, "I'm an optimist."

Chapter Thirty-three

UNAWARE I WAS ABOUT to attempt a fast start in a fixed race, I awoke Monday morning at five o'clock, sharp. At that moment, though unable to perceive the future, the next seven days stretched ahead of me like a week's journey through hell, with land mines guarding all corners and jolting surprises lurking beyond each turn.

Developments in both my personal life and the convoluted cases unfolded quickly. At first, some appeared insignificant. Many others, far more ground-shaking. Every last one packed a trainload of consequences.

Sam's urgent phone call, a few minutes after I awoke, set the tone: "Richard, I must see you. Immediately!"

"No sweat. I'll be at your house within the hour. Better yet, make that forty min—"

She cut me short. "No, I'll come to you."

"Any hint why?"

She began an explanation, then merely whispered, "Goodbye."

Since I had just spent two days plodding through company records, this would be our first face-to-face since Friday. In retrospect, we should've spent the time together, since my sleuthing hadn't fingered any of the sleaze-balls scamming the company. Oh, I uncovered one peculiar book entry: my ex-papa-in-law had made a substantial contribution to Reverend Goodall's Final Prophet. In cash!

While waiting for Sam, I primed and stoked the coffee maker. Already freshly showered, I slipped from my motley gray warmups into a faded plaid shirt, threadbare denim jeans, and a pair of decrepit sneakers on which I'd logged more miles than the average over-the-road freight hauler.

A glance in the mirror showed my sartorial elegance hadn't improved an iota. Trying for at least a minimal upgrade, I combed my hair and—not wishing to emulate the UnaBomber—dragged out the electric clippers and trimmed my shaggy beard.

Still no Samantha, I dialed her cell number. The operator mono-toned, "The unit you are calling is unavailable. Please try your call again later."

Angst-driven, I surfed TV news and weather, then admitted that I was interested only in news about Sam. Moving to a corner of the living room, I punched the computer's power button, tapped into e-mail, and clicked on the red-flagged mailbox.

Again, Cait insisted I join her in New York for a short visit. As if a lover's reunion wouldn't be enough, she included another enticing offer: tickets to "It Ain't Nothin' But The Blues," at Lincoln Center's Vivian Beaumont Theater.

If plans A and B were impossible, she had a possibly superior plan C. I paged down. Just then, flying gravel peppered the front sidewalk, a rock-solid announcement that Sam had skidded her red Metro to a four point, driveway landing.

Kicking aside my chair, I rushed outside. Leaving the door agape, I barreled down the sidewalk, reaching the car just as Sam opened the door.

Her lips set in tight lines, skin pale beneath the faint outside light, she struggled to retain her composure. "I'm hopelessly trapped, utterly desperate!" she cried.

"What is it, darling?"

"Please be patient. I've spent hours collecting my thoughts. Now, with you close, my defenses have crumbled, and I'm falling apart." She fell into my arms, blinking away tears. "Instead of talking, I just want to cry."

Gently, I kissed her and stroked her shoulders, then wrapping my arm around her waist, guided her up the sidewalk, onto the porch, and into the A-frame. Once inside, I removed and hooked her velour-collared, black wool cape on a coat rack, the austere house's substitute for a guest closet.

Certainly, Sam wasn't disheveled. She wore a three-button, charcoal jacket over a slate-gray wool dress, with silver, twisted-hoop earrings and a matching necklace adding a touch of elegance. She looked thoroughly competent and coldly businesslike, her appearance belying her emotions.

Of course, being a shallow jerk, I was struck by another facet of her outfit. The black, high-heeled pumps accented the shape of her calves, reminding me she had absolutely exquisite legs. Anyway, her dress was much too grand for an early morning visit to the A-frame, and furthermore, those weren't her normal teacher's duds. She usually dressed casually, her appearance youthful like her students. Obviously, she had a later appointment and needed to impress someone. Or she had a dreaded appointment and subscribed to the aphorism, 'Never let the bastards see you sweat."

Sam seemed preoccupied, not yet ready to share. She ambled aimlessly into the tiny kitchen and idly raised the shade, as if stalling for time or collecting her thoughts, then briefly gazed from the side window, onto the morning's dark wall.

I didn't push. When ready, she'd come around. While she dawdled, I poured and carried two cups of potently black coffee into the living room, to plop onto the scotch-plaid sofa.

Decision reached, Sam strode purposefully from the kitchen and, curling those gorgeous legs beneath her, sat beside me.

"So, is Joe Petry the problem?"

She nodded. "Last night, he called and proudly announced an

exciting surprise in store for me. With a curt 'No thanks,' I hung up. He continued calling well into this morning; having caller ID, I ignored him."

It was my turn to lift a questioning eyebrow. I did, adding, "And you didn't unplug the phone?"

"I know, Richard," she said, impatiently. "I realize I should have unplugged the phone, but I so deeply resent losing control of any part of my life. Even if it's only incoming calls."

When I was growing up, my mom always cautioned my sister and me that troubled people need a patient listener, not some egocentric interrupting with questions or solutions. After that one intrusive lapse concerning the phone, I followed Mom's advice and—except for understanding nods and an occasional "Hmmm!"—stayed silent. Of course, enforced silence places intense pressure on us know-it-alls who possess both a pipeline to ultimate truth and an urgency to share it.

Sam had expected an early morning call from her mother. She interrupted our conversation to dial her. "Please, Mom, I'm with Richard, so don't worry . . ." I liked her thoughtfulness in calling her mother. Even better, I was pleased they both found my presence reassuring.

Waiting, mind wandering, I rethought my mother's lesson. Mom, by suppressing me early on, might have committed irreversible damage to my tender psyche. What a tragedy! If I'd been allowed unfettered development, I might've had the smarts to out-think all the murderers, scam artists, and stalkers populating my cases. Maybe, then, those mysteries solved and me a renowned genius, perhaps Larry King would've requested a booking. After all, in this country, an authority in one area is considered a guru in all others.

"Mr. Richard Scott," he'd declaim, leaning so near I'd fight an urge to reach out and snap his red suspenders. "I understand you not only untangled a series of complicated criminal cases but, in your spare time, discovered solutions to the age-old problems of world hunger and lasting peace. For your adoring fans, please explain fully . . ."

While I soberly nodded my head, he'd glance over the top of his mike, toward an off-camera clock. "We have exactly three minutes until sign-off, which should provide adequate time . . ."

Snapping me back from my sidebar reverie, Sam said, "Goodbye, Mom, and take good care of George," and turned back to resume her story. I locked onto her every word.

"Our university group is flying commercial to London. This morning, with sleep impossible, I called Delta to arrange for a car at Heathrow. The computerized schedule advisory had malfunctioned, so I talked with a human."

Exasperated, she leaned far back on the sofa and raised her eyes in helpless supplication. "The agent asked that I repeat my given initial . . ." Her eyes still fixed on the ceiling, she pounded the cushion with both fists. "Because *two Petrys* are booked on Flight 4462 to London."

"Don't tell me—the second passenger is Joseph Petry!"

"Yes! Can you imagine my consternation?"

"My God! That was his exciting promise. He'll fly to England and stalk you there!" Propelled by a surge of adrenalin, I sprang to my feet and paced the floor, finally stopping with my back to the fireplace, my head just beneath the hook where the elk head's once hung. "Sam, even after the grief your ex has caused, that psycho creep is still convinced you still want him." I longed to replace the elk's head with Joe Petry's, either pinned to the wall, or discarded in the crawlspace!

My mind searched for answers. I don't pick fights, but goaded, I'm like a boxer who drops into a crouch and swings for the KO. When menaced, I settle into a fighting mind-set, and hammer away with fresh ideas until I win. Just then, I desperately needed a knockout idea. However, Since I'm a first cousin to all human juggernauts, confusion doesn't slow me. "Joe Petry will either cancel his flight plans, or I'll cancel him," I blustered. Involuntarily, my voice dropped dangerously low. Ultimately, that response spells danger for an opponent.

My muscular promise had strong, reassuring words for Sam, and that was my intent, precisely. Even I gained confidence! But how to back the big words? Easy—MIA!

Sam continued, "I planned to see Captain Redonzo, first thing today. Though there aren't provable grounds for his arrest, I want injunctive relief, strong enough to keep Joe at a distance, and most importantly, off that plane.

"Dreading an inevitable, embarrassing court appearance, but determined not to appear as a vulnerable, downtrodden and helpless victim, I dressed appropriately." She shook her head in frustration. "It's all so . . . so . . . extremely humiliating."

"Unfortunately," I added, "an injunction may merely infuriate him further and heighten the danger. While inaction might convince him he has carte blanche to do anything he pleases."

"Then what must I do?"

"I'm itching to take him on *mano a mano*, but with your life at stake, I can't take orders from my own testosterone. Nor do I dare to play God . . ." I groped for an answer.

"Sam," I said, wimping out. "Forget my hyperbole. Go ahead. Meet with Redonzo. Maybe we've underestimated his power. Perhaps, if Redonzo orders Petry to stay away, he'll listen."

"No!" Sam's strong voice showed new resolve. "I must never, never forget Lisa Bianco, who relied on our judicial and law enforcement systems—"

"—and paid with her life," I finished the sentence, my words brief, like Lisa Bianco's life had been.

"So, Richard, once again, you are my rock. I can depend only on you."

I wasn't totally surprised. Since I'm a big bozo with a winner's history in school, military, and business, people rely on me and trust me not to fizzle on promises. It's an ego stroker and pressure builder. That's both good and bad. I've always found extreme pressure and good performance to be the most effective partners.

"However, you must not—" She squeezed my forearm in emphasis. "You must not, this time, do anything rash. I don't want you hurt." Leaning nearer, she affectionately stroked my beard before planting a gentle, kiss on my temple.

"I promise. For now, the Buick—and Joe's crotch—are safe." Did that give Petry a broad safety margin? Couldn't say. I was flying by the seat of my pants.

I did persist in telling Sam that an unreadable flight plan offered an excellent training opportunity, while "Old Rocky Top," straight ahead, represented a rare photo op.

Sam prodded me about the previous *Herald Times'* announcement. "Will you definitely go to the Abram's Trace meeting?"

"Wouldn't miss it!" I exclaimed. "Jeanie Robbins provided an invitation." Yanking the invite from my vest pocket, and with a sweeping flourish, I handed it to Sam. Since it was gilt-edged, cursively printed, and greeted my company's CEO as "The Honorable President Winters," I felt theatrics appropriate.

"But this is directed to your ex-father-in-law—"

"Look, Sam, he's in the federal slammer; I'll accept on his behalf. Not only will Reverend Gabriel Goodall speak, Karl Sprader will be on the podium beside him."

"And who knows who else?" Sam commented. Glancing at her watch, she exclaimed she really had to run.

"What say we go for breakfast for the road?" I indicated our two untouched cups. "I'll brew a fresh pot. I never eat in, so food choices are on the skinny side. I can serve a toasted English muffin, with or without butter, or with marmalade. If that doesn't galvanize your taste buds, there's a frost-covered loaf of rye stashed in the freezer, so toast is a definite possibility."

Sam laughed her refusal.

Retrieving her cape from the hook, and silently scheming about the best approach to Joe Petry, I waltzed her to the car.

As I opened the Metro's door for her, she cautioned, "Richard, what will you say to Joe? And again, don't be reckless."

The brisk air smelled country-fresh. With my thoughts suddenly deserting Joe Petry and the whole perplexing case, I didn't respond.

Yawning, and then sucking in a hefty breath, I stood gazing around while Sam fumbled through her overstuffed purse. "Blast it! Where are those car keys?" she complained.

"Hey sweetheart, that's not a purse you carry. It's a mini compactor. Even insurance agent Felton Crenshaw doesn't pack that many goodies into his fat attache case."

Sweeping beyond the nearby stand of silver beech trees, my gaze settled on the dense thicket surrounding Rose Cutter's Quarry. Trees and a sheer cliff hid the dark water, but a thick, malevolent-appearing, gray haze marked its outline.

In contrast, according to WQIP-TV, the remainder of Indiana had been promised clear weather and that pleased me. Yet I knew a faint shiver, remembering the impenetrable fog that delayed my last trip to Midwest Detective Agency. I could still picture the coyote slinking in and out of a fog bank, its sharp eyes tracking my every move. On that day, like an evil omen, the nearby beech's skeletal limbs implored the heavens.

Today, mimicking the improved weather, my mental fog seemed to be clearing and, suddenly, a viable response to Joe Petry began to form in my mind. With it came a keen sense of optimism.

My gaze returned to the silver-gray beech trees. Some camouflaged creature on a lower limb slowly shifted position.

"Look, Sam," I whispered, pointing.

Growing legs, a tree knot metamorphosed into a silver-white opossum, with at least a half-dozen young clinging to her back. While we watched, Mama Possum crawled carefully down a limb, nosed her way into a hole in the trunk and, carrying her brood, disappeared inside the hollow tree.

"Even at Rose Cutter's Quarry, everything isn't about murder," Sam smiled.

"Hold that thought," I challenged, my voice light like hers. Definitely, we were on a roll. Our relationship had reached a new frontier. Sam had entrusted her life to me. My concern for her and hers had deepened, more strongly than ever. I was determined that she would not be hurt.

The Metro's tiny, lawnmower-sized engine ticked alive. "Just wait," I said. Leaning into the window opening, my lips brushed Sam's hair and face, her skin still chilled from the morning air. "I have a perfect, creative response planned for your ex . . ." I murmured, my lips losing their place in the conversation and straying from her cold cheek to her open, inviting lips.

Excited by the heady taste of lipstick, intoxicated by the faint fragrance of rose and narcissus and scintillating jasmine, I, at that moment, remembered those marvelous legs. My body consumed by a sensation having nothing to do with fraud, stalking, or murder cases, I fought an urge to try and entice her back into the house. "Sam, stay . . ." I whispered, conceding the fight.

"Oh, Richard, my love . . ." Her long slender fingers strayed to the ignition key, and for one hopeful second I thought she would stop the engine. But, as if of its own volition, her hand slowly returned to the steering wheel.

Straightening, I pulled myself away from the car.

Smiling, she reached outside and squeezed my hand. "Later," she promised, then slowly closed the window. Her eyes meeting mine and reinforcing her words, she waved and drove away.

Only when Sam's car had became but a faint honeybee hum in the distance, did I manage to force my mind back to the case. It was done with great difficulty, but as always, I focused completely.

My immediate scheme fit right into an overall plan for Joe Petry. It was a spit-and-polish, brand-new idea, having touched my mind just as I reached for the Metro's door latch. Its effectiveness depended on the twelve-gauge, semi-automatic shotgun. Only this project had a special twist with the involvement of a borrowed car, a camouflage outfit, a police scanner—and at least a truckload of good luck.

I grimaced into the morning, then smiled. Perhaps, in my investigations, luck *always* became the major ingredient.

Had I deliberately misled Sam when she insisted I play it safe while dealing with her ex's latest transgression? Hey! In my commitment to Sam, I promised not to again kick Joe Petry in the balls, nor attack his Buick. I hadn't guaranteed his safety. I hadn't ruled out using the shotgun. I might have been guilty of slightly tweaking the truth! But, basically, I was Honest Abe reincarnate.

Was my plan high risk? Without doubt. Worth the risk? With Sam's safety and peace of mind in jeopardy? That made it "no contest"—a shoo-in!

I would keep the pressure on. I would keep a roaring flame under Petry's butt and eventually I would remove him from Sam's life so she would be safe. I would ratchet the stakes into the stratosphere. Either I'd get Joe Petry off the plane and force him to focus his attention on me, or I'd . . .

I couldn't with absolute confidence predict my reactions. I did know, with certainty, that Joe Petry would be a fool to continue his pursuit of Sam.

Back inside the house, I switched the computer from its screen saver to the Internet. Cait's plan C wasn't good. If I couldn't visit New York, she'd meet me in Abram's Trace. According to her, the timing was fortuitous since she still owned property in Abram's Trace and had tax business to transact at the Cavalier County courthouse.

In case I nixed plans A and B, she had already hedged her bets by making plane reservations. The flight would arrive at Indy International, Friday, two o'clock—exactly one-half hour after Sam's departure.

No sweat! Ready to make my life an open book, I picked up the phone and tapped memory dial, prepared to tell Sam the new development. No! First, I would reason with Cait. I'd talk her out of coming. No! I'd meet Cait and *not* tell Sam. No? Still, nothing would happen between Cait and I. I wouldn't allow it; Cait wouldn't want it. Sure, for several months we had an idyllic romance, even living together, but that was water over the dam, or under the bridge . . . or wherever dead romances go to die. So why should I cause Sam additional worry?

"Hi, darling!" Sam answered. Compared to earlier this morning, her voice was cheerful and composed. "Did we overlook something?"

"Sorry, sweetheart." My guilt felt so intense I expected her to suspect a lie. "I hit the wrong dial button. We'll talk again, later—huh?"

There was one morsel of good news: Cait would be flying the same airline as Samantha, so arrival and departure gates should be close together. Saving steps, I'd be able to send away Samantha with a warm "goodbye" embrace at one gate and hurry to the next for a "Hello" kiss from Cait. Lothario, that I am!

One-half hour separated the two flights. Those ETD and ETA schedules would have to be NASA-tight or I'd be armpit deep in romantic complications.

Chapter Thirty-four

ONCE AT MY OFFICE, I dropped heavily into my ancient executive's chair. "Ahhh!," I sighed, grateful for a moment's respite. But my secretary buzzed through the door, long before my buns adjusted to the cushion's soft, well-worn leather.

"Richard," Jeanie admonished, "You are difficult—no, you're impossible!—to catch." Each hand held a packet of paper; she waggled both like semaphores. "I have several situations requiring your immediate attention. Which do you want first?"

"You make the call, or just give me whatever's on top of the thickest stack."

"Okay, I'll begin with the 'bad' and save the 'worst' for last. That one will send you into orbit!"

The first discussion covered personnel problems involving factory and office. One stood out. "Three times in as many months, the company hired and dismissed an hourly employee, Charlie Buford Crockett. With each rehiring, despite the job interruption, he returns with the highest pay allowable for his grade. The human resources department objects; his treatment is making a mockery of the company's hiring practices."

She presented Crockett's employee file. I read his stats: a qualified maintenance worker, forty-three years old, job history showed short stints in several states. Most of his life had been spent in the Bloomington area, where he dropped out in his high school sophomore year, then managed a G.E.D. before enrolling at Ivy Tech and lasting half a semester. His picture showed a balding man, close-set eyes glaring from a heavy, tough-looking, un-sculpted face. His size impressed me: Height, six-feet-six; weight, two hundred and forty-two pounds.

I studied his face more closely. "Christ, Jeanie, that face must take up half of this character's weight! You know, I've seen him somewhere before."

"Try to remember all the dark alleys you've ever visited. That's where Charlie Crockett's most likely to be found," she observed, venom dripping.

I didn't consider alleys. I pictured the crane operator, just before the Jag was bombed. But I couldn't make that profile fit Crockett's face.

The depth of Jeanie's anger intrigued me, yet I didn't fire questions. That's not my style. Instead, I waited for answers to flow naturally from our conversation. "Anyway, this situation falls within Seve Jensen's bailiwick," I said. "Please discuss it with him."

Jeanie colored a bright red. "I have! *Mister—*" She repeated it so I wouldn't miss her emphasis, "*Mister* Seve Jensen signed every deviation slip in Charlie Crockett's file. He even ignored a police record. And he suggested I pay more attention to the *honorable* President Richard Scott's business and keep my nose out of his."

Swallowing my gall, I stayed poker-faced while Jeanie droned on, relaying messages from several business colleagues who had been trying, unsuccessfully, to reach me. There were no messages about the mall job, so I figured Seve Jensen was staying on top of that.

Finally, she sucked in an exasperated breath, ". . . and daily . . . daily, mind you . . . I've dialed the eight-hundred service number to check for fraudulent purchases on your newly issued credit cards. Remember: I canceled the old ones. This report updates you." She slid it across the desk.

The credit card thief had moved across Florida to Sarasota, charging a boat rental there. "Gotta admire this jerk for taking such excellent care of *our* boat. A three-hundred grand investment deserves the best." I frowned. There was better news—charges in Forida ceased two days before the Vanden Plas and I got whacked by falling beams. Also I saw a recent credit card charge on I-75, south of Cincy. I frowned, thinking. "That the day's worst news?"

"No. You'll know when I reach it."

The next report covered Florida's latest hurricane. As usual, Jeanie was on top of her game. "Considering the gravity of this storm, I called your Florida insurance carrier. Your hurricane and homeowner's policies are paid-up and effective."

Jeanie had copied the Internet report, and read aloud: " 'Earlier today, Hurricane Aaron, packing winds of 120 MPH, walloped the Florida Keys.'

" 'Florida's west coast residents are being advised to shut off water, gas and electricity, post a note giving their destination, and take I-75 north to Georgia. We continue to be surprised by this storm's intensity.'

" 'In any event, radical weather pattern changes are especially alarming, when one considers that in ten minutes, a hurricane releases more energy than that contained in the world's nuclear arsenal.' "

I nodded at her recital. "Jeanie, in an offbeat way, I find the last terrifying fact kind of comforting."

She twisted her face into a scowl of disbelief.

"Look, unlike man's lethal mixtures, storms don't kill us with radiation, nor poison the planet for a million generations." Even as I said it, I knew the remark was motivated by the witches' brew Stella found in Indy.

"Now, Mr. Scott, prepare yourself." Jeanie handed me a letter from Scales, Ringster and Barbour, Attorneys at Law.

Dear Mr. Richard Scott:
    Our client, Consolidated Constructioners, Inc. has requested

that we represent them in their cause against your company.

During the years 1991–1993, Architectural Design and Elaboration, aka ADE, performed the design function upon their project, identified in your work documents as Job Number 2510 and designated in theirs: Sandpiper View Condominium High-Rise . . .

The gist of their argument was that, although in the early nineties I hadn't yet purchased Architectural Design and Elaboration, the liability for negligent design continued after the transaction. Consequently, they were holding the company, its subsidiaries, and its present owners responsible. They would seek indemnification for a long list of grievances, including all losses, costs or damages, interruption of business, and most importantly, reasonable attorney fees.

Jeanie had already requested a Dunn and Bradstreet report and received a return fax. Reading rapidly, I ran my finger from line to line in the report.

"It can't be! *Both* Reverend Gabriel Goodall and Karl Sprader are officers in today's version of Consolidated Constructioneers, Inc.!" I snarled, aiming the folder toward the waste basket.

Jeanie retrieved the report. Probably afraid the steam from my ears would parboil innocent bystanders, she scurried around the corner to her desk.

Within seconds, she returned to stand in front of mine. "You have an unscheduled visitor. A Mr. Roger Petry is in the lobby and urgently requests to see you." She shrugged. "I tried to discourage him, but he was very persistent . . . and looks so vulnerable, I just couldn't refuse without asking first."

I grinned. "You're a sucker for a sad story. Okay, I'll see him. Would you please escort this good-looking hunk from the lobby to my office?"

"With pleasure." She seemed on the verge of swooning. "God, he must be important! And sooo good looking!"

"It's the way he dresses, Jeanie. Clothes make the man."

Roger was wearing the same oversized, blue pinstripe suit he had on back at the Chez Royaliste Hotel. Also, he still sported the down-at-the-heels, green-and-white running shoes. I supposed them to be on their last legs, grimacing at my own silent pun.

The phone rang before I could speak or offer a chair. Roger crossed the room to read a couple of my framed bona fides then, attention shifting, picked up the "rose cutter" machining tool. After a close examination, he swung it hammer-like, with the cutting teeth thumping against the heel of his hand. Gritting his teeth, he tucked the rose cutter between his arm and ribs. Alternately, he rubbed his palms together, and licked and sucked life back into his bruised hand.

Much more respectfully now, he replaced the tool on the shelf and took a seat in an armchair near the front of my desk. He looked ill at ease, his long, graceful fingers fidgeting on the chair's upholstered arms, while his dark brown, expressive eyes flitted to and fro—like those of a young bewildered animal spooked by a trap.

Cradling the phone, I rose and extended my hand. "Hi, Roger! What brings you to this neck of the woods?"

Jeanie brought coffee. While Roger took a quick sip, I slipped a coaster to the corner of the desk. His cup rattled against the metal coaster before settling into a firm landing. He clasped his hands to stop their shaking.

"Mr. S, the pressure's awesome—always waiting to be busted for murder." He skidded forward in his chair. "I'm going for the DNA test. I've gotta prove I didn't knock up—uh, prove Janie McNamara's baby couldn't've been mine."

"You're smart, Roger. I'll call and notify Sheriff DeLyle." I reached for the phone.

"No! Wait till I'm gone, then arrange with the sheriff for me to have the test in Indy."

"But why, Roger? Indianapolis is only fifty miles away. If the police wanted you, they'd have driven up and cuffed you."

"I know, but, after what I went through right after Janie's murder, this town frightens me." Unfolding his slender frame from the chair, he climbed to his feet. "Fact is, that about covers today's business."

"While you're here, why don't you drop by and visit your mom or dad?"

"My dad? You gotta be kiddin'!" He sneered. "At one time, my own dad tried to make out with Janie. For awhile, I thought he had. I kept it secret to protect my mother." Then, his voice softened. "I would like to see Mom, though. But being this up-tight, I won't. On the way out of town, I'll risk a short stop at Breaking Fast Restaurants' office to see Clark Benefield. He's an awesome friend. He was right there in my corner when everybody else was saying, 'Screw you, Jack.'"

"Good luck," I said, dryly, walking around the desk to see him out. "If you find Clark Benefield, tell that 'awesome friend' I'd like an appointment. He can name the time."

"I'll give him your best. By the way, Mr. S, I need to make a call. Is there a phone in the lobby?"

"Use that phone," I said, pointing toward the desk near the window. "The phone in the lobby is constantly tied up, and the public one in the booth requires quarters and dimes. Save your shekels and buy that Chez Royaliste blonde a drink. Better yet, buy one for my secretary, Jeanie Robbins."

"Hmm, I'll consider it." When he smiled, his whole face lit up.

I exited the office while he was on the phone, speaking quietly, his long, graceful fingers wrapping the mouthpiece.

Roger's phone style was a far cry from his father's.

"Richard Scott, you rotten, conniving two-bit, gumshoe home-wrecker, I'll do what I want to do, when I want to do it—not what you tell me. I'll go where I wish to go, and I'll make the trip on a plane of my . . . my . . . pref—my . . . select—my own free choice—" Joe Petry ran out of steam, as if attempting to sort and re-stack the words now tumbling from his lips and into cellular phone cyberspace was just too much for his little brain. "Never, never—you hear me?—never, call me again!"

"Shall I interpret that to be a definite no?" I asked.

Having earlier received word that Professor Leveroux had completed his facial reconstruction ahead of schedule, Sam and I were driving to his Brown County home when we made the call to her ex. On the way, we stopped at the Hobnob Corner Restaurant in the tiny village of Nashville for breakfast.

Sam ordered the house quiche. I chose the three-egg omelet. Pictured on the front of the menu, it showed a whole raft of brightly colored ingredients that would be served with fruit preserves and toast. I needed to drop a couple of pounds, but infatuated with the omelet, figured next week to be a better time to begin dieting.

While the cook scrambled eggs and sliced fruit to go with the quiche, I had dialed Petry and opened the door for his diatribe. For a while, we listened silently. Now, smoothly modulating my voice, I tried reasoning, "Look, Petry, I have people watching your every move. You're booked on Sam's flight. I want you off that plane—now! Save yourself a fat package of grief. Cancel!"

"Is Samantha with you, Scott?"

"I'm alone," I lied.

Petry's voice grew in volume. With my fingers, I mimicked lip movements then, with a finger across my lips, handed the phone to Sam. Petry's voice rose to a higher pitch. She laid the phone in the middle of the table so we both might hear.

What an unbelievable paradox. Here we sat in a beautiful, century-old building, our feet planted firmly on inch-thick oak boards, while our thoughts concentrated on Joe Petry's ferocious, and ugly, irrational ranting. According to the menu's back page, this building was the oldest business in town and had housed everything from a lodge hall to a drug store. Nevertheless, I was willing to bet this was some of the best theater the place had ever witnessed. The electronic squawk of Petry's voice caught the attention of two octogenarian diners at the next table. They lifted their heads and registered disapproval. "The man on the other end of their phone conversation would be wise to call 911 and seek help," the prim, blue-haired lady announced to her escort. "Those two are driving the poor soul to distraction . . . perhaps to a seizure."

"They're also driving the poor man from the plane of his choice, dear." Surreptitiously glancing toward us, her man waggled his head at us. "Why are they be so strongly opposed to his traveling by air?"

Sam returned the phone. Cupping my fingers, I moved my lips kissing-close to the speaker. "Petry! Shut up!" I ordered, my voice now lowered to a growl.

Petry raised his voice to a still higher dynamic level. "Sam, can you hear me? If you can, please pick up the phone. Scott, listen up, you hammer-headed numbskull, give Sam the phone. Sam, don't let this creep come between us. We have something special. In the eyes of God . . ." Joe waited to hear Sam's voice. "Scott, are you on a speaker phone? Sam, in the eyes of our Savior . . . In the eyes of your loved ones, don't, please don't forsake your family values—"

I chopped his words with mine, "Petry, I'll regularly check the airline's passenger list. Cancel! Don't hang onto a reservation you'll never be able to use!" I folded the phone.

Unabashed, a pant-suited waitress standing at our elbows fussed with our orders. For ten minutes we tried, yet ended up merely picking at our food.

"Sam, your ex-husband is not only a cruel stalker, he's a magician as well. From a distance of nearly twenty miles, he's caused the best omelet in town to taste like a chunk of burnt rubber."

Smiling at the elderly couple, I signaled for the check and paid their bill as well as ours. I owed them. Two old-timers, enjoying breakfast out, shouldn't witness a grade B movie scene. At least, if they did, I could spring for the cost of admission.

Ten minutes later we parked and knocked on the front door of Leveroux' "House of Weeping Walls." Wearing a paint- and clay-splattered artist's smock, Professor Leveroux opened the door.

He greeted Sam with a hug and kisses on each cheek, then ushered us inside. "Samantha, how delightful to see you once again," he said, unwrapping his arms. He stood with his hands on her shoulders for another moment's appreciation. "It seems ages, even though I retired but two short years ago."

He turned and patted my shouler. "I have good news for you both. The reconstruction's gone beautifully."

"We only want to know why this house is called 'The House of Weeping Walls,'" Sam said, laughing at her rejoinder.

Leveroux smiled indulgently, but anxious to share his secret, ignored additional small talk. Moving quickly, he led us past the windows' panoramic view and directly into his studio.

The bust stood on a slender pedestal in the center of the room, its shoulders draped by a green velvet cloth, the head covered by a dark wig. "Hmm," I murmured, slowly circling the table, "I'm reminded of someone."

Carefully, Sam ran her fingers over its nose and cheeks. "He does have a strong jaw, doesn't he?"

Shifting from one foot to another, an eager Leveroux followed our every move. "In any art form, the artist's interpretative abilities determine the final product's quality. This genre presents challenges beyond a typical artist's purview."

"Could you explain?" Sam asked.

"As I earlier pointed out to Richard, the lower torso has provided invaluable information about race, age, coloration. I've emphasized the strong jaw, but wouldn't it be unfortunate if this gentleman has always hidden that strong jaw behind a full beard—" He nodded toward me. "As has Richard."

I snapped my fingers, the sound loud in the small studio. "Don't sweat it, Prof," I said, recalling the photo in the downtown Bloomington office. "I know this character's identity!"

"My God, Richard! Who is it?" Sam cried.

"Oh, dear," Professor Leveroux moaned, "What shall we do? Now the police will learn that I betrayed their trust."

"This is our missing Clark Benefield."

"Do you know him? I thought you never saw him?" Sam asked.

"Just pictures on his desk, but I heard his secretary Lisa Crum's excuses. Clark Benefield never hit the mattresses, or hid. When burning my house, he did a gainer into the sump pit, trying to survive."

"But what shall I do?" the prof persisted.

"We'll keep quiet. Bloomington's a small city, with all the big-gun businessmen well-known. The minute a likeness of this bust hits television and the daily newspaper, there'll be IDs galore. If there isn't, Sam and I can step forward."

We walked toward the front door. "Now, Professor, do tell us about the House of Weeping Walls," Sam insisted.

"Romantics recount the story of a schoolmarm's intended, who early one morning during the Civil War, left home to do battle with Morgan's Raiders. At the time they had launched an attack into southern Indiana and were reportedly retreating south toward the Mason-Dixon line.

"According to legend, while the schoolmarm's fiance was in hot pursuit of Morgan, his boat overturned and he drowned in the Ohio River. His body was never recovered. Even today, just like the fiancee did, this brick building waits and weeps for his return."

"How tragic." Sam sighed.

"Those who are more pragmatic suggest that, because the bricks were poorly baked from local clay, and because silicon sealant was unavailable, the ancient walls now absorb so much moisture that water practically flows from each mortar joint."

On that note, we gathered our coats, said our heartfelt and warmly appreciative goodbyes, and left.

During our drive home, I tried to add another piece to our crazy quilt. Sam put her hand gently on mine. "You know, Richard, you're becoming quite a bore, always reprising these cases."

"But, Sam, have you noticed that Reverend Gabriel Goodall and Karl Sprader seem almost to be in lockstep? They built the Indy apartments together. Now Sprader's in Bloomington and, together, they're suing my company for work done on the Sandpiper View Condominium in Florida.

"Rankles' letters show that Sprader had, maybe still has an association—maybe some sort of real estate connection—with my company. So did the dead man, Clark Benefield, who owned Benefield Enterprises. Both knew Seve Jensen, my second-in-command.

"And that's another thing, Richard! You're always leaping onto Seve Jensen," Sam said, her voice growing even more peeved.

"I guess I still picture him, *on his feet*, while rifling my files."

"He was merely checking your planner for a business contact's name, and he appeared to brace himself on your desk to take some of the pressure off his legs. You told me so, yourself."

"You're right, Sam," I conceded. Since I had just been told twice that "enough was enough," I let it drop there. But, when we were arguing, I noticed that we both passed right by Janie McNamara's murder without a word. I guess, on both that issue and the question—who helped Clark Benefield torch my ex-father-in-law's house?—we were dead in the water.

Chapter Thirty-five

I ENTERED MY COMPANY'S LOBBY, longing to ignore my confidentiality pledge to Professor Leveroux and announce to the world that Sam and I had just tagged a name onto the chunk of boiled meat found in my sump pit. Of course that showed a lack of sensitivity and wouldn't have been fair to the professor, but elation came easy. Why not? Clark Benefield and an unknown partner had surely arranged that midnight cookout with me designated as the flambéed main course. So what, if, instead, Benefield's own goose got cooked? Should I cry in my beer?

Giving short shrift to Clark Benefield, I plunged onward.

A figure far down the hall caught my eye. I did a double-take: Seve Jensen—walking!

His broad, muscular back toward me, leaning heavily on a tubular, wheeled invalid's walker, Seve trucked down the hall. A trifle unsteadily, but he was nonetheless perambulating.

"Jesus, Seve!" I shouted, sprinting toward him. "This is the best news I've had since I bought the place!"

He turned to face me. Days earlier, I had been infuriated when I discovered him standing behind my desk while snooping through my daily planner. Today, influenced by Sam's spirit of magnanimity, I buried all reservations about his integrity. Throwing an arm over his shoulder, I gave him an exuberant squeeze. "This is the greatest ever!"

"Yeah, Richard," he said, forcing an unpleasant smile. "But go easy on the ribs, or you'll have me moving from wheelchair, to walker, to a body cast, all in one day."

Pleased, but nonplussed that the barrier between us had grown so that we couldn't share his triumph, I gave his shoulder a final goodbye slap and turned away. Opening the door into my office's anteroom, I waved hello to Jeanie, who cradled her phone.

Wearing a dusty-blue, pinstriped pantsuit, along with a new pair of decorator-frame glasses and a tight smile, she held her palm over the speaker. "Once again, I'm in voice-mail hell," she grumped. "In today's world, nobody—but nobody—ever answers calls. However, if you'll please leave a message, they'll return your call, immediately. And never do."

"Yep," I agreed. "Nothing ever changes. Gemma, my old secretary at Capital Detective Agency harped on the same things. She'd be delighted to know you've picked up the torch."

"For all the good it does," she said, gesturing as if to slam down the headpiece, then reconsidering.

"Jeanie, will you please call Delta Airlines and see if a J. Petry is booked on Friday's Flight 4462 to London?"

In rapid sequence, she nodded "yes" to my request, handed me a letter from ex-realtor cum management consultant Leonard Rankles, unspiked a pink, message-reminder note from Hugh McNamara, the late Janie McNamara's father, and, finally, with a smile belying all the previous harsh words, spoke warmly to the party on the phone.

Breaking tradition, McNamara had phoned. Unfortunately, his wife Gertrude had "passed to the other side, and since I'm wanting to talk, I hope you can see your way clear to come down here for a short visit."

I stared out the window, juggling my schedule. Tomorrow, I'd drive the hundred miles, primarily to console him, but also hoping to uncover new information as well. While I kicked myself for my lack of altruism, Jeanie broke my train of thought.

"Mr. Roger Petry also called, hoping for information on some kind of test." She coquettishly puckered her lips, then apparently feeling out of character, blushed. "He's so sweet." She word-scurried on, "J. Petry's still booked on the London flight."

While counting three short days to change Petry's mind, I tore open the Leonard Rankles' letter.

Dear Dick,

Having failed to hear from you as quickly as expected, and being temporarily faced with a big-time cash-flow problem, I'm sending the top half of a two-page invoice for your quickest perusal.

I will expect a return check in the amount of $600, made out to cash. Once the check is in my hands, I will send the rest of the pages, which are mind-busters of the highest magnitude.

My six-C-note asking-price exceeds the previously agreed upon dollar amount, but I remembered you said the letters were worth killing for. I got a hunch this invoice is a real gut twister you'd die to own. With that thought hammering my mind, I've copied a section of it for your attention.

Yours,
Leonard Rankles, Esquire

The top part of the two-page invoice issued by Jacobi Realty and addressed to Consolidated Constructioners, Inc., read, "For services rendered, we will expect your earliest remittal. Details below . . ."

Unfortunately, not only had Leonard Rankles retained page two, he had scissored away the bottom half of page one. Obviously, Jacobi, plus Goodall and Sprader's company, had settled on the euphemistic term "services rendered" to describe their working relationship. I doubted the lower half of the page elucidated in detail. Still, I wanted to see it. If nothing else, I could admire the two companies' creative lying.

"Hmm!" Rankles Business Brokers' office was located near downtown. I could hand-carry and deposit six, crisp, green hundred-dollar bills, directly into Leonard Rankles' sweaty palm. Pity my visit would be delayed for two days. Still, I suspected that, if I mailed the money, Leonard would forget to send the documents.

I had no choice. Along with my private eye gig, I needed to keep my company fine-tuned, and that meant two days of meetings with both company employees and outsiders. They'd be far more enthused about making a buck than seeing me nail a murderer.

Theft having decimated my cash balance, I especially needed to sweet-talk our bankers. They'd choke on their own Palm Pilot planners if they ever knew a fraud case festered within ADE, one of their biggest borrowers.

To start the morning right, I took time off to visit the local Electronic Shack Outlet and buy a handy-dandy little police scanner. Guaranteed to operate on house current, batteries or a cigarette outlet, the directions didn't say, but I suspected, one could also crank or pedal it, if all else failed.

Returning, I called Herschel Peters. "Hey, Herschel, after work, how about dropping off the Ram pickup at my house?" Earlier today, I reviewed company vehicle leases and chose a new vehicle that hadn't yet been tagged with either the corporate ID number nor the flamboyant ADE logo. Where I was headed, I didn't want to be identified.

"Should I oughta have Minnie pick me up at your house?" Herschel asked. I pictured his great, beaked nose bobbing up and down while I considered the matter. "'Course, from your house, I could walk right across the field since I live so close." With the final revelation, his voice grew in volume and enthusiasm.

"No way, Herschel. I'll shuttle you home in the Jag." I lied about a plan to haul a few pieces of furniture to Goodwill Industries. The truck was actually the mainstay in my metaphorical proposal to haul Joe Petry's butt away from Sam's flight.

Back home later, and wanting surreptitiously to verify that Petry had settled in for the evening, I phoned his number. "Petry residence, Joe Petry, here." Hoping he didn't have caller ID, I hung up. Antsy, I waited for dark.

I passed the time by beginning an English mystery novel. Partway through the fourth chapter, I laid it aside to ponder the contents: although we Americans are masters at killing, why do the British still turn out the best mysteries? Are our writers too jaded from over-exposure to highschool and workplace slaughter? Are our minds so over-crowded with images of fatigue-clad killers wielding AK-47s and Makarov pistols? Is there no room left for imagination or conjuring shadowy figures brandishing letter openers as weapons or spoonsful of arsenic for the evening tea? Interesting theory. Sometime I might pursue it further . . . perhaps with Sam's and Professor Leveroux's assistance.

Since my Rolex was still deep-sixed in Rose Cutter's Quarry, I checked my new Timex. Eight o'clock! I checked the window. Plenty dark outside—time to visit Joe. I slipped into the second bedroom. Ever a thoughtful host, Barb's father had maintained a selection of various-sized camouflage coveralls for his guests.

Selecting the roomiest, I held it up and examined myself in the wall mirror. At least one of the old man's friends must've been a hefty critter. Still, I supposed the massive size would've made the camouflage outfit a more effective hunting outfit. Passing animals would've mistaken the hunter for an olive drab tent.

Anyhow, even though my tall frame appeared now amply padded, the coveralls were so broad I could pirouette inside them with neither my butt nor shoulder blades touching fabric. I discovered one bit of good news: The fully cut legs reached my loafer tops. Though that didn't exactly make this a Calvin Klein minute, my clicking on one out of two fashion requirements 'twerent bad.

Hurriedly, I snatched a ski mask from a closet shelf. After tugging the coveralls over a yellow sweatshirt and a pair of jeans, I selected a double-barreled, twelve-gauge shotgun from the rack. Tucking the gun and police scanner under my arms, I pocketed the .45 and sauntered through the living room as if I were a latter day Jesse James. Trotting down the sidewalk and past the Jag, I climbed into the Ram's cab.

I was glad Samantha wasn't witness to my preparations. She would've been crazy with worry. In truth, I too dreaded the evening. Although as a businessman I'm tougher than a jockey's hindquarters, given a choice I don't willfully hurt people. I fancy that I'm more lap dog at heart, than a bear-killer. I'm extremely competitive, however, and frequently my better instincts get submerged beneath a compelling need to win, win, win! Petry had aroused those instincts—in spades!

Still, when facing a cruel bully like Petry, I figure you've gotta play his game and maul him, or squash all pride from his self-image. For a creeping weasel like Sam's ex, a crushed ego might be the cruelest blow. So, tonight's exploit was for Samantha's benefit, I told myself.

During the last few years, many people had abandoned Bloomington and Stonecrop for upscale, rural housing estates, as had Petry. I located his spacious, two-story French manor limestone house at the end of a cul-de-sac on the north end of Cavalier County. A tall, hipped roof sheltered the second story's line of tall, skinny windows. A shaded lamp stood in one upper window. Downstairs, a light pierced the slit between heavy, pulled drapes. The rest of the house looked deserted.

Like the other homes, Petry's was surrounded by trees and heavy shrubs, with broad expanses of land separating neighbors. I presumed Joe liked the added seclusion. Certainly, my plans did. They called for privacy and would produce noise enough to rock the neighborhood.

His front yard's winter-stripped trees provided no cover. Afraid that Petry would see and ID my vehicle, I parked down the street behind a clump of evergreens. Before climbing outside, I added a touch of fierceness to my costume by pasting two strips of black tape beneath my eyes. Reconsidering, I ripped away the tape and donned the ski mask. I winked at my reflection in the mirror before trailing along the flagstone walk to a tiny inset porch. Covering the peephole with one gloved hand, I punched the bell with the other.

"Who's there?" Joe Petry called.

"A greeting from 'Lollipops, Orchids and More,'" I answered, in a happily lilting voice. Petry cracked the door. Glimpsing me, his eyes opened as wide as his horned-rim spectacle frames. I unleashed a violent kick.

The retaining chain ripped free of the doorframe. Grazing Petry's cheek, the door bunted his glasses into the living room. Then, the door swung farther. It crashed against a hidden piece of furniture just as I swung at Petry's jaw with the shotgun barrel.

He dashed across the room. I lunged forward.

He reached between two studio portraits of Sam, his fingers clawing for a pistol. In that brief instant, I glimpsed at least two-dozen of Sam's snapshots scattered around the room. My feet skidded on the waxed floor, but I quickly recovered my balance. I aimed the shotgun and released its safety.

My eyes caught his in a large mirror above the fireplace. "Move, and you're dead meat, Petry," I husked out.

To emphasize the point, I aimed over his shoulder and emptied one twelve-gauge barrel. The mirror disintegrated, our reflected faces vanishing in an eruption of pulverized glass. Smoke and acrid odors of cordite stung my nostrils.

"Drop it, Petry, or your ugly head disappears like the one in the mirror." On the heels of the shotgun's earsplitting blast, my oral order sounded faint.

He hesitated.

I re-aimed at his head, then raised my voice to compete with his and my temporary deafness. "Petry, I'll repaint the wall with blood. Yours!"

Petry cowered behind the cluttered coffee table, his face whitewashed by fear. His chest only partially covered by a thin, vest undershirt, he looked naked, shrunken and helpless. Finally, he dropped the Glock 19 onto the floor and collapsed into an overstuffed chair.

Thoughts raced through my mind. Somebody had stolen my Glock 19 from my house. I'd stolen another one from Petry's Buick. In Sam's house, Petry had threatened Sam with a third. Was this the third, or was it a fourth? Perhaps the weapons were growing on trees, and Petry owned the orchard.

As if a bachelor's loneliness hadn't been penalty enough, I had totally trashed his dinner. A half-eaten, double-decked burger had toppled onto a stack of onion rings and the whole mess now lay saturated by an overturned bottle of German beer.

A long strand of normally carefully combed hair fell down over his eyes. He brushed at it with trembling fingers, then wiped sweat from his upper lip with his palm.

Slowly, I lowered the shotgun's aim to his bony chest. Voice now low and ominous, I ordered, "Petry, I want you off Sam's plane. And I want you to stay away from Sam before she leaves. And when she returns as well."

On television, a serious looking Dan Rather was describing a NATO crisis in Europe. Slightly shifting aim, I fired off another round, this one blasting the picture tube and Dan Rather. Wow! I'd always had an urge to do that! Pity the TV hadn't been equipped with picture-in-picture. I could've whacked Brokaw with the same shot.

Recoiling, his back pressing harder against the backrest, Petry pissed his pants. The stain darkened the legs of his khaki slacks and dribbled onto the chair's cushion. He gazed longingly toward the Glock on the floor. I squeezed the .45 in my coverall pocket so he'd see its outline, then used both hands to chamber shells into the twelve-gauge.

Drawing myself to my full height, I then, real casual-like, enhanced the theatrics; pleased that Petry's momentary terror mimicked the constant fear he had forced on Sam, I moseyed across the room and pocketed his Glock. "Petry. This is a final warning. Leave . . . Sam . . . alone!"

Petry hadn't lost all his fight. "Scott, the cops will have you charged and cuffed before you're out of town."

I wiggled the shotgun so its blank, hollow eyes stared directly into his frightened blue ones. "Not until its too late for you, buddy boy!"

"Scott . . . please!" he whimpered.

"Petry," I virtually jeered, "I'm not acquainted with any Scotts. I'm just a good Samaritan out to eradicate the world's stalkers," I waggled the double-barrel more vigorously. "I'm a righteous man fighting an uncontrollable urge to blow you into hell."

I inched closer to him. Glass crunched beneath my shoe and I thought it was another shard from the mirror. It wasn't. I'd trashed Petry's spectacles.

Stooping, I picked them up. "Sorry, Petry, but these will need a tad of work." I speared a finger through each empty rim by way of explanation, and tossed the twisted specs onto his lap.

Totally disoriented, he tried straightening the bridge and earpieces, as if once the frame were reshaped, the lenses might pop back into place.

For a moment, I felt a touch of pity. But not for long—I remembered what he had done to Sam.

Wheeling, I dashed through the front door and sprinted down the street to the pickup. Whirling the Dodge's steering wheel with one hand, I switched on the police scanner with the other.

My trip home took me north through another residential area. On the way, I met a sheriff's squad car, its siren blaring. A streetlight showed the policemen talking on his two-way radio. The words from the scanner said, "Be on the lookout for a green Jaguar, licensed in Indiana, the plate number begins with a 49A prefix. That's four-niner-able . . ."

My scanner was definitely fixed on the right frequency. I was the cop's prey.

I raced home. The truck's tires screaming, I wheeled from the county road and sped up the drive toward the A-frame. Part-way there, I steered into the field, shifted the Ram into four-wheel drive and, helped by a running start, plowed my way up and over a steep ridge. I braked to a stop deep inside one of the pine groves guarding Rose Cutter's Quarry.

Quickly, I retrieved the .45 and the Glock from the coverall's flap pockets and stuck both pieces into my jeans. I stuffed my gloves into the flapped pockets, wrapped the shotgun, and felt my way to the edge of the quarry. I hurled the misshapen bundle over the escarpment—exactly where Jane McNamara took her final plunge.

Below me, the black waters were invisible. I waited for a satisfying splash. Nothing. I supposed distance had killed the sound.

I scurried back to the Ram and stuck my ear close to the scanner. "Jake, this is Sheriff DeLyle. Let's meet at the corner of Road 1000 and Cutter. We'll welcome Scott when he pulls into his drive."

"Right, Sheriff!"

"And turn off the damned siren! You'll scare him away."

I smirked into the night. "Not tonight, boys—not, tonight!" Mentally licking a finger tip, I marked up an imaginary point for Dick Scott's team. Now all I had to do was avoid losing by default.

Chapter Thirty-six

I SPRINTED ACROSS THE FIELD to the A-frame with my legs pumping like pistons. Simultaneously, headlights swept the final curve before Herschel's driveway.

I rushed directly from the front door to bedroom and stashed the .45 and Glock in the weapons cabinet. Then, back in the living room, I switched on the television and, leaving it to play to an empty chair, planted myself in front of the computer. Six minutes later, a car roared up the drive and skidded to a halt at the end of the sidewalk. I peeped between the drapes.

Sheriff DeLyle and his sidekick scrambled from the cruiser. The deputy brushed his palm over the Jag's cold hood. They exchanged glances, then both charged up the sidewalk, pounded across the porch, and hammered the front door.

I swung the door wide and drawled, "Gentlemen, to what, or whom, do I owe this pleasure?"

"Okay, Scott, knock off the bull!" DeLyle barked. "Where have you been for the last hour?"

"I took a quick look at Dan Rather. Objecting to his style, I tuned to the Net." I waved my hand at my computer. "It's a tough go being an Internet addict. Surf, surf, surf!" I flexed my wrists, my fingers poised over an imaginary keyboard. "And although you and your deputy are the best of company, I'd still like to know why you're here."

"Don't play that ignoramus game with us, Scott," DeLyle's deputy said, stepping close and locking his hard-blue, storm-trooper eyes onto mine. For a moment, he didn't speak further, but used the pregnant interlude to straighten his badge, hitch his pants, elevate his smoothly shaven chin, and tighten his lips.

I pictured him each evening, standing before his mirror and choreographing all the right moves before going outside to climb into the brown Merc cruiser. "We all work closely in these communities. Captain Redonzo keeps us posted. We know the trouble your lady friend has had with our friend, Joe Petry. We just left Joe at his front door. From what we saw through the door, I'd say his house has been totally wrecked. He alleges that you blasted the place apart while you were trying to gun him down."

"Alleges don't cut it!" Apparently irritated by the interruption, Sheriff DeLyle regained the floor, "Joe flat-out accuses you, Scott. And I buy his story. When we leave here, we'll be returning to his place for a thorough forensics examination. Anybody leaving a crime scene leaves something of himself behind, and I doubt you'll be an exception. That ski mask didn't fool Joe, or either of us."

I noted that both lawmen referred to Petry by his first name. Cops and ex-cops always have a keen sense of fraternity. One side of me liked that. Especially, since I'd borrowed the idea for tonight's gambit from one of their own. I wished I could share it with them.

DeLyle interrupted my train of thought. "With your permission, we're going to search your house, Scott. I want the shotgun. I want the coveralls. Since the Jag's hood is cold, I want to know who brought you home. I'll rack somebody else's rear as well. You either give us permission to search, or we arrest your sorry butt right here and now, and I'll wake Judge Roper and have a search warrant before sunrise."

I nodded okay, and followed that with a resigned, "Be my guest. Tread on my rights." Theatrically, I spread my arms wide, indicating the bedroom. "That's the closest door, so let this Hoosier inquisition begin there."

"Sheriff, what's he mean by this inquisition stuff? You want I should throw the cuffs on him?"

DeLyle shook his head. "Deputy, forget the semantics. Just search the bedroom. Begin with the closets and cover every inch of this house. I'll search the kitchen."

While I waited alone in the livingroom, my mind returned again to the magazine story that had inspired my attack on Joe Petry. I figured to tell Sam . . . but later. According to the story, a police officer in a southern city got tired of having a member of his family stalked. He aimed a shotgun in the stalker's face and said, "Look punk, you follow my wife one more time, I'll blast you into the next county!" His warning worked and the stalker moved out of town. Would my warning stop Joe Petry from stalking Sam? We'd see.

"Okay, Scott, I'll be back," a disappointed Sheriff DeLyle promised as he returned to the living room from some high-grade sleuthing through the pantry and china cabinets. "And if I wasn't so good-natured and accommodating I'd take possession of that arsenal in there," he said, nodding backward toward the still-open door to the bedroom. "Even though neither of the shotguns has been recently fired."

Smiling, I held open the front door. "Please return. Anytime. I always support my local sheriff." The sheriff's young sidekick pierced me with a Macon County glare. Raising one finger, I motioned DeLyle to stay. Glowering, he did.

"Sheriff, no matter what your opinion is about Petry and me, you owe me for my cooperation. Will you share the info on Roger Petry's DNA test?"

He glanced outside. His deputy had assumed a new pose. Both legs spread wide, the local version of Barney Fife stood with one hand hovering over his gun belt.

"Your colleague's not filled with trust," I observed.

"You haven't earned much," DeLyle said. "I'll be with you in a moment, son," he reassured his deputy.

He closed the door. Now, offstage, his expression softened. "Look,

Scott, I can't countenance your actions toward Petry. And although I don't like seeing women or children mistreated, in my bailiwick, vigilantism is way out of style."

Nodding without commitment, I waited.

"Since you reasoned with Roger Petry and brought him to me, I guess I owe you the information on his test . . ."

Chapter Thirty-seven

FIRST THING, NEXT MORNING, I called and gave Sam the information on Roger, then dialed the Chez Royaliste Hotel. A sleepy-voiced desk clerk answered.

"May I speak to Roger Petry?" I asked.

"Just a mo', I'll give you his room," the voice said.

After a dozen rings, my call automatically rerouted itself, and I pictured it clicking and beeping its way through Cleveland, San Francisco, and St. Louis, before returning downstairs to the lobby switchboard. This time a female voice responded, "Yes?"

"May I speak to Roger Petry?" I asked.

"Rog, honey, can you pick up on line two?" I recognized the blonde room clerk's voice, before she put me on hold and left me victim to a cascade of hard rock music. "I'm sorry, sir," she said, returning to the line, "Mr. Petry is like—uh, indisposed."

"Please tell him Richard Scott called."

"Oh, darn it to heck, he'll be thoroughly pi—uh, devastated. He said he'd rather have your call than a hundred-dollar tip. You'll call back?"

"Yep." I hurried out to the Jag.

In Bloomington, I picked up an early morning newspaper. The

Joe Petry story made the second page. According to Sheriff Casey DeLyle, "An armed and masked late-night intruder broke into a Stonecrop man's house and tied up and threatened the resident. There were no injuries and nothing was taken, although extensive damage was done to the house. A suspect has been interviewed, but no arrests have yet been made." In a subsequent interview, the victim was less certain that his original ID had been correct.

I supposed that, after the sheriff's initial visit, Petry rethought his position and decided to keep the case quiet. Good approach! Obviously, the police couldn't make a case since it was solely Petry's word against mine. Nevertheless, I didn't want the hassle nor the publicity.

Undoubtedly, Sam's ex had additional reasons beyond being frightened out of his wits. Surely, he was reluctant for Sam to learn he had now lost two battles: one to me; another for control over his bladder. In his eyes, the last would be the biggest pisser by far.

Tossing the newspaper onto the passenger seat, I drove to the office for catch-up duty. I cheated a tad. Later I made a call on Jacobi Realty.

Although it was early afternoon, the office was locked tight. Pressing my nose to the window, I peeped inside. Windemere Clairton's desk was missing. The company had ceased business.

Glad to be back to full-time sleuthing, I switched the CD player onto random play, settled into the bucket seat for some easy listening, and turned the Jaguar's streamlined snout toward the Ohio River and Hugh McNamara's house. I needed a couple of hours of relaxation, with no thoughts about crime.

Easily said. Within two minutes, I was back shooting case comments at the Jag's hood ornament, trying to rearrange my crazy quilt into a patterned tapestry.

My thoughts were spinning like a wheel. I supposed the Right Reverend Goodall might have the answer. "Brothers, the prophet Ezekiel raised his eyes to the heavens, and he beheld a wheel, and another wheel was spinning within that wheel and this holy man prophesied . . ."

With fifty miles to go I gave up, said, "Forget the case," and willed myself to concentrate on the music. Smiling in appreciation, I slung my right arm over the back of the passenger seat and tapped rhythm on the headrest. At that moment, the Jag and I ran head-on into a dreary rain heading north, but riding the same highway as we. Singing Michelins, and a duo of rattling wipers almost drowned the sweet sounds of "Sing You Sinners." Then right on cue, the music switched to Manhattan Transfer's "Rendition of Clouds" and after that, a Matt Munro recording promised "On a Clear Day You Can See Forever." It must've been a musical omen, because ten minutes before my destination, the waterlogged curtain lifted.

When I turned off into the two-lane gravel drive, a pale sun began probing for space between second-growth trees on the Kentucky side of the Ohio River. Bright beams danced and darted across the muddy water, reflections giving the afternoon a golden glow and painting Hugh McNamara's weatherboard house a friendly, yellow tinge.

I mounted the steep steps to my elderly friend's house. A brightly painted, red and yellow coal bucket contained remnants of last fall's geraniums, and propped open the screen. Gert's work? Feeling sad for Hugh McNamara, I reached to knock and my knuckles grazed a door already swinging open.

His greeting was succinct. "Have the police arrested Roger Petry yet?" he asked, holding wide the door.

"No—and they won't," I responded in kind. "Roger's DNA results prove he didn't father Janie's child."

Crestfallen, Hugh McNamara's shoulders noticeably dropped and the parentheses of wrinkles framing his mouth grew deeper. He was dressed as before, although today, the freshly laundered and ironed dungarees and lumberjack shirt hung more loosely on his frame. Maybe, in departing, Gert carried away with her a physical part of him.

"Naturally, I don't want to convict the wrong man," he said. "But I did long for verification. I wanted to tell—"

My quizzical expression must have quenched his words.

"But it might be safer to stay mum about our discussions."

I studied him a moment, then curiosity got the best of me. "Just who were you planning to tell, Mr. McNamara?"

"Scott, it won't affect much in this realm, but I wanted to walk through the Pearly Gates carrying an answer." Tears welling, he tugged a red bandanna from a rear pocket and wiped his eyes, then loudly honked his nose. He fell heavily into the ancient armchair. "I . . . I wanted to tell Gert and Janie the name of the killer, although I believe Janie died knowing. Be that as it may, I want to assure my two special ladies that justice will be done."

"Roger could've killed your daughter, even though he wasn't the sperm donor," I suggested.

"Nope. It'll turn out to be one of two other men and I'm wagering that the person who killed her did it because he didn't want to step up and accept the responsibility for fatherhood. Have you checked on Clark Benefield?"

"Yes. Sheriff DeLyle says his DNA sample also tested negative." I didn't mention that Benefield was dead. That announcement would have to come from DeLyle.

Struggling erect, he poured each of us a double shot of the Canadian Club I'd given him last trip.

"Kinda early for the hard stuff, isn't it?" I asked, nodding toward the sunlit window.

"Only if it's bad whiskey." We tapped glasses.

"While we're playing 'Pin the tail on the donkey,' how about sticking it to Seve Jensen?" I asked dryly.

"I don't believe he fathered Janie's child. Of course, I might tend to protect him for his parents' sake. After all, they're still neighbors. And the salt of the earth." Stopping, he massaged a patch of gray chin whiskers missed during this morning's shave. "I'm not wanting to admit that Janie slept around. But if we're to find the killer, I believe there's only one remaining possibility."

I set the shot glass onto the table and gave him my full attention.

The words blasted forth, "Her killer is still within the Petry family

. . . and it's certainly not Samantha!" He appeared uncomfortable with his accusation.

"Could you give me a little background, Mr. McNamara?"

"I've talked too much, and much too casually. Just let me say that Janie was scared to death of Joe Petry. Sam knows! Nobody can trust that man. He's a devil. I figured that, since acorns don't fall far from the tree, his son would be just like him. Maybe I was wrong."

Two prying questions later I gave up on the subject. "You said Seve's parents are neighbors. Could I have a sit-down with them?"

"Worth a try. They're just two driveways down the pike. The Jensen name's printed on the fancy mailbox that Seve bought, back when he was in college."

Five minutes later, I turned into the Jensen driveway. The fancy mailbox had a *Cannabis sativa* twig on its side panel, proving that, not only were the parents naive, they'd been victimized by Seve's warped sense of humor.

My words weren't meant to condemn a pot-lover's rap with "Mary Jane." My job's running factories and catching killers, not crusading against marijuana. After all, in the distant past, I, like a certain well-known personage, also had taken a couple of puffs, *without inhaling*.

The shotgun house, except for length, replicated Hugh McNamara's. Years ago, some enterprising builder must have made a living, constructing tiny, but sturdy, houses that would cling precariously, but almost eternally, to the edges of sheer Ohio River cliffs. He had certainly made his mark.

Today, instead of calling the carpenter, cash-strapped buyers tended to purchase flimsy house trailers that go airborne at the first strong gust of wind and end up as a tangled aluminum heap on the riverbank.

Timing my steps to land only on moss-covered and irregularly spaced stepping stones, I hurried to the front door. I knocked. I heard muffled voices and two sets of chair legs scraping a wooden floor.

The door opened. "Hi! Mr. Jensen? I'm Jerome Riddle, an old buddy of Seve's. We served together in the Gulf War. He here?"

The elder Jensen had enormous muscles and thick hair like his son. Sadly, age had loosened the knots in the muscles. The coarsened blond hair now resembled straw that had been left too long outside and become splotched and streaked by gray mold.

Not only was the house identical to Hugh McNamara's, the father's dungarees and shirt appeared to have come from the same store. But Jensen's had probably been hanging to the side of the showroom on the "Big and Tall" rack.

I couldn't get a clear look at Seve's mother. She peered around a doorframe like a female Kilroy who'd sprouted tufts of gray hair. A jerk of her head and she withdrew into the kitchen.

For a moment, the elder Jensen seemed confused by my Gulf War reference, but quickly recovered, "Seve never mentioned any friend named Jerome Riddle. You sure you're looking for the right man?"

"Yep!" Resolutely, I shook my head. "I was right there beside my good buddy Seve when he was injured. I was the guy that screamed, 'Medic!' at the top of my lungs. That was one tough day, with his wounds being so bad and blowing sand making the whole thing worse. Blood and sand; what a fu—, er, that is, screwed-up combo."

I wiped my brow with my palm. "Believe me, Mr. Jensen, he wouldn't forget ol' Jere. 'Course, he knew me as Jerry or sometimes Jere. Do either of them names ring a bell?"

"I'll tell him you called." He eased his big frame forward, trying to usher me toward the door. "Fact is, you should leave your address and phone number. We'll get the information to him, and he'll be in contact."

I wondered why he didn't want to hear more of my story. Most parents relish insights into their children's past.

Squatting beside an end table, I scribbled a Louisville phone number onto the blank corner of a *Courier Journal* ad page. "I'm moving within a week, so this'll have to do," I complained. "By any chance, could you give me Seve's number?"

"Sorry, our son's a very private man." His face colored. "But I'll see he gets yours." I turned as I started back down the stepping-stone walkway.

"Oh, by the way, Mr. Jensen, I like the unusual mailbox."

"Yeah, us too. Seve could be kind." Then the door slammed.

A lot of discomfort there . . . inspired by something unsavory in Seve's past? I snapped my fingers and uttered a strong, "You betcha!" I wasn't sure why.

Before heading north, I stopped for gas at an old-fashioned country store. Or maybe it was new-fashioned since half of it had been set aside for the sale of antiques and "Ukraine Woolens, 'Close-out Special.'"

Providing real authenticity, five denim-clad men huddled around a pot-bellied stove. "By any chance, you guys know a Seve Jensen?" I asked, sidling close. "I'm an old war buddy from way back."

They quit watching me to exchange glances with each other. The group's leader tipped his white Stetson hat higher on his head and examined me more closely. "I don't know what war you fought, but I know Seve," he said.

His toothpick worked its way across his lips during the short sentence. Carefully, he tongued it back to the other side. "The only war Seve fought was with Patrolman Hank Gerber."

"But, Seve was wounded in Desert Storm. Right beside me—"

My words brought a round of guffaws. "Yeah, I'll bet!" another offered. "Seve's only injuries came when he flipped that Ford into Deerlick Creek . . ."

I thanked them for the help, paid my pump bill, and sped up the road toward home. Now I had another problem.

Should I confront Seve? No. Being a liar doesn't make you a criminal. And I needed all the players to stay in place until the case wrapped, particularly Seve Jensen and Leonard Rankles. Especially Rankles. His place would be my next stop.

Chapter Thirty-eight

As USUAL, ON-STREET PARKING was an impossibility near Rankles' Business Brokers. From experience, I pulled into the Old Farmer's Bank lot just off the town square.

Raindrops dotted the windshield. Incipient clouds hung low and heavy over the roofs of taller buildings, their ash-gray bellies punctured by the courthouse dome and the bank's aluminum-staffed flagpole. The day wasn't freezing, but it was bone-chilling, with the cold dampness spring rains always bring. Feeling lucky, I climbed out of the car, not taking an umbrella or trench coat.

In front of the building, I located the ATM. Not ready to involve the company in what could end up as an embarrassing fiasco, I withdrew two thousand bucks cash from my own account. Six hundred would buy the Jacobi Realty/Consolidated Constructioneer's document from Rankles. Fourteen hundred would be seed money, or better put, bright green carrots—mutated, but enticing—to Leonard Rankles, a man living on the ragged edge of fiscal starvation.

I couldn't wait to wave the bundle under his nose. In hundred-dollar denominations, they'd be a real eye opener. In fact, the shock could very well fracture the axles on his darting eyeballs.

Dealing with Rankles was bribery—plain and simple. Bull-dusting myself, I rationalized I was merely purchasing a better understanding of enigmatic Karl Sprader, the vice president of Consolidated Constructioneers.

Already, I knew answers. Jacobi Realty had overseen our company property for my father-in-law, continuing to do so after he was jailed. Karl Sprader had some kind of an insidious association with Jacobi. The questions needing polish were: Did the relationship still exist? Could Sprader be involved in my company's money shortage?

Rankles' front office was dark. I surmised Leonard and Desiree, succumbing to the Chez Royaliste Syndrome, left early for a little personal R-and-R. On either a premonition or suspicion, I stuck my nose closer to the plate glass window. Glimpsing light in the rear room, I tested the knob. The door swung open to a dead-quiet office.

From my last trip, I remembered Desiree Martin's lunch. Surely, she had made a long-term commitment to the potato, soft drink, and poultry industries. The desk still held stray fries, a watered-down Coke, and a few golden-colored crumbs from today's chicken nugget lunch.

Yet her brown corduroy desk chair was missing. Very strange. Despite its huge, stainless-steel casters, I doubted she was out for a drive on it. Maybe she wheeled next door to see her boss. "Hey, Leonard!" I called, "Anybody home?"

The phone jangled. The raucous ringing filled the tiny office with an insistent demand for attention.

I abhor unanswered phones. I fought the urge to snatch this one from the hook, but it quit ringing. The office seemed quieter than before. And emptier.

Desiree's sunglasses, hairbrush, lipstick, small perfume spray, eyebrow pencil, eyelash brush, and open compact lay scattered across the desk pad. She must've taken her car keys with her, but a key with a tag that said OFFICE lay to one side, half-hidden by the desk pad.

"Would sweet little Desiree willingly leave her cosmetics behind?" I asked myself. "Never! Way out of character! She must have been spooked, and bailed out in a big hurry," I answered. An incipient foreboding began to seep into every recessed corner of my mind.

I swivelled her computer monitor. Either she, or inactivity, had triggered the screen saver.

My eyes strayed. "What's this?" I yelled, my question echoing within the empty office. Desiree's chair lay upside down behind the desk.

My pulse, slugged by a double shot of adrenaline, soared from its normal sixty-four to twice that. On the balls of my feet, poised for action, I wheeled around. "Hey, Leonard, last call!" I yelled, and charged through his door.

I glanced down—and halted my black, shiny wingtip in mid-stride. Blood! Struggling for balance, I grabbed the corner of Leonard's desk—and nearly plopped my palm into another scarlet pool.

Rankles still manned his desk. A devastating blow had turned his bald "power grooves" into a single, deep, and gore-filled lake.

I tore my eyes from Rankles and onto the swordfish's picture behind him. Splattered blood painted its head, the pike-like proboscis becoming an almost surrealistic part of the murderous attack.

Maybe the murder had something to do with Damocles' sword. Perhaps Rankles had told one too many big stories. Maybe his final tale had threatened the wrong person.

I thought of our last meeting and Leonard's little man's bluster. Today, with his skinny, blue-suited body slumped forward in his executive chair, his eyes staring through bloody, misshapen slots, he appeared far, far smaller, his dead eyes fixed on a spot beneath his desk.

I bent over, my eyes following his to the floor. For a clearer look, I tugged his leg aside. "Oh, my God!" I yelled. The rose-cutter tool from my office shelf lay between Leonard's grubby, brown shoes, its machete-sharp teeth matted with hair and flesh.

I straightened, mind agog. I was trapped! I would be the prime suspect. His letter to me provided motive. I owned the murder weapon. Unless my cleaning lady had done the world's most meticulous dusting job, my fingerprints would be on it.

Certainly I couldn't clear myself from a prison cell. I'd have to take the rose cutter with me. But first . . .

Then I remembered: Rankles stored the incriminating letters in his lower desk drawer. I yanked the handle—empty! Somebody—the killer?—had stolen the manila file. Now fighting panic, I moved to the filing cabinet.

Out front, car tires squealed, then ground against the curb. Voices! I listened.

Opening fast, the front door crashed hard against the wall. "The 911 call said there'd been a problem." I recognized the urgency in Raphael Redonzo's voice. "I assumed the call originated with an employee," Redonzo continued. "Now where is she?"

"You can see some chick really hauled outta here . . ." The voice was that of the young "spit 'n polish" who had been first on the scene the night Joe Petry held Sam hostage.

"This looks bad," Redonzo said. "Call Harry in from outside. We'll go over the place together."

The front door squeaked open. "Cap'n needs you, Harry!"

I cracked the back door, ready to flee. I hesitated—was the building cordoned off already? Recalling my last visit, I pictured Desiree opening the storage closet and disclosing a hidden stairway.

I crept across the office, skirting Leonard Rankles' chair, eased open the closet door, and shoe-horned my two-hundred pound body into a one-fifty space. I fumbled through the supplies, my fingers closing on a heavy stapler.

Leaning out, I hurled the stapler against the steel surface of the office's back door. I then tugged the closet door closed, leaving it barely cracked.

"They're gettin' away!" Three sets of flat feet thudded from Desiree's office.

Redonzo and Harry dashed through the rear door and split to cover both ends of the alley. Hot behind, "spit 'n polish" skidded in pooled blood and sprawled across the tiled floor.

"Holy Christ!" he yelped, then glimpsing Leonard Rankles, shouted, "Captain, for God's sake!" even more loudly.

Quickly on his feet, the deputy massaged a bruised butt,

complained, "Damn!" when he felt blood-soaked fabric, then hip-hopped through the back door. Favoring one leg, he charged awkwardly after his captain.

I waited. After an extended interval, the sound of police brogans pounding asphalt grew faint.

I scampered up the stairs to the second story. My eyes swept the room in a quick inventory. The floor was covered with records and discards, from boxes labeled Tax Records to broken-down empties. A dust-covered filing cabinet stood in a far corner. Stacks of manila folders and yellowed copies of the *Wall Street Journal* surrounded it.

I moved a teetering, three-legged desk to clear my path. Inadvertently, I plunked the keys on an Underwood typewriter—couldn't resist it—ancient enough to have been around when Captain Smith shouted, "Last call for Plymouth Rock!"

I longed to delve, but I had to get out. Like a treed critter, I searched for a way. I wove through more debris and reached a side window. It overlooked a fire escape, its bottom sill the only dust-free spot in the room, so I wasn't breaking new ground.

Undoubtedly the crime scene hadn't yet been cordoned off. I waited for Harry, the deputy, and the captain to return. The back door slammed shut; three excited voices jockeyed for attention. Picking the moment, I eased through the window and down the rusted ladder.

Three bottom rungs were missing. I vaulted off. Grimacing, I flopped down on the cinder walkway and rubbed a twisted ankle.

Fighting the urge to run, trying not to limp, I sauntered up the street. Rounding the corner, a police cruiser fishtailed the greasy intersection. Siren screaming, it roared down the street toward Rankles' Business Brokers.

Raindrops having threatened all day, now the gray clouds split. Rain swept the city, giving me an excuse to run. Ignoring the pain in my ankle, I charged down the street. My palms rust-stained from the ladder, my soaked jacket draped with cobwebs, my mind a blur, I climbed into the Jag.

I turned the ignition key. When the engine fired, my brain quit working. My ankle ached. Where to now? Awaiting a revelation, I kneaded the flesh around my sore ankle.

Undoubtedly, the killer took the incriminating letters. I didn't suspect Desiree Martin of either theft or murder; I imagined her dead.

I started to pull away. Braked. Sitting alone, the engine running, my dripping fingers clutching the wheel, new thoughts intruded: that dust-free sill in the upstairs room! Desiree must have escaped ahead of me—with the documents. I pictured her, terrified, hiding out. But where? Suddenly, I snapped my fingers. At least I knew the best starting point.

Chapter Thirty-nine

Next morning, I parked in front of Delilah's Temptation Bar and Grill, the place Desiree euphemistically called a 'club.' Except for my spot, all the spaces along the curb were vacant with meters flagged red. In the customers' side lot, one four-toned, Jed Clampett pickup nosed close to the tavern's brick wall. Following the sidewalk, a crumpled potato chip sack skipped past the front door like a tumbleweed.

The tavern's front door was centered between plate glass windows. Two pictures of dark-haired Serendipity Smith filled the windows on the left. In one, she wore a black, sequined dress; in the other, she was "almost" dressed in a go-go dancer's outfit.

From the opposite window, neon-painted lettering yelled a titillating promise: Hot Legs Competition Nitely—Wet T-Shirts Contest For Sweeties With Loftier Endowments. Above that, disembodied, thick lips framed a set of huge, square teeth—and provided a foot-long guffaw for the weak, chauvinistic pun.

My ankle somewhat improved, I ambled through the door, wearing an in-charge and confident demeanor. As expected, Jed Clampett was the tavern's sole customer. He stubbed a cigarette as if contemplating the world's big issues, while busily stirring his ashtray with the blackened end of a wooden match.

I supposed the rest of the tavern's clientele were either hard at work or uptown dunking donuts in stiff, black coffee.

Clampett turned to watch me from beneath a battered, greasy felt hat, one watery eye opened wide, the other trying to blink its way into focus. "You wanna beer, Mac? I could use some company." He proffered a crumpled pack of Camels and ripped the opening wider with a trembling finger, the nail and first two joints matching the tobacco's color. "Smoke?"

I gave him and the broken-backed cigarette a wave-off. Recalling my years-ago, week-end Army passes, I empathized. In those days, the sweet smell of hops were fully as enticing as a pretty girl's smile.

However, the next day was a downer. A guy remembers visiting the john. While he's gone, the girl—met but an hour earlier and now seen as the woman he wants to marry—vamooses on the arm of a knotty little guy with squashed ears and missing front teeth.

That experience, plus the odor of snuffed cigarettes, mingled with that of stale beer and wine, could make a man gasp, "Never again." Or cause him to yell, "Joe, pump another freakin' Bud," like Jed Clampett did as I edged along the bar.

I couldn't imagine big-moneyed Karl Sprader hanging out here, but I told the bartender's broad back, "I need to see Serendipity Smith."

Giving my reflection a casual once over, he slowly Windexed another glass shelf, then rearranged a half-dozen Gilbey Gin bottles before answering, "Yeah, you and every other creep able to suck the head from a cold one." He didn't turn from the mirror.

"I'm Serendipity," a warm voice behind me announced. I spun around, expecting to see the tantalizing creature pictured in the window. Instead, she was dressed in a zipper-necked, faded sweatshirt, blue jeans, and a dirty pair of scuffed Nikes.

Disappointed, but understanding, I gave her a gracious smile. I supposed that worn daily, the slinky dress might rain sequins onto the tavern floor like shimmering flakes of dandruff. Worse yet, the skimpy go-go outfit could cause the bartender to fog the glass shelves without pumping Windex. Or, maybe, Serendipity was actually a student and this joint was only her night job. I imagined her dear old parents, back in Des Moines or River Fork City, picturing her studying Plato or Descartes, not dancing, and certainly not giving a sexy pelvic thrust during her bump and grind finale—the part where she puts the "big move" on the red, velvet-covered post.

I flashed my private investigator ID. "Serendipity, Desiree Martin said she knew you. Do you have any idea where I might find her?"

"The police asked the same question, yesterday," she said, her voice pitched low, like the key in which I supposed she sang. "I'm sorry about her boyfriend, but I wouldn't be surprised if she killed him."

"Why?"

She traced the line of her bottom lip with the tip end of a red fingernail. "In one set, I play the crowd and sing to the husbands and boyfriends. It's all in fun." She pouted. "The other night, I sat on Leonard's lap and wiggled around a little, while whispering some seductive stuff into his ear. Desiree went violently ape. I mean she went ballistic!"

"Yeah, some girlfriends aren't totally sold on lap dancing," I said. "Probably raises expectations when couples get back to the bunkhouse."

"Leonard loved being the center of attention. When I saw him last, he was flush. That was rare. He even tucked a hundred-dollar bill in my bra." Her eyes went all dreamy while she savored one of life's special moments. "When he was busted, he ran a weekly tab. He always cackled real loud in that crazy laugh of his. Then he'd joke to the bartender, 'I'll pay the tab when I see Jesus.'"

"In tonight's prayers, you can remind Leonard that his tab's come due and with luck, he's at the right place to pay it."

Serendipity went blank.

Anyway, I figured the C-note came from me. Had he lived, with that taste, his poverty would've far outlasted the stolen letters. "Where does Desiree live?" I urged.

"Have you tried the—?"

The front door burst open behind me. Serendipity's eyes widened. She froze, her lips tight and pale beneath the thin lipstick sheath. "I gotta go!"

"No, by God!" Karl Sprader yelled. "Richard Scott'll do the running!"

I wheeled. And ducked.

Aimed for my ear, his ham fist whistled overhead.

In a quick reflex, I feinted for Sprader's chin, then punched deep into his gut.

My fist drove an agonized, "Oh nooooh!" from the bottom lobes of his lungs. He bent double, recovering only enough to grope for my shoulders, trying to clinch.

Tavern bad-asses sometimes fight for sport. I matriculated in 'Nam and Kuwait. I figure fights translate into blood. I grabbed his shoulders and whipped his body toward me, burying my forehead in his face.

He shook his head and blinked his eyes. Blinded, he tried to ID the concrete block that had just crushed the bridge of his nose.

I speared him in the groin with the toe of my wingtip. He collapsed onto a glossy section of the floor—the highlighted spot where last night's spilled beer had varnished the tongue and groove boards.

Brandishing a bat, the bartender charged around the end of the bar. I grabbed the steel-bound cushion from atop a bar stool and waggled it, shoulder high.

"C'mon, mother!" I growled, slapping the red-vinyl against the heel of my hand. "I eat fat-rumped bartenders for breakfast. And it's not noon yet!"

Glancing down, and getting a clearer look at my handiwork, the barkeep braked to a stop. For a long moment he studied Sprader.

Sprader, now on his side, lay in fetal position, comforting his crotch with two carefully cupped hands. He groaned, his Adam's apple bobbing convulsively. Seeking release, probably not wanting Serendipity to see his tears, his legs worked like he was running in place. His gait was that of an ailing horse that gallops from habit but is too weak to climb back onto its feet.

I was becoming super-proficient at this family-jewel kicking business. Sprader seemed to hurt more than Petry when I nailed him. I whispered, "Sayonara!" At that moment, I just had to like myself and my expanding capabilities.

Joe Bartender snuck back behind the counter and stowed the Louisville Slugger beneath the bar. "Now, hit the road!" he ordered. But he didn't wave the bat nor stray from behind the waist-high barrier. Nor did he lift the phone to call the cops. Could be, he figured the fight concluded, or he was afraid he might join Sprader on the floor. More likely, he figured Sprader would want to handle this thing later—his own way, with no outside interference.

I looked around for Serendipity. I wanted her to finish her tantalizing question about where to try looking for Desiree. But she had disappeared. I suspected I'd never hear those final words, now that Sprader had made the scene. I didn't.

Chapter Forty

JITTERY ABOUT THE TIGHT flight schedule, afraid Samantha's departure time for London might overlap Caitlin's arrival from New York, I picked Sam up at her door. I found myself hurrying—as if I could influence the schedule.

Carrying her three pieces of luggage to the sidewalk, I returned for the last one while she turned off lights and left a final message on a friend's answering machine. She checked the front door lock . . . once . . . twice . . . then compulsively twisted the knob a third time.

I put down her last bag and asked, "What's the matter? Afraid Joe's going to break in and trash the place, or that he's going to learn some new things you don't want revealed?"

She ignored me.

We walked together to the car with my yanking at the brindle suitcase's strap as if tugging at a recalcitrant George. I quickly loaded the first two pieces. With a loud, "Holy Momma!" I hoisted the last atop the others. "God, Sam! Do the airlines allow you to carry sample cases of rocks?" I groaned, crossing my forearms and kneading my shoulders. Both arms had been nearly twisted free of their sockets. I wanted privacy before hunkering down to examine my lower body parts for hernias.

"I must have my books."

"Yeah, I know . . . 'and my laptop, and my video camera, and all my jewelry, and my woolens for sure, my cottons, silks, and linens—just in case.'" I softened the criticism with a hearty chuckle. "Do you miss anything?"

We made the airport with a bare twenty minutes to spare. We thought.

Forty minutes later, the plane was still standing at the gate, and Samantha was still waiting to board. "You're fidgety," Sam said. "Are you nervous about something?"

I shook my head, but continued looking from side to side.

"I'll bet you're afraid of low-visibility take-offs. Is that it?" She gave me a peck on the cheek to make me feel better, then wiped away the lipstick smudge with a tissue.

Either the kiss or the tissue uncovered another layer of my guilt. "Oh, no," I blustered. "It's just that I'll miss you." I fiddled with the suede collar of her brown tweed jacket while surreptitiously checking my Timex and the dissipating fog outside. Sam's plane would leave thirty minutes late. If Cait's landed early, I'd have to dash between gates for my next affectionate "Hello."

God, however, sometimes untangles minor goof-ups for us humans. Saving my fanny, the PA system crackled to life, "Due to visibility problems, incoming Delta Flight 1009 from New York has been diverted from Indianapolis International to Louisville's Sanford Field. Outgoing flights will depart as scheduled . . ."

Bingo! Now, after another weekend of working and sleuthing, I would see Cait on Monday.

A few minutes later, Sam's plane roared off the runway. Relieved, I watched it climb toward low-hanging clouds. It banked and headed north for a quickie stop in Chicago, before a high, late-night transit of the Alantic.

I hustled out to the parking garage and climbed onto the Jag's soft Connolly leather seat. Already missing Sam, I sped south from the city toward the A-frame. I was seventy miles away from my present murder and fraud mysteries. But I was farther than that from discovering another new, and dangerous, enigma.

Fierce knocking shook the front door. I scrambled from beneath the top comforter, and pulled on my jeans and sweatshirt. Carrying my Glock for friendly company, I hustled through the living room. "Hold your horses!" I yelled, creatively coining a phrase.

Although it was daybreak, I couldn't see a face through the peephole. "Who's there?" I yelled. Maybe the wind drowned my voice. I leveled the Glock gut-high and yanked open the door.

"They're dead! Every single one's dead!" Herschel Peters yelled. Normally calm, he was wild-eyed, his face drawn and pale.

My first thoughts were for Samantha and Cait. But somebody would've called during the weekend. Stomach churning strong acid, I grabbed his arm. "Has there been a shop accident?"

He shook off my hand, sad expression undiminished. "No, not that! Come—I'll show you," he urged.

Outside, an almost vertical rain lashed the front porch. "Who? What?" I again reached for his arm and tried to pull him through the door.

He tugged his cap tighter on his head. "Come with me, please!" Spinning on one toe, he sprinted down the sidewalk toward the Ram, his fishing vest flapping beneath his arms like a bird's injured wings.

Yanking my ski jacket from the peg, I pulled it on while dashing behind him. The truck's engine was running and the wipers scraping the windshield. Herschel ground the transmission into gear and popped the clutch while I scrambled to get both feet inside the cab.

We bounced and bumped across the field toward Rose Cutter's Quarry. Mud wasn't a problem. We were skimming the ground like a hovercraft—going too fast to sink.

Herschel didn't park near the rim where Janie was stabbed. Instead, he circled to the far side of the quarry.

Accelerating madly, he aimed the truck toward a stack of

limestone slabs. I braced for a collision. At the last moment, he jerked the nose hard right and squeezed between the slabs and a pyramid of stark-white rock offal, corrected again and launched the truck downhill onto a hidden, double-tracked road.

Herschel's foot rode the brake as we careened our way deeper into the pit. We skidded to a stop at water's edge.

I smelled death. And it wasn't a personal reaction to Herschel's driving.

The truck skidded to a stop at water's edge. He jumped outside and ran to the end of a small peninsula. "The poor little things . . ." he lamented.

I joined him. Looking around, I placed my arm over his shoulder and gave him a hug. "Sorry, Herschel."

A layer of dead fish surrounded us on three sides. The lashing wind had pretty well aligned their bodies, belly to back, back to belly. They floated on the water, roofing its surface like multi-sized silver and pink shingles. A few mouths still sucked for water. An occasional gill pumped air.

"Look, Mr. Scott!" Herschel pointed. "I see a few carp, but most of those fish are frying-sized bluegills and bass." As he talked, he wrung his hands together. "Even the fingerlings and minnows are dead." He stomped a tiny foot on the ground. The long cap bill sheltered his face from rain, but his eyes were wet with tears. "I found 'em when I came down to fish."

Herschel's Shakespeare rod and reel still leaned against a sawed stone slab. His forest-green tackle box lay upside down, likely dropped there during his initial shock. Fishhooks, artificial flies, and brightly colored spinners and bobbers littered the ground. Waves lapped at a wicker creel.

A tiny kerosene heater sat in the lee of two Oldsmobile-sized stones. Most probably he planned to shelter there and warm his fingers while unhooking and re-baiting.

"Herschel, we'll run tests on the water and fish. We'll find out what killed them."

Farther out in the quarry, a thick-bodied black catfish rose slowly to the surface, half-heartedly beat the water with its tail, then lay bobbing on the surface. It appeared to have a second head. I squinted—it had grown a misshapen tumor. The growth was huge, befitting the fish's size.

Earlier I thought, "Dynamite." Now, I ruled that out as a cause of death.

"Running a whole bunch of tests won't bring the fish back, Mr. Scott." Herschel's voice was a mere, sad whisper.

"No, but whether it's dead people or dead fish, we autopsy to find reasons. Some bloody way, we've gotta protect each other and the environment." I took his elbow and guided him back toward the truck.

Herschel wiped his eyes with the corner of a carefully folded, orange shop towel, then shook out the folds and blew his nose. "Shame we can't learn things before the horse is already out of the barn." His downcast head nodded along with the words.

The rain had soaked through my ski jacket. Chilled, I tugged the points of my collar to block the rain from the back of my neck. I stood silently by the truck, my eyes moving point to point around the quarry. On the far shore, something spooked a flock of blackbirds. They fluttered a dozen feet into the air, then dropped back into the trees, as if too sodden to fly.

The wind died. Fat, vertically falling raindrops frayed the water's surface; tiny liquid mountains erupted to meet each drop.

The deformed catfish floated closer to shore, its spindly barbs like outriggers, the tumor causing it to ride unevenly in the water like a torpedoed ship.

What caused the tumor? What had changed and caused the water to kill so quickly?

I pondered the sequence. The tumor had required time to grow, but the fish kill had surely happened quickly. Decomposition had just begun. Voila! In addition to the malignant stuff already there, a new poison had been introduced in the water. But how? And what?

We climbed back into the truck. Herschel steered toward high ground. Surely long ago this road had been the removal route for the huge limestone slabs, for in the past the parent stone had once been dynamited and the pieces shaped on the quarry floor.

I hadn't been aware of the road's existence. Small wonder. My close-up visit had come late at night. It had been impossible to get the lay of the land, while dodging high-caliber slugs from a Glock 19.

Still, the road looked heavily used—and recently. Who had been driving it, and why? After all, the quarry was off limits for fishermen, except Herschel Peters. Maybe I was finding clues not there. The limestone shelf's natural paving might've blocked the growth of vegetation.

After a quick shower at home, I dressed and rushed to the office. "Jeanie, we've got killer water in Rose Cutter's Quarry," I said, my abrupt words dousing her welcoming smile. "Please, get the EPA on the horn."

She was sorting and filing an accumulation of papers from my weekend's work. Laying them aside, she leafed through the phone directory's blue pages while I described the fish kill.

"Poor things . . . poor Herschel," she said, her lips tight with anger.

"Let's line up tests. Tell 'em they have my permission for immediate diving. Follow the verbal okay with a fax. We must get to the root of this thing at once!"

Feeling like I had uncovered another murder—or more accurately—a serial killing, I stalked around Jeanie's desk and into my office.

Filled with anticipation, I sped down Highway 306. My visit to Abram's Trace was scheduled for tonight. The meeting would be held in the town's country club, so I called my longtime friend, maitre d' Samuel Jackson, to say I would be there. He was out and I left a message.

Reverend Gabriel Goodall and Karl Sprader, who seemed to play parts in my murder and fraud whodunits, were scheduled to star in a fund-raising production. I needed to learn more about them and their relationship to each other.

Another thought: I supposed Joe Petry would be there. Perhaps he and Sprader would get together and compare crotch injuries. At least the good reverend could pray for their mutually quick and full recovery. I doubted there would be a "laying-on of hands."

I also looked forward to seeing Caitlin McChesney for the first time in months. Cait presented a personal complication as well as a mystery. With Sam newly on the scene, my feelings for Cait had become totally confused.

Perhaps guys like me have problems with women because, in one sense, we keep establishing relationships with the same type of woman. My ex had been a deeply troubled woman who desperately wanted children, but could never have them. She tried suicide as an ultimate remedy to her problems.

Caitlin was a taller, business-oriented version of my ex; she had lost her adopted son in a divorce case. Now she seemed to be weighing options. If she and I reunited, her child would be lost forever. If she remarried Christopher, she'd regain the child, but be stuck in a bad marriage.

Samantha Petry shared similar personality and physical traits with both Barb and Cait. But with a stalker ex-husband and murder suspect son, her problems appeared even more complicated than theirs.

The women's history similarity was hard to figure. I often wondered if my relationship with them was oedipal. Perhaps, all three women reminded me of my mother? That kind of introspection brought me all the way to the hills surrounding Abram's Trace.

Trees in the area were sparse, with topsoil so thin and poor it wouldn't grow a crop, or if you fell on it, it wouldn't raise a lump on your head or body.

The highway next dropped into the rich Blacksnake River valley, where Abraham Lincoln once hunted bear. Here, also, Johnny

Appleseed saw a special vision of the Biblical Abraham before going north to Fort Wayne to die. The town was named either in honor of the founder of the Hebrew nation, or to pay homage to the savior of ours. Nobody knew for certain which, but as I remembered from living there, the townspeople still debated the matter.

I expected heavy traffic just beyond the Abram's Trace city limit sign. That's where the highway split the parking lots between two strip malls and, two blocks later, absorbed going-home traffic from Adroit Fabricators, the auto-parts factory once ramrodded by Caitlin McChesney.

Recollecting a recently read piece in a business journal, I slowed and looked to the side. The huge factory had been shuttered, employees fired, and its guts and product shipped lock, stock, and barrel to Mexico, courtesy of NAFTA.

That disgusted me. Rich capitalists move their manufacturing from country to country just so they can hire desperate people who'll work for the lowest wages while tolerating the shoddiest safety and environmental standards.

My slowdown snarled traffic. I read the twisted lips of the pickup driver behind me when he shouted an obscenity and shook his fist. I waved good-naturedly. Not allowing him time to inventory his arsenal and make a hard choice between the rifle in the gun rack and, possibly, a grenade in the glove compartment, I mashed the accelerator and sped on into town.

Two miles of framed one- and two-story white houses brought me onto the town square. I rounded the square. With the neoclassical, Monticello-type courthouse filling my rearview mirror, I drove east toward the Abram's Trace Country Club.

Now back on familiar turf, I waxed nostalgic. Not many months ago, I'd fallen in love while living in this town. Come to think of it, I'd also buried some friends, been stalked and shot at while chasing their killers. Maybe I shouldn't over-glorify the past.

I pulled into the country club, declining valet service, and parked my own car. Inside, I went straight to the bar. Samuel Jackson, my all-time favorite maitre d' cum bartender was missing. His replacement was delivering a tray of drinks to a corner table.

Waiting, I surveyed the white damask sea of empty tables and blue-patterned Limoges china. Nothing had changed. Even the carnations and fern centerpieces looked the same.

I remembered the first night I met Cait here. Light from the chandeliers' cascade of crystal drops and buttons had highlighted her auburn hair when she walked ahead of me to the table. This time, the memory didn't make my heart beat faster as I'd expected. Could be everything *had* changed.

"May I help you, sir?" the young, clean-cut African-American bartender asked. I turned to examine him more closely.

Maybe he was part of the new wave. He was dressed in a natty, blue wool suit and a red, floral print tie, not the maroon, uniform-like jacket, with the black velvet collar and the dark tie like Samuel Jackson always wore.

"I'm looking for Samuel Jackson. I'd appreciate a double Stolie while I wait."

"You must be Mr. Scott," he said, smiling and tipping the bottle of Stolichnaya vodka over ice.

"That a guess?"

"Mr. Jackson got your message and told me you'd be the gentlemen ordering the Stolie. None of our other customers order it by name."

After we gave the Pacers hell for a couple of minutes, I again asked, "Where can I find Samuel?"

"The crowd was unexpectedly large. The meeting's been moved to the Abram's Trace Community Center. The club's doing the catering, so Mr. Jackson will see you there."

While he served another customer, I knocked back the Stolie. I waved goodbye, received a snappy salute, and returned to my car.

Five minutes later, I steered between the limestone posts and onto the beech and maple-lined drive leading to historic Wynn-Dunne Mansion. I climbed onto the all-too-familiar porch and punched the doorbell; as I had with Samuel Jackson at the club, again I batted zero.

I noticed the pink stickie note attached to the door knocker: RICHARD, PLEASE COME AROUND TO THE CARRIAGE HOUSE. LOVE YA, CAIT.

Smiling happily, Cait waited at the top of the carriage house steps. "Darling, it's wonderful to see you," she whispered in my ear.

But I knew her well and sensed some reservation. After a quick hello kiss, I poured us each a glass of chardonnay. "Why are you slumming?" I asked, pushing the handle on my favorite recliner. "I thought this place belonged to 'me,' alone."

"It did, once, except for a few special nights, when it was 'ours.'" I didn't pick up on her hint.

After a slight two-count rest, she smiled confidently and continued, "Anyway, I'll be here only three days and didn't feel it worthwhile to reopen the big house. It's such a hassle . . . like bringing a cruise ship out of dry dock."

Dressed for the meeting, she was wearing a grey, pink-pinstriped pantsuit. The duster-style jacket, straight-cut and with but one button just below its lapels, reached to slightly above her knees and accented her long, willowy figure. Yet the overall effect was more business than pleasure. Intended? Of course. Everything Cait did was planned, to the most minute detail.

While we talked, she rose and used the mirror over the fireplace to add jewelry. "Do you remember this?" she asked, leaning close so I could see the incarnadine pendant on her woven silver necklace. The pendant, matching earrings, and even the wristwatch, were pieces I had given her.

"Give me just a minute," she said, and left the room. I got up and went to the desk. Columns of figures filled the screen on her laptop. I got the message: she was still preoccupied with her company's performance and never more than a room's distance, or two thoughts, away from the computer.

Feeling intrusive for peeking, I recrossed the room and flicked the TV onto the evening news. I watched three commercials and heard four news teasers by a perky, blonde newsperson. She kept making empty promises that she'd run some earthshaking stories after "Just one more important message from our sponsor."

"I'm back!" Cait exclaimed. "We couldn't be together for your last birthday, but you were forever on my mind. I've been dying for you to see your gift."

I ripped away silver, square-patterned paper, opened the rectangular box and exposed a glistening, sterling silver, Lorenzo de Medici Montblanc pen. It nestled in its silken bed, like an enticing lover. Definitely a pen collector's drool bait.

"You shouldn't have, Cait," I objected, but loved the fountain pen's heft when I made swirling motions above the coffee table's polished surface. As always, she knew the way to my heart. I doubted that the latest, graceful, silver ticket had cost less than four grand. But it was worth every last penny!

Abruptly I had second thoughts. And a guilt trip. Feeling trapped, seeking an out, I checked my watch and remarked that we'd best be going.

Following Cait's car toward the community center, I wrestled with my conscience. Between lovers—even ex-lovers—each bauble, virtually every gesture, has a *quid pro quo*, whether it's to prolong a questionable relationship or encourage a warmer kiss. Sometimes—no, always!—they each are equally difficult to repay.

I didn't want to hurt Cait by saying no to the gift. Yet I suspected our relationship had reached an end. So, how could I repay her—what was she expecting? A pound of flesh? I rubbed my chin whiskers pondering. Life's just too confusing for a simple man. Especially for one who's gutless.

When we parked side by side, my mind went quickly from confusion to shock. The car nearest us belonged to my second-in-command, Seve Jensen.

Within the community center, the tables were set for several hundred people. Both Reverend Gabriel Goodall and Karl Sprader stood at one side of the room in rapt conversation with a big-breasted blonde and her long lanky husband. Blondie talked fast and giggled a lot. Long-and-lanky tried to edge in a word here and there, but couldn't attract listeners.

When Cait excused herself to seek out the ladies' room to freshen her makeup, I looked around. No Seve Jensen in sight. Then I searched for Joe Petry. Surely he'd make the scene.

My cell phone beeped. "Richard, it's after midnight here in London." Samantha's voice came through strained and distressed, her words tumbling out, "Oh, Richard, Joe joined the flight when we stopped in Chicago."

"Where is he this minute?" I spoke so loudly that my strident question forced both Sprader and Goodall to tear their eyes away from the blonde and focus on me. Quite a feat!

"He's in the . . ." I was in a fringe coverage area for cellulars. Now, at the worst possible instant, the signal faded.

"Samantha!" I cried. "Where is Joe?"

When I said that name, both Goodall's and Sprader's glares became laser-like. A mirror might've shown two, bright-red, aiming-dots fluctuating between my forehead and chest.

The static cleared. "He's in the adjoining suite. He follows me everywhere I go. He—" The signal died.

Chapter Forty-one

I COULDN'T BELIEVE IT! All my posturing, all my hard-nosed threats had accomplished nothing. Joe Petry was in London, still stalking Sam and booked next door in the hotel. He might beat, rape or kill her. I must be losing my touch. I had expected Petry to be sitting right here tonight, at the head table near the elbow of his master, Reverend Goodall.

Stalkers excel in brutality. Sam's ex fit the mold. He owned both a fireball temper and a Glock 19, and never left home without them. He could compete with the most ferocious.

Now I had to find a way to protect Samantha with neither a hotel name nor a phone number. "Aha! I'll call the university. No, dammit!" Reading seven P.M. on my Timex, I reversed my field. The university offices would be closed. Desperate, I carried the phone as I paced . . . and fretted.

Cait's high heels clicked against ceramic tile as she rejoined me, and we moved deeper into the austere community center. "This table okay?" I gripped a chair back. An SRO crowd, nearby couples waited for our decision like perched vultures. We needed to quickly establish squatters' rights. This spot gave us a fairly good view of everything.

Cait sighted between obstructions toward the speaker's table. "Ideal. We can see perfectly."

I scanned the room. "I can't find Seve Jensen."

"Probably, after he saw you arrive, he departed," Cait suggested.

A woman pushing sixty, another nudging eighty, and two lovebirds in their twenties were already seated at the table. The chubby couple scooted their chairs in concert to avoid a moment's separation. One gray-hair winked knowingly, sharing smiles with Cait and me.

Pushing the season, the older woman looked skinny and cold in a flowered cotton print dress. I suspected she owned but the one, so dollars counted, temperatures didn't.

Her companion's head peered from a fuzzy blue turtleneck like a chipmunk from its burrow, eyes flitting in search of a killer tomcat. Grinning shyly, she passed a colorful brochure across the table. Cait nodded her thanks and tucked it into her purse.

The courting pair wore vibrant yellow, Abram's Trace school sweaters. Identical pullovers, excess weight, and inseparability made them appear so amorphous a single head would have sufficed.

One of Samuel Jackson's waiters snugged a cart near the table and unloaded plates heaped with pot roast, mashed potatoes, and acorn squash. He backed that with red Jell-o with fruit cocktail and pine-apple upside-down cake. The Jell-o was bright as a barrier light, the cake as big as a battery to blink it.

"Richard, the meeting's been hyped as a political fund-raiser," Cait observed. "But this seems more like an old-fashioned church dinner."

"Makes sense. Politics and religion form a compelling mix for Bible-thumpers. No telling the dollars Goodall can raise for a combo candidacy and preacher cause."

"You sound piqued. Cynical?"

"In Indy, Sprader and Goodall built family apartments on ground they had contaminated. I suspect Sprader bushwhacked me inside my own home. Goodall robbed my mom and others of their life savings. Both may have defrauded my company. Their friend Petry couldn't be here because he's busy in London, stalking his ex-wife."

"Who just happens to be your girlfriend?" Cait's question hit the air fully as dry as the Stolie martini I craved.

Interrupting, and saving my life, another server centered the table with a huge tray of piping hot buns, briefly distracting Cait. She sniffed appreciatively. "The aroma reminds me of Grandma's baking."

"Yeah, strong enough to raise the roof." I indicated our neighbor, busily whisking crumbs from his school sweater. "Enough, anyway, to make him swap his girlfriend's lovely, plump hand for a second bun."

Cait didn't smile.

"You've just heard the world's first bun pun," I concluded.

Breaking with custom, a third server arrived with tofu stroganoff and fruit compote for diners battling high cholesterol or tradition.

Raised a Baptist, I'm programmed. Hearing "Rock of Ages," I immediately recall a misspent past and fixate on guilt. When served either pot roast or roast beef, I "feel the spirit." I expect the next plate to be carried by a man in a blue, shiny-bottomed suit soliciting contributions.

Right on time, Karl Sprader rose to say grace. "Thank you, Jesus, for this repast," he said. "And for bringing Brother Goodall to watch over us . . ."

I almost choked on my fruit punch. "I hope Sprader's main squeeze, go-go dancer Serendipity Smith, arrives before the benediction," I said. "Maybe she'll slink onto the stage, straddle the velvet pole and really bring the crowd to its feet." Cait had too much class to respond. Having become the table's center of attention, I didn't have the guts to explain.

For twenty minutes, the huge square hall grew silent, except for a low hum of voices, the clink of silverware against china, and an organ recording that filled the chinks between sound bytes. Throughout the interval, Gabriel Goodall and Karl Sprader maintained a animated whispered conversation.

Only Goodall and Sprader sat at the head table, although there were place settings and name signs for three. The third sign was turned down. I longed to peek.

Finally, Goodall whipped the napkin from his neck. He patted his lips with an uncharacteristic daintiness and clinked his knife, not so

daintily, against his water glass. The crowd quieted, save for a few
mavericks still spooning Jell-o and one klutz who capsized a coffee
mug. While the awkward bozo mopped up his mess with one hand
and motioned for help with the other, his wife chewed resolutely on
his flaming-red ear.

With a thin-lipped show of impatience, Goodall tapped the knife
more vigorously against the glass. Now the room quieted. Everybody's
attention was riveted on the front table, and the crowd's anticipation
virtually palpable.

I felt apprehension. A sixth sense warned me—something brewed
here beyond politics and religion. Unable to put my finger on it, I felt
a cold chill of arcane warning.

Lumbering slowing to his feet, eyes searching the room from end
to end, Goodall lifted the ends of a colorful bar-striped tie, a la W.C.
Fields, patted his white-shirted stomach, and stifled an imaginary
belch. That earned him a smattering of applause.

He winked and smiled appreciatively. "Now, in the name of family
values, the right to bear arms, and Hoosier-brand common sense,
listen closely to my message." He lifted his trademark, pearl-handled
.45 from the table. "If any man, woman or child sees fit to contest
tonight's message, this might be the final arbiter." The comment
brought a nervous titter.

The comedic warm-up ended, he retook his place at the table. "As
proclaimed in Exodus, 'The Lord is a man of war.'" Now resembling
a leashed attack dog, he strained forward, elbows planted firmly on the
tabletop, his dark, deep-set eyes once more sweeping the room.

People craned toward him. Their faces like sunflowers, they lifted
their eyes as if following the sun.

"Surrounded by evil, we must never turn the other cheek." His
upper body springing upright, he hammered the table with a fist. That
brought a solid round of applause.

"Amen, brother, amen!" A plaid-shirted man at the next table
cried.

"I *will* say it straight! My message will be"—he paused, his voice lowering to a rich, mellow bass—"as divinely inspired as the Ten Commandments. Those same precious Commandments, now banished from our schools—"

"But never from our hearts," our eldest table-mate croaked, then caught my eye and lowered hers in embarrassment.

"Amen, sister. You will hear the mighty sounding of horns, not the tinkling of bells—"

"Brrip!" my cell phone interrupted the holy moment, beeping for attention. Desperately trying to punch the phone into silence, followed by the eyes of three hundred indignant people, I raced from the hall.

"Samantha!" I said outside, willing her to answer. Any other voice would spell bad news.

"Darling, I've called and called," Samantha said. "I couldn't reach you on your cellular, so I tried your home and you didn't answer there either."

"I'm at the Abram's Trace political meeting, remember?" I didn't add, "With Caitlin McChesney." Instead, I asked, "Where's Joe?"

An exasperated breath and hesitation, before, "This morning, as I was planning to visit Elstow Abbey and Chicksands Priory, I caught the very early milk train to Bedfordshire, where John Bunyon preached and was imprisoned for eleven years while writing *Pilgrim's Progress*—"

I cut in to slow the tumbling words. "Sam—for God's sake!—where is Joe?"

"Can you imagine? When I got off the train at Midland Station, he was waiting inside the depot."

"Ooh, boy! What in the world did you do?"

"I pretended to be overjoyed. We even embraced. Richard, I believe he fully expected a loving response."

"Of course! He's a stalker, hon. In his twisted mind, you've finally regained your senses. Remember, even after your divorce, he insisted you wear your wedding ring." I gripped the phone so tightly I half expected it to shatter. "What happened next?"

"It was drizzling rain. I pretended to have misplaced my umbrella. Joe skipped happily away. 'Since you didn't bring an umbrella,' he said, ' I'll collect you one in a mo', sweets.' "

"He's already speaking the mother tongue," I observed dryly. "Surely you picked that moment to grab a taxi." I squeezed the phone harder. "Please say you did!"

"How did you guess? Anyway, postponing my visits, I went directly to the station and caught a return bus to London." Again, her voice became excited, "Joe careened into the station, just as the bus pulled away. I crouched low in my seat. He followed for miles in a rented car. When he was finally convinced I wasn't aboard, he tore past the bus, swerved onto the interchange, and merged into the M-5 traffic for London."

"I suppose the bus stayed on the secondary roads, so he was gone for good."

"Exactly."

"Well, all's well that ends well," I observed, coining another clever phrase sure to exasperate Shakespeare.

"That was hardly the end—" The signal faded again for a moment. I tensed, anticipating more minutes of anxiety. "Last night Joe knocked on the door between our suites. When I didn't answer, he splintered the door with a chair."

"But wisely, you'd moved in with a friend?" I asked, holding my breath.

"God, it's uncanny—again, you've read my mind." Sam explained that the hotel manager called the police. "Joe insisted that I, not he, wrecked the door. While the bobby was sorting through our disgusting emotional mess with his superior, Joe disappeared from the hotel."

"To be swallowed by a dense London fog, I hope." The signal strengthened. Listening closely, I heard background traffic. "Where are you staying?"

"At the new Hotel Exeter, near Piccadilly. In the distance, I can see the statue of Eros."

"Stay with your friend again tonight. And you mustn't leave the hotel alone." She didn't answer. "You must promise—I insist."

"Oh, all right, Richard, I promise."

"One other observation, Sam," I said, covering all bases. "Eros was the Greek god of love."

"So?"

"Just in case his presence influences you," I paused for effect. "Is your friend a guy or a gal?"

She chuckled. I laughed along with her. The signal died again before she could answer.

When I sneaked back inside, people were stamping their feet, just as Goodall's radio audiences always did. Reverend Goodall stopped speaking and lanced me with a look calculated to melt collar buttons. I glared back. Joining the pissing contest, Karl Sprader and the audience also zeroed in on me.

I figured the whole group could fixate on me for only so long. After all, I'm not that good looking. I was right.

Breaking the spell, Sprader rose and moved Goodall to a podium. Now an overhead light accented the good reverend's overhanging brow, recessing his eyes, distancing him, yet melding he with his audience.

"God bless you, children!" Holding his open palms high over his head, he pumped his arms enthusiastically. "You know that I answered the Almighty's call to run for the U.S. House." He lowered his head as if overwhelmed by his decision. "My road will be long. My task arduous. My journey *ex-pen-sive*." He elongated the last word, hammering each syllable. His face twisted in anguish. "My reward is not of this world, but of that blessed realm beyond . . ." His voice faded, his face lifted in supplication, his eyes still hidden at the bottom of deep, dark wells.

Abruptly, his hands raised in triumph. Some in the audience waved theirs.

"He certainly keeps 'em off balance," I whispered to Cait.

She nodded. "And afraid. Just to keep him happy and unthreatening, they'll follow him to perdition." She caught her error. "Make that Heaven."

"Wherever. Point is—they'll keep the faith even if it costs the rent money."

He waved a check high above his head. "This ten thousand dollars comes from your own city's Buick agency. You too must give generously! Heed the law of reciprocity. Your gifts will be returned tenfold—nay, a hundred-fold! Your riches will be beyond imagination, your rewards beyond comprehension, your return greater than your most fervent dreams of paradise!"

He took a sip of water, then paced away from the podium. His eyes, suddenly visible again, flitted from table to table. Bright firebrands, they touched each eager face while crossing the room, and again upon their return. "Come all ye, come, come forward! Bring thine offerings to the altar . . ."

Most carrying greenbacks and checks, a few digging deep into pockets and change purses, people filtered to the center aisle and trooped forward like lemmings to a cliff. After a brief consultation, our pant-suited lady left our table clutching her own ten-dollar bill, a dollar-fifty from the lovebirds, and a green wad from her partner who stayed behind to ride shotgun on their straw purses.

A stooped octogenarian clasped the edge of our table to steady herself, then dropped heavily into the empty chair beside Cait. Gasping, she pored over the last page of a grubby check register, and dropped her ballpoint while painstakingly trying to scratch out a check.

Cait disappeared beneath the tablecloth. "I found it, dear," Cait said to the elderly lady as she resurfaced, the pen held high.

"Would you please fill out the name and amount? I go in for cataract surgery next week. Would you believe, I'll only be on the operating table for a half hour? And I may be able to get rid of my glasses. It's like an Ernest Angley miracle."

Cait quickly completed the check and made a bank balance subtraction. She also helped the woman to the front table.

When she returned, I asked, "What was the amount, Cait?"

"Thirty-seven dollars, leaving a balance of two dollars and twenty-six cents."

"It's called the 'widow's mite.'" I touched her arm. "Keep your eyes open. Somebody may trudge forward carrying a live chicken or a jar of home-canned peaches."

Contributions collected, Reverend Goodall opened the floor for questions. Answering a question about unusual threats to the Holy of Holies, Goodall paused for another sip of water, then leveled an angry blast at British television's *Teletubbies*.

"I think he plans to indict Tinky Winky," I whispered to Cait. "Is he joking?"

"Surely," she answered, rolling her eyes.

Goodall stalked from the table. In vain, we waited for a smile from him, a titter from the audience, or a clever punch-line. Sweat streaking his face, his skinny fingers locked on the podium like talons, Goodall agreed with other prominent Christian far-righters that the TV dolls were stalking horses for Gay Pride. He dabbed sweat from his brow. His handkerchief seemed to glow beneath the bright spotlight.

"Won't we whites soon become the country's minority?" another voice inquired.

Heads turned to locate the speaker. Looking ill at ease, a fiftyish man decked out in overalls climbed slowly to his feet. He stood with eyes downcast, shielding his face behind a Farmall cap bill. When applause rippled through the audience, he raised his head and smiled sheepishly.

"Emphatically, yes!" Goodall cried. "We must fight both integration and immigration." He raised his hands. "In the words of our esteemed Senate majority leader: we need to protect our freedoms from the 'dark forces.'" He twitched his first and index fingers to each side of his head, signifying quotes.

I wanted to bolt from the hall. I looked at Cait. With a

questioning frown, she indicated the door. Though disgusted, I reconsidered, shook my head, and stayed put.

Samuel Jackson stopped topping water glasses and lowered the pitcher. He glowered at a chuckling Karl Sprader, then glanced toward me.

Compelled to object, I rose to my feet. Rationalizing that the moment wasn't exactly right, I dropped back into my chair.

I could feel Cait watching me, and knew when she turned away. Having also witnessed my shoddy performance, Goodall and Sprader exchanged satisfied glances. Nobody had challenged their implicitly racist comments. Shrugging in disappointment, Samuel retrieved the pitcher and moved slowly along the table, face glum.

Suddenly quiet, Goodall moved around the podium and leaned his hips against the head table, observing the audience, his blue-suited body a metronome, hypnotically swaying to and fro, to and fro. As if mesmerized, many in the audience swayed in unison.

Voice softening, abruptly shifting subjects, he discussed the church's new building program for retirees. "Give one final love offering to the church and to my campaign," he pleaded. "For that gift alone, you can live your senior years in luxury. You will sit at my right hand; I will be a loving caretaker until you go forth to meet your God . . ."

A local farmer rose to give the benediction. Waiting, he shifted anxiously from foot to foot. Reverend Goodall waved a tumbler, signaling for a final refill. Samuel Jackson obliged.

"The reverend runs on water and malarkey," I muttered.

"Pardon?" Cait said.

I shrugged. "Never mind."

When Samuel approached, Goodall placed an arm over his shoulder. Giving the maitre d' a condescendingly tight hug, he waved theatrically to the audience. Samuel now became another stage prop.

His mouth tightened. I strained forward in my chair, sensing an explosion. The .45 still rested on the table. Surely it was empty. Would Samuel be foolish enough to grab it?

He took Goodall's glass, filled it. His hand swept forward, drenching Goodall's face. Rapid fire, he emptied the pitcher over Karl Sprader's head.

The hall fell silent.

Reverend Gabriel Goodall raised his face and arms heavenward. "Protect me from mine enemies, precious Lord! "

Sprader cowered, buried his face in his arms, and dodged backward. His chair crashed to the floor. Recovering, he raised his eyes just above the tabletop and reconnoitered the room. Reassured, he scrambled to his feet. Now more confident, he scraped together a handful of his neighbors' napkins and blotted his face and hair.

Samuel Jackson, back plumb-line erect, head high, eyes straight ahead, marched slowly and regally from the room. I charged after him and caught him as he opened the door to his car.

"Samuel," I said, "I'm so sorry."

He turned. "Mr. Scott, why didn't you speak? Had you objected, I might not have reacted so impulsively and rashly. As we've agreed so often in the past, somebody must *always* take a stand." He didn't show anger, just disappointment, like Cait had when I started to object and weaseled out.

Samuel's Ford pulled slowly from the lot. Cait and I stood on the steps watching, then returned to our own cars. A news photographer caught the whole sequence. He snapped again just as Cait placed both hands on my cheeks and kissed my lips.

Chapter Forty-two

AFTER FOLLOWING CAIT BACK to the carriage house, I morosely uncorked a 1994 Pine Ridge cabernet sauvignon. Solemnly, we clicked glasses. I felt as if I needed a straw so I could go for the dregs, having bottom-fed so long on Goodall's unadulterated dreck. Now, I had trouble raising my sights.

"Your friend Mr. Jackson will be fired," Cait observed.

"Yeah, I know . . . and I'm responsible. If only I'd objected." I wanted reassurance, but Cait didn't speak. "Wanted" and "deserved" aren't synonyms. "I'll find a way for him to get his job back," I finished lamely.

Cait had changed into a loose-fitting, unbelted wool robe, and a pair of scruffy house slippers the moment we got home. She looked fully as beautiful as before, yet ill at ease. Understandable. Our personal situation remained knotty and unresolved. Neither of us had the guts to broach the main subject.

Cait read aloud from the brochure provided by our erstwhile tablemate at the community center, "Under Goodall's plan, retirees who purchase condos from the church, are assured of a 'lifetime home,' no matter *the length of their lives, or the state of their finances.*" Cait emphasized the last sentence.

"I'll lay odds Goodall's henchmen run a very tough background check," I said. "I'll wager the basic thing they look for is big bucks beyond the condo's original purchase price."

"Uh-huh . . . but what happens when the condo owner dies?" she asked.

"Goodall's contributors go to their heavenly paradise, of course!" I sneered, raising my eyes and wineglass toward the carriage house rafters. "If, on the other hand, they've held onto their stash and not shared with Goodall, their ticket's not punched for that trip. Instead, *they* take the one-way, River Styx voyage—with the big-time fireworks."

Cait groaned. "No! I mean, who gets the condo?"

Accustomed to reproach, I continued without embarrassment, "The property is gifted to the church, what else?"

"I don't see that here." Cait carefully scanned pages.

"You won't. I learned about the program when they hassled Mom for money. Before I cottoned on, she contributed her bundle, although not a condo's worth."

"Well, well! This place looks pretty nifty," Cait indicated the picture of a beach-front high-rise.

"My God, Cait!" I exclaimed, looking at the brochure. "That's the Sandpiper View, designed years ago by ADE. I didn't know Goodall's organization had purchased it until last week."

"So?"

"Goodall's organization has accused my company of defective architectural work and is suing us for a bundle. It all happened before my time." Agitated, I got up and took a short walk around the room. Fortunately, my steps led directly to the liquor cabinet. Hey, I once lived here! I knew the road.

Returning, I refilled Cait's wineglass. Still trying to forget the disappointment on Samuel Jackson's face, I sampled the cognac, found a bottle of ginger ale, and mixed myself a Hennessy cocktail. Once more on top of my game, I sat down again.

"In more ways than design, the building is definitely a trap," I said. "When he victimized my mother, I concluded that, geographically, Goodall located retirees and seniors at the farthest point possible from their families and friends."

"Makes sense," Cait said. "Older people, all alone and sometimes confused, are easier prey."

"Yep, and the first check written is usually only the beginning. Eventually, their investments and bank accounts are picked clean. At Goodall's leisure—"

"At Goodall's *and* Sprader's leisure," Cait corrected. "By the way, Richard, I accomplished something more when the elderly lady made her contribution—" She handed me the third name sign, the one that had been turned face-down on the head table.

"My God," I erupted, hurling the sign across the room. "So it *was* Seve Jensen's car parked outside. He was supposed to sit at the front table!"

"He must have seen us come in, as I said."

I agreed, "And sneaked out the back door."

Abruptly growing quiet, Cait rose and approached the fireplace. Her back to me, she stood fiddling with pictures and whatnots on the mantle. "Richard, we must discuss our own situation," she said determinedly. She swung slowly around to face me. "I still love you, Richard. You must know that."

I rose and came forward to hold her in my arms. "And I've always loved you, Cait," I whispered, adding complexity to an already impossible predicament. Soon, I might add rodents to my diet: for a second time tonight, I had metamorphosed into a weasel.

Still, my words weren't hollow. If a man can't love two women at once, for sure he can feel strongly enough that he can't bear to hurt either.

"Richard, we can't go on." Her words came out slowly, and I sensed the separation between composure and breakdown to be gossamer thin. "I must protect my son from Christopher, even though it destroys the relationship you and I have."

"I understand," I said softly, kissing her cheek. I tasted salty tears and, even through the bulky robe, I felt the pounding of her heart. "What will you do?" My voice soothing, I reached beneath her robe and gently stroked her shoulders.

"Chris and I will remarry."

"Caitlin! That's the worst possible choice!" I exploded, "Christopher is a consummate ass!"

"I have no choice . . ." And that ended it.

I had always heard that the world would end, not with a bang, but with a whimper. Well, Cait's words spelled finis to our love with those last four words.

I spent a sleepless night, alone, on the sofa. Cait didn't fare better. Several times, I heard her moving restlessly around the carriage house. The house grew quiet a little before daybreak when, finally, she slept. A second goodbye could only harm us both.

Creeping quietly down the stairs, I left. My steps carried me past a hundred memories, a thousand tender moments, an infinity of unrealized plans and hopes. A nightlight glowed inside the country kitchen where a dear friend had been brutally murdered. No lamps burned in the mansion's windows, but memories of our days of togetherness filled every room. It was there, once upon a time, where Cait and I were in love.

I cranked the Jag and waited for the wipers to scratch through the thick, soft frost. Squinting between blade marks, I drove down the road, away from Cait . . . and toward Sam.

I planned to begin a new life with Sam. But she was thousands of miles away. And with Joe Petry close by her, she could be hurt or dead. Those thoughts chilled me more than the forty degree temperature.

Chapter Forty-three

I DROVE DIRECTLY FROM Abram's Trace to the factory office. "Other than the lobby guard, I'll be first in today," I promised myself, glancing at the dash clock, and exiting the car's warmth. "Jeanie and the rest won't be here for at least an hour."

Surprise! When I turned the corner to the front entrance, I found Police Captain Raphael Redonzo waiting inside the lobby. He faced the front entrance. Undoubtedly, he had waited awhile. He was leafing through a metalworking magazine. Nobody does that unless they're in the steel business or utterly bored.

My mind exploded into a maelstrom of possibilities, none good. Would it be rotten news about Sam? Had the police discovered my incriminating letter to Rankles' Business Brokers? I pictured Leonard Rankles' corpse and the bloody rose cutter between his feet. Had Redonzo tied the murder weapon to me?

This visit would be a first. The captain and I didn't usually meet early in the morning for coffee, donuts, and amusing conversation.

Buying time, I turned and chose a side door. Thoughts ordered, I sallied around the card-sorting guard's desk and approached Redonzo from the rear. "Good to see you, Captain!"

Startled, he came to his feet. We shook hands. "How can I reach Samantha Petry?" he asked.

"I have her London number, although its early morning there, and she'll be sleeping. Anyway, she can't be reached in her own room," I said ruefully. That raised his eyebrows.

I described last night's phone call. I recalled for him the night when Petry attacked Sam, "I suppose you're still foursquare in good ol' Joe's corner, eh?" The thought of their special relationship raised my hackles.

I know that having the "big bucks" allows me to be insolent when it strikes my fancy. If I were poor, I'd toe the line or risk trumped-up charges and a quick trip to the clink.

Redonzo stayed cool. "Then I'll notify you," he said. "You tell Samantha Petry that her son, Roger, has been charged with Leonard Rankles' murder."

"You've lost your mind."

The guard quit shuffling papers. Not every day does a company president and the town's police chief discuss murder suspects in the factory's lobby.

"Let's talk in my office," I suggested.

Neither of us spoke going down the hall. I had a feeling that once the whatnot shelf came into play, we'd more than make up for the conversation lapse, and in short order.

I held open the door and he entered. Redonzo chose the chair slightly to the side of my desk. He put his blue uniform cap on a desk corner and unbuttoned his Ike jacket so it wouldn't pull, bind, or wrinkle.

He carefully hiked his trouser legs before sitting down. He was wearing one brown and one blue sock. Perhaps he was color blind. Still the oversight could wreck life for a perfectionist like him. Banishment to Elba might be a possibility. Early retirement could be the answer.

"When Mr. Petry went in for DNA testing, we also recorded fingerprints," Redonzo said. "His are all over the death weapon."

"This is preposterous!" I thought back, picturing Roger in my office as he examined the rose cutter tool. Still, I couldn't admit to being inside Rankles' office and seeing the rose cutter on the floor between the dead man's feet. Redonzo would have to name the murder weapon. My job was to feint and jab, do a little soft shoeing, and kick the dirt until he did. "How was Rankles killed?"

Redonzo tried drawing a word picture. Running short of adjectives, he ripped a sheet of paper from my desk pad and drew a rough sketch.

"That's a stone cutting tool. I have its twin," I said nonchalantly. My eyes never wavered from his. When walking a precipice, never look down. Perhaps I could teeter my way to the other side. I remembered the unmatched socks. Redonzo wasn't perfect either.

"May I see it?" His voice was casual, like mine.

A confident man showing a simple relic, not one plodding deeper into a murder investigation, I strode to the shelf. My back to him, I rehearsed words of astonishment.

I glanced at the shelf, then wheeled around. "My God, Captain!" I exclaimed, my eyes blinking with surprise. "It's gone! The cutter's gone!" I hoped to see a rerun of my performance during the Emmies, wherein I might thank my producer, my agent, and Grandma Scott who taught me to love . . .

Redonzo rearranged his long body in the armchair, but didn't speak.

"If my cutter turns out to be the murder weapon, I can clear Roger," I said. "He examined the tool in detail when last we talked. Undoubtedly, the killer wore gloves. Voila! Clear as a bell, you have the wrong man. Release Samantha's son, and go for the real killer."

"Not quite. You own the weapon—and your prints are on it too."

"So arrest me instead of Roger," I bluffed.

"We knew you owned the piece. Officer Larkin saw it when he was in your office soliciting for PAL. Logically, your prints would be on it. As for Roger Petry—" He rose from the chair. "You're sweet on his mother. Undoubtedly, you'd go to great lengths to protect her son."

I walked him to the lobby. Just as when we came in, we didn't talk on the way out either.

Being a gentleman, I didn't tell him about the brown sock.

On my way back to see Jeanie Robbins, I dropped in behind Seve Jensen, who was hurrying along the hall. "Hi, Seve!" I called. Seemed like I was always talking to his broad, muscular back.

Gearing to a slower pace, he turned and offered a desultory, "Hello," but then, without another word, he detoured into the accounting department. I couldn't be certain, but his limp appeared to worsen when I spoke.

"I should've checked my voice at the door," I mused to myself. "It's like carrying a dangerous weapon. My friendliest greeting causes the sick and injured to relapse."

While I had been away, Jeanie had kept track of the Florida hurricane, and had a sheaf of newspaper and Internet reports to share. Seems that, after ripping the guts out of the Florida Keys, the storm weakened and, like a spent brute, staggered up Florida's west coast before stalling for a few days near Pensacola.

Gathering strength, it charged back down the coast and took a quick whack at the Tampa-Clearwater beaches before establishing temporary residence outside Sarasota's barrier islands.

"During the evening," one report read, "wind gusts exceeded one-hundred-twenty miles per hour with storm surges carrying sixteen-foot waves. In a cruel twist, the only death occurred hours later, well after a hurricane-spawned tornado smashed its way through a local condominium complex. While Bernard Glantz was observing clean-up operations down below on the beach, his eighteenth-story balcony collapsed, plunging him and his French poodle to their deaths . . . During recent weeks, the Sandpiper View Condominium has been the subject of a highly publicized lawsuit. . . ."

No denying, the Sandpiper had been figuring heavily in my life of late.

Collecting my emotional bearings, I squished more deeply into my leather chair. Could be, I was making a symbolic run at the womb.

Before I could wriggle deeper, Jeanie peeked around the corner. "Mr. Scott," she whispered, holding her hand over the cordless phone's mouthpiece. "You have an urgent call on line three."

I picked up. "Yes?"

I recognized Laureen Smith's voice, immediately. "Mr. Scott, Rose Cutter Quarry's filled with people."

"Run that by me again, Laureen," I said, hoping her description wasn't literal.

"This morning, while dusting out the living room, I heard voices over to the quarry. I snuck over. There were two yellow vans parked down by the water. For a couple of minutes, I didn't see nobody, then two men bobbed up out of the water." Her voice quavered. "Mr. Scott, they were all black and shiny like them channel cats that Herschel is always a-fishin' for."

"I'll be home in a jiffy!" I told her. Aiming the phone towards its cradle, I sprinted for the parking lot.

Chapter Forty-four

I SLID TO A STOP ON Rose Cutter's rim, slammed the Jag into park, and jumped out. In the quarry's midbasin, a diver broke the surface, his black hood centering a silvered corolla of air bubbles. He treaded water, then lifted his goggles and watched wide-eyed as I made my open-field dash down the rock-cluttered road.

A heavy-duty van encroached on Herschel's favorite fishing spot. A young-stud diver finished hosing his diving gear and dropped his skinny buns onto the van's running board.

I planted myself directly in front of him, my legs anchored like stanchions, my hands on my hips.

The diver drawled, "I'm Ed Clausen with EPA," before languidly unfolding his tall, thin frame and climbing to his feet.

I was abruptly aware of the incompatibility of my recent daytime desk duty and nighttime Stolies with two-hundred-meter dashes, and steadied myself on rubbery legs. "I faxed permission for you to dive," I said, handing him a business card. "I didn't know I'd receive two divers and a truck by return fax. This isn't your typical fishing camp, son." I punctuated my remarks with a wheezing gasp that closely resembled a death rattle. "What do you hope to catch?" I didn't explain that fish hadn't been the only victims hooked in this water.

He leveled a quizzical squint. "In extreme situations, I'm quick on the job," he said. "Also, I'm hands-on. I supervise. I do field work. This big yellow box is my field office." A thumb aimed over his shoulder indicated the van. "Sometimes, it's my bedroom and kitchen."

"Do you always park downwind from a fish kill?" I hadn't eaten. Now, I fought to retain this morning's coffee.

He smirked. I sensed that, contrary to my first impression, Ed Clausen was mostly business. I liked that. "Okay, more importantly," I asked, "what caused the problem?"

"Tests show that this"—his sweeping arm covered the whole of Rose Cutter Quarry—"is one of the state's worst pollution problems. In this type situation, water leaches through the karst formations. Nobody escapes the poison. Not Hoosiers. Not even the river rats downstream in Memphis, Natchez, or New Orleans. Pollution is democratic; everybody shares."

He still wore a set of fins, but, while talking, unzipped the wetsuit. It hung crumpled around his middle. His upper body remained covered by bright-red long johns. He hadn't picked up the sun-bleached hair and a beach-bum tan on the banks of Hoosier quarries.

A welter of equipment lay near his feet. A mask, snorkel, hood, weight belt, air cylinders, buoyancy compensator, information console, and diving gloves topped the miniature mountain. A loaded spear gun lay to one side. It made me wonder: maybe Clausen had found a quarry creature not yet discovered by Herschel Peters.

"Yessir! There's evil stuff here. If you're an ecologist, be pissed. If you caused it, be afraid. My department will feast on your ass." Abruptly, he stopped speaking and examined me with a pair of intense blue eyes. "*That*, my friend, is a promise from yours truly."

"Look, pilgrim, before jury impanelment and trial commences, tell me your findings."

"You've got beryllium, dioxin, arsenic, lead—" He paused to tug his legs free of the wetsuit before continuing the litany. "PCBs, liquid solvents, toxic sludge, filtering clay . . . Look, I can keep naming, but the list's abominably long. We'll provide a list in the deposition."

"But why the fish tumors? Those fish stayed healthy, growing big, then suddenly died."

"Don't kid yourself!" Clausen scoffed. "The tumors aren't new. For years, those fish have contained enough mercury to charge a thermometer." No longer scrutinizing me, now thoughtful, he watched as his partner across the quarry climbed onto a rock shelf to rest. With a start, I realized it was the same rock I had occupied after being bushwhacked inside my house.

"See, Mr. Scott, the problem begins when the owners close a quarrying operation. Left-overs get dumped in the quarry. Everything from steel cables to derricks, from broken wheelbarrows to five-gallon paint cans."

"Surely that's not a huge problem."

"No, but, it shows a classic screw-the-environment attitude. Fortunately, the owner's stuff is mostly inert and only rips holes in your butt or wetsuit. Worst case, it might snag a safety or oxygen line. Big-time problems arise when somebody dumps industrial waste."

"But what *new* poison killed the fish?" I insisted.

"Nothing's new." He shrugged.

I raised my eyebrows until they nearly met the hair on my widow's peak. "What do you mean?"

"Months or years ago, most of the killer agents were brought here in containers, from fifty-five-gallon drums, to—believe it or not—a small truck tanker filled with PCB oil. The junk tanker isn't near the access road, so obviously, it was backed to the quarry rim, unhooked, and dropped into the basin. The trailer drove away. The problem stayed hidden. For years."

"Now, I presume, the tanker and the barrels have rusted through."

"Right. Eventually, there'll be more leakage. The problem will mushroom."

I looked out over the basin, carefully avoiding the sight of Herschel's favorite fishing spot. Out in the middle, the crystal clear waters sparkled beneath the late-morning sun. "My God, Ed, do you realize how many young people swim in these places. Many quarries are okay, but the kids still swim in even in the worst."

"Yeah, but you don't know the half of it," he snapped. "Wait just a mo—" He ducked into the van. Three minutes later he reemerged, now dressed in jeans and a multicolored ski jacket. "Look!" He handed me a six-inch square aluminum sheet, its surface pitted and discolored like it had been fired in a furnace and then chomped by an furious, steel-toothed giant. "Earlier today, this aluminum was as shiny as your watch. For fifteen seconds, I suspended it in chemicals found in one of those submerged barrels. Now look at it."

"Case made," I agreed.

"Hold the agreement, Mr. Scott," Clausen warned. "You'll want to see your attorney. Maybe hire the whole freaking firm."

He eyed me, waiting. I stayed quiet, already knowing the implications. "Look, Mr. Scott," he continued. "You own this property. Possibly, the refuse came from your factory. You are our top suspect. You could face a huge cleanup charge."

"Hey! Stow the Miranda bit. If I had anything to hide, why would I call you?"

"Yeah, that's the reason we're talking at all now. However, you can bet your sweet bippy—not the county, the state, the feds, nor the companies involved will want any part of this clean-up expense. Everybody will pass the buck to another player with deep pockets." He thrust both hands into his jeans as if making the point.

"We're talking huge bucks," I agreed, my voice tight. I recounted an article from yesterday's paper that stated recently "the court assessed a local company a hundred million dollars for clean-up work."

"Big, whooping deal," Ed Clausen scoffed. "In that case, the company will arbitrate the figure way down to a half-hearted clean-up job. Or none at all. Hell, in most cases the deepest pockets disappear."

"Say again?"

"Huge companies bring jobs. Then they poison the land. Or they hire trash disposal people to do a cover-up for them."

His voice deepened when he stooped to slip his sockless feet into a pair of boat shoes. "Later, the company busts ass to Mexico where there are no environmental regulations. Unemployed people are left with poisoned water, higher cancer rates, and afflicted children." His words were corroded by bitterness. The thought went through my mind that he might've breathed acid onto the piece of aluminum.

"Since I'm not protected by PAC money, I suppose I'm about the right-sized pigeon to go after." I growled. "That means I've gotta find the original polluters."

"Be careful," he warned, not disagreeing. "People commit murders to stay off lists like yours."

"Without doubt," I agreed. "By the way, why the spear gun?"

"Just a safeguard. Some people would also kill to stop one of my investigations." Inside the van, a phone beeped and Clausen turned to go.

I waved, then slowly climbed the hill. I recapped: Previously, I investigated murder and fraud. Now I faced bankruptcy.

I remembered Jacobi Realty once managed this very piece of land. I recollected that the firm had a tight relationship with Karl Sprader. I pictured Sprader and Reverend Goodall together.

Could Leonard Rankles' lost letters and documents tie Goodall and Sprader to this disaster? Where was the secret file? Undoubtedly, it was with Desiree Martin. But where was Desiree?

New thought: Should I invest in a spear gun like Clausen's? It would be more difficult to steal than a Glock.

Although the sun was at my back, I shivered. I was still sweaty. Maybe, my quick, post-run cool-down explained my sudden chill. I wondered.

Chapter Forty-five

THE QUARRY DISASTER UNDER my belt—for the moment—I spent another long, lonely night. I checked e-mail. Good news. No message from Cait. I called Captain Redonzo to make certain Roger was aware he hadn't fathered Janie's baby. Under his present circumstances, that was surely small comfort.

I avoided calling Samantha. I didn't dare say that her son, Roger, had been jailed for murder. Not when she was in London and most vulnerable. Yet, I wanted updates on her ex. Joe Petry was still a blockbuster bomb with a lit fuse.

Sleeping, or trying to, I endured a debilitating nightmare. I dreamed I invented a new bowling game. In my version, there was but one pin—me! The contestants stood in a circle and had at me with hand grenades.

I awoke after midnight and reset the alarm. Turning on the computer, I listened impatiently to interminable squeaks and squalls while logging onto Internet. Perhaps AOL was telling me to climb back into bed.

Surfing, I found an early-morning flight from Indy to Sarasota, but had to schedule a late-night return. I booked anyway. I was determined to visit Gabriel Goodall's Sandpiper View condos.

The ride into Indy airport ended at dead-on six o'clock. After shoving my .45 beneath the seat, I tucked the morning paper inside my briefcase and hurried from the parking garage.

My cell phone beeped as I cleared the passenger entrance. "Mr. Scott!" Herschel Peters cried, his voice clear as a bird's call. "I know who messed up the quarry! When can we talk?"

"Tomorrow. Early. I'm at the airport." Cellular conversations are insecure. Sometimes, the signal can be intercepted. Herschel and I needed a face-to-face.

"Oh, dadgummit anyhow!" Herschel complained in his strongest terms ever, followed by a disappointed, "Okay, Mr. Sco—" By then I was deep inside the airport and distance trashed the signal.

I wanted to return home. "Still, I can't have bodies raining down from defective condo balconies," I said under my breath. "Come to think of it, maybe that's the way Sprader and Goodall dispose of their enemies!"

I thought I had whispered. Maybe not. The young couple beside me got up and moved. Probably hoping for a flight without a nut case.

Aboard the plane, I opened the morning daily and saw the Abram's Trace story occupying the front page. One pic showed Samuel Jackson leaving the community center after dousing Reverend Goodall and Karl Sprader with water. Cait and I were shown kissing while watching him go. Explaining that picture to Samantha would take some creative words, I told myself. Sam's being in England was good. For now!

Three hours later, I landed in Sarasota. I herded my rental Lumina several miles south on Tamiami Trail, took a hard right over an intracoastal bridge, and parked in a San Simon Key public parking lot.

I approached Sandpiper View from the beach. That was how Hurricane Aaron and the tornado had made their grand entrances, so damage would be from Gulf side, and obvious.

Today, in the late morning, the beach looked delightfully tranquil. The sky had but one cloud, and that a jet contrail. The glistening white sand beneath my feet felt as loose as granular sugar and just as quickly filled my shoes.

I retreated to the water's edge and its ten-foot rim of solidly packed sand. My sunglasses were still back in Indiana, and the bright glare away from the water hurt my eyes, but even without them, I could enjoy the damp sand's fawn shade. I had to give way to a mixed group of old-timers wearing faded bathing suits, brown-leather skins, and varicose veins. After staring at my dark slacks, wingtips, and blue poplin shirt, they held a whispered mini-conference and lowered their eyes in disdain.

My route also screwed up brunch plans for a flock of sandpipers. With their beaks rat-tat-tatting sand, and their legs a-blur, they chased the retreating surf. When the water returned, they scurried inches ahead of it before sprinting down the beach to outdistance me. They reworked the territory as soon as I wasn't there to hassle them.

"You should sue Goodall for naming that crummy condo after you," I told the sandpipers. I thought I heard one pipe its agreement, but couldn't be sure. Of course, when you're searching for breakfast on the half-shell, there isn't time to stop and bitch.

Pitying the sandpipers, I withdrew to the loose sand. That disturbed a gathering of gulls. They didn't deign to fly, but separated like a gray-white stream to let me through. They were still sullen as they refilled the space behind me. Momentarily, I felt like a small-time Moses, parting my own peculiar sea.

A first look at the condo brought me crashing back to reality. It was a beige stucco building with terra cotta trim. Each apart-ment boasted its own wrought-iron-enclosed balcony. The balconies were supported by ornate steel arms, left visible for aesthetic purposes.

Plywood sheets covered several windows. On the third floor, a crew had begun repairs. I hoped they wore safety ropes.

So this was the building my father-in-law built. Except for twisted remnants, one balcony on the eighteenth floor was completely missing. I pictured the balcony shearing away. I visualized a momentary pause when it ripped the bannister from the balcony below. I could imagine Bernard Glantz's terror when he and his poodle rocketed into open air.

Wanting a closer look, I followed a wooden pedestrian bridge over a dune line of sea oats and wild flowers onto an exposed aggregate sidewalk. From there, the walk wended its way between palms and hibiscus.

At first glance, these retirees were having it pretty good after all. Or perhaps I had become intoxicated by the fragrance of jasmine, oleander, and invested greenbacks.

I knocked at the maintenance manager's office. A stooped man of seventies' vintage opened the door.

"I'm Richard Scott, here to inspect storm damage," I said. I'd considered a pseudonym. As subject of Goodall's negligence suit, however, I had the right to inspect damages. I offered my business card.

Trying to zero in on the fine print, he pumped his arms back and forth while tipping the card at varying angles. "After what happened to Mr. Glantz, I kinda expected you," he answered. His yellowed false teeth clicking in time with the words, he added, "My name's Glarney. Hugh Glarney."

We took an elevator to the eighteenth floor. Hugh Glarney punched the number, then retreated to the far side of the elevator and peeked at me from a corner of his eye.

His cell beeped on the way up. He speared his ear with a knobby index finger, then vigorously reamed the air passage. After cursorily examining the tip of his finger, he unfolded the phone. "Hugh Glarney, at your service!" he croaked.

He listened intently. "Yes, Mr. Sprader, Mr. Richard Scott's here now. You want him?"

A loud voice erupted from the headset. Snapping the unit against an open palm, Glarney crushed the voice into oblivion. "I'm seventy-eight and working for fun. I won't abide much abuse."

He used a passkey to enter the apartment. Our shoes were deathly quiet on the thickly padded, maroon carpet. The apartment was furnished with heavy-duty, dark furniture. Like my wingtips, and the velvet drapes, the furniture didn't belong here, not overlooking a gleaming white beach.

I sniffed the air. Obviously, Bernard Glantz and his wife had liked fried food and at least one of them had smoked, heavily. Glarney pulled back the drapes in time to see me recoil.

"Bernie loved his cigars. He smoked them big, thirty-five-dollar Cubans. Some was this long." He paused and held his palms several inches apart. Not happy with his description, he circled two fingers to show girth. "Them Cuban cigars is what killed 'im."

"You mean he didn't fall?"

"Humph!" Hugh Glarney, exclaimed. "You see, Mr. Scott, Bernie liked to fish. He'd take his boat out on Sarasota Bay and fish for sheepshead and mangrove snappers. He was lonely, and sometimes he'd take me along. The day he died, because of the storm, he left his boat at the dock and fished off the north bridge for snook and sea trout."

He picked at his nose, face sad. "Them cigars killed 'im."

"Please explain?" I urged.

"Well, Bernie always enjoyed a cold beer and a cigar after fishing. Delores—that's his wife—got so she wouldn't let him smoke inside the house. She made him go outside. If she had let him smoke on that couch," he nodded toward an overstuffed sectional, "he'd still be around today."

One end of the couch was pockmarked with burns the shape of moon craters, so I figured Bernard Glantz was given time to destroy at least one lung and a sofa arm before his wife hung out the No Smoking sign.

Glarney grew even more glum while chipping away at one of the craters with his thumbnail.

"So you might say that his wife and not the cigars conspired to kill him, eh?"

"Yeah. Guess so. Still, I thought it kinder to blame the cigars. I wouldn't want her to carry that kind of guilt."

"Does Mrs. Glantz still live here?"

"Nope. The little lady can't bear to be in the place now. It's not safe nohow. Say you're a sleepwalker. You open them sliding doors. You step onto the balcony for some ocean air. Zoooom!"

He aimed a gnarled finger toward the courtyard. "Your butt ends up plastered on that fancy sidewalk, just where Bernie cracked the concrete." He looked at me accusingly, and I suspected that along with the Cubans and Mrs. Glantz, he was now blaming me for Glantz's death. Quickly, he lowered his eyes.

Not responding, I dropped to the floor, carefully bellied myself forward, and hung the top part of my body over the sliding door jam to inspect the damage. "If you'll furnish the hacksaw, we'll cut a sample from that beam, Mr. Glarney."

"See them fresh saw marks?" he asked. I nodded. "I already cut you a piece. Just remember the shape of that edge. The piece downstairs will fit it exactly."

I already knew what the metallurgical tests would show. For certain, during building construction, a criminal act had occurred.

Hugh Glarney locked the sliding doors and pulled the drapes. "While we're here, you mind if I take a quick look around the apartment, it being vacant and all?"

On my nod, he departed to check the bathrooms, air conditioner condenser, and the water heater for leaks. I sifted through a stack of letters and sympathy cards left lying in the kitchen next to a phone. One was from a daughter in Indiana. Glarney returned before I could read all of it, but it mentioned a suit against the Right Reverend Gabriel Goodall. Quickly, I jotted down the address.

"Who might that be?" I asked, lifting an eight-by-ten portrait from a hall table.

"That's the Glantz's daughter, Marilyn. She's now—" He removed his cap so he could better scratch his head. "Dagnabit! I can't remember her married name."

Back downstairs, Glarney cleared me of guilt and again blamed the cigars. "You know what?" He asked. "That big Cuban Montecristo was still in Bernie's mouth and still burning when the medics got to his body. He musta clenched that baby all the way from the eighteenth floor to the sidewalk.

"Old Bernie sure did like them cigars . . ." he continued grousing when I said goodbye and pulled shut the door behind me.

Two steps later, it reopened. "Marilyn Glantz married a guy named Lawrence," Hugh Glarney exclaimed, triumphantly.

Somebody would pay for the death. I'd see to that. But I couldn't make a case against Cohiba Esplinado nor Montecristo number-2 stogies, so I figured the Cuban-cigar importers would come clean. Still, Miami nationalists might try to hang the rap on Castro.

With a sinking feeling, I realized that Consolidated Constructioneers might be right. Somebody in my own company could've caused the death.

If so, even though it didn't happen on my watch, the blame laid solely at my door.

Chapter Forty-six

THE NEXT DAY WAS "designed for the vicious, with scheduling by the insane." But the morning broke slow and easy. The picture didn't last.

Again, despite the late-night flight from Florida, I was the first honcho into the office parking lot. Scrambling from the car, I held my briefcase in one hand, clutched my coat collar with the other, and tried to sidestep stray raindrops. An icy torrent overtook me when I was nearing the door. Briefcase roofing my head, I sprinted for the lobby.

The blue-uniformed guard met me with a full-dentured smile and a fat roll of towels. "Mr. Curl, is that rain, or a tsunami?" I joked, while trying to worm a piece of bulky paper into one waterlogged ear passage.

He merely smiled, ignoring my comment. I liked having this old-timer inside the lobby to greet visitors, and well remembered his squared shoulders and snappy salutes when he manned the plant's guard gate.

Nonetheless, after his last greeting, when he still worked the gate, I had driven past him and got bombed by steel beams inside the factory. I hoped seeing him again wasn't a precursor of another disaster.

"You could use an umbrella, Mr. Scott," he observed, lifting the London Fog from my shoulders.

"Yeah. Luckily, I'm inside for the day."

From long practice, he folded the wet raincoat over my arm with the outer panels inside so my suit would stay dry, then, smiling, he held open the hallway door and gave the back of my collar a bonus adjustment when I walked through. Then he called after me. "Three or four days ago, a visitor came by saying he had to deliver a package back in the factory. He said you asked him to do it, but since he didn't have proper authorization, I wouldn't let him in."

"Good work, Mr. Curl." I walked a dozen feet then stopped. On a hunch, I turned and walked back into the lobby. "May I see your visitor's log and the sheet where my anonymous visitor signed in?"

The guard quickly showed me the sheet. I didn't recognize the name, but the handwriting was distinctive. Searching through the file, I saw where that same visitor had made other visits and been admitted by a substitute guard when Curl wasn't on duty. His last visit had been the evening before I flew to Florida and visited Sandpiper View. Quickly, I ran copies.

Once in my office, I searched the office's break area for high-octane coffee, but settled for an almond-roasted blend and loaded the coffee maker. While Mister Coffee spat steam and gurgled promises, I booted my PC. Standing behind my desk, I leafed through yesterday's mail. Today I wanted to get down to company business and discuss the mall job with Seve Jensen—and the money shortage if he had anything to add. Even if he stonewalled me, I would call Joseph Schwab, the company accountant in Indy.

Those were my plans. Then I ripped open an Express Mail letter—and veered off into an entirely unexpected direction. Marilyn Lawrence, Bernard Glantz's daughter had written to request an "immediate meeting."

She couldn't possibly have known I had pilfered her address and phone number while at her parents' condo, so she furnished new ones upstate in Merrillville. Idly tattooing my chin with my fingertips, I considered the implications. "I bet she wants to include me in her suit against Goodall," I groused aloud. "Still, she'd surely do that through her attorney."

I continued, mulling happier possibilities. "On the other hand, maybe she knows of my sour relationship with Goodall and wishes to share information about a common enemy."

The Mister Coffee spat a final obscenity. Answering its ribald summons, I sloshed in coffee, and not finding a spoon, swirled the cup to dissolve a skim of powdered sweetener. Plopping into my leather chair, I noted the earthenware mug and the coffee were precisely the same murky color.

I considered another of life's mysteries. Why does almond-flavored coffee exist? World over, pub crawlers devour mixed nuts. Leftover almonds, closely resembling dead slugs, line the bottoms of picked-over bowls.

Now the ugly pits, unloved by everyone, had been collected, camouflaged as connoisseur coffee, and shilled to Jeanie Robbins. I smiled, thinking I might warn her against sleazy coffee peddlers— "right here in River City."

That mystery unresolved, I grew serious, reflecting on yesterday's trip to San Simon Key. I was certain my company made design recommendations, but I doubted they furnished the steel used to build the Sandpiper. That would mean my company didn't cause Bernard Glantz's death.

Better yet, my meeting with Glantz's daughter might be a case breaker. Anticipating, I longed to pour another cup of Almond Divine and fire a cigar like one of Glantz's Bolivar Belicoso Finos. I imagined myself luxuriously kicking back in my leather chair, hoisting my wingtips onto the desk pad and, with my head wreathed in a dense blue cloud, celebrating my own perspicacity and good fortune. Those were the happy thoughts.

Downside. Gagging on the smoke, Jeanie might demand a

transfer. Just then, with one eye on her watch and the other surreptitiously observing me, she hurried through the door.

"Would you believe," She sucked in a deep, exasperated breath. "At the end of my driveway, a school bus smashed into a deer? Nobody was hurt, but since it was raining, I played nursemaid to forty kids while waiting for a replacement bus."

Although the day would bring events much worse than a dead deer, or forty kids running wild in a split-level, I wasn't anticipating that at the time. "Jeanie, you got a minute?"

She finished shaking rain from her umbrella, then double-timed to my desk. "Yes, sir?"

"Jeanie, yesterday I promised Herschel Peters an early call. How about getting him on the squawk box?"

"I'll phone the tool crib. He never flies far from his nest." She grinned at her own analogy.

I felt ashamed. My calling the speaker phone a squawk box had probably triggered it. Still, good-natured Herschel would've smiled too, had he been there and recognized the comparison.

I returned to paper-shuffling. Thirty seconds later, Jeanie leaned over my desk, a perplexed expression on her face. "The shop foreman says Herschel didn't come in yesterday, nor today." She paused. "He's never absent. I'm worried."

"And I. Have you called his home?"

"The foreman has. Several times . . ." Her voice trailed off.

"Worse yet," I groaned. "I rang earlier, hoping we'd talk on the way to the shop. Neither he nor Minnie answered, so I supposed he had already left for work."

I maintain that human instinct provides rock-solid answers to most problems even before all the facts are in. Now, apprehension clawing my gut, I grabbed my coat, bailed through the office door and charged down the hall. An unsmiling Seve Jensen glanced up as I flashed by his office door. We didn't speak. I didn't slow until I was behind the steering wheel and cranking the engine.

Minutes later, I wheeled from the county blacktop. After

hammering the bottom of every water-filled pothole on Herschel Peters' gravel lane, I hurtled to a stop in front of his house.

I raced up the sidewalk, onto the porch's freshly painted, nut-brown floor, and stabbed the doorbell. My body charged with adrenalin, my quivering finger an inch from the button and aimed for a second try, I looked around.

The modest bungalow reflected personalities. And the rotten day. A combination glass and wrought-iron shelf held three tiers of decorative pots. Spindly, winter-killed stems protruded forlornly from each.

Beside the sidewalk, a battered wheelbarrow held half submerged bags of topsoil. Carefully placed bricks outlined a flower bed running the length of the porch.

So Minnie had been preparing for spring planting. Yet when it rained she allowed the potting soil to get soaked. I wondered why she hadn't come outside to take care of business.

I supposed Herschel had made the intricate, wooden scrollwork running overhead, decorating the space between porch columns. Same for the old-fashioned, colorfully painted wooden swing and the Adirondack chairs that almost whispered, "Brush away the dust, friend. Sit down, and let's talk a spell."

I hoped that both Minnie and Herschel would be around to keep up their end of the conversation.

Again, I punched the doorbell. While the musical chimes climbed and descended a diatonic scale, I pounded the door with my fist. I leaned over the glass shelving and squinted into the bow window. Tightly drawn drapes hid the room.

I yelled, "Herschel!" Zilch. "Minnie, you there?"

A clock cuckooed the hour. Eight o'clock.

Involuntarily, I smiled. An agonized moan from deep inside the house squelched any humor. I backed off a couple of feet and slammed the door with my shoulder. The door held firm. "Herschel, you must've fashioned this sturdy mother yourself," I griped, while massaging life back into a crushed shoulder.

Although feeling guilty about wrecking the house, I hoisted a chair and rammed its legs through the bay window. Wielding one of Minnie's clay pots, I hammered away glass splinters, wriggled beneath the drapes, and into the living room.

"What in—!" Against the far wall, red and yellow display lights played across an electronic display board. My eyes blinking to adjust, I yanked open the drapes.

"Jesus!" I yelled.

Minnie Peters lay sprawled on the piano bench, her back to a dark, lacquered electronic organ. Her head teetered on the music stand, both eyes wide open, fixed on the ceiling. One arm dangled beside her. The other lay draped over the ivory keys. Her face was nothing more than a bruised-purple, featureless mass.

She wore a nondescript pink housecoat. A torn hairnet dangled from a hidden bobby pin. Sheet music littered the floor around her floppy, orange house slippers.

I'm a 'Nam and Gulf War vet. Dead I know. Not pausing for confirmation, I detoured Minnie. Charging down the short hall, I shouted, "Herschel! Herschel!"

Grabbing a door frame, I swung myself into the master bedroom, stepped onto a throw rug, and fighting for balance, skidded to a halt. "Oh, Lord, no!" I cried. Herschel's diminutive body lay wedged between wall and bed.

I stood rock-still, my eyes locked on the scene. A string of dried blood split the middle of the sparkling white sheets and splattered the bedroom's flowered wallpaper. I deciphered the gore like a bear hunter reading tracks. Herschel had been lifted overhead and hurled across the bed. Still airborne, he had smashed headlong into the wall, his blood splashing the panel.

Herschel moaned, "Oh, Minnie—please, help me, Minnie . . ."

My deep shock turned to hope, then escalated to scorching anger, but I kept my voice as calm and reassuring as I could. "She can't help, Herschel," I soothed "But just lie quiet—I will!"

Cursing under my breath, I grabbed for the bedside phone, then thinking about fingerprints, I uncradled my cellular.

"You've reached nine-one-one," a young female's bored, dispassionate voice announced.

"Hurry!" I demanded. "Send the sheriff and an ambulance to Rose Cutter's Pike. I've got one murdered and one critical." After thirty seconds of confused direction giving—I can recall street names, but what genius can remember the intersection of county road 1100S and 250E?—I folded the phone and tried to comfort Herschel.

It wasn't easy, because of the way his upper body was wedged between the bed and wall, and I knew he shouldn't be moved. I didn't dare lean over the bed: movement might cause him to slip further down on the floor. I managed to squeeze a leg between the mattress and wall and sweep my suit coat over his body.

Help's on its way, old friend," I said, gently patting his lower leg. "It won't be long now . . ."

I had to know if we were alone in the house, so I went looking. Near the back door, my feet crunched glass. The Peterses would've heard a break-in, I surmised. The killer must've broken in while they were away, then waited for them to come home, park the car, and come inside from the attached garage.

I stopped, scratching my head. They were both dressed for bed, so I supposed the sadistic attacker had let them get comfortable before he struck. My emotions had settled, but the new thought resparked blistering anger.

I stooped, my eyes sweeping over the mottled green vinyl. A bloody, ball-peen hammer lay beneath the dinette table, its head matted with hair and flesh. I forced myself to move closer, then recoiled in shock. My company's brass ID tag had been tacked onto the butt of the hammer handle.

I retraced my steps. I wanted to stay near Herschel, but decided to go outside. If the police and ambulance driver blew their directions and overshot the drive, I'd be ready to give chase.

Keeping the front door sanitary, I climbed through the bay window and back onto the porch. I dropped onto the swing, hyperventilating in the cold air, coming to terms with the carnage inside.

Siren blaring, the sheriff's car wheeled from the country road and splashed its way nearer. As if propelled by a wave of noise, a bright red ambulance barked, bawled and growled in hot pursuit. "That racket should penetrate raised windows and driver's daydreams," I said to nobody, and slowly climbed back onto my feet.

Exiting the cruiser, Sheriff Casey DeLyle led the way up the sidewalk; his deputy goose-stepped inches behind. A quick stop might've spelled romance for them both. "They inside?" the sheriff demanded. I nodded yes.

"You do that?" The deputy indicated the shattered front window, and leveled a strong kick at the door before I could nod affirmation. The door held, and he grimaced, probably fighting an unmacho urge to massage his big toe.

"You might try opening the door from inside. That's a Herschel Peters lock. He builds to stop tanks."

"Yeah, but not killers," DeLyle observed dryly.

DeLyle's deputy limped across the porch. After frustrated looks at the door—and me—he reluctantly straddled the window casing and squirmed inside just as I had earlier.

Five minutes later, Herschel was aboard a gurney and headed toward the ambulance. I held an umbrella over his head while the two ambulance jockeys maneuvered down the porch steps and along the sidewalk to the ambulance's open doors. He appeared dead, his lips never moving, his chest expanding not an iota.

Figuring that even an unconscious, hurt man might crave a human touch—something warmer than the cold, plastic pillow beneath his head—I took one of his cold, skinny hands in mine. I glanced at his other hand which was resting on his chest.

"Sheriff!" I called. "While somebody else was getting a dinner, Herschel got a snack." DeLyle trotted down toward us. I pointed: Herschel had a tuft of hair clutched in his hand. I knew somebody had a sore scalp: the tuft was held together by a patch of flesh.

DeLyle collected the hair in a plastic bag. The medics maneuvered Herschel into the ambulance. Minnie stayed behind.

The sheriff and I watched silently as the ambulance slowly swayed down the gravel drive. Usually, Herschel and Minnie were together, except when he worked. Now, the separation would be forever. I verged on tears.

The rain grew from shower to cloudburst. DeLyle and I retreated to the porch. "Scott, you have any suspects?"

"None," I lied, although among my confidential shopping list of possibilities, I pictured Karl Sprader, Seve Jensen, and whoever tried to drop the beams on me. As a silent afterthought, I included Joe Petry. But he was still out of town. Wasn't he?

My mind in a whirl, aware I was concealing information, I didn't even mention Herschel's telephone call to me at the airport. I remembered his words verbatim. "Mr. Scott! I know who messed up the quarry."

"How'd you happen to find these folks?" DeLyle asked.

"Herschel Peters has always been Big Ben dependable. When he didn't show for work, two days running, I knew something was wrong."

His lips twisted into something resembling a half-smile, Sheriff DeLyle interrupted. "Company presidents don't usually go searching for tardy and absentee employees."

I described my special, neighborly relationship with Herschel. To better make my point, I nodded toward my house, its black, A-shaped roof clearly visible between two shallow hills. "By the way, Sheriff, did you find the ball-peen hammer?"

"Yeah, first thing. It got my attention. Your company furnished the rose cutter weapon for Leonard Rankles' killing. Now you've provided a hammer for this latest murder. You and your company are constant presences, Richard Scott."

Before vanishing, he turned back toward his drenched assistant. The deputy had just finished anchoring a line of yellow police tape to the handle of Minnie's wheelbarrow.

The downpour had formed a mini-lake near the bottom of the drive. Turning from the county road, a car split the mud-brown waters. Twin curtains splashed higher as the Buick sedan accelerated up the drive.

"That'll be Doc Warner from forensics," DeLyle said. "You can go, Scott. But not far. We'll need to talk."

"Will you provide a round-the-clock guard for Herschel?" I asked.

"Yes. I know—Peters saw the murderer."

I climbed aboard the Jag and steered down the drive. "I hope he lives to tell who he saw!" I said, again to myself.

As Sam had to Janie McNamara, I made a solemn promise to the Peters, one dead, the other nearly. "I'll find whoever's responsible. Herschel. You and Minnie can bank on it!"

For two long days following the attack on Herschel and Minnie, I had either manned my office, studied financial records down in accounting, or walked the factory looking for the yellowbelly who bombed me with the beams. I was up-to-here with interruptions, my psyche a muddled pool.

After sundown, I spent longer-than-workday nights sleuthing the booze joints where Desiree Martin might be known. No matter how exhausted I got, I kept reminding myself that she had worked as Leonard Rankles' secretary—and almost surely, she was still carrying around vital documents, just like the one I purchased from Rankles for five hundred dollars. With those papers in hand, I might learn just how Karl Sprader and Reverend Goodall fit into my crazy-quilt case. I could solve the company's missing-cash mystery. Best of all, I figured that Desiree had been a witness to Rankles' killing.

With so much at stake, I kept searching for her. I played a concerned boyfriend. I reminded everybody, "I gotta find this pretty lady. She's uh-drivin' me ape . . . That's ape with a capital A. Add a capital S if you wanna complete the phrase."

I shared a drink with anybody questioned, and bought for the house when I thought it would help. Adding veracity, I kept pace, drink for drink, pretzel for pretzel.

Sympathetic, trying to help, my drinking partners sent me on wild-goose chases that extended miles south, and north all the way to Indy. Some of them volunteered to go along to share the driving and drinks. Especially the drinks.

Nothing worked. Even Serendipity Smith was MIA.

Finally, the effects of the cheap booze caught up with me. My nerves were shot. My gut ached like an impacted wisdom tooth. My head was the healthiest thing about me, and it throbbed in time with an erratic heartbeat. I needed sleep, desperately. It was early evening and I was I was just dozing off when a car stirred the gravel at the end of the sidewalk.

I slipped into a pair of sweats. "Wait a sec!" I snarled to whoever was pounding the front door. I slipped into my sweats and raced to the front door. Then I thought of Minnie and Herschel. Not risking the door's peephole and a bullet through the eyeball, I lifted a corner of the window drape.

Doing a double-take at who I saw beneath the porch light, I yanked open the door. "My God, Sam! Where did you come from? You weren't due for days!" I held out my hands. Sidestepping my embrace, leaving my lips to pucker in the wind, she skedaddled past and stomped straight into the living room. So much for the "absence makes the heart grow fonder" bit.

"Some things can't be discussed over the phone," she said, in a voice not heard since high school when she caught me smooching Laurie Peabody in the rear seat of Joe Klein's hotrod.

Pale, eyes bleary from lack of sleep, Sam was dressed in her favorite outfit, the dark slacks and brown tweed jacket she'd worn when I took her to the airport. She had to be upset big-time, not to stop at home and change.

"Is something wrong?" I asked, introducing a banality. She didn't answer. "Did Joe Petry return on your flight?"

"No, after fleeing the bobbies, he immediately flew home from England."

"Not surprising." I played it cool, not pressing. "I suppose he wanted to get the hell out of Tombstone before the Brits issued an APB. That could've kept him from boarding an outbound plane. "But you see what that means!" I exclaimed. "Your ex was here in time to attack the Peters."

Sam's eyebrows lifted. I described the bloody scene at Herschel and Minnie's. "Herschel called me at the airport and said that he knew who polluted Rose Cutter's Quarry. I suspect somebody tried to kill him to keep him quiet. They obviously thought they had succeeded. His wife died because she was a witness." I didn't tell Sam that her son, Roger, had been jailed for murdering Leonard Rankles.

Deep in thought, very much alone, she paced the room. Her eyes fell on the torn pocket I'd left on the bookshelf after being bushwhacked in this very living room. "Where did you get this?" she demanded, running her fingers over the gold-embossed insignia.

"You know a New Orleans Saints fan?" I asked, hopefully.

"Fan, my foot! This fleur-de-lis is from a shirt I bought Joe years ago, when we visited France."

I described my heroics, in this very room, when I ripped off the pocket. She showed slight interest.

Talk about downward spirals. She had arrived incensed for some unknown reason. She had just proven that her ex had tried to kill me in my home. Now I had to tell her about Roger.

"Please, Sam, sit down."

"Is it Roger?" she asked, her mother's intuition on full boil. Nodding, I sat on the couch beside her and took her hands in mine. Her face a mask of concern, she didn't respond. "Roger's in jail." I tried keeping my voice low and comforting as if a gentle tone could make a cruel message, more tender.

She clutched my hands spasmodically. "No! It can't be!"

I told her about the rose cutter tool used to kill Leonard Rankles, and about the former Jacobi real estate man who had ventured into his own brokerage and consulting business before his stash of stolen letters *probably* got him killed. "Roger's fingerprints covered the murder weapon."

Rising to her feet, she dry-washed her hands. "What shall I do?"
"What shall *we* do?" I corrected.

Her glare could've pierced a bulletproof vest. Reaching inside her jacket pocket, she produced and unfolded the newspaper photo of Caitlin McChesney and me kissing, her lips curling contemptuously as she thrust it at me.

Now I understood. First, she'd been stalked in England. Second, she had rushed home and discovered the picture of Cait and me. Next, she'd heard about the attack on Minnie and Herschel. Following that, she'd found the emblem from her ex's shirt. Finally, I'd told her that her son was in jail and charged with murder.

Welcome home, Sam!

"Sam . . . Cait came here to say it was over between us. For all time. That was a goodbye kiss." I beseeched her. "Please, believe me."

Sam's expression remained relatively unchanged while her eyes bored deeply into mine. I knew she was trying to fathom the depth of my honesty . . . or betrayal. Moments later she turned to leave. As an afterthought, she pulled a small parcel from her purse and laid it on a table beside the door.

I followed her outside and held open the car door. I touched her arm as she sat down, but she shrugged away my hand.

"I'll find a way to clear Roger," I promised, but the Geo's put-putting engine muffled my words. Her expression when she raised the window clobbered any new ones.

Going back inside, I tore a red bow and silver wrapping from the parcel she'd left behind. The package held an antique, delicately fashioned, tulipwood dip pen with a solid brass nib holder and gold nib. Lovingly, I hefted it, feeling its balance. Holding it closer, I could see that long usage had worn the wood shiny and ink-stained the nib. As I've said before, I adore experienced pens that have written lots of messages about the range of human emotions, from love and happiness, to sorrow and desperation.

I imagined Samantha's thrill when, somewhere in England, she stumbled upon such a objet d'art. I wanted to kiss her and tell her how much it meant. "Still, It's probably lucky I didn't open the package while she was here. After seeing that picture of Cait and me, she might've stabbed me with the bloody thing."

Chapter Forty-seven

SINCE TOMORROW WAS D-DAY for visiting Marilyn Lawrence, the woman whose father, Bernard Glantz, had high-dived from a Sandpiper's balcony, I added intrigue to the mix. On the way home from work, I planned to swing by Arvet Consolidated. The company had done business with mine, and Scott Benefield had handled the transactions before he was killed torching my house. My previous visit to his office moved me to still suspect fraud.

En route, I stayed overnight in Indianapolis. As advised by my newest barfly buddy, I prowled several south side booze joints. Batting zero in my Desiree Martin search, I crashed for the night in my own Indy condo.

Next morning, after shaving and showering, I slipped into khaki chinos and a favorite sweater, then logged onto the Internet. The red flag snapped erect. I had e-mail. I clicked Jeanie Robbins' message: "Serendipity Smith wishes to meet you at Delilah's Temptation Bar and Grill. She said it's urgent. You and she must talk."

I typed, "I'll be there." I corrected that to: "I'll be there *tonight!*" Enthused at the meeting's potential, I typed in two additional marks for emphasis and clicked "Send now." Carrying my laptop, with the .45 tucked inside my briefcase, I departed in haste for my trip up north to see Marilyn Lawrence.

Climbing aboard the car, my bleary eyes focused straight ahead, I strained to see beyond the Jaguar hood ornament. I steered past the condo guard's vacant quarters and onto a morning-muffled street. After two miles of trees, upper-middle class homes, and a half-dozen four-way stops, the secondary street fed into a main drag.

Brightly lit restaurants and service stations clotted the I-465 cloverleaf. I stopped for rejuvenation.

Gingerly balancing a cup of scalding, McDonalds-to-go coffee, I merged onto the freeway. Speeding north, I'd traveled fifty miles before sane Hoosiers awoke and made first swats at their snooze buttons.

After two more scalding-hot carry-outs, and another hundred miles of uninterrupted corn and bean fields, I slowed for the last exit before Gary. Standing like giant exclamation marks, towering smokestacks marked the end of I-65 and the gateway to big-steel country.

Pulling to the berm, I rechecked my map. My choices were east toward South Bend and Notre Dame, west toward Chicago, or straight ahead. The last would lead through a sliver of Gary and across a steel mill complex before dunking the Jag's front wheels into Lake Michigan.

I swung east and hustled to the Chesterton exit. My last time there, my wife Barb and I had carried a picnic lunch and stopped for beer, chips, chicken sandwiches, and lovemaking atop a sandy knoll in Dunes State Park.

Now, living a new life, but feeling guilty and nostalgic for the old, I turned south, moving still farther from Barb and what once had been.

Damn, life is baffling! We reject people and situations, scramble for replacements, then secretly long for what we've lost. If we ever do recover the original, we yearn for the other and reach for the next. Talk about going around in circles . . .

I stopped for directions at Amoco. Yeah, men do that—sometimes. The cashier's booth stood between two pump islands. Squeezed inside, the heavyset occupant appeared to be wearing the booth in lieu of a bulletproof vest.

Eyes lowered, lips working, he painstakingly tallied a thick stack of bills. I pecked on the window. He marked his place with a stubby finger. Cupping a palm behind one ear, he shrugged at his inability to hear and resumed counting.

Silently cursing today's impersonality, I leaned close to the cash slot. Aiming my words so they ricocheted beneath the glass and into his ears, I yelled, "Is Blue Harbor Estates nearby?"

"Push the green button for high-test! Yellow for regular! We no got blue." Third try, he shook both fists and added a string of accented words that would earn him a stoning in Bagdad.

Sidling past me, a suited man slipped a twenty-dollar bill beneath my nose and into the cash slot. "I live in Blue Harbor," he said, pointing. "Turn right at the second light. Go a mile." He massaged a pale cheek, reconsidering. "Make it two."

The suit retrieved a dollar change. I smiled, "Thanks, for the info."

Feeling good, I even winked and snapped a salute toward the cashier. Nonplussed, he must've paged through some cerebral disk of possible insults. Finding nothing, his scruffy beard parted to show a big-toothed smile and he waved goodbye.

Three minutes later, I punched the intercom button at 1202 Meadowlark Drive. "This is Richard Scott, PI."

Chilled, impatient, shifting from foot to foot, I turned around to survey the manicured grounds. A red brick sidewalk led down a gentle slope toward a manmade lake, paralleled the shore for a few feet, then descended to a wooden boat dock. Obviously, the Lawrences had nabbed themselves a hefty portion of the great American dream.

"One minute, please!" Scratching its way through the speaker, a curt, masculine voice sounded colder than lake water.

Within seconds, an unsmiling, exec-type opened the door. Fidgeting with his brightly colored power tie, he motioned me into the foyer. "She's expecting you," he grumped, without further introductions.

Missing a final twirl, he unthreaded the Windsor knot. He yanked the pointed ends even and mouthing, "She's on her way," was off like a shot, down the hall and around a corner.

With my burgundy tassel loafers planted on gray, variegated granite, I sensed chill through my leather soles. The crystal chandelier's sparkling bulbs and draped buttons didn't lighten the room's mood, or mine.

Just down the hall, a woman wearing warmups and no makeup exited a doorway and moved lithely toward me. I remembered Marilyn Lawrence from the Florida portrait. This more mature version was, however, not only my age, but a half-dozen years older than Mister-Windsor-Knot, whom I took to be her husband.

"Thanks for coming," she said. "Please follow me." Heeding orders, I trailed her slim, gray-clad figure through a triple-width arched doorway and into a very high-ceilinged great room. She indicated a sofa. I sunk into its mound of plump, minimattressed cushions, and had to wriggle my butt to stay upright.

After fifteen seconds of clipped pleasantries, she asked, "Would you care for coffee?"

"Sounds great," I smiled. "Thanks," I added, peering up from my nest. I appreciated the overture. A clod might've said, "Sorry, I've already sucked enough coffee to float a squadron of kidneys."

While she perked, I scanned. Carpeted with a beige, boucle textile and furnished in light colored woods and fabrics, the room appeared to be a work in progress. A few books, pictures and odd pieces of mantle bric-a-brac added touches of color. With its soaring ceiling and sparse furnishings, the great room had the coziness of a cathedral nave.

I wanted to introduce Marilyn Lawrence to all my main squeezes. I had admired Cait's antiques; I liked Samantha's upbeat house; and I recalled that Barb always warned against decorating when depressed. Marilyn Lawrence could use decorating hints from each of them.

Again, but like always, with a start I realized that all my relationships now carried the sobriquet "ex."

Ms. Lawrence returned with a silver vacuum pitcher and poured coffee. For the first time, I noticed her fresh, Florida suntan.

On cue, she said, "I'm just back from Mom and Dad's place on San Simon Key." I *was* a perceptive spook.

Her voice had caught when she said "Dad." Remembering my own father's death, it was easy to imagine how grief influenced her attitude. Yet, I doubted sorrow to be the full explanation.

On guard, curious about my invitation, I slowly stirred my coffee. "I just visited Sarasota."

"I know. Mr. Glarney, the building manager, told me." Round blue eyes dominated her narrow face. I fancied that with a touch of makeup and a happy smile, she would've been very pretty. Also, I detected a smidgen of warmth.

While I waited, she collected her thoughts, smoothing her straight, blonde hair with her fingertips. "My mother and father were robbed," she announced.

"But why call me?"

She bored ahead with, "We've sued Goodall and FIPRO for defrauding my parents. They weren't rich, but well off. Now, all their money has been given to FIPRO."

Before answering, I stirred vigorously, having trouble keeping my anger in check whenever I remembered that FIPRO was an acronym for Final Prophet. "Gifts freely given aren't fraudulent," I suggested.

"No, but my mother had Alzheimer's and was incompetent to make contracts. Both before and after Dad's death, checks to Goodall's organization were issued against her account. And Dad's. Some, Mom wrote. Others, Goodall's secretary forged."

I interrupted. "So sue the secretary."

"No. The secretary admits writing and endorsing the checks, but on orders from Goodall. She deposited the monies into his account—also as ordered."

"But why call me?" I persisted. "My company's accused of contributing to your father's death."

Her eyes sparkled with indignation, her lips became tight lines. Momentarily, I pictured her father plummeting from the balcony. Her fury was probably targeting me. "Until proven differently, I shall blame Goodall," she said, clearing the air.

She leaned across the coffee table. Her hand strayed nearer, and I thought that, desperate for emotional support, she might reach for mine. Instead, she drew back. I breathed a quiet sigh of relief. "Most importantly, I need you. You'll be the most convincing complainant of all."

I stayed quiet, my interest escalating.

"During the course of the suit, we uncovered a list of those who've issued checks to Goodall's organization. Your mother was among the most prolific."

"Forget it," I shrugged. "My mom's checks and that lawsuit are ancient history."

"Were you aware that your mother still regularly sends money to Reverend Goodall?" The words had been whispered, and she almost choked on "Reverend," but the tone was triumphant.

Pounding the coffee table so violently that our china cups rattled inside their saucers, I came to my feet. "Are you certain? Christ! Goodall took all Mom's money years ago. Now, thank God, I'm pleased and able to pay her bills. But without help, she'd be destitute."

I remembered our last visit. Surprised when mom complained of a cash shortage, I wrote an adequate check. Now, I massaged my beard, puzzled to find she had excess funds. "I can't believe it!" I exploded. "Mom must be sending Goodall her piddling Social Security checks. Those were to be her mad money."

"Will you join our suit?"

"Certainly!" My voice had become a low rumble. "I'll go after him tooth and nail."

For the first time since we met, Marilyn Glantz Lawrence smiled. "How shall we begin?"

"Initially, I'll need metallurgist's info on your parent's condo." I mulled over the situation for a moment. "In the meantime, I believe tonight's visit with Serendipity Smith could help."

Ms. Lawrence arched her brows. "Seren—? Uh, is Ms. Smith your assistant?"

"Nah. She's a go-go dancer. And Serpentinity's sister," I joked.

Now, Ms. Lawrence appeared totally confused. I tried to explain.

"It's a bit complicated. Serendipity Smith knows Desiree Martin who worked for—"

"Enough!" She rolled her eyes.

Planting my elbows atop the squishy cushions, struggling for purchase, I pried myself aloft. "Take it from me," I said, moving toward the front door. "With Serendipity Smith helping us, we'll soft-shoe our way into a courtroom. Goodall will be dead meat."

Her palm lightly touching my forearm, she smiled, "Thank you, Mr. Scott." We had a good, solid tie—our shared hatred for Reverend Gabriel Goodall.

I couldn't know it at that moment, but Serendipity's assistance would reach far beyond Goodall. Nor, could I anticipate that, like everyone else in my perplexing cases, she'd pay a heavy price for helping.

Chapter Forty-eight

BACK IN THE CAR, I angled cross-country toward Fort Wayne. Now, I'd see Arvet Consolidated—the company that had been the recipient of numerous, big-dollar checks from Architectural Design and Elaboration. I reached its location before noon.

The visit was short. The company didn't exist. The address was in the middle of an Indiana corn field.

I should have known! Or, at least, suspected.

At dead on eight o'clock that evening, back in Bloomington, I parked in a side lot, tucked the .45 beneath my jacket, and sauntered around the corner to Delilah's Temptation Bar and Grill. Serendipity's promo signs had been ripped from the front windows. Torn corners and tape fragments outlined where they'd been.

A new sign boasted: TONITE FOR THE FIRST TIME! IN PERSON! SEX BOMB TANYA TROUVEAU WILL SING AND DANCE! Obviously, there hadn't been time for pictures. But nevertheless, what had happened to Serendipity Smith?

My gut twisting tight, I shoved open the door. Except for Serendipity's absence, everything appeared normal. Near the back wall, musicians were setting up shop. Searching for the lost chord, one picked stray notes from deep inside an electric guitar. Tanya, Serendipity's replacement, struggled with a balky brassiere hook. The drummer ripped a fast beat from the snare, then leaping to his feet, hammered dents into the cymbals. Feigning alarm, Tanya fumbled the bra strap and, smiling coquettishly, covered both breasts with her palms and backed close to the guitarist for help.

On an overhead screen, Bulls and Pacers muscled for rebounds. The Caterpillar cap crowd had gathered, but Jed Clampett had dibs on his favorite stool. He was still sucking a broken-backed Camel. He and the bartender were deep in conversation, probably swapping world views or tips on the financial markets, when I entered.

Peering from inside Jed's smoke cloud, the bartender eyed me. His smile evaporated like rain from a hot rock; he reached beneath the bar. "I want you outta here, Scott. Fast!" he yelled, and charged around the bar waving his ball bat.

Trying to ward him off, I grabbed the fourth chair from a three-man table. "Bartender, when are you shifting from baseball to basketball season? I'm getting bloody tired of that bat."

He feinted then, swinging for the fence, sheared away two chair rounds. I yelled, "Remember Sprader. He bled and dropped in the spot where you're standing!"

"By God, I ain't Karl Sprader!"

"Listen, fathead! Serendipity invited me here."

"She didn't tell me. You've caused enough trouble already. You've cost her her job and her looks." His eyes flitted toward the empty, front windows and back to me. "So hit the blacktop. Now!"

"She'll have to ask me to go!"

Three cold-eyed locals, a mountainous Hoss Cartright and two Little Joe sidekicks, inched forward in a flanking movement.

I yanked out the .45. Aiming it stomach level, I swivelled the barrel so its black, empty eye touched everybody in the bar. When I tipped the barrel lower, the tavern went quiet. "I've never kneecapped before, but I can," I said, my voice deep and rough enough to chip splinters from the wooden floor.

The three wannabe bouncers shuffled backward to rejoin their Budweisers. The bartender eased back around the bar.

I angled my way toward him. "Let's have it! What happened to Serendipity?"

"You'd know better than anybody."

Growing restless, the crowd again began to mutter. I decided to make my point quickly. "Check your facts with Serendipity, pal," I said, reaching across the bar and yanking a ballpoint from his shirt pocket.

"Tell her to call me here." I jotted my cell and home phone numbers on a blank bar tab. Wide-eyed, the bartender fixated on the pen. Wielding it like an ice pick, I speared the paper, pinning it onto the vinyl armrest.

I stalked to the door. Deliberately, I turned around. "Next time you pull out that Louisville Slugger, I'll feed it to you, sweet spot first." I offered a final thought. "If I don't hear from Serendipity, I'll do it anyway."

Back in the car, I dialed Samantha's number. "Sam, let's talk."

"I can't. Not now." After a moment's reconsideration, her voice strengthened. "Please, Richard . . ." Her voice tired, the dial tone clipped off her last words and my hopes for reconciliation.

Spinning the steering wheel, I turned the Jag's nose around toward Bloomington Hospital.

"May I see Herschel Peters?" I asked the candy striper.

She laid aside a *New York Times* crossword.

Her long, bony finger did a solitary dance on the keyboard. "I'm sorry," she frowned, "Mr. Peters is still listed in ICU. You won't be able to see him this evening." I turned to go. "By the way," she asked, "Do you know a seven-letter word for a female orator?"

"Try o-r-a-t-r-i-x. "

Her lead pencil scratched the paper. "It fits with x-ray. Thanks."

I rode an elevator to the third floor nurse's station. Inside the glass cubicle, a straw-haired nurse whispered into a phone. Another clicked reports into a computer terminal. She'd been in the business long enough to go silver, and her name tag read, CLAIRE KELLY,R.N., SENIOR NURSE.

An old man maneuvered his wheelchair down the hall, grizzled head bowed, an open-backed gown showing a waxen, mole-splattered back. First one veined hand, then the other powered the wheels. Tiny, almost imperceptible, zigs and zags measured the chair's progress.

A rumpled, blue uniform hurried by pushing a load of trays, the cart's wheels squeaking for the old guy in the wheelchair to give way. The sight, and my reason for being here, caused me to picture Herschel in a wheelchair. Just the thought enraged me—and heightened my resolve for revenge.

Down the hall, a uniformed deputy lounged beneath an Intensive Care sign, so I knew where Herschel Peters was presently housed. On second thought, I supposed the wheelchair would be an upgrade from the ICU's tubes and wires.

Feeling trapped, I fidgeted. Supposedly, hospitals have an overriding odor of medicines and cleaning agents. Not for me! My nose distinguishes hidden components. I detect urine, feces, rancid flesh, and foul air from sick lungs. I suspect that I'm getting a whiff of my own destiny, and it scares hell out of me.

Finally, the computer terminal fell silent. "Ms. Kelly, I need an update on Mr. Peters."

Eyes wary, she glanced first at the deputy and then back to me. I showed an ID. She looked relieved. "He's still listed as critical." She pointed out that there had been a reduction in his brain swelling. "He's holding his own."

"Call me if there's any change." I handed her my card.

"I'm sorry, but first, the family must be notified."

Herschel had no kids. I pictured Minnie on the music bench, her dead eyes staring overhead toward the ceiling. "I may be the nearest thing to family, he has left."

I spent another long evening fighting the urge to dial Sam at home, willing calls from both her and Serendipity.

I didn't phone. Neither did they.

Just after midnight, I got a surprise call from the nurse in ICU. "This is Claire Kelly, at Bloomington Hospital," she said, her voice somber.

"How's Herschel?" I held my breath, deathly afraid of the news.

"It's not Mr. Peters," Ms. Kelly said. "It's Samantha Petry. She wanted me to call and tell you she was here at the hospital."

"So she's checking on Herschel herself?"

"You misunderstand. She's in critical care; she's been badly beaten."

I reached the hospital within thirty minutes. I looked into her room. Working feverishly, doctors and nurses were hunched over Sam. I couldn't get a clear look, but her face looked badly bruised. She was lying very, very still.

Claire Kelly saw me and came outside. "For the remainder of the night, Ms. Petry will be under sedation. You may see her during normal visiting hours tomorrow."

I was disappointed, but at least I could stay nearby. Going to the waiting room, I picked up the visitor's phone and called my housekeeper, Laureen Smith. "Do you still have the keys to Benefield's office?"

"I forgot to turn them in." She sounded defensive, maybe expecting a reprimand.

"I know this sounds strange, but could you meet me there at four in the morning?"

The phone went quiet. "I'll pay you . . . and I have to be there before the secretary makes the scene," I explained. "I've got to see inside that safe." I didn't tell Laureen that my company had been losing millions of dollars and that I might discover who had stolen it.

I sat in the waiting room until three A.M. Reassured by the night-shift nurse, I said goodbye and rode the elevator back to the bottom floor. Outside, I breathed deeply, trembling like an aspen when the outside air reached my lungs. My jacket zipped to the top, I slowly climbed the concrete steps to second floor parking.

Optimism is difficult after a night spent in a hospital's intensive care unit. Yet, I sensed I was closing in on a bunch of perps. Before an arrest could be made, I'd have to arrange for special transportation.

When I wrapped the cases this time, I'd need a bus to haul all my enemies to jail.

Chapter Forty-nine

Laureen Smith, clad in a crisp, blue uniform dress, but smiling sleepily, met me in Benefield Enterprises' upstairs lobby. Meticulously, she sorted through the tangled keys on a jangling, choker-sized key ring. Seeing her assortment, I predicted she could unlock every office she ever cleaned.

Finally the door swung open. On edge, anticipating a mother's lode of incriminating evidence, I longed to push Laureen aside and rush into the walnut-paneled office. But I didn't.

Her broad figure blocking the doorway, she paused to sniff the air. "This place is certainly musty. 'Course, it hasn't had a good cleaning since Mr. Benefield went to make his peace with God." Crossing herself, she hustled inside.

I sniffed too, but my nose must've been keener than Laureen's. I got a strong whiff of Van Cleef and Arpels cologne, a fragrance I used to wear.

"I'll stay outside in the lobby," Laureen said. "If the downstairs door opens, I'll begin vacuuming. You'll know we've got visitors."

I nodded conspiratorially. "And I'll dart into the restroom."

Making myself at home, I plopped down in Clark Benefield's softly upholstered chair. First off, I felt guilty wriggling my hefty buns into the depressions made by his late, lamented butt.

Then I remembered that although after Janie McNamara's murder he had seemingly protected Roger Petry from the police, he also had a past romantic involvement with Janie himself, and just might have killed her. Topping that, Benefield had been accidentally or intentionally parboiled in the sump pit while torching my father-in-laws house—and but for my own good luck, he might have roasted me. Now, today, there was the matter of Benefield Enterprises and its involvement with my company ADE, and possibly its missing money. Guilt assuaged, I placed my laptop on his fancy, rococo desk and flipped open the screen.

Ready to compare his computer records with mine, I powered up his PC and stroked the key pad. Once again, as if still holding an electronic grudge, the secretive bugger screamed ACCESS DENIED and PROGRAM TERMINATED in huge yellow letters that filled the screen.

Surmising that it would be hard copies or nothing, I surveyed the office. Bingo! I rushed across the room to a three-drawer, fireproof filing cabinet.

"Oh, no!" Scrapes and gouges covered the gray cabinet's sheet metal surface. The drawers had held fast, but a top corner on one jutted out, and the handle hung askew.

Laureen charged in from the lobby. "What, for heaven's sake, is wrong?" she demanded.

I remembered the telltale trace of cologne. "This morning's previous visitor must've sledge-hammered this baby." I wiggled my finger inside a jagged hole. The lock mechanism had been punched deep into the center of the door. "Laureen," I said, my voice gone morose, "unless you've brought a cutting torch on that key chain, we're dead meat."

Her lips curling in disdain, Laureen unsheathed her massive key collection, while I reshaped a coat hanger per her instructions. Firing orders, she maneuvered the key, while I steadied the lock with the wire hook plus a silver letter opener from Benefield's desk.

Grunting loudly, I yanked open the drawer. "Eureka!" I gave Laureen an exuberant, politically incorrect hug. If she charged sexual harassment, her Heimlich-strong response provided a defense. I could countersue based on busted ribs.

The first drawer bore my company's Architectural Design and Elaboration, Inc. label—with the acronym ADE pencilled beside it. The second drawer carried a Pasha Industries label. The third had been assigned to Arvet Consolidated.

The scam involved a complicated paper trail. The concept was kid-simple. Our top brass had authorized Benefield Enterprises to hire outside companies to perform work for my company. ADE then issued orders to Benefield for both legitimate and phony jobs. For the phony jobs, Benefield wrote orders to Arvet Consolidated, the ghost company. My company paid Benefield for work never done. Bypassing Arvet Consolidated, the checks were deposited directly into a Pasha Industries bank account.

Now I understood my company's cash shortage. The owners of Pasha, whatever that was, had stolen it.

Orders and checks from my company had been okayed by somebody with the initials "P. M." I clicked onto my laptop's company icon, provided double passwords, and keyed my way into the accounting department. The initials stood for Peggy Murdock, the smart-ass girl with an attitude I recalled seeing so often in Jeanie's office.

Her job description didn't authorize check-signing. However, she doubled as Seve Jensen's secretary. Since the latter position provided extra clout, nobody questioned her signature.

I called the office. "Jeanie, on the QT, please run a D and B check on Pasha Industries."

Playing a snoop's role, she whispered, "What are you looking for?"

"I need the owners' names." Deep in thought, I cradled the phone. In my heart, I already knew.

I scurried back to the filing cabinet and found that checks from Jacobi Realty had also been diverted from my company to Pasha Industries. Now, I desperately needed the documents Leonard Rankles once offered to sell me. We could, must, establish connections between my company and Consolidated Constructioneers Vice President Karl Sprader, ADE financial officer Seve Jensen, and almost certainly Reverend Gabriel Goodall. I might discover ties to Joe Petry, or perhaps a link to whoever had attacked Minnie and Herschel Peters. Could be I'd even ferret out a yet undiscovered criminal perp. Surely, Leonard Rankles' sweetie Desiree Martin had the damning letters. I had to find her before Rankles' killer did. Or she, also, was dead meat.

Could Desiree's data prove Roger Petry's innocence? If so, then— maybe—Samantha would come back to me.

"Ah, shucks, Sam," I'd say, averting my eyes, and scuffing my feet in the dirt. " 'Tweren't nothin' but brilliant sleuthin'."

She'd kiss me before I could take her into my arms . . . Still in my flight of fancy, I abruptly visualized her lying in the hospital. Except for welts and bruises, her pallid face blended into the lactescent pillow case. My smile quickly died.

When I left Benefield's place, it was still too early to visit the hospital. I bought a newspaper at a corner stand. Today's *Herald* was short on news on the front page so I skimmed my way to a third-section "Political Viewpoints" insert. Later in the week, House candidate Reverend Gabriel Goodall would be featured speaker at Stonecrop's Metro Community Center. "Come one, come all!" the first article screamed in bold type. "Admission is free. Contributions to Reverend Goodall's political and religious crusade will be gratefully appreciated."

I wanted to go, but doubted I could hide inside the vague confines of the "Come one, come all crowd." I flicked on my Palm Pilot and scanned the date. We'd see.

Then, brilliantly inspired, I reached for my cell phone. Sitting back in the Jag's front seat, I dialed Marilyn Lawrence's number. She answered first ring. "Ms. Lawrence, here's a meeting you might wish to attend . . ." Then, I dialed another number, and another, and another, in each instance making the identical request.

Tossing the paper in the backseat, I rushed to the factory and walked the aisles, once more looking for the crane operator who'd tried to snuff me. Again, I shot craps. Then I checked my Timex and raced through a side door to the parking lot.

I rehearsed my most creative dialogue lines during a fast drive to the hospital. Once there, I pulled my chair kissing-close, my knees presses against Samantha's tubular bed. She was still sedated and sleeping, but I lay my cheek against hers and whispered the only things that really mattered: "I'm so sorry, darling . . . I love you so much . . ."

Sam stirred and whispered, "And I love you . . ." before fading back into sleep.

I stayed beside her, shifting only for an attending nurse, moving only when I stroked her hand or arm or brushed her hair with my fingertips. Finally, her eyes fluttered open and she managed a weak smile.

I could no longer wait. I had to tell her—she had to know. "Sam," I blurted, "despite the photo of Caitlin and me kissing, that romance is dead, and had been even before the picture was snapped."

"I believe you. I do need you," she murmured. "I do understand."

Gently, I ran my fingertips over her face. She flinched when my fingers touched her neck, then whispered, "Oh, Richard, hold me close."

Obliging, I caressed her shoulders, my hands moving slowly and tenderly over her shoulders and back. I kissed her cheek and her neck. Finally, her breathing slowed. I gingerly removed my arms and crept across the room to wait, watching as she slept.

After an hour, Sam's eyes snapped. With a startled expression on her face, she looked around the room. She smiled when she saw me and I returned to the chair nearer her bed.

She appeared fully awake and I let her talk first. "Last night I returned late from class. I was taken completely by surprise. I parked the car—"

I interrupted, unable to hold myself. "You and that alley garage! In future, please park on the street."

"I know, I know," she agreed, placating me.

Still, I knew she'd continue to take risks rather than give up ordinary rights to her own home.

"Anyway," she went on, "I was unlocking the back door when I was grabbed and hurled against the brick wall."

"You bloody well know Joe did it."

"I believe so. But the light was poor, the man was masked and didn't say a word." Struggling to retrieve some lost detail, she reached for her forehead and winced when her fingers brushed a pink and red bruise. "I'm sorry Richard—I can't say with certainty that it was Joe."

I could see Sam was riding a thin emotional edge. She rubbed her palms together, fighting not to tremble. Again, I took her in my arms. But now, my thoughts were about Joe Petry, my mind seething with fury. Gently, I kneaded her shoulders, careful not to touch her neck. After a while the tight muscles began to relax.

Becoming drowsy, she stopped talking. Still in my arms, she dozed. Just like before, she again awoke with a start. She wrenched herself away from me. I wondered how long it would take her to forget. I must be there for her.

"It's okay, Sam. It's okay. You're safe."

She rose up and swung around and sat quietly for a few minutes, her bare feet dangling from the tall bed. I asked a passing nurse to refill the water pitcher. After a sip of ice water, Sam resumed talking as if there had been no interruption.

"Once again, Miss Jarrett saved the day. She saw the trouble from her upstairs window and screamed to high heavens." Sam paused. "Joe—or whoever—threw me to the ground and bolted down the alley. Moments later, I heard a car door slam."

"The case is closing, Sam. Soon you'll be back at the old grind. You'll be checking your clothes and hair in the hall mirror and hurrying off to class."

"God, I hate to be shallow, but I dread class, looking like this. My bruises changing to black and blue, and finally a putrid yellow and green." Taking her purse from the drawer in the side table, she fished for a compact and examined the bruises on her face, giving each welt a minute appraisal. "I'll look like an eggplant." Unexpectedly, she chuckled. "Richard, can you love an eggplant?"

"It's my favorite fruit," I said, deadpan, then playfully chucked her beneath the chin.

Then and there we quit talking and I dialed Sheriff DeLyle. He answered first beep. "Sheriff, we have new, pertinent information."

His voice hollow on the squad car's speaker, he said he was on his way to interview Sam, and was but a mile away.

"Let's meet in the guest's lounge," I suggested, then looked to Sam for a nod okay.

While Sam gingerly dabbed on some lipstick, I peeked around the corner. Three minutes later, Sheriff DeLyle marched from the elevator and into the waiting room. "Okay, Scott, what is it?" His tone held more than a hint of cynicism.

Sam began to describe the mugging, but the sheriff said that Captain Raphael Redonzo had already provided the lowdown.

"Ah! But neither of you have seen this." I pulled the torn shirt pocket from my briefcase and laid it in his palm. "This belongs to your buddy, Joe Petry."

Ever so casually, he traced the fleur-de-lis with his fingertips. "So?"

"I misplaced this piece of evidence after being attacked in my house. Already, you have a blood sample from the broken window. This cloth ties Joe Petry to the crime. How about pulling him in for blood and DNA samples?"

"You mean, try hanging that crime on him, since neither of you can provide evidence about this one?

"That would help!" I eyed him caustically, about to erupt. "At least it would give Samantha a breather from being stalked."

After a few perfunctory questions, the officer climbed slowly to his feet. His campaign hat had been balanced on the chair arm beside him. Pulling it on, still watching us, he used two fingers to measure the brim's distance from his crooked, battle-scarred nose.

"You're on the right track, Scott." He eyed us closely to be sure he had our rapt attention. With infuriating slowness, he made a minor adjustment to his Sam Browne belt, then hiked the pistol holster a half-inch before lowering it slightly. "Yep! You're on the right track, but I'm riding a faster train, and I'm ninety miles ahead of you both."

With that he stalked from the room. I figured he wasn't offended, but like all good politicians, couldn't help playing the crowd. Even the tiniest.

"Richard, do you think he's already run tests on the blood samples?" Sam's voice sounded hopeful.

"And without delay, he'll arrest your ex? Get real, Sam," I chided. "I suspect the ol' boy system is still operational. He's protecting Joe."

Suddenly, at that mention of Joe Petry's name, I reflected back to my visits with Janie's father. Hugh McNamara's comments came hurtling back into my mind. Without a word to Sam, I dashed out into the hall.

"Sheriff!" He turned, a puzzled look on his face. I walked close so I wouldn't be overheard. "Please check the blood samples against the droplets found atop Rose Cutter's Quarry the night Jane McNamara was murdered."

Looking displeased, not answering, he speared the elevator button with a big, stubby thumb. I gave the wall a quick once-over, half expecting to find a jagged hole like the one somebody had punched in Benefield's fireproof safe.

Deep in thought, I returned to the guest lounge.

"What was that all about?" Sam asked.

"I told DeLyle to handle the new information cautiously. I stressed that we wouldn't want to provoke Captain Redonzo."

I tried pondering my next move, but concentration became impossible. I had a terrible premonition. Sam had already been hurt by Janie McNamara's death, her husband's cruelty, and her son's arrest. If my suspicions were on target, worse trauma lay mere hours away. The case had become a runaway locomotive—I couldn't stop it. I could only be there for her after the wreck.

Sam rifled through her purse and pulled out the incriminating

Abram's Trace photo. "Please dispose of this." As if finding it offensive, she held it by the tip of one corner.

For the first time, I noticed a smaller photo of Gabriel Goodall and Karl Sprader on the reverse side of the newspaper cutout. I reached for it and stuck it in my pocket. Then, giving Sam a kiss and promising to return later in the day, I left her to rest.

As I walked through the parking lot toward the Jag, my cell phone beeped.

"This is Serendipity Smith. I want to see you immediately—and Desiree will be with me."

Agreeing to meet in an hour, I suspected somebody was listening in. "Tell my old bartender buddy to swap that Louisville Slugger for aluminum. The sweet spot's bigger—"

"Screw you, Scott!" The barkeep husked out.

Chortling, I folded the cellular and tucked it back into my briefcase.

On the way to Delilah's Temptation, I swung by the office to see Jeanie Robbins.

The owners of Pasha Industries were as yet unidentified. She had received word from the metallurgical testing lab. The report on the material in Bernard Glantz's condo was multipaged and more complicated than a lawyer's brief. I tucked it inside my briefcase for later reading.

On a hunch, I detoured through human resources. With no time to lose, I snagged a couple of updated personnel folders. Squeezing them in next to the metallurgist's report, I sped on down the hall.

This time, when I reached Seve Jensen's office, I stepped inside. He was standing before the window, his back to me. Did he know the extent of my investigation, I wondered as I stared at him from the rear. Was he aware that the insurance company now questioned his war injuries . . . and doubted that he'd ever served in the military? If he's learned of my trip south—when I talked to both his parents and his friends—he must know that I would eventually confirm the insurance company's suspicions.

I opened my mouth to speak, then changed my mind and backed slowly out the doorway. Under the circumstances, what could I say?

Striding purposefully across the parking lot, I glanced back toward Seve's office. He hadn't moved. I could distinguish his features. Twisting his head, he spoke to somebody behind him and turned back toward me. Eyes narrowing, he faded into the office.

Serendipity called again. "Change of plan! Desiree says our meeting has to take place at her old office."

I wondered the reason. Yet, I dared not risk discouraging Desiree. "Look, Serendipity. We'll be trespassing. Either Captain Redonzo or Sheriff DeLyle will have our butts."

"If we can't meet there, Desiree will cancel the meeting."

"Wait!" I pondered legalities. "Ask her if her job has been officially terminated. If not, we can go there as her guests."

"Just a minute." She muffled the phone, and a moment later Desiree came on the line. "My paychecks are still being deposited in my bank account," she whispered. "And there's been nobody around to fire me. Not with Leonard dead . . ." Her little-girl's voice faltered, before rising to a wail. Sobbing uncontrollably, she hung up.

Calling back, Serendipity said, "The meeting's still on."

Within five minutes, she called again, this time to say that Desiree had lost her key.

I recalled seeing it on her desk just before I discovered Rankles' body. I dialed Laureen Smith. "Laureen, could you open Leonard Rankles' old office? You could? Good! Can you meet me there in five? Thanks."

"Why, for God's sake, would Desiree want to return to the murder scene?" I queried myself. It didn't take a high-powered nose like mine to smell the fish in this peculiar deal.

First one there, I surveyed the scene, driving slowly by the Rankles' Business Brokers office. The front door still carried Leonard's name, but the Jacobi Realty sign beneath it dwarfed the logo.

On the lookout for police or killers, I parked a half block away. For once, there were a few parking places on the street as well. Within a few minutes, Laureen's car scraped the curb in front of Rankles' office. Five seconds later, Serendipity's Mustang snugged in behind Laureen's muddy little Toyota.

Still sitting in my car, I watched as Laureen keyed the lock, and stepped aside so the others could troop through the door. Serendipity's purse was tucked beneath her arm. The Delilah Temptation's bartender carried the Louisville Slugger over his shoulder like a woodsman's axe. Desiree's hands were empty. But where were Leonard Rankles' documents?

I got out and nodded to Laureen as she climbed back into her car, then, shifting my briefcase, twisted the knob and hurried into the office. "What on earth happened, Serendipity?"

Her blue sunglasses matched exactly the color of her navy sweater, but even wide lenses couldn't conceal the two shiners. Obligingly, she lifted the frames. "Karl Sprader accused me of ratting on him when I talked to you. Isn't this terrible?"

"Yeah, and that ain't all!" The bartender exploded. "She wouldn't level with me and I was convinced you'd clobbered her." Leaning the ball bat against a chair, he gently stroked the pretty dancer's hand. She kissed him lightly on the cheek and he fashioned his rough features into a twisted smile.

Edging reluctantly into the next room, Desiree froze in front of Leonard Rankles' desk. I followed closely.

Rankles' blood had been swabbed away, except for splatters on the three-sectioned picture above his desk. A dark smudge still covered the swordfish's lower jaw.

Desiree trembled, sucking in her breath.

I imagined her thoughts. Short days ago, she had been the center of Leonard's world, playfully vamping me while her boyfriend smiled his appreciation. Now he was dead and she was on the run. I had become her only hope.

"Can you describe what happened?"

Lips quivering, she fingered tears from beneath her eyes. I laid a protective arm over her shoulder and offered a tissue from a box on the corner of Leonard's desk.

When the killer attacked Leonard, she'd been primping at her desk. Her words rushed out, "I heard yelling. I peeked into Leonard's office. He was already unconscious, but this man kept beating him on the head. Then he saw me. He threw this crazy-looking, shiny hammer to the floor and came flying around the desk after me."

I knew that "crazy-looking, shiny hammer" had to be the one-of-a-kind rose-cutter tool from my office's what-not shelf.

She dropped the soaked tissue into the wastebasket. "I knew I couldn't help poor Leonard, so I ran outside and jumped into my car."

"I surmised that somehow you escaped up the stairs." I described the dust-free, outside sill when I made my getaway.

She smiled. "It should be as well polished as them big, black shoes you usually wear. That's the route Leonard took when people came looking for money." She puckered up again.

"But what about the documents?"

She wiped her nose on the turtleneck's ribbed cuff. "Leonard knew them documents could get him killed. He had already hidden 'em."

"So we're out of luck," I groaned, "because either the police or the killer will have found them."

"Nah! No way! They'll be right where he left them." Confidently, she tugged open the door behind his desk.

She leaned inside. I peered over her shoulder. "I gotta get a screwdriver." Quickly straightening, her body pressed against mine, her ample breast brushing one of my biceps. A mischievous smile flitted across her face.

Using a screwdriver she retrieved from Leonard's desk, she pried beneath the third stair step. Hinged, it lifted open.

A thick rubber band had snapped in two. A dozen envelopes lay loose beneath the step. "Holy Mother!" I cried. "I almost stepped on them when running from Redonzo."

Desiree refused to touch the documents. "Read 'em. Then, get 'em to the police. Call me when I can quit hiding." She ran her fingers through her blonde hair. The black roots were just beginning to show. "And get on the stick. I just gotta get back to Chantelle's Hair Salon. Anyway, the bank must've scraped his account to find money for my last paycheck. I'm needin' another job."

I unloaded my briefcase on Leonard's desk. I pointed to Roger Petry's picture. "Do you recognize this man?"

"I've never seen him in my life."

I handed her the newspaper photo taken in Abram's Trace. "That's you kissing a pretty lady," she teased. For a second time, she smiled as she had the day when Leonard Rankles introduced us. Quickly, the smile faded as I turned over the photo. She didn't recognize Reverend Goodall or Karl Sprader.

I opened the personnel folder brought from the office. Her shrill scream filled the tiny office. "My God! That's him! It's him! I'll never forget his face!" Her face colorless, she dropped weakly into Leonard's chair. Sobs wracked her shapely body.

This was a more recent picture of Charlie Buford Crockett, my sometimes phantom employee. He had lost weight since his last picture, the one shown me by Jeanie Robbins when she complained that Seve Jensen allowed Crockett to receive undeserved pay raises.

So now we knew—Crockett had killed Leonard Rankles. I recalled the crane operator's profile just before he dropped the beams and flattened the Jag. I nodded. Yes, this man had also tried to kill me. I couldn't be sure, but I suspected that he also had tossed the lighted match inside the wrecked Jag.

Standing beside Desiree I wanted to celebrate, but I couldn't. Crocket was not the brains behind the killings. The toughest part of my sleuthing was yet to come.

Calming down, Desiree said she'd like a few keepsakes from Leonard's desk. While she opened drawers and scratched through key rings, old business cards, name tags from long-ago meetings, and the remainder of the clutter that settles to the bottom of desk drawers, I reprised the case mentally.

The tapestry—or crazy quilt—still lacked too many threads for a complete pattern. I still didn't know who killed Janie McNamara nor Scott Benefield. I couldn't name the thieves who trashed my company's finances. Nor could I identify who had attacked Minnie and Herschel Peters. And I was far from closing the case on Reverend Gabriel Goodall and his sidekick, Karl Sprader.

But obviously, when I finally wrapped the case, I would need Sheriff DeLyle's help. He'd be the engineer. Without his clout, I was a passenger. With it, I was the conductor. I'd run the train and announce the stations.

But I couldn't forget: Desiree had provided answers; I still needed her official statements. I couldn't let her get away. "Desiree, how about a phone number? We need to deal direct."

She had just finished examining a snaggle-toothed comb from Leonard's desk. Her mood turned sour. I suppose she pictured the comb slipping through her lover's scanty locks. Or maybe the sight of his dandruff brought him close.

"No way!" she exploded. "I'm sticking with Serendipity. You call her. She'll call me." With that, she flounced through the door and rejoined her friends in the next room.

I had another question for the pretty dancer. "Serendipity, do you still have a key to Karl Sprader's house?"

"Yeah," she said, looking puzzled. "Although I'm now staying at my new boyfriend's apartment."

"Look, I need a body sample from Sprader. A hair or a nail clipping would do fine."

"That won't be a problem. The drain in his bathroom always looks like King Kong just showered."

I wrote down Sheriff DeLyles address and told her to Fed-Ex him the sample. Remembering that Tanya Trouveau had taken her job, I slipped her a twenty-dollar bill to cover the cost. She could keep the change. Next, I called the sheriff and told him to expect Serendipity's special parcel at his office.

Then I had a second thought. "Expect one from me too. I'm

sending a copy of the threatening letter I received when I first took over this case, along with Charlie Buford Crockett's signature from his company employment file. I'll also throw in samples of Joe Petry's, Seve Jensen's, and Karl Sprader's writing. Compare their handwriting to that in the letter.

"Is that all, Scott?"

"Nope. As a bonus, I'll include a page from the visitor's log at my factory. The line in space thirty-three should be compared to the handwriting of Petry, Crockett, and Sprader. Please send the whole lot to forensics and we'll find out who's been making late-night, unauthorized visits to my factory."

When I left, Serendipity was holding one string on a shopping bag, the bartender the other, while Desiree dumped the contents of her top desk drawer inside. I double-timed up the street, and backed my car's rear into an alley. Traffic was sparse. A cruising deputy slowed his car and turned his head when he passed.

Finally my three Musketeers left the office. When Serendipity's car turned the corner, I tagged close behind. I lay back, waiting, while she collected body samples from Karl Sprader's house, but followed more closely until she dropped Desiree in a rugged neighborhood on the old Northside of Indianapolis.

I punched the address into my Palm Pilot. It was good having an address. With the case riding on Desiree's slender shoulders, a phone number wasn't enough.

Now, if I could just keep her alive!

Chapter Fifty

THE MICHELINS SEEMED to sing a different tune as I fled south. I couldn't catch the lyrics, but I believe they mentioned the end of the case's crater-scarred, convoluted road.

Back in my office, I pored over the metallurgist's report. It took only a few minutes to compare that data with the building's blueprints and the recommendations my company had made. The condo would be near salt water. As part of a modernistic, far-out design, the prints called for exposed, unpainted beams. The prints specified an expensive, special-quality steel. The steel used hadn't followed the specs, but instead had been the lowest grade available. Weakened by salt-water rust, it had collapsed.

Either my company or Goodall's and Sprader's company had killed a man. I love a mystery. But not one where I'm both foil and leading suspect. I kept reading.

Consolidated Constructioneers, Inc., the company owned by Reverend Goodall and Karl Sprader, may have tried to save on the cost of materials and bought the wrong stuff. That could be construed as murder, but would probably go to a jury as manslaughter.

My company, Architectural Design and Elaboration, could've made a mistake—a glaring, design error that cost poor Bernard Glantz his life when the balcony collapsed. My company and I would then be declared criminally negligent. I might even face a manslaughter charge and end up with new lodgings in Florida. Not along the beach, but in a Sing Sing knock-off.

I continued to turn pages. Finally, holding my breath, I read the conclusion and decided to phone Marilyn Glantz. But not now. I decided to delay the uncomfortable call.

But the discomfort wouldn't leave.

"Jesus Christ!" I yelled. "Bernard didn't deserve that!"

Just before reaching the hospital, I called Sam and suggested we meet in the hospital cafeteria. She was in the middle of a treatment, so I arrived first.

I plopped down at a table near the door and sat fidgeting. With my big news, I couldn't wait to see her. In addition, according to a foot-tall, red-lettered sign, the cafeteria was pricing tossed vegetable salads by weight and throwing in the dressing free. Hey! I had to find some way to recoup that stolen two million simoleons.

Finally, Samantha came in. I jerked out a chair. "Sam, we now know Leonard Rankles' killer. Roger is innocent! Desiree will make her statement to Sheriff DeLyle and Roger will be released."

Sam rocketed to her feet. "My darling! How could I have doubted?" She kissed me full on the lips.

After a few seconds, I opened my eyes. Senior Nurse Claire Kelly stood behind Sam's shoulder, observing. "Unless you're too committed, Mr. Scott, you should come back to the third floor. Herschel Peters just awakened for the first time. He's asking for you."

"Whoopee! This is great news! Sam, I'll be right back."

Chapter Fifty-one

I WAS STILL ABSORBING Herschel Peters's case-shattering testimony when Sheriff DeLyle had me paged over the hospital P.A. system. The page directed me to the guest lounge.

Inside, the sheriff sat alone.

The television, located high on an adjustable shelf and tuned to a hospital infomercial, showed a young, fuzzy-faced M.D. who had just wowed the world with a description of titanium hip-joints and the joys of replacement surgery. The camera cut from the doctor to a group of his laughing, fully recovered patients playing grab-ass on a verdant lawn. None looked a day over thirty.

Ignoring the television's noisy tumult, his face a tight, expressionless mask, Sheriff DeLyle energetically leafed through a tattered, elderly copy of *Vogue*. From the doorway, even over the TV's full-blast volume, I fancied I heard pages rip and tear.

He spied me. He threw aside the magazine and shot to his feet, his knee bumping a glass-topped table. For one moment, I thought he might vault over it in his rush to confront me. Smiling, I ambled across the room, hand extended.

He was confused by my amiability and responded with a limp rag. "Earlier today, my deputy saw you enter Leonard Rankles' office," DeLyle barked.

"And . . . ?"

My laconism lit the fire. "An hour later I got word you were still lurking in a nearby alley." His crimson face grew incendiary; the words got hotter. "I'm taking you in, Scott." He unhooked a pair of handcuffs from his belt.

"I was in the office as a guest," I said, my words measured and simple. "Desiree Martin's still a company employee, and you've broadcast no public APB on her whereabouts." I lowered my eyes, but resisted aw-shucks-ing and scuffing the shag carpet with my toe. "I had no idea you were searching for her. It would be a shame if you embarrassed yourself by arresting me."

The "company employee" bit punctured his case. Reluctantly, he holstered the handcuffs. "Where is she, Scott?" The heat had dissipated; the threat remained.

"Can't say. Don't even know where she lives. But, definitely, she witnessed the killing. Through an intermediary, I can reach her."

He half-heartedly requested a name; I refused. "All right, Scott, I'll let you off this time. We'll meet in three days, and you'll be there"— he jabbed a stubby finger at me—"with proof!"

Getting the picture, I agreed. The time interval allowed him time to receive Serendipity's and my package and arrange for a quicky DNA test. "When we meet, I'll produce Desiree. She'll make a statement. I'll also deliver Rankles' incriminating documents."

"Okay, Scott, you do that. In return, I'll make a couple of startling announcements of my own."

As always, DeLyle was a brown-uniformed contradiction. We walked from the hospital together. Going out of his way to accompany me to my car, we warmly shook hands when I was seated, and he softly closed the door while I punched the key into the ignition.

Also, as always, I felt guilty for not sharing the incriminating documents. Still, they were locked securely in my office. A disturbing question plowed through my mind. What if I had a nighttime visitor too? Would my office safe be any sturdier than Clark Benefield's? In the meantime, I had a little scene to set up. What I proposed would blow the sheriff's mind, the murderer's cover, and the case.

Minutes later I was walking down the hall toward my office. Erupting from Seve Jensen's door, a shaken Peggy Murdock ran into me.

"Got a minute, Peggy?" I called after her.

Not answering, she detoured. Two steps at a time, she charged up the stairs toward the accounting department.

Maybe my secretary would be more talkative. "Jeanie, have you received the D and B report on Pasha Industries?" Jeanie had tears in eyes when she handed me the report. After reading it, I was ready to borrow her hanky.

Loaded for bear, I paged Peggy Murdock. This time she answered and said she'd see me, "In a sec."

When she strolled into my office, I said, "Peggy, you're facing a monstrous problem. You'd better sit down."

She did, with studied casualness, and crossed her legs. Her short, stretch-wool skirt rode up dangerously high. She observed me for a long moment before tugging down the hem. After a bit of recreational ogling, I returned to her face.

"You don't have a thing on me," she bluffed.

"I have an eyewitness. Your boyfriend, Charlie Buford Crockett, killed Leonard Rankles. I suspect you two are in cahoots. If you help me, I'll talk the sheriff into going easy on you."

At the mention of Crockett's name her eyes wavered. "Well, I did pass your credit cards on to Charlie—but that's all. Gosh, Mr. Scott, I wasn't even sure he would use them."

"Yeah, I'll bet," I said, familiar with the drill. "Undoubtedly, you were the brains behind the credit card scam. You suggested address changes, so bills would be delayed and Crockett could stay ahead of the investigators—and me."

"That sounds much too complicated for me," she objected.

I pressed on, "Crockett charged gasoline south of Cincy, on my credit card. Was he traveling north to kill me?"

A tiny smirk touched her face, but was just as quickly erased. She was learning fast, probably practicing for the jury. "All the guys thought having your credit cards was a big joke. Anyway, nobody goes to jail for stealing a few lousy dollars on a credit card. His buddies laughed their heads off."

I pointed to the report just provided by Jeanie. "Some of your cackling buddies may face murder one." I read a few terse lines from the report. "And that's just the beginning. If you come forward now, you have a way out. You delay, and somebody else will grab the sheriff's hand."

She collapsed against the back of her chair, her confidence shot. "What . . . what can I do?"

Sitting forward, I displayed my toughest, hard-nosed scowl. "Talk to no one about this . . . and go back to work as if nothing has happened. I'll handle the rest."

I watched her reclimb the stairs. This trip, she took them one at a time, each step taking greater and greater effort, as if she were struggling to scale a towering mountain.

While watching her, I understood why I never managed to encounter Crockett on the factory floor. Undoubtedly, Peggy had always called ahead to warn her boyfriend I was on my way into the shop. There had been a thousand nooks and crannies in which he might hide.

Just before she reached the top step, I interrupted her climb with a question: "Was your boyfriend the guy who shadowed Sam and I when we visited the Bedford cemetery?" She stopped walking, turned around, and came slowly back down the stairs . . .

Next morning, early, I called Serendipity to formalize our plans. She said Desiree had changed her mind about another meeting. I asked for a three-way telephone hookup so I could talk to Desiree.

"Nope! I won't go the sheriff's office. And that is that!" Desiree flatly stated.

"But why?"

"Somebody will shoot me, dammit!"

I couldn't argue that point. "Okay, then how about meeting at my place by Rose Cutter's Quarry—say on Friday?"

Reluctantly she agreed. "All right—I guess. What time?"

"Twelve noon."

"Well, all right . . . If you can have Chantelle meet me by ten? I need your help a bunch, Richard," Desiree wheedled. "I'll come early to see her. My hair's a mess. Now I have this dinky little pimple coming. It's right on the very tip end of my nose. And . . . it's icky—and it'll still be there when we meet."

She waited for sympathy, so I murmured into the phone until Serendipity came to the rescue with, "Desiree, I promise. I'll call Chantelle."

"This case has shot my nerves," Desiree complained. "You guys are trying to kill me."

"Right now, a bunch of guys would be willing to take on that job. I'm the good guy who's trying to save your life." I waited for the comment to sink in before continuing, "Desiree, you're our chief witness. You're about to knock over the first domino."

"I don't feel like playing games, especially dominoes. I might consider poker. You ever play strip? Naahh! I just want to testify and get on my way to the Calliope. There's a great flick showing there. See, Rob Lowe is captured by this guy wearing a turban—"

"I'll pick you up at eight sharp, honey," Serendipity said.

Finally. D-day. Zero hour. I waited.

Ten o'clock. No Chantelle. No Desiree. No Serendipity.

Eleven o'clock. Same story. I made call after call. Chantelle had left her building, but my other calls ended, trapped in voice mail. Marilyn Lawrence called me. I explained that Goodall had bought defective material, that negligence had led to her father's death.

Finally, a few minutes before twelve, a knock rattled the door. Carefully applied make-up hid Samantha Petry's multitude of welts and bruises. "God, Sam, you look great!" I gave her a careful squeeze, before nuzzling her neck. I liked the feel when her cashmere sweater tickled my nose, and her skin's special, seductive aroma. "It's a treat seeing you in street clothes."

"It's great being out of the hospital, except for the moments with you," she said, offering her lips.

Just as we kissed, there was another knock, and I opened the door to the morning's odd couple. "Sam, meet Peggy Murdock and Herschel Peters," I said.

Methodically, Sam surveyed Peggy's peroxided bangs, pullover and blue-jeans, eyeing her to the tips of her lug-soled oxfords before nodding coldly. Warming to Herschel, she searched for an accessible spot between bandages then, maneuvering past his cap bill, kissed him on the cheek.

"Please wait here for a few minutes," I said, showing Peggy and Herschel into the bedroom-cum-storage room, "Sheriff DeLyle will arrive shortly."

Sam and I scurried around making ready for the meeting. First thing, she put on Diana Krall's "Peel Me a Grape," bringing entertainment to a house sorely needing it. For my part, I strong-armed a poker table onto its side, wrestled it through the second bedroom door and, balancing it as if it were a cumbersome wheel, rolled it to the middle of the great room. A sullen Peggy didn't volunteer to help. I waved aside Herschel's offer.

While I collected chairs from the kitchen, Sheriff DeLyle pounded the door. Sam greeted him.

He surveyed the room with a jaundiced eye. "So far you've got a mighty tiny party, Scott," he grumped. "Where's Desiree Martin?"

"Peggy Murdock and Herschel Peters are in the next room; Desiree's on her way," I promised. "In fact, not more than an hour ago she delivered the Leonard Rankles papers."

Carrying a tray, Sam had just walked through the door from the kitchen when she heard my blatant lie. She stopped so suddenly the coffee sloshed in the carafe.

I assigned seats, took one, and snapped the tab on a Coors from Sam's tray. Sam poured coffee for the sheriff. Both he and I placed our Panasonic recorders in the center of the table.

We hadn't talked in detail. "Sheriff," I suggested, "while we're waiting, we'd better review this whole complicated case." With that, I spread a collection of files on the table. My case files and notes provided a picture of the relationship between characters, organizations and events in my case. They chronicled a story of environmental crime, fraud against my company, and murder. The sheriff's forensic reports would complete the stories.

DeLyle pored over the papers, pausing only to ask questions and sip his coffee. After a few minutes, he again rose to his feet. Hooking his thumbs over the edge of the poker table, he leaned forward and looked directly at Sam. "We'll get into those details again, later," he said, indicating the case notes he'd just finished. "Right now, I have a few sorry matters that I want to discuss with this lovely lady." He directed his attention toward Sam. "Ms. Petry, you're not going to like what you're about to hear, and I'm sorry. But, telling it like is . . . well, ma'am, that's my job."

He flipped to the second page of a forensics report. "I've followed a trail of blood from that broken pane over there"—he indicated the back door—"to Jane McNamara's killer.

"We ran DNA tests on your son's blood. That told us he didn't father Jane McNamara's baby. But we remained certain he killed Leonard Rankles. Now, Richard here"—he hooked a thumb toward me—"reassures me that Desiree Martin's testimony will clear your son of that murder, but . . ."

Sam nodded silently, yet steepled her hands in front of her face. No question about it, she dreaded the remainder of his story.

DeLyle seemed to like the attention. Deliberately stalling for time, he lifted the carafe to warm up his coffee, then hesitating further, he gazed longingly at my Coors it was as if he thought life were cheating him.

"Go ahead, Sheriff," I urged, wishing to keep him happy and

communicative. "Even on duty, you need support when you're wrapping a case."

"By golly, I believe I will! Get me a cold one like yours."

I eased into the kitchen and returned with a bowl of pretzels and the beer. DeLyle popped the tab, took a generous slug, then slipped the tip of a fat pretzel into his mouth. Quickly, he nipped his way to the other end. The sound mimicked a squirrel nibbling an acorn.

He picked up the dropped thread of his narrative and said, "So far, Ms. Petry, you've got to be liking what you're hearing. But be prepared, things are about to go to hell in a handbasket."

He lifted the Coors for a second time as though buying time to allow Sam to steel herself. She reached across the table and I took her hand in mine.

Diana Krall had just finished "Garden in the Rain," and the room grew deadly quiet. Roughly, DeLyle slammed the beer can back onto the table. Aluminum striking oak cracked like a gunshot.

"Let's go way back. Jane McNamara's killer nicked his hand when he shattered the bottle over a rock prior to stabbing her." He sucked in a deep breath. "Then, when Scott gave me the torn pocket, I knew I had sufficient grounds—along with others, I pulled Joe Petry in for a blood sample. Wanted his as well as your son's for the comparison tests."

Sam's face turned completely white—except for the cover-up makeup now blotching her face.

The sheriff turned another page of the report. "Number one: Joe Petry fathered Jane McNamara's fetus. But that's not all."

I gripped the table rim, waiting and knowing, although—for Sam's sake—dreading to hear the rest of the story.

"Like I said, that's not all, not by half."

Involuntarily, a terrible mewling issued from Sam's throat. Ever so slowly, she slid back her chair, the chair legs grating against the darkly varnished floor. Teetering a bit, she rose to her feet.

I knew she feared the new announcement would further implicate Roger. I reached out to help.

"Sam, darling, please!" Waving me away, she walked rapidly to the bathroom, head high, lips forming a firm, straight, white line.

Standing outside the door, I heard water running in the sink. I rejoined Sheriff DeLyle.

In two minutes she returned, wearing no makeup, to reseat herself and stare straight ahead, chin lifted, showing her inherent determination to see it through. Now, every bruise showed, each welt strengthening the case against Joe Petry.

While I waited for DeLyle to resume, his eyes fell on the tables' fourth empty chair. "Okay, Scott, where is Ms. Desiree Martin?"

"No sweat, Sheriff. She's on her way," I bluffed. "First, for God's sake, let's finish with Joe Petry's story. You're making Sam a nervous wreck—"

At that moment, a braking car scrambled the gravel at the end of the drive, interrupting my delaying lie. I rushed to the door to welcome Desiree.

Desiree turned to wave at Serendipity, who remained outside in her car. Desiree's hair, now trimmed shorter, looked as if each strand were uncombed with no two hairs lying parallel.

"Nice hairdo," I observed, a bit dourly.

Desiree assumed a hurt expression. "I stopped to see Chantelle. But she works better in her shop." She turned to face the sheriff. "Anyway, I couldn't meet the most famous lawman at Delilah's Temptation—and maybe all Indiana—without a new hairstyle and some decent clothes."

"So you went shopping as well?" I asked.

"Yep." She pirouetted, displaying a tight, loose-weave sweater and a short velour skirt. Raising one pretty leg, she kicked out a black demi-boot for the sheriff's inspection. "Aren't these absolutely the greatest? Don't you just love those big, chunky heels?"

Sheriff DeLyle smiled uneasily.

Fashion show finished, Desiree eased seductively into the fourth chair. Running a finger over the tip of her nose, she unclasped her compact for a closer examination.

While Desiree scanned her schnoz, the sheriff and I flipped the switches on our Panasonic recorders. Just as she had for me, Desiree repeated her detailed description of Leonard Rankles' murder, complete with all the trimmings.

I retrieved Crockett's employment file from my briefcase and held out his picture. For the record, I asked, "Do you recognize this man?"

"He killed Leonard!" Desiree wailed, again breaking into tears, just as she had in her office. "Fact is, I saw him earlier today when we drove by the Metro Community Center!" She turned her attention from the sheriff to me. "Richard, he was entering through a side door with them two old farts—the ones in that picture you showed me when we met in the Leonard's office."

"Sheriff, those 'two old farts' are Reverend Gabriel Goodall and Karl Sprader, who were pictured in a newspaper clipping after their Abram's Trace meeting."

"I don't like this! Not one bit!" DeLyle exploded. "Goodall and Sprader will put Leonard Rankles' killer back on the lam. That happens, we'll never prove this case!"

"Okay," I said, standing. "Then let's get to the reverend's political meeting."

Moments later, still adjusting our coats, Sam, Desiree, Peggy Murdock, Sheriff DeLyle, and I charged down the sidewalk toward our cars. Still unaccustomed to crutches, Herschel Peters struggled to keep up. I slowed to help.

Herschel and Peggy rode with Serendipity and Desiree, Sam and I with the sheriff. Gravel flew from the Mustang's tires as Serendipity punched the accelerator and led us down the drive.

Her pace wasn't rapid enough for the sheriff. "My God! We'll be too late going this speed!" He drove onto the berm, bounced through a shallow drainage ditch, and passed the Mustang. Although Sheriff DeLyle drove at top speed on the way to the political meeting, we still managed to keep discussing my case notes.

We trouped into the community center just as Reverend Goodall concluded one question and waited for another. Sprader, seated beside

Goodall, rose to his feet. "Reverend Goodall, will you let the federal government confiscate our guns?"

Surveying the crowd, Seve Jensen, sitting to Goodall's left, nodded solemnly. The others at the table smirked.

Just like the one at the Abram's Trace meeting, this audience craned forward, hungry for answers. Building suspense, Goodall focused on the audience, carefully tugging his French cuffs and adjusting his gold cufflinks, their diamond clusters sparkling beneath the overhead lights.

Their attention riveted on Goodall, neither Sprader, Jensen, nor Joe Petry noticed our arrival. Sheriff DeLyle's deputy—acting as sergeant-at-arms—did. Looking uncomfortable, he smiled weakly but didn't otherwise acknowledge us.

I searched the crowd for Charlie Buford Crockett. Obviously catching on, Peggy Murdock leaned over my shoulder and whispered in my ear, "Charlie's in the second row." When I strained to hear, she grasped my arm and drew me closer, pressing her breast against me. "He's third from the end." When Peggy sat back into her seat, Sam brushed my brown Ike jacket as if it were soiled.

"The Second Amendment guarantees our right to keep and bear arms. We must interpret it closely." Reverend Goodall waved a check above his head. "This cashier's check—this love offering —is from the weapons association," he said, proudly. "Weapons are your rightful heritage." He raised his trademark .45 above his head, the pistol's silver barrel glistening as it bobbed up and down. I knew absolutely he had gone over the top in his zeal to attract money from the weapons industry. Again, I felt a tinge of sadness, remembering what he had once meant to Mom and Dad when his ministry first began.

The crowd was totally into the political campaign's here-and-now and cheered exuberantly. Two rows in front of our group, a woman waved a homemade "Goodall for Congress" cardboard sign, while her husband gently stroked her sweatered shoulder with a calloused, sunburned hand.

"We must remain vigilant. Together, we'll bring God to this

government. We must prepare for the Rapture; we must gird ourselves for that moment when the righteous are taken bodily into heaven." Pausing, his smile beatific, he lifted his eyes as if visualizing the glorious event. "We must fight evil. As an esteemed leader in our Christian Right warned, 'Almost surely, the Jewish Antichrist is already among us.'" An angry, supporting mutter hopped from table to table, dying only at the back wall.

Exactly as I had at Abram's Trace with Caitlin, I wanted to bolt from the hall. I caught Samantha's eye, and she grimaced in response. "This time, things will be different," I promised myself. "I won't wimp out. Far from it. Today, I'll see this man destroyed."

I raised my hand. Goodall acknowledged one nearer the front. "What's your stand on the environment?" I recognized Ed Clausen's soft voice.

I was pleased the environmentalist from the EPA had responded to my telephoned invitation. That made me curious to see how many others had shown up at my instigation. Scanning the crowd, I saw the late Bernard Glantz's daughter, Marilyn Lawrence, one row behind Clausen. Murder victim Janie McNamara's father sat a dozen seats to her right, his silver hair and translucent skin setting him apart from the crowd. I had hoped he would be here—he had so desperately wanted the truth before dying. Today he'd know.

Goodall stroked his palms together while reflecting on Clausen's question. "Man has dominion over the earth and all its creatures," he answered, his voice sober and earnest. "We won't be deprived of God's treasures by any half-baked coalition of atheists and leftist environmentalists."

His voice went from scathing to unctuous, "Most certainly, our stewardship of this earth will be loving and godly. I love Indiana's lofty forests." He raised his arms, his voice soaring like the trees. "And I adore her peaceful, clear-running streams," he concluded, his voice fading to a whisper, like softly running water.

"Except he wants his trees clear-cut and on the ground," Sam whispered.

"Yeah, and I know how he feels about water," I said, picturing Herschel's favorite fishing spot littered with spiny skeletons. Propelled by white-hot anger, I leaped to my feet.

Glancing toward the darkened rear of the room, Goodall responded to my figure not my face. "Yes, you back there near the back—you have a question?"

"I'm Richard Scott," I announced. "While Jacobi Realty managed my property, Reused Resources—a company owned by you and your colleague Karl Sprader—dumped chemical waste into Rose Cutter's Quarry—" The hall erupted in sound. Every head turned toward me. Nobody smiled.

Goodall grabbed the mike from its mount. "How dare you, Scott!" he chided as if speaking to a child. Abruptly his face tightened, his voice swelling into a scream. "Leave this room, immediately! We have no place for two-bit, muckraking investigators."

I shouted in return, "In my possession, I have Leonard Rankles' documents." When first sitting down, I had landed on a thick stack of discarded political handouts. Now, for effect, I waved the whole sheaf in the air. "These documents show how your vice president, Karl Sprader, conspired with my company's financial officer, Seve Jensen, to dump chemical waste in Rose Cutter's Quarry. They record each and every shipment—"

Voices filled the room, the sound a bumblee's angry drone. I kept talking, trying to explain how the payoff money first flowed from Sprader to Jacobi Realty, an innocent participant, before being divided, with some going to ADE to make the transaction look legitimate, but with most being diverted to Pasha, the company owned by Jensen and the late Clark Benefield, who perished in the house fire he helped set. Finally, the noise completely drowned my voice. Replacing words with drama, I whipped my arm and tossed the pamphlets. The paper sheets sailed aloft, skimming overhead, before fluttering into the crowd.

Grabbing the mike, Goodall turned toward the deputy. "Officer, throw that man out!"

Springing to his feet, Sheriff DeLyle knocked over both our folding chairs. The clatter of steel against concrete quieted the crowd. "Don't even think about throwing anybody out, Deputy!" he yelled.

Scrambling to the end of the row, I charged down the aisle. The sheriff overtook me as I reached the head table.

"Reverend Goodall, I'm placing you, Karl Sprader, and Seve Jensen under arrest for conspiring to have Charlie Buford Crockett murder Leonard Rankles," DeLyle shouted. "Desiree Martin witnessed the killing, when Mr. Rankles was bludgeoned to death."

The crowd noise strengthened, the buzz fragmenting into angry shouts and threats. Several men dashed through a nearby maintenance room door.

"Why would we even bother to murder some bush-league business operative, Sheriff?" Goodall demanded when the crowd noise subsided.

"You three coconspirators had motive aplenty, Reverend Goodall!" DeLyle answered. "Rankles' papers proves your participation. And unless you could destroy those records tying you and Sprader to the pollution of Rose Cutter's Quarry, you were facing a twenty-million-dollar clean-up bill."

DeLyle glanced toward me, making a silent appeal for backup. "You're right, Sheriff," I said. "And although my investigation already had the perpetrators on edge, the fish kill at Rose Cutter's Quarry brought the whole thing to a head." I pointed toward Herschel Peters who had both crutches under his arms and was leaning on the table for support.

"Mr. Herschel Peters will testify that, as he sometimes does, he went into the factory late at night to repair a piece of equipment, and that while he was sitting behind the broken machine and quietly reading an instruction pamphlet, Seve Jensen, Karl Sprader, and Charlie Crockett walked down the aisle and paused just a few feet from Herschel to talk.

"According to Herschel Peters, Crockett seemed to be getting scared and threatening to provide state's evidence to you, Sheriff. As

Herschel recollects, Sprader told Crockett, 'You hauled the stuff out to Rose Cutter's Quarry when you were working for my company.' Then he warned Crockett to keep quiet so the three of them and Reverend Goodall could weather the storm. Sprader said that otherwise, Crockett would hang with the rest of them, or end up dead like Leonard Rankles—and be blamed for the whole thing." I pointed toward Herschel. "While they were talking, Herschel tried to sneak away, but Jensen saw him leave."

"I've never in my life entered Richard Scott's factory. It's my word against that pipsqueak," Karl Sprader snarled, indicating Herschel.

Sheriff DeLyle moved closer to the table and Sprader. "You're dead wrong, Sprader. The guard at ADE clocked you in the moment you signed the visitor register, and although you used a fictitious name, handwriting forensics proves you signed the name and were there the night Herschel says he overheard you."

I glared straight at Sprader. "Once you saw Herschel trying to sneak away, you had no choice. You had to silence him. You tried to kill him, and convinced you had succeeded, you did kill Minnie Peters because she witnessed the attack against her husband and could testify against you."

The sheriff joined back in and pointed his finger directly at Sprader. "The DNA in the hair and skin found at the crime scene matches the nail clipping samples Ms. Serendipity Smith provided from your home, so forensics proves you attacked Herschel and Minnie Peters."

"And," I said, "Seve Jensen joined the Rankles' murder conspiracy not only to protect himself in the pollution case, but because he knew the pollution investigation would lead directly to Pasha Industries, the dummy company owned by him and the late Clark Benefield— because that company had also been used in his more recent scheme to defraud monies from my company."

I didn't try to explain in greater detail above the crowd noise. Didn't need to. The sheriff had in his possession my notes explaining how Seve had both legitimate and phony purchase orders from ADE sent to Benefield Enterprises, and that when ADE paid for those phony jobs the money had been deposited into a Pasha account, just like the checks had been when Sprader and Goodall paid Jensen for allowing them to pollute Rose Cutter's Quarry.

Seve Jensen's voice erupted in a guttural oath. He was determined to reach me and stormed up from the far end of the table. DeLyle's deputy blocked his path. He climbed onto a chair, mounted the table, and leaped to the floor inches away. "You can't prove anything, Scott," he snarled, fists cocked.

"Wanna bet?" I asked, balancing on my toes in a boxer's stance. "Once I saw the battered safe and smelled your Van Cleef and Arpel cologne, I knew you'd been in Benefield's office to destroy evidence." I feinted, lashing out, my fist grazing his chin. "The records showed you and Clark Benefield had been defrauding the company for years, even before I returned as president."

Jensen circled me, searching for an opening. I planted a straight jab on his nose. Staggering, he flopped backward onto a chair. He struggled to his feet and wiped blood from his nose before collapsing back into the chair.

DeLyle surveyed the room. "Where'd Crockett go? "

While the sheriff and his deputy looked around the crowd for Crockett, I turned toward Herschel, who was standing just behind me. "I'll be glad to testify, boss," he said, reading my mind. "I'll testify for you . . . and for Minnie."

It was impossible not to admire Herschel's spunk. He was brave! Just being here had taken a lot of guts. "Thanks, Herschel, I really appreciate your help. DNA and fingerprints on the ball-peen hammer will back you up."

DeLyle had been unsuccessful in his search for Charlie Buford Crockett, my "loyal" employee who not only had killed Leonard Rankles, but had given me an up-close-and-personal touch of his temper by bombing my car with a crane full of beams. DeLyle mounted the head table. Seve Jensen lost interest in me and disappeared into the crowd.

Yelling, "Everybody, quiet!" Reverend Goodall began pounding the table with his fist. The sound was lost in the crowd's noise. Pushing forward, the crowd milled around us.

"Let's get 'em," one big, economy-sized, overall-wearing farmer said. Earlier, I had seen him duck into the maintenance closet. Now he yanked a clawhammer from beneath his bib and came at me. I fended him off with a chair.

Desperate to recapture the meeting, Goodall grabbed his .45 from the table. Holding it by the barrel, he again pounded the table—much harder than he had with his fist. "Quiet!" he yelled.

Losing patience, he raised the pistol, chest high, and slammed the grip against the table. With a thundering crack, the pistol's explosion shocked the room into silence.

Goodall clutched his glistening white shirt. Blood soaked the cloth and streamed from between his fingers. "Scott, you bastard." But his snarl lost its punch as his eyes dulled. He fell forward across the table. The farmer dropped his hammer and melted into the crowd.

I hunched over Goodall, pressing down on his chest, stanching the blood with my handkerchief. Somebody booted me in the back, spearing a kidney, then thrust me aside.

Snatching the pistol from Goodall's fingers, Charlie Crockett dashed toward the nearest exit.

Sheriff DeLyle yelled, "Halt!"

Crockett whirled, brandishing the pistol. The sheriff's service revolver roared first. Crockett sank to his knees.

Screaming, "Charlie! Charlie!" Peggy Murdock ran to him.

Crockett wrapped Peggy in his arms, never letting go, even after they fell together to the floor. Maybe it was love; or, could be, he feared his next destination. There'd be no Cigarette Boats on the River Styx.

Within minutes, ambulances arrived for the dead and wounded. Close behind the meds, a swat team cleared the hall.

Their bodies stiffly erect, Marilyn Glantz Lawrence and Hugh McNamara crossed the hall to the front door. Turning, they caught my eye. Almost imperceptibly, she nodded, then walked outside. Janie's father gave me a grim, but satisfied smile before following her through the door. Fair enough! Both Marilyn's and my mother had been defrauded. Now we had our revenge—and money could be returned from Goodall's estate. Mine would go from there to a worthwhile charity.

Hugh McNamara could now die in peace and carry his message to the other side. He could also explain that the monument's wide-brimmed hat was now ever-so-slightly cocked, a little bit jaunty, since Janie's killer had been caught and the *four* of them—Janie, her baby, and Hugh and Gert, the grandparents—were finally together.

But there were still too many players in this drama, and they weren't all accounted for. Not yet!

"Sheriff, Joe Petry's gotten away," I growled. I placed my arm over Sam's shoulder. "Sam, let's get out of here. The sheriff can locate your ex later."

She held a finger over her lips and pointed with the other hand. Following her gaze, I saw a polished, black shoe protruding from beneath the table's red, white, and blue bunting. Giving a huge heave, I yanked outward on Petry's foot. He held onto an opposite table leg, so Sheriff DeLyle jumped from the table and grabbed the other foot.

Petry lay spraddled on the floor, his hands covering his face, while DeLyle read his Miranda rights. This time, Petry's control remained strong; the brown pants stayed dry. "Joe Petry, your DNA proves you not only fathered Jane McNamara's baby, but also held the broken bottle that stabbed and killed her." As an afterthought, he added, "And the blood on a window pane proves you invaded Richard Scott's house and attacked him."

As we followed the sheriff outside, Samantha asked, "When we were back at your house, why didn't the sheriff just say that Joe not only fathered Janie's baby but also killed her? It would've been much easier on me."

As I nodded in agreement, She continued, "Richard," Sam said, "for you, the biggest mystery has yet to be solved."

"Oh, I doubt that. Not with half the town either dead, wounded, jailed, or already buried."

Sam said no more, her personal mystery still hidden behind an enigmatic smile.

Sheriff DeLyle gave Sam and me a lift back to the hunting lodge. Too many questions hung unanswered in the air. We were still discussing them when we pulled up in front of my house.

"Are you absolutely certain that Seve Jensen and Clark Benefield worked closely with Reverend Goodall's organization?" the sheriff insisted, switching off his engine. "That conspiracy tie must be strong—or our case will be weak."

"Most assuredly," I answered. "Remember: Seve Jensen's relationship with Goodall goes way back. When we were competing for the company, Jensen not only planned to use the proceeds from a fraudulent insurance settlement, he planned to borrow additional money from Dollars for Mankind, another one of Reverend Goodall's fronts."

A happy thought intruded. "Now that the good reverend has shown his true colors, my maitre d' friend Samuel Jackson will get his old job back—and be hailed as a hero besides."

"So, Richard, who killed Clark Benefield?" Sam asked. The sheriff's face fell when she directed the question to me. "Sorry," she said, making amends and redirecting the question, "Sheriff, what's your conclusion on Benefield's death?"

DeLyle adjusted his Sam Browne belt so it rode lower on his paunch. "We'll never know for certain. I suspect Jensen and Benefield burned Richard's house, since they had valid reasons to either frighten him away from the investigation, or possibly even kill him. I'll always suspect that since the big house was almost finished, they believed that Richard was sleeping there, not in the A-frame."

"So they did want to kill Richard?" Sam asked.

"I'm certain of it, but can't prove it. But I'd wager Benefield's death was accidental, and he became trapped when the furnace flicked on and sparked the gasoline fire."

"And possibly, my point is incidental," Sam said. "But it just occurred to me. We've never identified the writer of the threatening letter, nor the character who shadowed us in the cemetery, nor the letter sent to Richard's secretary, Jeanie Robbins, in which he was warned about the pollution in Rose Cutter's Quarry."

"That's not totally true," the sheriff objected. "Forensics examined Karl Sprader's, Joe Petry's, Seve Jensen's, and Charlie Crockett's handwriting and compared it to the letter. Definitely, Crockett wrote the threatening note that warned Richard away from the case."

I interrupted. "We don't know who sent the letter to Jeanie, but I suspect that, since it wasn't threatening in nature, it probably came from a local environmentalist. And as for the person who shadowed us in the cemetery—once Crockett became involved in the case, I deduced that he was the only suspect large enough to fill that huge coat our cemetery stalker was wearing. Peggy Murdock confirmed I was right; in between trips to Florida, where he went to fatten up on my credit card, he found time to shadow us at the cemetery. Seve Jensen put him up to it."

Mentally cataloguing information before tossing in another final comment, I said, "Also, since Seve Jensen will be charged with complicity in the murder of Leonard Rankles, I doubt the insurance company will pursue the fraud case. However, Sheriff, that original green Jag was my favorite. I'd like to hang Crockett's buns for destroying it."

"No problem," the sheriff said, restarting his cruiser. "What's another charge, more or less? We'll get 'im for destroying your property as well attempting to kill you. That's in addition to the murder one charge he already faces in the killing of Leonard Rankles." With that, we climbed out of the car and he drove off.

Sam and I watched as his brown cruiser made a three-point

turnaround and accelerated down the lane. He waved over his shoulder just before topping the hill. We walked into the house.

"We forgot a couple of mysteries, Sam," I said, wrapping my arms around her shoulders. "First, why an 'elephant cage' at Chicksands Royal Air Force Base. Second, why did Henry the Eighth destroy the Gilbertine religious order?"

"British locals called the U.S. Air Force's huge, circular antenna an elephant cage. As for Henry the Eighth, let's talk about that over dinner and drinks," Sam said, grinning.

Her eyes swept around the room, pausing only for a split second at the window framing Rose Cutter's Quarry. "I certainly don't wish to live here." She brightened. "Of course, my house in town will be ideal for the two of us."

"But what about Roger? On at least a temporary basis, won't he be moving in with you?"

"No, he has a new girlfriend. He and Jeanie Robbins will be living together."

"Oh, no!" I started objecting, then reconsidered. "Jeanie only works for me. Undoubtedly, she can do just as she pleases. And Roger . . . well, he owes me no explanation at all."

Samantha placed her arm through mine and gently urged me toward the door. "That's not totally correct, Richard. If you count forward from our special night in Indianapolis, to Roger's birthday . . ."